Kelly,

I'm so, so glad I met you and look forward to many more days in the sun hitting the yellow or b... or a chita porchside :)

— Crystal

FALLING THROUGH TREES

FALLING THROUGH TREES

CRYSTAL KLIMAVICZ

DEEDS PUBLISHING | ATLANTA

Cover design and text layout by Mark Babcock

Published by Deeds Publishing
Marietta, GA
www.deedspublishing.com

Printed in The United States of America

Library of Congress Cataloging-in-Publications Data is available upon request.

ISBN 978-1-941165-12-6

Books are available in quantity for promotional or premium use. For informa-tion, write Deeds Publishing, PO Box 682212, Marietta, GA 30068 or info@deedspublishing.com.

First Edition, 2014

10 9 8 7 6 5 4 3 2 1

ACKNOWLEDGMENT

AT SOME POINT ALONG THE way, what began as a purely cathartic and self-fulfilling process to work through the grief and guilt of losing a mother to suicide turned into *Falling Through Trees*.

I would first like to recognize Jeffrey Stepakoff, a successful television writer, producer, and author. If it wasn't for his encouragement of my story idea at my local public library, this book may never have happened. I would also like to acknowledge Christina Ranallo from PenPaperWrite, for providing an outstanding workshop that got Falling Through Trees off the ground, and fellow aspiring writers on Scribophile for reviewing the original opening chapters.

Finally, I need to thank my husband and two children for putting up with the countless hours I have spent hovering over my Mac these past few years and, of course, Deeds Publishing for believing in my story and bringing it to print.

The simple truths within these pages are that my parents divorced when I was young, I have a younger sister who is a wonderful woman (as sweet as "Molly" yet much, much stronger), and that we lost the mother we share. We also have a brother who will be "revealed" in the next book in the Kate Harriman series.

All other scenes, situations, and characters portrayed in these pages are derived from my imagination for the sole purposes of writing a novel. My hope is that hearts will be touched by the underlying threads of family difficulties, of growing up and finding your way, and of the indescribable pain of losing a loved one to suicide.

I have met many people who have been touched in one way or another by such a sad and bitter ending to someone's life, and my heart goes out to them all. For me, just one woman is behind this novel, my mother, Cindra, whom I miss dearly each and every day.

Thank-you,

Crystal Ann Klimavicz

"All change is not growth,
as all movement is not forward."

-Ellen Glasgow, an American novelist who portrayed
the changing world of the contemporary south
(April 22, 1873 – November 21, 1945)

"Things alter for the worse spontaneously, if
they be not altered for the better designedly."

-Francis Bacon, the founder of empiricism
(January 22, 1561 – April 6, 1626)

CONTENTS

PART III

PART I

1. THERE'S ALWAYS A BEGINNING

AS A TEENAGER WITH DULL-BROWN hair and legs that were far too short, I was no runway model back then, that's for sure. Thanks to my overly curvaceous grandmother, though, I was rather developed in the female department. And let's face it—even a short mousy teenager with a full 'C' cup will draw some attention to herself from time-to-time.

I also seemed to make friends fairly easily, and at some point along the way I learned to put on a smile even when I didn't quite feel it inside.

I was fifteen years old, a freshman at Belleview High School, when I first met Tom Harriman. He was older, a junior, and of course I already knew who *he* was. Everyone did. Tom was the star quarterback for Belleview—a team that couldn't seem to lose—and he was by far the most popular boy in school.

Yes, Tommy was quite well liked—attractive and cocky, with just enough brashness to make the teachers laugh and looks that could melt a girl's heart. He was a good catch and everyone knew it.

Including Tom.

I didn't know much about boys then—looking back, I really didn't know anything! But I could tell with a girl's instinct that I'd caught his eye. I'd been walking home from school one day when he and a couple of his friends came round the corner onto my street. They were hootin' and hollerin' as boys will do and making fools of themselves. I saw Tommy do a double take as he passed me by, though I pretended not to notice. A few minutes later, he shouted out something to me. I couldn't hear exactly what he had shouted with all the noise the boys were making, but then I heard the word "boots" carried off in the wind, and I knew.

He had teased me about the damn rain boots I had on, and when I turned around I saw the other boys pointing at them and laughing. I'm sure my face turned beet-red.

His friends were right to laugh, though, for I remember that those damn boots were as ugly as sin; Lord knows how I hated them so. A nasty mud color, they were the cheap version made to look like Wellingtons, yet one of them leaked at the sole on the bottom, and the other never quite fit right. And even though my Mother tried to convince me that they were brand new, I could tell that they were just some hand-me-downs or maybe bought second-hand at the local Goodwill.

Mother made me put them on almost every day for school, rain or shine. If I tried complaining about having to wear them, she would always say the same thing in that annoying, singsong voice of hers, "Elizabeth, honey, in Maine there's *always* the possibility of rain, so it's better to be…"

But I'd usually just cut her off and mimic her with my eyes rolling dramatically. "I know, I know, Mother… It's better to be safe than *sorry.*"

Eventually, I figured out how to outsmart her, though. I'd leave home wearing the boots like a good daughter should. Then, when I got around the corner and out of sight, I'd change into the black Mary Jane's a friend's sister had given me that I stashed in the bottom of my school bag. Every day, I'd half-hide those old boots under the same bush at the corner of my block on Elm and Lincoln, hoping they'd be gone when I got home. But they were always there, waiting for me; I guess no one else wanted a pair of ugly rain boots, either.

Anyway, boots or no boots, I was pretty amazed when Tommy Harriman noticed me, that's for sure. You see, until then I'd never had that kind of attention. My home life growing up was small, with an overbearing, cigar-smoking, poker-playing father, and a submissive mother who lived at his beck and call. As the middle child of three kids, I always felt like the fifth wheel on a cart that surely didn't need one. Our dad, a retired army sergeant, ran that house like a colonel herding a band of deserters. And my mother, well she just scurried about the house picking up after my brother and sister and me and waiting on dad hand and foot. Oh, she'd rush us kids off to church services with her whenever she could, either to praise God or get away from our own father, who knows. It never seemed like much of a life to me.

Thankfully, as a traveling insurance salesman, our father didn't stay home much anyway, and mom did most of the raising on her own. Maybe it was a good thing that he instilled the fear of God in us kids early on, but Mother kept us on a tight leash just to be sure.

Yes, I led a fairly sheltered life, but with a devout church-going mother and a domineering father, *really*, what could you expect?

Looking back now, I don't remember seeing much love between my parents. They never really fought, but that's probably because she did whatever he wanted. I swore back then that I wouldn't live like that when I got married. From family photos, I know that my father was a handsome man back in his day. He must have done quite a job of wooing my mother, because she'd told me once that they dated less than three months before they got married. Of course at some point I did the math in my head and figured out that my sister had been born just six months later.

I guess the apple doesn't fall far from the tree...

Anyway, nothing could have surprised me more than Tom Harriman liking me. After he and his friends passed by that day, right as I was about to duck into the safety of our old gray house, he yelled out to me, "Hey, there! What's your name?"

I remember I turned around on the top step, my hand still tight on the doorknob, and yelled back as saucy as I could, "Elizabeth... Beth, my name is Beth!"

Then I darted inside with a huge grin plastered on my face.

I guess, though, that's why they say some things are just meant to be. For that one day—and Tommy Harriman—altered the direction of my life forever.

The next day at school, he found me in the halls and we started hanging out together whenever he wasn't with his friends or playing football—during recess, after school at the soda shop downtown, and sometimes at the public library (the one place we could get some privacy). Soon after, he brought me to his house to meet his family. He had four siblings, all older girls and all still living at home. As the youngest child and the only boy, he was babied and coddled by his sisters. That certainly didn't help matters.

Tommy usually got what he wanted, even at the expense of others, and you could tell.

With that many young females running around, his house was rather crazy, and it was *the* place to be for the neighborhood kids to hang out. It was very different from my quiet, little home on the other side of town. Whereas my parents never raised their voices to each other and only grudgingly acknowledged each other's presence, Tommy's parents fought like cats and dogs and yelled constantly. They never seemed happy together. His mother told me once in a rare moment of candor that it was all because she was Italian and Tommy's dad was Irish and that their union had been doomed to failure from the start.

Poor Tommy, his relationship with his parents wasn't so good, either. Whenever I saw him with his father, their conversations were stilted and uncomfortable and often ended quickly. I'm sure his dad must have wanted a son early on, but I guess by the fourth child he'd just had enough and didn't care anymore.

As for his mother, I soon learned like the others before me that it was best to avoid that woman like the plague. She was a force to be reckoned with, God rest her soul. And I'm not just saying that because she ended up being my mother-in-law. No, Tommy and his sisters all tried to avoid her biting tongue and harsh whippings, and the rest of us stayed out of her way as best we could. Sometimes I think it was her irrational behavior and the discord between Tommy and his father that did him in.

I remember how cold his house always felt. Not the kind of cold that makes you run for a sweater, but one that gets at you from the inside and tenses you up like an icicle. Yes, the lack of real love in their home was a sad state. Looking back now, between his childhood and my own, it's no wonder that he and I didn't know what it took to make a marriage work. We'd never seen a good one!

I know I'd been looking for attention when I met him; maybe love was trying to find me, as well. In the innocence of our youth we were both searching for something new, something we'd never experienced before.

Yes, I fell head over heels for Tommy, but he chased after me, too—with all the drive of a crazed teenage boy! I could tell the other girls at school were envious, and I loved every minute of it. We dated for two years before his persistent teenage hormones finally wore me down. By then, I was a junior in high school and Tommy had recently graduated, working to take some courses at the community college if he could save up enough money. We were at the drive-in theater one Saturday night—I can't even remember what that damn movie was—and nervous as hell and with more guilt and excitement than I'd ever felt before, I let him go all the way for the first time.

There was nothing magical about it, I'll say that much; just some awkward groping by two kids in the back seat of a car. It ended before I'd even realized it. But at sixteen you just don't know all that yet, you know?

Anyway, it's odd how life turns out, though. For it was from that first fumbling encounter that I would soon learn a new life grew inside of me; and everything began to change.

2. KATHERINE HARRIMAN, ATTORNEY AT LAW

"ALRIGHT, MR. SHEFFIELD, LET'S GET this meeting started," Kate muttered to herself in the prodigious room that had served as her second home for more than five years.

If anyone else had been in her office with her, they would have seen a prepossessing and poised woman who appeared to be the picture of self-confidence. She sat rather stiffly behind her grand mahogany desk, attired in the usual grey pinstriped Burberry suit and white silk blouse underneath. Her manicured hands were folded neatly together and rested on top of the desk, the thumbs forming a perfect triangle between them. Tucked underneath the desk were long slender legs, crossed tightly at the ankles. Her legs received appreciative glances from both sexes on any given day as she strolled with purpose through the office halls. One Jimmy Choo-clad foot now tap-tapped at the air in rapid-fire as the only physical evidence of its owner's impatience for her meeting to begin.

At fifteen minutes before the hour, four o'clock could not arrive soon enough.

Kate looked down again at her prepared notes on Sheffield's case, carefully laid out in multiple folders across the desk. Her overly efficient assistant, Sam, had color-coded the folders with pastel Post-its so she could easily identify the contents of each one. The presence of the folders represented a mere formality, however, for Kate already knew each and every detail inside by heart.

Her eyes darted to the Grandfather clock across the room, and she emitted a heavy sigh as the hands slowly ticked the time away. Like a sentry footman, it guarded against all those who were admitted into her domain. The towering piece leaned heavily against the wall beside the door, the ticking of its gears echoing loudly in the room.

On the other side of the door stretched a wall-length credenza. Housed on its shelves were over a hundred books of all the notable legal cases dating back to the eighteen hundreds. The black and maroon binders, their spines labeled in crackled gold lettering, were an impressive display. Even more impressive, however, was the fact that the woman they belonged to could recite almost any case within them without once referencing their pages. As a result, a layer of dust had settled on the tops of most, and they remained there more for show than any actual use.

There were no family pictures in the room to be seen. No personal mementos that would offer guests a clue as to the woman who belonged to it. Only one overgrown cactus was on display on the massive credenza, a *Ferocactus pilosus* species that had long since outgrown the confines of its small potted container. The cactus was something that required so little maintenance that it could hardly be called a real plant. Its bulbous form towered next to four empty coffee mugs that were all lined neatly in a row at one end of the stand.

Sam knew well enough not to interrupt her during meeting preparations, so there the cups and the cold remnants of her Jamaican bold coffee remained.

Kate gazed at the cups longingly and sighed, knowing that it would be too late in the day for one final cup. In a flash of annoyance, she recalled her previous client, Bobby Burrell. A dowdy investment banker who came across as annoyingly fastidious and—she felt quite sure—suffered from OCD or some other undiagnosed illness. His neurosis had annoyed Kate to no end during the case. For some reason, he had retched at the mere smell of coffee so Kate had had no choice but to limit her intake when he came around. At one point, she'd thought about throwing the case just to be rid of the poor bastard, though she knew her pride would never have allowed it.

Like Burrell and so many others before him, her newest client, Bocephus (Bo) Sheffield, had contacted the Parker & McClellan law firm in a flurried state of panic. He had also demanded that Kate Harriman personally represent his case and said that he would accept no other representation. Kate had grown accustomed to such requests over the last few years after her many accolades in the courtroom. She had also grown accustomed to the subsequent looks of undisguised envy from the other attorneys at the firm, and she relished every one.

Now, thinking about adding yet another win to her already impressive portfolio made her heart race in anxious anticipation.

A sudden knock on the door interrupted her thoughts. "Yes?" she called out.

Sam slowly opened the door and poked his overly blond head inside, "Mr. Sheffield's secretary just called, Kate," he said with a smile. "He should be arriving shortly."

Kate opened her ruby painted mouth to offer him cursory thanks then simply nodded and looked back down at the notes on her desk.

Sam knew that Kate needed Sheffield's meeting to begin on time. The day marked her fifth-year anniversary dinner with Ethan, and they had decided to celebrate with a nice dinner out tonight. Sam had made their reservations for them over a month ago at the prestigious Le Noir restaurant on the east side of town. From their imported wine selection to the haughty wait staff, the upscale bistro offered a reputable dining experience for only the upper echelon of Atlanta society. Kate most loved their Frutti Di Mare dish—seafood was one of the few pleasant reminders of growing up near the coast in Maine that she allowed herself. She was very much looking forward to the evening… and to whatever lustrous gift Ethan decided to bestow upon her. However, for Kate, being *seen* at Le Noir was far more important than the celebration of any alleged marital milestone they may have achieved.

A movement caught her eye, and she looked up, surprised and somewhat irritated to see Sam still standing inside the doorway.

"What is it, Sam?" she snapped, wondering how she hadn't noticed that the door hadn't click shut with his exit.

He hesitated and stared at her expectantly before taking a small step into the room. He closed the door quietly behind him then, clasping both hands in front of him, took a deep breath and allowed the words to gush out.

"Kate, I overheard Parker on his phone earlier today. I'm not sure who it was with, but… well, I think you should tread lightly on this Sheffield case. I know you are after another win, but be mindful of who you'll be up against with this one, ok? Politics always makes for bad medicine, and I think the partners will be watching this one closely."

She knew that it took a lot of nerve for Sam to extend such a warning to her, so she tried to sound sincere in her reply without being condescending, "Thank you. I'll try to keep that in mind."

However, the wryness of her tone was not lost between them. They both knew that she would do whatever it took to ensure herself and her client another victory, no matter whom it involved.

Sam nodded with a resigned smile and quickly turned to scoop up the empty mugs on the credenza with a quick glance toward her before leaving the room. The click of the door closing behind him resonated softly; she could smell his expensive cologne lingering in the air. Kate knew that she was fortunate to have Sam. He had been by her side since she started with the firm, and he had stayed late many a night to assist her with case preparations. *I wonder if I've ever told him*, she thought briefly then just as quickly cast the wayward thought aside.

Stealing a glance outside the window, she saw the tops of the elms from below as they swayed in the autumn winds. In the back of her mind, watching the fallen leaves get swept up in the wintry air, she knew the small dip in the Atlanta temperature was nothing compared to the chilly digits they would already be experiencing back in Maine where she had spent her childhood. She shivered involuntarily, though much more at thoughts of the past than for the weather. Bad memories that she kept stored away threatened to resurface—the sorrow she felt growing up at home, the desperate feeling of wanting to get away, and those final years before she could finally escape and leave home. In that moment, her mind scurried in the darkness like a thief in the night, trying not to conjure up her childhood days; days that had been filled with sorrow, loneliness and anger that she had since worked so hard to forget.

Kate squeezed her eyes shut, and of its own volition her body began to rock back and forth in the overstuffed desk chair as she forced her mind to push back down the memories that threatened to haunt her.

Then, from the furthest recesses of her mind, *his* face emerged. Laughing at her, mocking her, scorning her, then another look, one she didn't understand at first, before he…

Click, click, Fwiing! The chime of the clock resonated loudly in the room. Her eyes flew open, and Kate exhaled slowly as she looked around the room. Grateful for the disruption to her errant thoughts, she shook her head hard, as if to rid her mind of what resided in it, and wished it could be that easy. As the seconds ticked by, she stared at the door in front of her, willing it to open and proffer her new client. The anticipation of Sheffield's imminent arrival coupled with the prospect of winning another case meant that the past was, for the moment, forgotten with the anticipation of Sheffield's imminent arrival, coupled with the prospect of winning.

It made her pulse begin to quicken and her heart beat faster. The corners of her mouth turned up at the edges before it became a full smile. The anticipation of Sheffield's imminent arrival coupled with the prospect of winning another case meant that the past was, for the moment, forgotten. The corners of her ruby painted mouth turned up into a Chesire-cat smile.

3. MOLLY CURTIS,
MOTHER OF TWO

"IT LOOKS LIKE A CYCLONE hit in here," Molly spoke softly, with an attempted smile, as she looked around. She stood in the middle of her living room with her hands planted on her widened hips and sadly surveyed the chaos around her.

Clad in her usual navy sweatpants and oversized T-shirt, Molly looked at the lot of children's toys, doll, books, and games that littered the furniture and floor. In the adjoining kitchen, piles of breakfast dishes still covered the counter top and the never-ending mound of dirty laundry on the landing of the stairs remained a formidable heap. Emitting a heavy sigh, she bent over with a small *oomph* and picked up a few Dr. Seuss books from the floor. Then, disheartened by the extent of the mess, she simply tossed them back down and slowly straightened up again.

"Lord, I don't even know where to begin," she mumbled and walked back into the outdated, though brightly lit, kitchen.

Standing at the sink, she glanced outside with remorse at the rain that still came down in buckets, hearing its rhythmic pelting against the glass. In typical Maine fashion, autumn had delivered yet another storm, despite the weatherman's assurance of sun, so she and the girls had been forced to spend the day indoors. With two rambunctious children under the age of six to entertain, that became quite a feat. During the morning, Molly had tried to keep them busy making hand puppets out of paper bags, baking chocolate chip cookies, and playing dress-up. In between, the girls had done well to entertain themselves, dancing around the house with their pink frilly tutus on and playing school.

She looked on with a broad smile as the girls came down the stairs, one behind the other, and darted into the living room. They chased each other around the couch, laughing wildly and shrieking with delight. Molly hoped no more injuries or bruises would mark the day. Emma had already experienced a run-in with the coffee table, which had produced a nice little Robin's egg on her forehead; Molly knew that Jack would surely fret over it when he arrived home. Not long after that incident, Alice had tumbled off the back of the couch, landing sharply on a pile of her Barbie dolls. From the ear-piercing screams, Molly had at first thought that her daughter must have broken something. But the drama of the moment eventually passed, and no more bruises or markings arose... *at least not yet, anyway*, she thought wryly.

At that moment, as if her daughters had somehow read her mind, Molly heard a loud shriek. Molly's breathing stopped as she looked their way. Her back tensed up as she waited for screaming to ensue, but only their laughter continued and she gratefully exhaled. *Just a typical day for the Curtis household,* she thought, then with a small frown she unconsciously rubbed at the side of her head. For a moment, she closed her eyes tightly against the disorder that encircled her and tried to pretend that it just wasn't there.

Turning to note the time on the microwave in the kitchen— *three thirty five on the dot, good*—she decided to begin dinner preparations a little earlier than usual. As the weekly menu on the family blackboard stated, she planned to make turkey lasagna with a side salad. The meal had become one of Jack's favorites, at least the lasagna, anyway; Molly knew Jack only ate anything crunchy and green because she asked. He would tease her, saying that with her big doe-eyes she could get him to eat mud if she asked him to.

In her ancient oven, the lasagna always took longer to bake than anticipated, so she knew she needed to get started on it soon. She'd been asking for a new oven and stove unit for ages, but with one income and two children, there were always other things that demanded their money first. Molly stopped, suddenly feeling a momentary sense of panic. She couldn't remember if she had fresh lettuce in the fridge or not. She turned on her heel and yanked the fridge door open, her eyes frantically searching for signs of a light green head inside. Finally, spotting the cellophane orb half-hidden in the back, she breathed a sigh of relief. She scooped everything she needed into her arms, turned around, and dropped it all onto the island counter top.

While she started dinner preparations, Molly quietly hummed *You Are My Sunshine* without being aware, and the girls continued playing together in the other room. As she stood at the sink and filled a pot with water, she hoped the girls would be good long enough for her to finish getting everything ready for supper.

Molly liked to have their supper done and on the table by the time Jack came home at night. After working at the mill all day while she stayed with the girls, she felt it was the least she could do. Her "work" (though she hated to even call it that) as a stay-at-home mom was exhausting for sure.

Gosh, how could it really be called work when I love being with them so much? She smiled as she worked, her hands deftly washing and slicing vegetables and shredding cheese. As mothers will do, she periodically looked over to check on them without even realizing it as the girls continued to dash around the room.

Alice had recently turned five, and Emma was two and a half years younger though barely an inch shorter in height. By appearance, they could almost be identical twins. Both girls had curly brown hair and saucer-like brown eyes, just like Molly. Their red lips pursed like dolls when they weren't laughing, and they browned equally in the sun. She referred to them as her "Little Brown Beauties," though never in front of them for Alice would object with a scrunched-up face and tell her that brown was a "yucky" color. Though they looked similar in appearance, Molly knew better than anyone how deep their difference ran. Alice took after Molly with her sweet personality and a heart that burst with love for everything and everyone. She wore her heart on her sleeve and already behaved like a teenager on many a day. Often the peacekeeper in the family, she showed a more nurturing nature and was forever being helpful with her baby sister. Changing Emma's clothes as if she were her own baby, washing her up and getting her dressed in the mornings. More often than not, however, it was with shoes on the wrong feet, a shirt ill buttoned, and hat askew.

Little Emma was the opposite in so many ways. Though the younger of the two, *she* behaved like a wild one and was a real tomboy. Most of the time, Molly found herself protecting Alice from Emma instead of the other way around. Silly, impish and quick to react, even for a two-year old, Emma loved to make people laugh, and her silliness shone through at the oddest of occasions. Her playful impish personality reminded Molly so much of Jack that it sometimes startled her.

"They are beautiful," Molly spoke softly to herself and sighed as she looked back around her home. "It's hard to believe that they're responsible for all this chaos."

Well, almost, she added with a small smile and raised brows.

"But, as they say," she continued, forcing a brightness in her voice that she didn't truly feel inside, "a messy home is a happy home, ri-?"

Molly stopped short and shook her head in chastisement. "Lord, I have *got* to stop talking to myself like this. People will think I'm going crazy!" She shook her head in frustration. Yet with another frown she thought, *sometimes I think I am losing it,* then shook the idea away like a bad dream upon awakening.

Peering over at the girls again, envious of their boundless energy, she decided that she should try to calm them down before things got too far out of hand. Quickly washing her hands and wiping them dry on her checkered apron, she took a few steps away from the kitchen and took a deep breath to gather up her strength. Yet, as if on cue, the two pig-tailed heads suddenly dashed around the corner into their playroom, red-faced and laughing, and the house suddenly went calm.

Molly waited just a moment then peeked around the corner from the kitchen into the room—one that was intended to be a formal dining room, but had ended up housing all the girls' toys when they were properly stored away. Grateful, she saw them playing nicely together, having already created some imaginative game with their tea set and dolls. She breathed a small sigh of relief.

"Well, that's more like it," she said softly.

The girls barely glanced up at her when she spoke, accustomed to hearing their mother talk to herself during the day. They continued talking to each other, each one taking on a role of tea server and guest, and included the dolls they liked most in their tea party by lining them up in the chairs around the little table. Molly looked on as Alice carefully set out the small cups and dishes, talking softly about who should sit where and how many biscuits they should all get with their tea. Then she leaned over to pick up a nearby book. She pretended to read to her sister and dolls that had joined the tea party at the little table, as Emma served them all tea.

Molly smiled, for she knew that Alice couldn't actually read all of the printed words yet. She had simply heard their bedtime stories so many times that she could recite them by heart.

Little Emma reached out to grasp her hand, and seeing that small but loving gesture, Molly's heart seized up with love. Then, stealing another glance at the clock behind her, she darted back into the kitchen to finish dinner. She sighed loudly, already feeling worn out and tired from the day. It had been such a long one, being trapped inside with the rain, that she felt as if the day should already be over and done with. But her mind began to rattle off all the day's unfinished tasks that would require more energy than she may have to give, and she knew the day was far from over... *finish supper, give the girls their baths, get Jack's lunch packed.*

In that moment, thinking about everything that she still needed do, her body tensed up, and Molly felt the familiar surge of panic begin to creep in. Her face scrunched into a grimace, and she felt her spine cinch tight and her neck tense. She hated to be overwhelmed, and too many days lately that's exactly how she felt. Lately, the thousands of little things that had to be taken care of throughout the day were enough to cause her a level of anxiety that she didn't think was possible. Her heart began to beat faster, and the sensation felt like small explosions ricocheting inside her body. Sensing that her anxiety might lurch out of control—*Again?!* her mind screamed out in frustration—Molly quickly darted down into the bathroom and locked the door behind her, alone and away from any questioning looks from her daughters.

She squeezed her eyes tight and tried counting backwards from one hundred as the doctor had suggested. Whispering the numbers slowly and carefully, Molly hoped to ward off the threat of panic in her mind that lately seemed as if it would smother her soul.

4. SUCCESS IS EVERYTHING

DURING HER EXTENSIVE PREPARATIONS FOR Bocephus—*God, I hope he goes by Bo*, Kate thought with mild aggravation—Sheffield's case, she had learned that his family had started an adoption agency over sixty years ago. Sheffield had taken over the business twenty years before, after his own adopted parents had passed away. He renamed the agency *Matters of a Lifetime*, and since then he had made a name for himself in the industry. Under his heavy-handed yet warm-hearted tutelage, the agency had flourished, placing thousands of children in new homes around the Southeast.

Kate discovered through her research that the adoption industry had experienced a sort of "transformation of intent" over the years. Initially, adoption had primarily been the answer to the growing number of orphans that existed during the post-depression era. Then at some point during the early twentieth century, the industry's focus shifted from offering a home for children of all ages to primarily providing infants for couples who could not procreate. The system ceased being solely about the children and turned into a hugely profitable business.

Sheffield's agency, however, had always maintained the creed of putting the children first, no matter what, and sought their own profit and gain second. One article Kate had located concerning Sheffield's moral business practices described him as "a businessman who was honest to a tee" and "truly adored by his faithful staff." He had even been referred to as "Papa Bo" by his staff, despite the fact that he had never had any children of his own.

Kate was pleased that he had a solid reputation. It made her job that much easier.

The reason behind her elation at bringing in Sheffield's case, however, had much more to do with the opposing party involved than any sense of do-goodness. For just as Sam had warned her moments before, the lawsuit against Sheffield had come from none other than the city's Mayor, W.T. Thomason and his heiress wife, Greta McConnell Thomason Pearson. The formidable pair was recognized locally as the perfect parallel of power and money and had become a political force to be reckoned with, though most would agree that Greta was the one who truly ran the day-to-day show. She was known as a smart and savvy business woman who had been born with a silver spoon in her mouth, and she usually got whatever she wanted. Kate was well versed enough in local news and political affairs to be aware of Greta's biting reputation in the community.

According to Sheffield's initial statements, Mayor Thomason had been more than agreeable to most of the children presented to the couple for adoption over the years. It was Greta who had found some reason to decline each and every one, with a snub of her nose and a jerk of her head. Over a period of two years, Sheffield had looked on as she turned away dozens of children before he had had enough. He finally told Pearson so in no uncertain terms and threatened to cancel their contract for good. The next day, Greta had allegedly charged into Sheffield's office and delivered the lawsuit herself, slapping the papers down on Sheffield's desk for "failure to fulfill contractual obligation." Then, sputtering something about "taking you for everything you're worth," she had stormed out of his office in a huff, with her flustered chauffeur trailing behind her.

Thinking about Greta Pearson and what a privileged life the woman must have led made Kate's back bristle and her eyes glint. Her own upbringing had been devoid of any wealth or niceties—*or much of anything good for that matter,* she thought bitterly— so the excitement and anticipation at coming up against such a powerful woman as Greta Pearson—and the opportunity to bring her down—was almost too great to bear.

Kate felt like a greyhound waiting for the starting gate to be thrust open and all but panted as she sat behind her desk ready for Sheffield's meeting to begin.

Her eyes slid over the small, coiled glass snake that sat on the edge of the desk, and she couldn't help but smile. The piece, often the icebreaker with clients, was the result of an office prank earlier in the year after a large number of high-publicity trial wins that she'd earned. The local press, who had been more than liberal in their praise of her courtroom achievements had described Kate Harriman as being "tough as nails and a lawyer to be reckoned with," with an "uncanny ability to strike at her opponents when the time was right." It was the latter sharp-edged description that had prompted the deliverance of the snake figurine. Kate had found the small sculpture perched on her desk late one afternoon. The following day, she'd noted the unrestrained snickers from the others in the office and had pretended to be annoyed; she, of course, had her reputation to uphold.

But inwardly, she had been beside herself with indulgent glee. For being compared to a snake in a world still primarily dominated by men was an accomplishment in her eyes. Her shrewdness and astute perceptions of jurors and testifiers were virtually unprecedented, and her reputation as a closer grew quickly. Early on, she found that she could be as effective in the courtroom as any man, if not often more so, whittling lying testifiers down to tears, creating doubt in jurors' minds where none should be found, and winning case after case.

After the newspaper articles came out, somehow the epithet "Lady Viper" got started around the office, and eventually the local press caught on to Kate's new nickname, though some surmised that Kate had alerted the press herself. Her fellow attorneys would call out the name in the halls as they passed her by, and each time Kate smiled inside with unfettered delight.

Since then, the glass snake secured its distinguished place on the front corner of her desk for all who entered to see. For her, it served as a constant reminder of her hard-earned accomplishments in life and how far she had come.

5. COUNTING THROUGH THE FEAR

"EIGHTY. SEVENTY-NINE, SEVENTY-EIGHT…" MOLLY STILL stood alone in the bathroom, counting to try to calm herself down when a sudden knock on the door made her jump.

"Mommy! I have to go really bad," moaned the small voice of her oldest daughter from the other side.

Molly could hear the shuffle of tiny feet and recognized the "potty dance" of a child who had held it for far too long. She forced herself to open her eyes and look in the mirror, afraid, as always, that she would see some crazed monster staring back.

Yet the face that peered out of the glass looked to be the same tired-looking woman as always, with permanently etched worry lines and troubled eyes. Molly peered closer and thought she saw more lines around her face than before. Fleetingly, she wondered if a new worry line found its way to her face with each passing day and sighed heavily.

"Mommy, are you in there?" Alice pleaded again as she rattled the locked doorknob.

Molly's mouth was dry, so when she spoke the words were high and crisp, "Yes, I'll be right out, sweetie."

She subconsciously pushed a lock of hair behind her ear that was long overdue for a cut and shook her head hard, trying to ward off the bad feelings. Reluctantly, she pushed open the door and quickly left the safe confines of the bathroom. She brushed past her daughter to dart back into the kitchen, as Alice pushed her way inside the bathroom. The little girl barely looked up at her mother as she struggled to pull down her skirt, half close the door, and hobble over to the toilet.

Molly stood in the middle of the kitchen, turned to the windows, and breathed deeply, trying to relax. She felt as if the floor

shifted and swayed under her feet and that the walls were pushing in. She hated herself for it. She stared blankly outside and
watched as the rain continued to beat down, unconsciously mas-
saging the pounding that persisted inside her head.

A few minutes later, Alice exited the bathroom, throwing a
questioning glance toward her mother when the usual callout to
make sure the toilet was flushed and hands were cleaned did not
happen. But her mother remained perfectly still, with her back
to her, and didn't even notice the little girl walk by. Alice rejoined
Emma who had moved back to the living room, still preferring
at her young age not to be alone in a room where she couldn't
see her mother. The girls resumed their pretend play, engaging in
their secret little world.

When Molly eventually turned around to look at them, her
heart ached. She desperately wished that time could stand still
and her girls could stay like this forever. They were innocent,
sweet, and carefree, unaware of the inevitable troubles of life and
the harsh realities of growing older that would hit them someday.
She knew that they were blissfully oblivious to any problems or
danger beyond a lost toy, a broken crayon, or a misplaced puzzle
piece. She ached to run over and hug them in close to her and
squeeze them tight. For in those simple moments, Molly could
pretend that nothing else in the world mattered. It served as a
cloaked pretense of happiness, she knew, but it was one that still
managed to block out the fear and worry that needled its way
inside to her core.

Just get busy, Molly, and do what needs to be done. Just get busy, she
told herself. Then she laughed out loud as it reminded her of Dory
on the *Nemo* movie that she'd seen a dozen times with the girls.

"Just keep swimming, just keep swimming," sang Ellen Dege-
neres, the voice of little blue fish that helped Nemo's father, Marlin, find his son again. She played a character who was forever
blithe and eternally optimistic. Her constant cheerfulness drove
poor Marlin to the brink of insanity.

Maybe that's how Jack feels, maybe I'm just Marlin the downer,
Molly thought with bitter sadness.

She sighed, knowing that Jack behaved like a saint for putting up with her these days. Between her panic spells and taking care of her mother—which some days felt like another fulltime job beyond the daily demands of motherhood—sometimes it just became too much. Jack never complained, though, and had hardly a bad word to say about any of it. She loved him even more for it.

"That's my Jack, always happy. Lord, I wish I could be like that just for a day," she mumbled with heartfelt remorse.

Forcing her limbs to start moving, she began to clean off the counter and load the dishwasher, unaware that her face had taken on a look of extreme melancholy that didn't let go. It wasn't long, though, before shrieks from Alice interrupted the calm in the house and the girls needed Molly's motherly intervention once again.

"Mommy! Emma took her diaper off!"

Molly turned to focus her unseeing eyes on the girls barely in time to see a little plop of brown land onto the floor behind Emma as she stood in the living room. The little girl looked quickly up at her mother then ran laughing to the other side of the room with a Hansel-and-Gretel-like trail falling behind her.

"Nooo, Emma! Stop, honey!" Molly shouted. She ran over to Emma and scooped her daughter up in her arms, laughing at the absurdity of it all. The realization that something could still be on her daughter's dimpled little bottom barely occurred to Molly as she drew Emma's squirmy body in close. Emma giggled and wrapped her pudgy arms around her mother's neck. Molly's heart ached with love.

"Enuf, mommy, enuf!" Emma squealed and tried to wriggle out of her mother's tight grasp.

Wiping Emma off and putting a new diaper on her, Molly experienced that familiar surge of regret at having just two children. When she and Jack got married, she thought that they would someday have a house full of kids. She knew how lonely it felt to grow up without siblings around, as her older sister had left home when she was just eight, and she wanted nothing like that for her own children. The days of playing solitaire, doing word searches, and calling around to different friends' houses desperate to find someone to play with were long past for her. However, with one family income—steady but not stellar, as Jack liked to joke—after Emma arrived, she'd had no choice but to agree that two children would have to be enough.

But as she glanced down at her pant legs—dirtied with the fingerprint marks of jelly, peanut butter, and something else she couldn't identify—Molly managed a small half-smile. She knew with sadness that, finances and circumstances aside, two children were all she could handle anyway. Particularly with everything else going on.

"Mommy, when will Daddy be home?" Alice called out in her sweet toddler voice.

"Oh, soon, baby, soon," Molly gushed, feeling equally as anxious for Jack's arrival.

She finished cleaning up Emma then headed back to the kitchen. Glancing again at the clock and seeing that Jack would soon be home, she smiled with memories of her husband and the good times they had shared. She felt just the same toward Jack as she had five years ago on the day they met. She had seen enough bitter divorces to know *not* to take her marriage for granted.

I only hope that Jack still cares for me the same, the small voice pleaded inside her head.

Taking a deep breath, Molly squeezed her eyes shut and attempted again to push the anxieties of her life away, anxieties that constantly threatened to surface and forever crowd out any goodness. Rubbing her head and feeling the tension wrapped up inside like a taut rubber band, she stopped moving and closed her eyes. Placing both hands on the kitchen counter, she stood still and waited for the feeling of anxiety to pass. However, the pain inside her head began to pulsate louder, and her muscles began to spasm. When her knees almost gave way, it took every ounce of strength she had not to shout out for help, even while knowing that there was no one nearby who could.

She turned her back to the girls with teeth clenched, not wanting to scare them any more than she already had. Too often, she saw them looking up at her with a measure of fear in their own eyes, and she hated herself for it. Taking a deep breath, she willed the moment to pass and waited for the heavy blackness inside her head to fade away.

Molly knew that it had been the trials and tribulations of taking care of her *own* mother that had created most of the anxiety in her life, on top of everything else that she did as a mother and wife. Each week, Beth had seemed to need more and more from her and could handle less and less on her own, even though no one understood why. Sometimes her catatonic states would turn into extreme fits of crying in just a split-second, other times she tried to initiate endless conversations with Molly that were seemingly about nothing and went nowhere. Being a caregiver for someone who was sometimes irrational and sometimes crazed had added a dimension of stress that Molly simply didn't feel equipped to handle. She did whatever she could to help her mother, but sometimes the pressure and her mother's failing condition were just too much to bear.

With her eyes clenched tight, she gripped the counter harder and said with as much conviction as she could muster, "I am not like her, I am not like her..."

She held on tightly, trying to ward off the feeling that she was standing near the edge of a precipice about to fall in. Finally, after she didn't know how many moments had passed, the anxiety subsided, and her body relaxed. Molly slowly opened her eyes, yet the numbing thought that she really could be just as twisted inside as her mother and would someday end up just like her, would not let go.

6. HINTS FROM THE PAST

KATE LOOKED AROUND THE OFFICE that had served as her second home for the last five years and felt a familiar surge of pride. The room boasted of success, and she had fought for it each step of the way, letting no one get in the way. She had been given nothing and earned it all—the large corner suite, the impressive view of the city below, the grand mahogany desk that seemed to engulf the room—and felt a strong measure of pride.

Beside her, the phone intercom buzzed loudly, interrupting her thoughts. *Right on time,* she noted with a glance at the clock. Sam's voice scratched through the antiquated phone system.

"Mr. Sheffield is here now, Ms. Harriman. Shall I send him in?"

"Yes, thank you, Sam."

Seconds after the words left her mouth, her office door was thrust open. In strode a large man clad in a startling blue periwinkle seersucker suit. His hefty frame seemed to overtake the doorway. In one hand, he held an old-fashioned worn leather briefcase; in the other, a long wooden cane. He appeared to be quite portly, reflecting a mixture of old age and days of good eating. A thick crown of shockingly white hair encircled his head, causing him to appear almost surreal. A smile that seemed to reach the top of his head covered his face with a clown-like quality about it.

He spoke loudly, his voice overtaking the room, in that timeless Southern drawl that could still occasionally be heard on the streets downtown, "Good afternoon! Ms. Kate Harriman, I presume?"

He stood there smiling broadly in the doorway of Kate's office and entered no further as she rose behind her desk.

She thought he appeared rather foolish, like the cat that swallowed the canary, as he stared openly back at her with that broad grin. *Hey, I'm not the canary here, buddy, let's keep that straight.* She nodded and stared straight back at him from behind her desk, arrogantly waiting for him to come in.

As if he'd read her mind, Sheffield began to amble toward her desk. Kate noticed that despite his formidable size he still managed to exude a refined sort of class. He was quite well dressed in a suit that appeared expensive, even if slightly faded from wear. He looked as if he came from a bygone era, a time before a mass influx of northern transplants had taken over the city and the once distinct lines between North and South had merged more incongruously together. He set his briefcase and cane down beside her desk and stood upright again, allowing a small gasp of exertion to escape his lips.

With one of her overly confident and prepared smiles, Kate extended a firm hand in greeting. "Hello, Mr. Sheffield, it's good to finally meet you."

"Well, I'll be! You're even prettier than you sound on the phone," he exclaimed as he reached forward enthusiastically to shake her hand. Kate's slim fingers were immediately engulfed in his pudgy grasp as he pumped it up and down.

She pretended to ignore the compliment, though inwardly she felt pleased. Kate knew in a guiltless form of narcissism that she looked damn good for her age—tall and slim, "femininely fit" as she liked to describe herself. She smiled coyly and unconsciously swung her head to the side, causing her long auburn hair to tumble in soft waves around her shoulders. The action evoked a small smile of thanks from her guest, as she knew it would.

She tried to extract her hand, but Sheffield held it firmly in his, not yet ready to let it go.

"Yes, I can see now why you have the reputation that you do, my dear." The ridiculous grinning smile never left his face as he held on to his now sweaty grasp of her hand. His eyes gave her an admiring once-over then strayed nonchalantly down to the glass snake on the desk.

Kate followed his gaze, then looked back at him squarely. "Oh? What reputation is that, Mr. Sheffield?" she prompted with well-feigned innocence.

"Well, we *all* know that you've been dubbed the 'Lady Viper' for your many accolades in the courtroom, Ms. Harriman. Let's not be shy about it!" he exclaimed as he finally relinquished her hand.

He absentmindedly reached down to glide his hand over the cool glass piece. Kate offered him another small smile as she discreetly wiped her hand on her skirt and sat back down, motioning for him to do the same at one of the two high-backed chairs next to him.

"Shall we get started then? We *do* have a case to win."

"That we do, Ms. Harriman! That we do."

Sheffield agreeably sat down, wedging his ample body into the chair's cushioned frame. Not put off by her business-like demeanor, he immediately began talking about his agency, describing the "many *wonnerful* things" that they had done for families over the years. Most of his discourse Kate already knew through her preliminary research, so maintaining her usual eagle-sharp focus became increasingly difficult with each passing moment. Eventually, though, aided by her not-so-gentle prompting and a quick reminder of her hourly fee, Sheffield swung the conversation around to the Thomson/Pearson case.

In retelling the story of the scenario with Greta, Sheffield confessed with the telltale averted eyes of a guilty man that he *may* have shouted a few derogatory words to her as she'd left his office the day she'd delivered the lawsuit to him.

"It's not like I tol' that uppity woman what a pain in the ass she had been," he declared defensively then grumbled under his breath, "Though I certainly could have, you know, and then some!"

Sheffield shifted in his chair and huffed a little from the effort. The buttons of his blazer threatened to come undone at his midsection with each breath. He stared out the window in thought, breathing hard. Despite the fact that Sam kept her office at a pleasant sixty-eight degrees, Kate noticed small beads of sweat had formed on Sheffield's brow. He clumsily wiped at them with an old-fashioned looking lace handkerchief that seemed to come out of nowhere then deftly tucked the cloth out of sight again like an accomplished magician.

When he didn't immediately continue, Kate again prompted him, somewhat impatiently, "Go on, Mr. Sheffield."

He complied, grudgingly at first, then telling her in increasing detail about his relationship with the Mayor and Pearson, about the work his agency had done for them over the years, and the rude interactions with Pearson at every exchange. Slowly, the hands of the old grandfather clock edged past five o'clock as Kate struggled to maintain her patience while listening to Sheffield's ongoing diatribe. As he talked on, his indignant anger escalated a few times more, and he allowed a steady stream of expletives to fire rapidly off his tongue. It reminded Kate of those cheap cracker-jack fireworks sold at grocery stores—no bang for the buck, just lots of noise. One wayward comment made reference to seeing Pearson's "overly tight behind" as she had stormed out. This elicited a chuckle from Kate that she did her best to hide.

It was at that moment that Kate realized with a measure of surprise that she may actually like this Bocephus Sheffield. The unexpectedness of the thought caught her off guard. Normally, a client was just that—a client and nothing more. Merely a stepping-stone for her career. She spent time with each of them with the intent of learning more information to help win their case, that was all.

Yet Kate saw something in Sheffield that she couldn't help but admire. *Well, at least a jury should do the same,* she thought with measured satisfaction.

His voice suddenly bellowed out her name, causing her to jump just a little in her chair.

"Ms Harriman!"

Looking directly at him as if she'd been focused on him all along, she answered, "Yes, Mr. Sheffield?" A forced look of attentiveness rested on her masked face.

"I was asking how long will this thing take to resolve? Why, just gettin' ready for our meetin' today has already eaten up my time like a crow on a carcass!"

Kate turned her head and had to bite her lip to keep from laughing out loud at her convivial client's choice of words.

"Well, that remains to be seen, Mr. Sheffield, but rest assured that I will work toward a swift and successful resolution on your case."

"I know," he said softly. A momentary darkness passed over her face as he turned and gazed out the window. "It's just that casting all those children aside like that is a real tragedy for us all. Kids *need* a good home, and I just don't know how could someone do such a thing."

At those words, Kate's heartbeat quickened and her breath caught in her throat. The emotion emerged so strong that she shuddered involuntarily as if a cold chill had snaked down her spine. The movement caught Sheffield's eye, and he looked at her questioningly. Kate looked down at her desk to try to hide a further reaction, hating what had come over her. Inside she was seething, for her emotions had betrayed her. Busying herself with a folder, she pretended to search for something while avoiding Sheffield's eyes. As the silence grew louder, the seconds felt like eternity. She struggled to recover in the moment, but it was Sheffield who finally broke the quiet. He spoke with a slight edge to his voice.

"Ms. Harriman, what just happened? You look ill all of a sudden."

She answered a bit too forcibly, forcing herself to look up and face him, "I'm fine! It's nothing, I was simply reminded of something... about another case," her voice trailed off. She knew it came out full of uncertainty and she despised her displayed weakness.

Sheffield sharply drew in his breath before he responded.

"You know," he said quietly, "I've been around a long time, and I've seen quite a few things in my lifetime. I know damn well when something's wrong, now what is it that caused you to look so queer?"

The odd use of the word caused Kate to somewhat relax. She exhaled quietly and offered up a small smile to Sheffield, releasing tension in her body that she didn't know she'd been holding.

Then, speaking as casually as she could, she attempted to assure him.

"Really, everything's fine, Mr. Sheffield. I had just been thinking about a recent case—another win, actually. That's all. " And though the reassurance sounded hollow even to her ears, Kate could sense that Sheffield struggled, wanting to believe her.

A few seconds passed before she could attempt to offer what she hoped was a confident smile. Her voice sounded louder than she'd intended when she spoke again. "Shall we continue then? There is much work to be done here."

Sheffield looked at Kate with his head cocked to one side and his eyebrows raised. He shifted in his seat and finally spoke in a conciliatory tone, "All right, but you *will* tell me if there's anything wrong."

"Of course, Mr. Sheffield, of course," Kate said, her voice coming out in a strange singsong way. It reminded her of how her mother used to try to appease her about something they'd been fighting about. She had used that same irritatingly fake tone that had always grated on Kate's nerves. Kate shook her head involuntarily and spoke more confidently. "Yes, I assure you, there is absolutely nothing to worry about."

Inwardly cursing her momentary weakness, she forced herself to let the moment go. Yet just as she began to congratulate herself for bringing the meeting back under control, Sheffield's next question shook her to her very core.

"Well, tell me then, Ms. Harriman. Will you be needing to see any other adoption records of ours? If so, how many years back would we be talkin' about for all those abandoned children who need a home?"

Kate looked up sharply at Sheffield. She felt as if he may be toying with her, yet sheer logic told her that couldn't be the case. Her smile completely dropped away from her face, and her mouth went dry. An overwhelming and unreasonable sense of panic threatened to overtake her. She stared back at Sheffield with unblinking eyes and didn't even attempt to offer him an answer. She simply shook her head back and forth. Struggling to maintain composure, she thought that maybe—just maybe—by remaining quiet she could somehow make the moment disappear.

Turning away from Sheffield's questioning gaze, she caught a glimpse of her pained reflection in the window glass and blanched inside. The woman who looked back was pale, almost hollow, though Kate's innate sensibility told her that it had more to do with the afternoon sun than anything else. Closing her eyes, she fought hard against the pain of the past that had been buried inside, then swallowed hard and slowly turned back to face Sheffield.

With the pleading desperation of a lost soul, Kate smiled wanly back. She willed the demons that haunted her inside to disappear as she struggled to find an answer.

7. NOTHING EVER STAYS THE SAME

WHEN TOM AND I FINALLY told everyone about the baby, I was already five months along. They screamed and ranted and raved while Tommy and I just stood there and listened. As the news traveled around school, our friends all looked on with awe, knowing what we had done. Our teachers shook their heads in reproach. Some people encouraged me to give up the baby so I could finish high school and graduate along with everyone else. Others suggested to me in more subtle and hushed tones that I should go away for a while and "just take care of it."

I remember how scared I felt, but what girl wouldn't be?! I wouldn't dream of doing anything to my baby, though, and Tommy's fear of sullying his good-guy reputation in town was enough to prompt a hasty proposal. We were married in a small courthouse ceremony about a month later. My little Katherine was just barely starting to show under the hand-me-down baby blue dress my tearful mother had given me to wear. The service was brief. I think the only one smiling was my annoying younger brother who pretended to make farting noises with his armpit in the back of the hall.

Those few months after were just a blur. We lived with Tommy's parents until we found an inexpensive little apartment in town. Then two weeks before my due date, she was born. I delivered naturally after three hours of God-awful, mind-numbing pain. They say the mind will forget pain, but that's just rubbish. I certainly appreciate the epidural with her sister ten years later!

When my contractions began, it was early on a Sunday morning. That didn't work out so well for Tom, because he was never much of an early riser on the weekends. I remember he was snoring like a hibernating bear when I finally woke him up. By then,

I'd already been in labor for a few hours, and the pain was almost unbearable. He didn't believe me at first when I told him we needed to get to the hospital right away—as if he'd seen so many other pregnant women, the oaf! He actually rolled over and fell back to sleep. My screams must have finally convinced him, though, because he jumped out of bed, got dressed, and quickly ushered me outside into that old orange Duster of his. He drove like a demon to the hospital, all white-knuckled on the wheel. I remember he kept yelling at me to stop distracting him with my screams. By the time we made it there, my contractions were less than a minute apart, and she almost popped out of me right on the hospital steps!

My baby girl was beautiful, though. Once they'd washed her all up and handed her to me, I looked down in my arms to see a full head of dark red hair and fine porcelain-like skin. I know she got her hair from Tom's crazy mother, but it looked much more adorable on my baby girl. She looked just like an angel. As soon as the nurses let Tom into the room, I looked up at him and said as surely as I had ever said anything in my life, "Her name is Katherine, just like my great-grandmother. She was such a sweet woman." Then under my breath, I'd called Tom a jackass for not believing me about my labor pains. All the nurses had laughed.

I guess it was a sign of things to come with my Katherine, though, for I learned later on that my grandmother's name didn't exactly match my little girl. No, she had a fiery fierceness inside her right from the start.

Things were tough in those first few years. Tom had already enrolled in a nearby community college, but once Katherine came he'd had no choice but to stop his studies and take a full-time job to support us. His father got a job for him down at the town mill. It was dirty but steady, and it paid the bills. For me, instead of finishing high school with the rest of my classmates, I had to quit school and learn how to be a mother. Katherine was full-time work, and though I did take on a few hours at nights at the mom-n-pop hardware store to help make ends meet, money was scarce.

At first, I thought that Tom and I were happy together, but maybe we were just so tired that we didn't know any better. While my friends were out going to football games on Friday nights and hanging out at the local drive-in, Tom would fall asleep in his Lazy Boy and I was alone in bed by nine o'clock, exhausted and worn thin.

By the time Katherine had turned three, she had a full head of gorgeous auburn curls and a fiery personality to match. I remember people would stop me on the street and comment on how pretty she was. Being twenty with a toddler was a difficult thing to hide in a small town, but with her curly red locks we definitely stood out everywhere we went. The ones who knew me looked at me with judgmental eyes—eyes that were hypocritically raised to God each Sunday morning at church, I know. And strangers would look back and forth between us, trying to figure out if she could really be mine.

They would all say the same thing, though. "Oh, what an *adorable* little girl she is!" I'd simply thank them quietly and walk away.

Adorable on the outside, maybe, but on the inside Katherine was as obstinate as any child could be. Lord, she was a handful! She often drove Tom and me to the ends of our wits with her stubborn antics. Early on, my father nicknamed her "The Firecracker." That lasted until she was about five, when he called her that one day and she walked right up to him, put her hands on her hips, and used the most condescending tone I'd ever heard used toward my father.

"Grandpa, I am a lady now. And you are *not* allowed to call me that anymore!"

I laughed so hard! No one had *ever* talked to my father that way. The look on his face was priceless.

Anyway, taking care of a small child, let alone one with such a strong will, became more difficult than I could have ever imagined. And as time went by, the challenges of being married *and* being a parent began to settle in hard for Tom and me. It wasn't long before we realized that the union of our personalities on paper proved quite disastrous in real life. We were different, yet as time went on, those difference weren't the kind of opposites that attract—or so that ridiculous expression goes. We fought about everything, all the time, and eventually grew apart. Those last years that we were together were filled with high-volume screaming matches and—I am embarrassed to say—a fair amount of profanity.

We were trying to be grownups and raise a child while we were still kids ourselves.

Yes, things were hard then, but what hurt me most is that Tom seemed like he stopped caring. Most nights, he was either sitting in his recliner guffawing at some damn TV show, or going out drinking with his friends like life was normal. He started to come home from work later and found excuses to be somewhere other than at home with Katie and me on the weekends. Somewhere along the way, I turned into an angry young woman—overtired, underappreciated and unloved—and Tom avoided it all, finding more and more reasons to spend time away.

I'm sure he had his own share of annoyances with me, as well, but we all have our own versions of life and sometimes that's all we really have to live by. I know that I tried to make things work between us, though as I remember those days now that I'm older, I can see that my pleadings with Tom came out more like nagging.

"Tom, you never pay attention to me anymore! It's like we're strangers living in the same house… Tom, are you even listening to me?"

If he gave me an answer, it was always the same and full of irritation, "Elizabeth, I'm tired, and I work hard. You know how it is at the mill. Just let me relax when I get home, dammit!"

"You *could* do that… if we didn't have a three-year-old running around!" I'd scream back in exasperation.

Our barbs went back and forth, often well into the night. Sometimes, he would just get up and walk out the front door, leaving me still hollering at an empty room. *God, how I hated that man at times.* But now I just hate myself for allowing everything that happened to me, and to my daughter, affect our lives so. I feel like I ruined my dear Katie's childhood, even though I loved her so much. And lately, with all the craziness that's going on in my head that no one seems to be able to fix, I've put poor Molly through too much pain, just trying to take care of me.

Probably the only reason I hesitate about going through with this now is that I won't be able to tell either of them how sorry I am. But I do believe that sometimes, no matter what, saying you're sorry just isn't enough.

Sometimes, you just need to let go and as I look around me at this lonely place I've called "home" for so long, I know that's what I have to do.

8. KATE

BO SHEFFIELD JUST STARED AT Kate; a confused look shrouded his face. He finally spoke with a shake of his head. "Ms. Harriman, I know you are the one of the best, but I'm a little bewildered as to what's going on here."

Kate steeled herself to look at him directly and took a deep breath.

"I assure you, Mr. Sheffield, everything's fine." Meanwhile, her mind frantically searched for a way to divert the conversation.

However, as Sheffield pushed forward in his chair as much as his widened frame would allow, it quickly became obvious that he was not convinced. He wagged a plump finger toward her, and his face became red with the effort of his movement.

"Now look here. I've been around people long enough to know when something's up. Now what the hell is going on?"

"It's nothing," she said then spoke with celerity in a futile attempt at distraction, "And yes, I'm just as disgusted as you are for Ms. Pearson's actions. I've read your bio, Mr. Sheffield, and I know that you do good work for those children."

Attempting a casual a look of impassivity, she continued as best she could and simply stated, "I promise you we're all good here, Mr. Sheffield."

She could feel the color slowly coming back to her cheeks and forced herself to look Sheffield steady in the eyes. She put on her best courtroom face and waited in silence as she hoped that he would believe her.

Finally, he raised his eyebrows and asked in a condescending yet hopeful tone, "Are we *sure* about that? Because I do want this to work out between us. I wanted you to represent me the moment that Pearson woman left my office and disparaged me so."

"Yes, I know…" Kate unconsciously paused for effect just as she would in the courtroom and then continued deliberately with a show of confidence that she did not yet feel inside, "Your question concerning past records simply reminded me of another case. One that we won, you'll be pleased to hear."

As the crafted lie rolled off her tongue, Kate allowed her words to sink in. The moment seemed long, but when she looked back up at her client she knew she was back in control. The apprehensiveness had all but left Sheffield's face, and his demeanor had relaxed.

Kate pushed a loose curl behind one ear and smoothed a non-existent wrinkle on the sleeve of her blouse. She could tell that he needed one more "push" to seal his satisfaction, so as casually as she could, she stood up and said something about needing some additional papers. Slowly, Kate walked around her desk to the credenza behind him. She could feel Sheffield's eyes follow her as she walked across the room; it was a dilatory strategy she sometimes employed in the courtroom, one that rarely failed to work with members of the opposite sex.

With a sneer she thought, *God, so predictable, men just never grow up.*

As she pretended to search for something in the files, she allowed herself a few extra moments to collect herself—and provided Sheffield with a distracting view of her backside. Then, grabbing a few miscellaneous papers out of a folder, she moved back around the desk and sat down with her shoulders pulled back and her chin held high. With an attorney's intuitiveness, Kate immediately sensed upon seeing his face that the tension in the room had melted away. She breathed a sigh of relief.

Facing Sheffield squarely with her professional mask firmly back in place, she flashed him one of her most winning courtroom smiles. "Shall we continue?"

"All right, Ms. Harriman, but you *will* tell me if there's something I need to know."

"Of course, and in return, you need to promise to trust that I *will* take care of this."

He smiled back and accepted her assurance, his body visibly relaxing. She knew she had him.

"I know," he said, still grinning broadly as he settled fully back in his chair, "That is precisely why I came to you, Ms. Harriman."

Then with a somewhat mischievous look, he quickly added, "And I know I'm old enough to be your father, but please… call me Bo. Hearing 'Mr. Sheffield' like that always makes me look around for my Pop, God rest his soul."

A sudden knock on the door caused them both to jump. Kate and Sheffield looked at each other self-consciously then his laughter bellowed out. His jowly face turned pink from the effort, and he mopped his sweaty brow again, though this time without much success. Kate glanced up at the clock and noted that Sam's interruption had come right on schedule—six o'clock. She let out a barely audible sigh of relief as he opened the door and stepped in.

"Excuse me, Ms. Harriman, I wanted to remind you that you have a client call shortly."

As always, his professional demeanor was perfect and on cue. But with a curt nod, she waved him inside rather impatiently, as if his interruption had occurred in the middle of an important meeting, "Thank you, Sam. Please come in."

Looking back at Sheffield, she asked in an overtly questioning tone, "I believe Mr… Bo and I were just finishing up here?"

"Yes, yes, I probably *should* be going. That God-forsaken drive at rush hour will only get worse, right?" Mr. Sheffield accepted her prompt with alacrity and started to shimmy himself up out of the chair.

"Before you go, Bo, allow me to officially introduce you to my assistant, Sam Beckman. Sam will be working with me closely throughout your case."

She motioned for Sam to approach and rose from behind her desk for their introduction. As Sheffield shook Sam's hand and pumped it firmly, he looked the young man up and down. Sam looked over at Kate questioningly, but she just shook her head slightly, letting him know that it was all right. Then, giving him a quick though genuine smile, Sheffield released Sam and turned back to Kate. He took hold of her own hand again and held it tightly as his steel blue eyes held her gaze.

"I realize that my agency is paying a hefty price for your services at three hundred an hour, but the assurance of a win is worth it," he paused before continuing with a wink, "I'm sure I'll be getting some news from the 'Lady Viper' real soon."

Kate gave him a firm nod of her head in return and felt a surge of pride for bringing the meeting under control again.

"You will, Bo. You will. The Mayor and his wife don't stand a chance," she said. With another nod of her head, she motioned for him to follow Sam out.

"Ha! Don't I know it," Sheffield bellowed out as he lumbered out of her office behind Sam with his cane and briefcase again in hand.

Kate's smile remained as she watched Sheffield leave and the door close behind them. The smile was proof that the woman behind it thought she had everything and everyone under control. She sat down at her desk and let out a long and much needed sigh.

She was, after all, Kate Harriman, Attorney at Law, just as the prominent bronze plaque on her large mahogany desk declared.

9. MOLLY

AS THE GIRLS PLAYED IN the living room and Molly anxiously awaited Jack's arrival home from work, her thoughts drifted back to the day that she and Jack had first met.

It was six years before, on a warm October Saturday afternoon. A time of year that Mainers typically refer to as "Indian Summer," a period of one week, maybe two, after Labor Day when summer returns for one final burst of warmth before the inevitable New England cold takes hold again.

She had just turned twenty-three and graduated from one of the smaller universities nearby, a school where she wouldn't get swallowed up in big classes, or be too far away from home. She didn't have a clue what she wanted to do, so an English degree had seemed about right. Maine's job market offered limited options anyway, and after graduation Molly had no interest in relocating somewhere else just for a job. Unable to find any serious work with her major that interested her, she took a waitressing job at a local restaurant—happy to ride it out for a while and wait for the right opportunity to come along.

That opportunity did come one night at the university's rival football game—though not in the form of a job as she had been expecting.

Jack Curtis had been in Maine visiting his parents; as retired empty nesters seeking quiet and solitude, they had recently moved from Boston up to Maine. He came to the game to meet up with some of his old college buddies from Molly's school rival, and a mutual friend introduced them. When Jack mentioned that he had grown up on the outskirts of Boston, Molly perked up. Boston was the one place outside of Maine that she knew anything about, and she told him that it was near where her sister lived although she'd never been down. He told her with a playful grin that he had loved being a city slicker, but he wanted to be closer to his parents as they got older and hopefully settle down someday.

He had joked that as a state whose motto is *The way life should be*, he'd felt that he should at least give the place a try. "An entire state of folks can't be wrong, right?" he said with a playful wink, and Molly couldn't help but smile.

She liked Jack from the start, and as they talked the two seemed to forget all about the football game that night.

Molly remembers that Jack had seemed shy at first. He told her that he had recently ended a short-lived though difficult relationship. And though he had tried to hide the hurt, Molly thought she could see right through to it, and her heart went out to him. He had looked so handsome sitting next to her in the bleachers that day, that Molly felt like pinching herself to make sure it was all really happening. Tall and strong, with leathered hands and broad shoulders, he looked as if those shoulders could carry anything. She couldn't imagine any woman *not* liking such a kindhearted man who could make her laugh so. She listened attentively as he told her about his life, his new job, and his fun but crazy family—anything, it seemed to her, except the ex-girlfriend back in Boston who had broken his heart.

As they talked and laughed, it looked to those watching as if they had known each other all of their lives.

With Jack's surfer blond hair boyishly waved to one side and his impish smile, Molly never thought to ask him about his age until their third date. She was surprised at the notable gap between them, but by then those ten years—the same as between her older sister—simply didn't matter.

She had already made up her mind that Jack Curtis was the one.

During the blistery winter months ahead, he wooed Molly with handpicked flowers, store-bought chocolates, and silly love poems. By springtime, they decided to move in together, and Jack soon asked her father for permission to marry her. It was a conventional wedding with five bridesmaids and groomsmen and Jack's younger nieces as their flower girls. Outside of the church, hundreds of daffodils blanketed the walkway to the old Model-T Ford waiting for them. Everything was just as Molly had always dreamed about for her special day.

Furthermore, everyone that Molly cared about was in attendance; even some remote cousins had flown in from Indiana for their wedding. The church was packed with family and friends from both sides. Everyone, it seemed, was present except for her older sister who had left a hasty message the week before and said she couldn't attend because of a busy court schedule.

The crisp five hundred dollar Macy's gift certificate that Kate sent a month later did little to assuage the pain that Molly had felt from her sister's absence.

The wedding was beautiful, though, and the honeymoon that followed was better than she could have imagined. She and Jack spent a long weekend in Newport, Rhode Island for the annual Wharf Seafood Festival, and they happily spent their days strolling the music-filled streets eating fried treats from the sea and licking ice cream cones like kids. Their nights were consumed with sweet, passionate lovemaking that brought Molly to tears in adoration of her husband.

With just a few short relationships with college boys behind her, she had saved herself for this and the act of giving herself to Jack meant everything. Jack could feel her inexperience that first night and took things as slowly and gently as he could. The remaining nights—and some days, though only with the curtains fully closed—she would timidly ask him to make love to her, and the glow that she felt after seemed to last well until the next day.

Six months later, Molly shyly began telling family and friends that they were going to have a baby. She swelled with the growing baby and loved every part of being pregnant—from the first-trimester nausea to the shoes that would no longer fit on her puffed up feet. After Alice was born, motherhood instantly consumed her, and Molly threw herself into it with her heart and soul. Little Emma arrived two years later. More than a few times, Molly told

Jack with a mischievous grin that *he* should be the one exhausted at the end of the day as he was "so much older," but with two little girls to take care of, Molly was usually the first one to give in to sleep each night.

She loved him with her heart and soul, and every night as she lay in bed nestled tightly in Jack's arms, Molly could almost believe that the worry and the badness in her life could go away.

10. KATE

AFTER SHEFFIELD LEFT HER OFFICE, Kate worked on finalizing her notes from the meeting; her fingers pecked away at the keyboard like chickens eating corn. Her mind still reeled from the disconcerting realization that she almost lost control, so pulling the thoughts out of her head proved more difficult than she'd anticipated and she felt the time ticking away.

A soft knock interrupted her again, and before she could speak, the door slowly swung open and Sam tentatively peeked inside. He started to speak, but she quickly cut him off and motioned him in with a jerk of her head.

"I'm finishing up my notes, Sam. Come in," she said, impatiently waving him over to the side of the room.

"Okay." Sam entered quietly and closed the door behind him. He stood placidly by the window and scrolled through his iPhone while he waited, looking up at her every few minutes to see if she was done.

As she typed, Kate peered over at him from the corner of her eye. Clever and astute, Sam had proven his ability on cases with her time and again, often staying late into the evenings to assist with projects and even working weekends when necessary to help her prepare for trials. He also watched over her like a mother hawk, picking up the pieces of her social obtuseness around the office whenever she needed the intervention. She knew that even though she may not be well liked by her peers, they didn't outright hate her because Sam had covered for her arrogance and brashness on many an occasion. *Well, you don't get anywhere in life being nice,* she thought. She felt no remorse for her behavior.

She looked Sam over from head to toe and noticed that even though they were nearing the end of the workday, he still looked as if he had just stepped off the catwalk. He had always dressed impeccably and displayed the latest fall fashions around the office. Today he wore a trim dark gray suit of some top-rated men's brand—of that she felt sure—and a lavender floral tie of just the right length; he appeared the epitome of class and professionalism, dressed better than many of her fellow attorneys on any given day.

Kate abruptly stopped typing her notes and stood up behind the desk. She walked around to the chair that Sheffield had sat in just moments before and hesitated, deciding whether or not the seat still bore any suffering from its sweaty tenant as she peered down at it. She finally opted to sit down then turned to Sam and motioned for him to do the same in the chair next to her. As he took his seat, he stared at her with such a look of expectation that she almost laughed out loud.

"Sam, for God's sake, what is it?"

"Well... how did your meeting go? I can only guess that everything went well from the smug look on your face."

Kate knew that Sam loved to win almost as much as she did, and she had been thrilled when he'd been assigned to be her assistant when he came into the firm. She had already made a name for herself in the legal community as a winner. His Type A personality, eagle-sharpness with detail, and ability to work with Kate's often strident and barbed temperament without getting his feathers ruffled made them a perfect pair.

"Yes, Sheffield's agency has done the right thing, and I'm confident of another win." Then she added under her breath as if to convince herself, "*Everything* went just fine."

"That's fabulous," he said with a small clap, not picking up on her tone. He then added drolly, "Though certainly not a surprise."

"Well, you know I plan to make partner after this one. Here, or at another firm if I have to," Kate said with an undisguised glint in her eye. Then she uncharacteristically whisked a hand in front of her, proclaiming loudly, "Though I'm already envisioning the new name on the marquee outside—'Parker, McClellan

& Harriman' and I have every intention of making that happen before the year is out." Her bravado was met with clapped hands, and Sam smiled deliciously back at his boss.

"Oooo, listen to you, Ms. Eager. Usually so calm, cool, and collected," Sam laughed loudly. "I like it, but perhaps we should finish the case first?"

Kate agreed and stood up, immediately all back to business at hearing Sam's words and more than ready to end their little tête-à-tête. Walking back around her desk, she felt a measure of relief. Everyone seemed to require such a high degree of small talk during daily interactions, but she found it tedious and wasteful. Even with Sam.

"Yes, that we should."

She began to clear up the paper stacks on top, moving files around and putting folders away. After a few moments, she turned and saw Sam still standing there. Having already dismissed him in her mind, it took her a second to realize that he had not left the room. Without being aware, her tone was laced with mild annoyance when she spoke, "Sam, why are you still here. And more importantly, why are staring at me like that?"

"Aren't you at all excited about going out tonight?" he finally blurted out excitedly, deftly ignoring her tone and rudeness. "Le Petit Noir is just to die for, and who *knows* who you'll see there!"

When she didn't respond, he approached her desk and prodded her again, seemingly oblivious to her unreceptive body language. After years of working with her, Sam knew that if he pushed her farther, Kate would eventually give in and open up a little.

"*Well, I'm* curious even if you aren't. What do you think Ethan got for you this year? You know, I looked it up online and apparently, wood and silverware are the five-year gift suggestions for you heteros. What is *that* all about?" Sam's nervousness increased his loquacity as he fidgeted with the snake sculpture on the edge of her desk.

Then, he shuddered—though at the gift idea or the thought of being straight, Kate wasn't sure—and she chuckled inside.

She sat back down in her desk chair for a minute and gazed out the window thinking about past presents from Ethan and some of the disappointments. Then she turned to face Sam and answered, "Who knows, Sam? Sometimes Ethan's been great with my gifts. Other times… well, let's just say that a number of them have already been forgotten."

"He had better treat you right tonight, or I just may need to have a few words with that man," Sam said in mock seriousness. He crossed his arms over his chest and tilted his head to one side, trying to look stern. But to Kate he simply looked even more gay, and she snickered inside.

She shot Sam a look that let him know that he would soon be stepping out of bounds with her and suggested that he discontinue his line of discussion. He rolled his eyes before looking away unabashed and pretended to smooth out a non-existent wrinkle on his slacks. Then, well accustomed to her sharpness after their years together, he waved off the silence with a playful grin and suddenly produced a small colorful box. He leaned over the desk and thrust it out at Kate. He smiled down at her so oddly that Kate wondered for a moment if he'd lost his mind.

"Well, *I* decided to get you a little something that I just know you're going to love," he announced with undisguised glee.

Kate looked up and down again between Sam's face and the box in his outstretched hand. The velvet square that rested there looked to be much more than a "little something." She wavered a little, but curiosity prevailed, and she grabbed the box from his palm. She stared down at it, noting the gold scrolled lettering around the base of the box, and debated whether or not to fully accept it from her assistant.

"Go on. Open it!" he prompted excitedly and sat back down in the chair.

Not to quell Sam's obvious enthusiasm—and because greed got the best of her—she did. Inside rested a piece of jewelry that she knew more than reflected the comfortable salary that Sam earned as her assistant. It was a heavy silver bracelet that lay on a bed of thick black velvet. She could see some sort of writing on the underside of the bracelet. Peering closer, she read the words that were etched in cursive print around the inside—"For Kate Harriman, LV."

She looked up questioningly at Sam, but before he could speak, she realized that the initials after her name stood for "Lady Viper." Kate smiled deliciously and removed the sterling bracelet from its velvety bed to hold it up in the light. She could see that it would be a stunning accessory with the new dress that she had purchased for dinner tonight.

A few weeks before, Sam had picked out the gown for her at a nearby boutique. They had been walking back to the office after a court date one afternoon when he saw it in the window and pulled her into the store. He had seen the dress in a fashion magazine and immediately knew that it was designed for his boss. When Kate emerged from the dressing room moments later with the high-slit dress on, Sam clapped his hands and emitted a loud squeal. He then loudly announced to the other shoppers who were already gawking at her, "We'll take it!" As they walked backed to the office, Sam had laughed when Kate told him that with his eye on fashion she grudgingly had to admit that gay had trumped female once again.

"Sam, this is too much... and for my anniversary?" she said now, even while sliding the piece onto her slender wrist and noting its expensive brilliance. "You do know that gifts for my marital anniversary are not compulsory for your job here."

"Yes, I know... I have to confess, this gift is actually to recognize *our* time working together. Though *you* may not remember, Kate, it's been five years since I've been putting up with you here," he announced. With a sly look on his face he added, "And, of course, I've enjoyed every minute."

"Well, if you put it like *that*..." she retorted wryly.

Sam looked at the bracelet draped on her wrist, quite pleased with himself.

"Oh, you are going to look so fab tonight, Kate, I almost wish *I* was your date!"

"Yes, Ethan would love that," she said. "Did I ever tell you? He doesn't believe that you prefer your own gender, you know. After he saw us talking together once, he actually asked me if you and I ever snuck into the closet for a quickie."

Sam laughed loudly, tossing his head back. The thought brought a smile to Kate's face as well, though more for a memory with Curt, an old college flame, that popped into her head. *God, that guy was a piece of work,* she thought. Her body heated up in all the right places just thinking about the times she had spent with him during her last two years in undergrad. Curt was their university's star hockey player and the most passionate man she'd ever slept with. Their lovemaking had been unequaled—even compared to Ethan, she had to admit—and on late nights when she found herself alone, she still liked to remember their times together.

One drunken night, while his roommate slept in the next bed, Curt had coaxed her into his dorm closet for a quickie. After some initial fumbling in the dark, Curt had fallen down directly onto his hockey stick and broken his arm. When his mother visited them the following weekend, he'd made up some lie about the cast and hockey practice. Kate had stood beside him with a reddened face. She remembered how his mother had just smiled and winked at them both.

The memory made Kate laugh out loud, which elicited a quick and defensive retort from Sam.

"Hey! Being with me isn't *that* funny, you know," he said in mock protest and crossed his arms defensively in front of him.

"No, Sam, I was thinking about someone else," she replied, rather impatiently. Then with a tip of her head and arched brows said dryly, "Though it really *is* quite funny."

There was an awkward pause for a moment before Sam blurted out with a distasteful look on his face, "I did go there once."

"What?" Kate asked, only half listening and not comprehending him.

He pointed toward Kate's midsection before shuddering and looking away, "Though I couldn't bring myself to ever do *that* again!"

"Alright, alright," she retorted and put up her hand in mock protest, "There's no need to provide any more details on that, thank you very much."

There was another moment of awkward quiet between them then impulsively Kate leaned over and gave Sam a brief and stiff hug. He was so surprised that he almost tipped out of the edge of the chair before righting himself in it. Kate did not want to hug him, but she knew Sam would appreciate it, and she felt pleased with herself for extending the gesture to him.

"Thank you for the gift, Sam," she delivered the words a little too stoically, obviously not accustomed to saying them.

"You are very welcome," he replied, not at all put off by her gauche manner in accepting his gift.

"So, are we done here now?" she asked, already rising up from the chair. "I do need to take care of a few things before I go."

"What? You need to leave, girl! Your reservations are for eight o'clock, and if you're more than ten minutes late at Le Noir, they *will* give them to someone else."

Kate smiled at him knowingly. Sam may have been looking out for her, but he was most likely hopeful to get out of the office himself to go out for the night. Most of Kate's evenings consisted of quiet nights at home pecking away on her laptop while Ethan engaged in his own activity somewhere else in the house. Sam usually went out on the town, though. He loved to be around people and parties as much as Kate tried to avoid them. He had chosen not to be a promiscuous gay man, but he did enjoy a little fun whenever he could.

"I'll leave soon. You go now, though," she said as she walked back behind her desk. She called out after him as he left the office, "And give Mr. Right a kiss for me tonight!"

She watched as Sam stopped, tossed his head back and laughed, then sashayed out, leaving Kate alone in her office at the end of the day. Once again. She looked around her, moving only her eyes as they circled around the large room, and felt a twinge of the loneliness that too often seemed to mark her life.

11. IT ALL BEGINS TO CRUMBLE

AFTER ANOTHER YEAR WEIGHED DOWN by the same frustrations with Tom, neither of us knew what to do. Tom spent more time away. Our marriage fell into a rut that we couldn't climb out of. One day in a fit of anger, I tossed out the word "divorce," and Tom readily agreed.

I knew our Katherine suffered through it all. When Tom and I fought, she would run upstairs to her bedroom and hide in the back of her closet. She would stay in there for hours, with only her stuffed animals and dolls. When I went up to check on her, I'd hear her talking to herself, "It's all right, everything's going to be all right." That just made me cry harder as I left, for I knew that even though our Katherine was strong, behind her proud exterior there was a pile of pain festering inside of her.

I took Katherine and moved to an apartment across town. The place was nothing great. The walls were scuffed and worn by many tenants before us, and it had a ratty backyard the size of my bathroom. But our neighbors were friendly and the abundant sunlight throughout the rooms made up for their lack of size. More importantly, it was as far away from Tom as I could be and still keep Katherine in the same school district.

After the divorce, Tom and I only spoke when we had to and for Katie's sake. He begged for me to come back a few times that first year. And I tried to feel bad for him, but I just couldn't after all the heated arguments that we'd had and the loneliness that I'd felt while being married to him. That was well before I'd found out what he had done to me with that floozy down at the mill.

It's probably a good thing I didn't know back then, because God knows what I may have done to that man if I had.

Anyway, for the next year I focused on my life with Katie and just tried to keep our heads above water. I got a job at the new grocery store that came to town. With all those hours and Tom's alimony, I managed to get by. We didn't have much, but I am proud that we never went on food stamps or accepted charity like some of the other divorced women I knew.

As a twenty-five year old with a six-year old child, my life wasn't easy, that's for sure. I suffered through a few blind dates here and there that my coworkers had set up for me. But I never met anyone worth much and generally tried to avoid dating all together. It's a small town, too—really, even smaller back then—so there really wasn't much to choose from. As a single mother, most nights I ended up too tired to go out anyway and preferred early evenings at home in my own bed with Katie sleeping next to me. Even when a date went well, the evening always ended quickly once I told him that I had a pre-teen daughter with me at home. The guy would clam up and get all clumsy or rude with me. One of them, I remember, even demanded that *I* pay for the damn dinner!

Eventually, on one otherwise uneventful day about three years after my divorce, an unfamiliar and handsome face appeared in my checkout aisle at the store. I guess that's usually when something big happens, right? When you least expect it. Because by then I'd given up on finding anyone and certainly wasn't looking for Mr. Right to sweep me away.

The guy bought beer, hamburger meat, and chips, like he was headed to a cookout or something. He seemed to be in such a hurry to pay that I thought he'd hardly noticed me as I checked out his groceries. He had a rugged look about him, a look that makes a woman feel like she'll be taken care of. Surprisingly, he came back in the next day, looking nervous and acting strange as he waited in my line and stared my way. The cashier of the line next to mine shouted that her register was open, but he ignored her and kept his eyes glued on me. I knew something was up. I thought at first that there may be something wrong with him, maybe he was a serial killer or something, but I don't think I ever told him that.

Anyway, it was finally his turn with his groceries and he stood in front of me. He was big and tall and looked down at me with big brown eyes and a grin from ear-to-ear. I could tell right then what was coming because I wasn't scared. And I felt warm in a place that hadn't felt any warmth in a long, long time. He gave me his money and brushed my hand, and I felt a bolt of electricity go through me, just like they talk about in the movies. When he spoke, his voice was low and smooth.

"Hey, there. I… uh… came through here yesterday," he said quietly.

"Yeah, I remember," I said, trying to be cool, even though my heart was racing inside as I avoided his eyes and handed him his change.

I decided that I wasn't going to make it easy for him. No, I'd already done that with one guy. So I said nothing more and bagged up his things, handing him everything like we were all done. He didn't leave, though. He just stood there staring at me with his money in hand, before finally blurting out loudly, "Well I was wondering if you'd like to maybe get dinner some night?"

Embarrassed, I looked around to see if anyone else had heard him. My coworkers were all turned away, but I knew they had and were pretending they didn't. Before I could change my mind, I hastily wrote down my phone number on his grocery receipt and handed him the slip of paper.

"Great!" he said with a broad smile. He started to rush toward the door.

"Hey?" I had to call after him, "you want to tell me your name?"

He turned and called back with a sheepish grin, "Oh, right, my name's Robbie." Then he was gone.

As soon as he walked out, the other cashiers and even some of my longtime customers cheered for me in the store. I know I must have blushed. I teased Robbie later on that the only reason I said yes to him, was because I didn't want to flat-out reject him in front of everyone. But to be honest, I needed a date something fierce. It had been a while since I'd been out. Really, it had been a *long* while since I'd *been* with a man. And we women have needs too. I wasn't one of those women who could do a one-night stand. No, I had to love the guy before I could go to bed with him. And seeing Robbie's strong hands, his tall frame, and that weathered face, I think I'd started fantasizing about being with him before he even made it out to his car!

I barely found a sitter for Katie the night of our first date and almost thought about leaving her at home with the TV on and the doors locked. I was so desperate to go out. One of the other cashiers—with three kids of her own—must have felt bad for me; she ended up coming over to stay with Katie and even helped do up my hair before I left.

I guess I probably should have realized that something that started out so desperate wouldn't bode well for any of us.

Robbie and I had our date a few nights later, as planned. He took me not to the one fancy pasta place in town like most of the others had, but to a drive-in burger joint in the next town over called Juicy Burger Boys. It's actually still there—right off Route 1—and has become a relic of sorts with us locals. Back then, it was a place where the waitresses served food on roller skates and the onion rings were as big as the burgers. He and I got along well from the start. I liked that he seemed so different from the rest of the guys, and in the middle of our first date I decided to tell him about my Katherine and just blurted it out. I'd caught him unawares, and he probably surprised himself when he said he already liked me too much for it to matter.

We dated over the next year and were married one year later. With my mother's overzealous intervention, the wedding quickly turned into a big formal ceremony—the one every girl dreams about, the one that I didn't have the first go-around with Tom. We held it in the biggest Congregational church in town, and I felt like a real princess that day. I was twenty-seven years old then, already with a ten-year old child, and Rob was thirty-two. We hastily said, "I do," and kissed long and hard in front of more than a hundred family and friends. Little Katherine looked so beautiful that day. I'd asked her to be our flower girl; she had wild daisies pinned in her hair and wore a cute pink frock that I'd made especially for her.

The wedding was really a blur, as they always are, but I will never forget the expression on my little Katherine's face each time I'd look over at her—blank and wide eyed, just staring at everything around her. She looked like she didn't know what to do or where to turn the whole time. I'm sure she was just trying to understand the turn of events in our lives, to make sense of it all. Katie was always such a strong-willed girl, though, that I should have known that all the changes in our lives would soon come between us.

She stayed with my parents while Robbie and I were off on our honeymoon, and he moved in with us right after. I think it wasn't until then that Katherine realized just how different he was from her dad. For where Tommy was a sports jock, Robbie would spend his time outdoors working on his truck or chopping firewood. Tommy enjoyed a beer or two most nights and the occasional cigar, but Robbie had never smoked and rarely drank anything stronger than black coffee. Tom was stocky and athletic, had turned mostly grey by the age of thirty, and was the life of the party wherever he went. Robbie, on the other hand, was quieter, a head taller and ending up balding around the temples like men will do. My two husbands were as different as two could be… in most ways, that is, except what really counts, I learned.

Maybe that's what attracted me to Robbie in the first place. Maybe I foolishly thought that the same thing wouldn't happen to me again from someone so different.

I can see now that I put too much of myself into both of my husbands, though, as different from each other as they were. If I'm honest, I guess I simply lost myself in them. Maybe that's why they both did what they did to me.

As the months went by, I spent less and less time working at the grocery store and instead wrapped myself up in my new life with Robbie like it was some expensive mink coat. Life really *had* seemed good for the three of us… in the beginning.

But if I knew this all back then, I would have done things differently. I wouldn't be sitting here trying to decide if I should put a gun to my head and end all the pain and craziness I've had trapped inside for so long.

12. THROUGH A CHILD'S EYES

"MOMMY, WHY DOES GRANDMA LOOK SO sad?" Alice's question brought Molly out of her reverie about Jack. She looked over to see Alice peering at a framed five-by-seven picture on the bookshelf; the little girl had a puzzled look on her pixie-like face.

Molly saw that it was the picture of she and the girls with her mother that Jack had captured last summer. The girls were eating pink cotton candy puffs at the annual clambake festival. Molly had worn her favorite sundress, the one with the white halter-top and daisies lining the hem. Though it was only May then, she already had a tan, so the dress had looked nice against her browned skin.

She smiled, remembering how Jack had teased her all day, saying she looked like a teenage virgin. He had playfully pinched her rear, making her blush and look around to see if anyone noticed.

For weeks before the festival, Molly had begged her mother to join them. After many excuses, Elizabeth finally agreed, and they all went together. When they drove over to Molly's childhood home to pick up Beth, she had walked out her front door and been all smiles, giving the girls big hugs and loud kisses. She'd looked so good that day, wearing the new outfit that Molly had given her for her birthday. A striped navy and white top with khaki slacks that looked classy and befitting for a fifty-plus-year-old woman. She could see that Beth had even taken the time to do up her hair and put on some makeup for the occasion.

Everything had seemed good and they'd all had a fun time eating fried clams, going on rides, and playing a few of the silly carnival games. Elizabeth had offered to go on a few of the kiddy rides with Alice and Emma. This produced ear-piercing shrieks of delight. *Yes, it had been a good day with mom.*

Yet with bitter sadness, Molly realized with a sinking feeling that even her five-year old could see, just from the photograph, that something was wrong.

She walked over to the bookshelf and stood next to Alice, peering at the picture and seeing it as if for the first time. She could see the pained expression on her mother's face that she hadn't seen before, the haggard hurt in her eyes, the smile that didn't quite reach her eyes. Peering closer, Molly now recognized the forced smile on her face and understood that it was the same sad smile that her mother had put on for far too long. It was worn thin and old, but it had somehow fooled them all.

Molly reached down and grasped Alice's hand, holding it tightly.

"Aw, honey, that was just a big day for Grandma," Molly's forced laugh sounded fake even to her own ears. "All that fun and excitement with her favorite girls? I think it was too much for her, sweetie."

Alice seemed to accept her answer, and she ran off to play with Emma, the conversation already forgotten.

Molly stood there staring without seeing and desperately tried to remember when all the problems for her mother had started. After mentally flipping through the pages of the past, she found it so odd that she could recall the exact day she had met Jack as if it was yesterday, yet she couldn't put a finger on the moment when her mother's behavior began to change. She sighed heavily. For though she had known deep down that her mother hadn't been okay, admitting it was much more difficult than trying to deal with it. And as her mother's behavior slowly yet inexorably transformed into something that nobody understand over the last few years, *just* dealing with it is exactly what she had done.

Sometimes, Molly would watch as Beth stomped her feet like a child and cried out in exasperation. Other times, her mother refused to leave the house, preferring to stay alone in her bed with the bedroom door locked, hiding from the world. Her tantrums turned into shouting in a split-second, yet before anyone knew what to do, she would change again and weep like a child.

Whenever her mother needed her, Molly was there. She did not know what to do, and she barely knew what to say, but Molly was there by her mother's side doing the best that she could. Nobody knew what to do, or what was wrong. Not her father, not their church pastor, not any of the doctors around town that her mother had gone to seeking help. Certainly not Elizabeth, herself. She couldn't seem to handle life anymore. She just couldn't seem to handle life. She was constantly wrought with anxiety and sadness, and some days she seemed to be a mere shell of the woman she once was.

Molly did her best to shield her girls from their grandmother's decline. At her best, she hid her fears and forced a happy face around them. At the worst, she ran upstairs and hid in the shower, letting the water wash away her own tears.

How am I supposed to make this all right? She thought with exasperation as she looked around at her own demanding life. *Motherhood, marriage, and mayhem are what I'm surrounded by here!*

"I don't know how to fix her!" she called out louder than she intended, causing the girls to briefly look up from their games.

For a moment, Molly felt her insides constrict and turn themselves around as she struggled to control her own anxiety as it again threatened to consume her. She felt a hollow emptiness in the pit of her stomach. In a strained voice, she turned and called out for Alice and Emma to get cleaned up for dinner. Yet they were so engrossed in their make-believe play that they didn't hear her.

Seeing them sitting there, together with their books, Molly suddenly remembered a scene that she'd witnessed at the library just the week before. The incident itself was insignificant—certainly nothing out of the ordinary—yet it was something that now made her heart skip a beat and her mind turn in on itself with dread and a gnawing fear. She had volunteered to read to a group of first-graders in the children's section as Emily sat attentively by her side, so happy to have her mother there. At one moment, Molly looked up to see a grandmother reach over to gently brush a loose strand of hair out of a little girl's eyes. It was a simple gesture, hardly worth remembering, but that small act of normalcy now made Molly go numb inside as she realized that her mother was not like that grandmother at all. And *not* at all okay.

It took Alice's observation of that picture to bring her understanding to the surface. Molly was instantly chagrined. As she stared again at the photo, Molly saw then just how lost her mother had become. She smoothed the creases that seemed permanently etched into her own forehead and turned away, her heart even heavier and tears pooling in her tired eyes.

"Mommy!" Emma called out sharply. Molly's attention snapped back to the present.

"Emma, honey, let's not shout," she admonished the little girl a little too sharply.

"But, Mommy, what's that funny smell?" Alice retorted as she pointed to the kitchen. She crossed her arms in front of her defiantly with her chin thrust out.

"Oh, shit! Nothing, honey," Molly said as she rushed over and grabbed at the oven door to see the lasagna juices sizzling on the oven floor. "Mommy's just cooking dinner, sweetie."

She took a step back and almost tripped over a Dora doll lying on the kitchen floor, cursing under her breath again.

"Mommy, mommy! Emma's eating somefin' off the floor."

Molly turned sharply on her heel with a stifled scream of exasperation, just in time to see Emma put a large green chunk of something unidentifiable in her mouth. With a scowl, she turned up her nose as soon as her taste buds made contact with the item and promptly spat the offending piece out onto the floor.

Yeah, wouldn't it be nice if we could all get rid of our problems that easily, she thought with bitter sadness. The corners of her mouth turned down.

Emma's face mirrored how Molly felt inside as she tried to wipe the offending taste off her lips.

Wiping away tears that began to spill over, Molly threw out a half-hearted admonishment to Emma then began to set the table for dinner just as she had done a thousand times before. The pounding in her head continued; it felt as if it would explode off her shoulders, and she braced herself for the next wave of panic with each placing on the table.

13 . KATE

TEN STATES AND OVER A thousand miles away, Kate finally left the office and headed home. Though on the road for less than five minutes, she already felt the usual level of frustration mounting from the slow commute during rush hour traffic. Her irritation rose with each passing mile.

Some nights—the nights she could partly enjoy—she was able to drive just over the speed limit with the windows rolled down while listening to the radio and enjoying the smooth ride of her three-month-old, five-series BMW. Yet most times, the Beamer could only crawl down the road like a snail, leaving a trail of sluggish irritation in its wake. Kate loathed the wasted stretches of time in her daily commutes, and tonight was no exception.

In the intersection ahead, she saw a police car with flashing blue lights stopped behind an SUV. As she passed by the young female driver with the long face, Kate felt a sense of annoyance for the woman. Having received numerous traffic citations over the years, Kate could empathize with her. All of her own tickets had been negotiated away in county court, but in her mind speeding tickets were an unnecessary evil of the road. Each time she'd been pulled over, Kate felt the injustice just as strongly—knowing that the offending officer could be at that very moment allowing some hardened criminal to get away with something terrible, somewhere else.

As she edged the BMW onward, unable to break any speeding laws today, a line on the radio caught her attention. It was from the Average Joes, Atlanta's bawdier talk show duo and by far her favorite morning radio program. Crass and derogatory, the ribald pair often made her laugh out loud with their scorn of anyone who behaved with untoward idiocy. She often agreed with their controversial radio programs, especially after witnessing in court just how far the general populace will go in an attempt to justify their own ridiculous and foolish behaviors—*even* under oath. Kate's experience with a number of such denizens of society over the years had only confirmed the lack of esteem or intelligence in the general human race. She had little respect for the majority of people in the world and chose to avoid the rest.

Trying not to tail the beat up Ford Fiesta in front of her too closely, she looked across at the car crawling along beside her. Seeing a dry cleaning bag hanging in the backseat reminded her of Ethan and his promise to pick up her clothes on his way home from work tonight.

"Hmmm… will he or won't he remember?" she mused out loud with skepticism dripping off every word.

Kate rolled her eyes and sighed. Those seemingly innocuous points of marriage often frustrated her the most. Small things—like letting the trash bin get too full or leaving shoes in the doorway or brushing his teeth for far too long—often drove her over the edge. During these minor incidents she delivered biting comments that she knew she'd regret afterward. Her marriage, in general, often brought too much consternation into her life, much more than she'd ever anticipated. She wondered if other women experienced similar frustrations with their husbands, though without any girlfriends to confide in and share with, she didn't know.

As if on cue, a low humming vibration diverted her eyes down to her phone. And though she half-expected to see her mother's name showing on the screen, as Beth had been calling her so often these days, she saw that it was just Ethan. He sent a text letting her know how much he was looking forward to their dinner at Le Noir tonight.

Kate rolled her eyes skyward again. She felt that Ethan often behaved like the woman in their relationship, and his unmasculine show of sensitivity was annoying. He was usually the one to remember to send thank-you cards for gifts or make the obligatory call for family birthdays. She hesitated before deciding not to reply and tossed the phone back inside her Louis Vuitton bag.

Kate sighed and looked down at the perfectly cut two-carat ring on her finger as her hand gripped the steering wheel. She knew that everything outside of her career had taken a backseat, including Ethan and their marriage, and she had made no excuses for it. The courtroom had become the one facet of her life that she truly loved, a place where she could experience control, power, and a professional success that most people only dreamed of.

Kate exhaled again. She knew Ethan was a good man, quietly handsome, intelligent, and honest. And she *was* comfortable with their lives together. However, even after five years, sometimes she still couldn't believe that she had actually married and sometimes still felt that urge not to be tied down, to run off alone and be free. Some days, it felt like she lived in a one-act play that never seemed to end.

She remembers what a surprise it was when she informed her family about the marriage. Her mother's shock was unmistakable over the phone; she had been momentarily speechless and then gasped with questions as to how it had all happened. Her sister's incredulous reaction was also not well disguised.

Kate had impatiently answered their questions and promised to keep them posted on the nuptial plans. Yet typical of her disinterest in any romantic inclinations, she later arranged a quiet, remote wedding with little fanfare and no family guests in attendance. She and Ethan exchanged their vows on Astwood Cove, a secluded beach on the Bermuda Island, with only a local hotel employee as their witness.

Kate didn't tell anyone at the office, even Sam, why she intended to take time off. She simply closed her office door and returned to work the following week wearing the huge diamond ring that she'd told Ethan to buy, immersing herself in another new case as if nothing had changed.

"Shit!" she yelled out as the car next to her almost swerved into her passenger door. "Watch where you're going, you imbecile."

And with that, Kate suddenly remembered that she had promised to call her father yesterday to check on him.

"Dammit!"

Her busy mind immediately began concocting the lies she would tell Tom about why she hadn't bothered to phone him. She tried to recall the details of his hospital admission earlier in the week for a spinal epidural to alleviate chronic back pain. The doctor had said that it was the result of his advanced age and too many years playing contact sports in his youth. This was to be the first epidural of a possible three that he could receive before resorting to the next and final option of spinal surgery.

When he'd told her about the issue, Kate had informed him with her usual measure of superiority that his back troubles were actually the result of spending an exorbitant amount of time sitting in front of the TV.

"Not all of us live and breathe perfection, Katherine," was his response. It was an awkward attempt at levity that she did not receive well.

"I'm not perfect, Tom," she had reported smugly then added with an obvious hint of bitterness in her voice, "I just make smart decisions."

She now felt a flash of guilt that she'd completely forgotten about his epidural then quickly pushed it away. She hated guilt as much as she hated ignorance. They were both weaknesses. In her mind, weak behavior paved the road to a life of disaster.

"I'll just call him tomorrow. There's no need to let another disappointing conversation with Tom ruin my night."

She could hear that her words sounded shallow and selfish, but in her usual act of self-preservation, she took a deep breath and let it go. For her, the relationship with her father had been permanently, undeniably altered when he had made the choice to hurt her mother by cheating on her. Kate felt that could never be corrected, no matter how often she did or didn't talk to him. Their relationship had suffered.

Her mind couldn't help but drift back to her childhood days with her parents before the divorce. She grimaced, remembering with a child's intuitiveness that her parents had a rocky relationship for as long as she could remember. After the screaming fits dominated their nights and weekends, she knew it was only a matter of time before her parents would end up like the family who had lived next door—broken and divorced. It wasn't until she was in college, though, that Kate learned from her father's oldest sister exactly why her parents had decided to end their marriage.

In a moment of weakness, her aunt had confided in Kate that back then her father had apparently had a difficult time keeping his eyes—or rather, his hands—off one of the secretaries at work. He had cheated on Elizabeth for the last two years of their marriage, hiding behind a thin veil of deceit and lies. When Beth discovered the truth, she immediately took Katherine and moved out. Kate always knew her mother was bitter about the divorce, but she understood even back then that it had been her father's choice of infidelity that broke her mother's heart.

Chagrined for spilling the beans, her aunt had made Kate promise not to tell her father that she knew of his indiscretion. Kate never did, but over time that knowledge created a wall between her father and her, and their relationship had never been the same. She solely blamed her father for the divorce and held his cheating against him like a sword of condemnation. At some point, she stopped referring to him as "Dad" and began to use his given name, Tom. Eventually, she called him "Tom" directly when they spoke on the phone. And though they had never brought up the past, that was her way of letting him know that she knew exactly what he had done.

Now, more than fifteen years later, Kate's arguable defense for their still distant relationship was that she had simply become too busy with her career. And over the years their sporadic phone conversations had been noncommittal at best, barely covering the courses of their separate lives. They would blandly discuss the weather or one of his favorite TV shows. If Tom did disrupt the mundane to ask Kate a question about herself, the inquiry was so unexpected that all she could do was sputter out some hastily unformulated response in return.

It's no wonder I don't call him more often, she thought wearily, *we simply don't have enough to say to one another.*

Yet as the minutes went by, she let her guilt get the best of her and finally picked up her cell to scroll through her contacts for his name. When she finally hit "Tom" and heard rings then the usual click of his answering machine connecting, Kate was instantly relieved.

"Well, at least I tried," she muttered. She ended the call without leaving a message. She cursed his name under her breath again as she swerved to avoid another near collision. Shouting more obscenities at the offending driver, Kate turned off the highway, relieved to be nearing home.

14. MOLLY

MOLLY HESITATED WITH THE PLACE settings before setting five plates down around the table. She couldn't remember if her father would be joining them tonight. She vaguely remembered inviting him over for dinner after he helped Jack build the deck out back over the weekend. Then, deciding to put the extra setting on the counter instead, she returned to the counter and resumed the last cuttings for their salad.

These days, her father disappeared more often than not, so she rarely knew where he was or when he would show up. Off on some camping trip with his buddies most times, Molly guessed. She never said a thing about his absences at home, just like they didn't openly talk about what had been happening to her mother. Molly understood that her father didn't have a clue about what to do for Beth, either, and she grasped at the notion that he felt as helpless as she did, just trying to believe that everything would be okay.

He called her sometimes, but most often it was when things got tough at home and he needed her help. He'd beg Molly to come over and help with her mother. Every time, Molly would go, holding back the tears as she hurriedly strapped the girls into the minivan and obediently raced to her father's rescue. Molly tried whatever she could to calm her mother's fears and make things right again, while Robbie stood off to the side and looked on helplessly at them both like a lost child.

However, lately Elizabeth's outbursts had become more and more unmanageable; sometimes they would paralyze her into a statue-like state, leaving everyone dumbfounded. She needed help with the smallest of tasks—simple errands such as picking up groceries or mailing a letter. A few times, Molly even had to drive her mother back home when Elizabeth couldn't remember how to, from places around town that she had been to a thousand times before. Molly's defensiveness and guilt about her mother's declining condition wrapped themselves up in her head like a hungry boa constrictor that wanted to choke the life out of her from the inside.

With that thought, Molly started and nearly jumped where she stood. Her head snapped up, and she looked around, as if she couldn't believe the thought that entered her mind; it coursed through her body like a sharp jolt of electricity. Her body went stiff as her mind frantically searched for an answer. Salad tongs hovered in midair over the plastic bowl. Her hands had stopped moving.

She realized that she had not heard from her mother even once today.

After the uncountable number of phone calls day after day for the last year or more, it was almost unthinkable to not receive a single one. Molly could taste the bitterness of fear in her mouth, and a cold numbness began to seep into her bones. She foolishly looked around again, feeling as if the strangeness of the moment should be visible, perhaps just hanging nearby in the air.

"How did I not realize this before now?" Molly said sharply under her breath. Yet with a look around the house—and with the constant pounding in her head that made it so difficult to think—she quickly had her answer. Molly dropped her face into her hands and let out a small moan. Then taking a deep breath and trying to calm the angst that already started to fester inside, she reached for her cell phone and called her parents at home. No answer. *Of course, when **I** really need to reach her, she doesn't pick up,* her mind screamed out in frustration as the phone rang and rang.

Her parents had balked at the idea of buying an answering machine—they argued that everyone who needed them knew where they were anyway—so the phone continued to ring. She called her father's cell next but got no answer there, either.

Molly's anxiety rose fast, and her breathing quickened. She ran over to the home phone in the den to check for messages, scrolling through missed calls, knowing that sometimes Alice or Emma would get hold of the phone and play with the buttons. But once again there was nothing. She forced down the panic inside. Her mind raced to think of anyone else who may have talked to her mother. Most of their extended family had already passed away, and as an only child with both parents gone, her mother had few people left to reach out to.

"Who else can I call?" Molly swore under her breath, wondering if she should just put the girls in the car and drive straight over to her parents' house. Then like a rush of fresh air, she remembered her mother's friend, Lena.

Lena lived near her parents' house and probably saw her mother more often than anyone else these days. They were neighbors, but they had also become very good friends. Molly knew that she might know where Beth was, and if she didn't, she could walk over and check on her.

"Surely, they would have talked together today," she spoke under her breath, trying to reassure herself.

She searched for Lena's number, grateful that it had already been programmed into her contact list. Lena had given it to Molly a few months before when she and Elizabeth were going out for the day and Elizabeth had once again forgotten her cell at home. Molly had been so relieved that her mother had a close friend to talk to these last few years. She knew that even though the two women were quite different in their nature, Lena had been good to her mother.

Just as she was about to end the call, Molly heard a click and a short "Hello?" on the other end.

Molly tried to keep the worry out of her voice, feigning a calmness that she did not feel inside; her mind screamed out the question that her mouth did not. "Hi, Lena! It's Molly, Elizabeth's daughter. How are you?"

"Molly! How are you, dear? It's nice to hear from you. How are those precious little girls of yours I always hear so much about?"

"Good, thank you, they're growing fast," Molly politely answered then paused before blurting out her question to Lena. "I... I was just wondering if you'd talked with my mom today?"

"Well, no, dear, I don't think I have... Why?"

"Oh, well, I haven't heard from her all day and thought maybe you had..." Molly let her voice trail off and tried to keep the disappointment out of it.

As panic welled up inside her, Molly wondered if the feeling was similar to what her mother experienced during one of her own attacks. Molly asked Lena again in hopes that a different approach would produce the response she so desperately wanted to hear.

"So, do you two have any plans to get together soon?"

"Well... we just went shopping the other day, but we haven't discussed doing anything else. Why are you asking, Molly? I'm a little late for a hair appointment now, but I'll be sure to stop by her house right after that to check on her, if that's okay. I've got to run now, dear!" With that, she ended the call.

Left holding the phone and with no answers, Molly's fear got the best of her. "Where is my mother?" she yelled out in exasperation.

Alice and Emma looked up quickly. They were used to their mother's mutterings, but they were startled by her loud outburst. Her sharp tone and the odd look on her face produced a swift and immediate reaction from the girls. Alice began to whimper, which turned into full-blown cries once Emma joined in, and Molly quickly ran over to them, kneeling down to draw her daughters in close.

Theirs tears tapered off as Molly whispered to them over and over again, "It's okay, it's okay," even though her head screamed, *It's not okay, nothing is okay!*

She squeezed her eyes shut against the thoughts that tormented her. But her imagination ran wild with the terrible possibilities for why she hadn't heard from her mother yet. She shuddered involuntarily and kept the girls tight in her embrace until they abruptly broke free and scampered around her with shrieks of delight.

"Daddy! Dada!"

Molly spun around on her heels, almost falling over, grateful to see Jack in the foyer closing the door behind him. She regained her balance and breathed a sigh of relief, quickly trying to brush away the tears that had threatened to spill over.

"Hey, how are my three favorite girls? Did you miss me today?" Jack knelt down and scooped up Alice and Emma, one in each arm. He looked over at Molly teasingly and said, "And how was your day with the best mom in the whole world?"

Both girls shouted with glee and wriggled in his grasp.

"Hi, Hun," Molly managed a small smile, but her words were lost in their cheers.

When he motioned with one free hand for her to join them, she gratefully stood up and stepped into his embrace. Jack set the girls back down, making some comment about Emma's forehead just as she knew he would. Molly didn't move away, so he allowed her to bury her head in his flannel-covered chest as she unconsciously smelled that familiar sweaty lumberyard scent that she'd grown to love. She felt her body relax just a little and looked up at him, hoping that he would see the need she felt inside when their gazes met. But when he smiled back but said nothing, she knew he had not seen through to her and kept herself from getting angered by his obtuseness.

"Jack, can I talk to you for a minute?" she asked, nodding her head toward the kitchen. She took a small step away, "Alone."

"Sure," he said, looking at her questioningly as she grasped his arm and led him into the adjoining room.

She called out to the girls, looking over her shoulder, "Alice, you and Emma can go watch TV for a few minutes. Dinner will be ready soon, ok?"

Cheers erupted for the extra TV time, and Jack looked down at Molly more closely as they walked into the kitchen, trying to figure out what was going on. When she turned away from the kids and stopped to face him squarely, she finally said the words that were smoldering in her mind.

"Jack, I just realized that I haven't heard from my Mom today. And I can't seem to reach her. I think something's up."

"Okay…" he said slowly, waiting for her to continue.

"No, I really think that something may be wrong."

"Hun, I'm sure she's just been busy."

"No, Jack," she shook her head adamantly, "I tried calling over there a few times, and I just tried my father's cell, but no one picked up." The pitch of her quavering voice increased with each word. "I'm really worried."

"Alright, calm down," he said, mirroring the words Molly had used with Alice just minutes before, "Maybe she just forgot to check in and got busy with something today. Maybe she's out doing something?"

"No, Jack. You *know* that Mom calls me *every* day. This just isn't like her…" her voice trailed off before continuing, "I even called Lena. You know that neighbor of hers she gets together with? But Lena hasn't talked to her today either."

Jack placed his hands reassuringly on his wife's shoulders. However, the tone of his words came across more condescending than helpful. "Now, honey, I'm sure everything is fine. I mean did Lena feel that anything was wrong? You know you can get worked up sometimes."

Molly's reaction was swift.

"Dammit, Jack, I knew you'd say that to me! Don't you treat me like I'm acting crazy here." She barked out the words at him and abruptly pulled away from his touch.

Jack kept his silence for a moment then took a deep breath and chose his words carefully. "Okay… then let's think about this for a minute," he said, rubbing her arm and trying to smooth down his wife's ruffled feathers. "Do you remember the last time you talked to her? Maybe that will help you figure out where she is."

She looked up at him and said firmly, "Jack, do not baby me. I know I spoke to her yesterday, right after dinner—I can remember standing in the playroom watching the girls while we talked. But nothing since then. I *know* there's something wrong!"

Sudden shrieks of laughter from the living room caused both parents to look back toward the girls. Emma chased Alice around the room; Alice's pigtails flew behind her and Emma almost tripped on a stray doll. The two girls were engaged in their fun, oblivious to the struggle and uncertainty around them. Molly watched on, and for the moment she relaxed and turned back to look at Jack.

Then, in a softer voice, she said to him, "I just wish there was someone else I could call…"

Molly stopped mid-sentence. With a catch of her breath, she slowly turned around to gaze upon the girls in the other room. They were tickling each other, and Emma fell onto the floor in fits of high-pitched giggles. Molly's gaze took on a faraway look as she stared at them, like someone who'd just discovered a long-lost secret, yet she said not a word.

"What, Molly? What is it?" Jack peered around her and tried unsuccessfully to read his wife's face.

Molly didn't hear him. She was too focused on the scene before her. Then without answering him, she picked up her cell and began to quickly scroll through her list of numbers.

"Hun, who are you looking for?" he repeated impatiently.

She started to answer him while still looking down at the phone, softly as if she was talking to herself. "I don't even know if they talk…" She shook her head, her voice trailed off.

"Who, Molly? Who are you talking about?" Jack's sharp tone made her look up.

She smiled at him half-heartedly, thinking of someone who hadn't been a part of her life for as long as she could remember. She was simply the only other person Molly could think of who could know something about her mother. Yet even as the name rolled off her lips, the absurdity of the idea almost made her laugh out loud.

Molly forced a small grin as she looked up at Jack and quietly replied, "Katie, Jack… I'm calling my sister, Kate."

She slowly brought the phone up to ear and hit "send" with uncertainty and a measure of fear in her eyes. So focused on the call, she failed to see the trepidation in her husband's own eyes.

15. KATE

AS SHE EXITED THE HIGHWAY and turned off toward home, Kate smiled with satisfaction. Their subdivision was conveniently located in the sprawling suburb of Chapin Hill, twenty minutes north of Atlanta. With little traffic or crime to worry about and a variety of jogging parks nearby, Kate felt it was the ideal place to live.

Yet even more importantly, it was a well-developed area that represented the true reflection of it's inhabitants' prosperity and growth. Kate knew that most of its residents—many of them doctors, CEO's and lawyers—also earned six-figure incomes, and she loved seeing the luxury cars and SUVs throughout the neighborhood that reflected their status and wealth. Everyone's successes were proudly on display for all to see, from the three-car garages to the lush landscaped lawns decorated with the latest nursery buy and manicured hedges. For Kate, this classy and upscale locale represented everything that she had worked so hard for.

But even more importantly, the town was located far enough away from the back-road little town that she grew up in and from everyone she had left behind.

As she turned onto her street, her phone rang through the Beamer's Bluetooth. She glanced down, expecting to see her father's name on the caller ID.

However, the name that appeared was someone *else* in her family whom she rarely talked to and generally tried to avoid. Kate hesitated another second deciding whether or not to take the call then inhaled sharply as she hit "accept" and answered.

"Hello?"

"Katie? Hi, it's Molly. How are you?"

"I'm fine. Good, really," Kate's voice sounded fake and overly cheerful to her own ears. "How are you?"

"Okay... it's been a while since we've talked," Molly started hesitantly.

"Yes, it has, I know," Kate replied, instantly on the defensive. "Work's been very busy, and I've had to put in some long hours at the office."

"Oh, what are you working on these days? Any murders in the courtroom?"

"No, Molly," Kate stifled a sigh. "I handle corporate law, so murders are out of our legal realm."

Kate hoped that she didn't sound as condescending as she felt.

"Oh, well that's good, I guess."

Neither of them spoke for a few seconds, leaving an uncomfortable silence. Kate was the first one to talk in an uncharacteristic attempt to fill the void.

"I actually have a new case that just came in. It should be a good one, concerning the Mayor..." Then she stopped herself, feeling that someone in the role of "Suzie Homemaker" wouldn't be able to fully comprehend what she did anyway. Molly started to say something, prodding her on, but Kate cut her off to divert the conversation to something she knew would work better.

"So, anyway, how are the girls doing?" she asked with feigned interest.

"Oh! The girls are good. Alice really likes her school, and Emma's finally sleeping through the night. Alice had a sore throat last week, but thankfully the rest of us didn't catch it. I didn't know if she was..."

Yet by the third sentence, Kate had already blocked out the majority of Molly's words. Just as she knew Molly would, her sister went on and on about her daughters, and Kate's irritation at having to listen to her chatter rose proportionately. For Kate, those "how are you?" questions were merely a form of politeness, certainly not intended for anything of more detail or significance. Yet as Molly's words about her kids tumbled out, it quickly became apparent to Kate that her sister did not feel the same.

It's not that she wasn't interested in her nieces' wellbeing, though admittedly she barely knew them. Kate simply felt that after Molly's kids were born, any opportunity for the two of them to talk was forever gone, and she gave up calling her altogether. For what had sprouted during those initial and infrequent conversations was more information than she ever thought possible about diapers and rashes, runny noses and wheezing coughs, the occasional throw-up that didn't make the bucket, and anything else kid-related. Kate could not relate to or understand any of it.

As Molly prattled on, Kate's mind began to formulate a way to quickly end their call as she wound through the side streets toward her neighborhood.

"Katie, are you still there?" Molly's sharpened question interrupted Kate.

Dammit. "Yes, I'm here," Kate responded before allowing an innocuous lie to roll off her tongue far too effortlessly. "There's always a dead spot on the way home from work, so I'm afraid I didn't catch all that."

You're going to get caught in one of those little fabrications someday, she chastised herself.

"Oh, well, I was just telling you about my girls… Anyway, I actually called you for a reason, though." Molly paused then jumped into her question, hoping she didn't sound too crazy, "Katie, I haven't heard from Mom today, and… well… I think something's wrong."

Kate retorted a little too curtly, "Molly, I'm sure she's fine… and you know I go by Kate now, if you could please remember. It's not Katie anymore."

"Oh, right. Yes, I forgot, sorry," Molly's apology tumbled out, and Kate could hear the girls scream loudly in the background. Though Kate knew there were only two kids—*Still just two, right?* she questioned it herself for just a moment—the noise level in the background indicated many more. Kate grimaced at the sound coming through the phone.

"Well," Molly continued, "I thought that it was odd that I hadn't heard from her today."

"Who? Heard from who, Molly?"

"Mom!" For the first time during the conversation, Molly's usually gentle voice portrayed her impatience, and her words were marred with impatience. "I'm talking about Mom. I know you and she don't talk much, but…"

Those last words finally got Kate's attention, and she snapped back a quick, razor-edged retort. "What do you mean, Molly? Mom and I talk all the time!"

"What? You do?" Molly clearly sounded taken back. "Kate, I- I- I had no idea. I mean, she and I talk a lot, but I didn't even know that you two were really in contact these days…" Her voice trailed off.

In the silence between them, Kate struggled to process what Molly had said. Her mind raced around itself, trying to understand why Molly didn't know that she and their mother talked. Feeling defensive, she sat up straighter in the driver's seat and gripped the steering wheel. Her palms rolled back and forth over the leather grip. When she spoke, her voice was short and crisp.

"Molly, are you saying that you are completely unaware that mom and I talk?" She knew that she was feeling overly indignant at the insinuation, but her response to Molly's next round of questions pushed her over the edge, and anger got the best of her.

"Well, does mom call you, Kate? Or do you call her? How often, really? I'm just so surprised…"

With that, Kate was instantly pissed. Knowing that she needed to end the conversation soon before she said something to her half-sister that she would later regret, she abruptly cut her off.

"Molly, I don't actually have time to talk right now, and you're breaking up, anyway." She hoped she'd hid the curtness behind her words, even as her insides seethed with anger.

"Oh, okay," Molly replied, never the type to push back. "But call me back as soon as you can, okay?"

Molly had responded just as Kate knew she would.

"Yes, I'll call you back later." Once again, the lie fell out of Kate's mouth far too easily as she knew that she wouldn't.

"Soon, though, okay? Because I really think…" Molly pleaded, overly agreeable.

But Kate was mad, disgusted with her sister for her agreeability, and pissed off at the implications of her newfound knowledge. She abruptly cut her off, "I will, Molly, I will," and ended their call.

As she wound through her neighborhood streets, the more she thought about Molly's words, the more irritated Kate became. Though at whom, she wasn't sure. *At Molly for not knowing? At their mother, for apparently keeping their relationship a secret?* Or at herself... for recognizing that Molly's perception of her family involvement wasn't that far from the truth. Yes, she did talk with their mother, though it was much more often than she would like to or usually had time for. For theirs was just another relationship that had never measured up to what Kate had thought it should be... especially after.... Her thoughts cut off; she refused to think back to what almost happened. She wound through her neighborhood streets, seeing but not seeing the children playing in yards and women pushing strollers on the sidewalks, as her mind forced down old memories that again threatened to surface. Fury mixed in heavily with the old standby guilt, and the emotions continued to bubble up high. Before she lost control, Kate decided right then that she wouldn't allow herself to feel bad for a situation that had already been created for her.

"Nor will I allow disappointment to win where I have no control!" she screamed out within the confines of her car. The sound seemed to ricochet inside the fine interior. She opened the window and allowed it to escape.

Keep it together, Kate. It will be much better for both of us if you wait and call Molly back tomorrow. You can call Tom then, too. Everything can be dealt with tomorrow. She talked to herself, forcing her thoughts back to the present and casting her guilt aside like last year's shoes. With great effort, she let it go.

"You know there's a reason everyone in my disappointing family is purposefully far away," she argued out loud. "And I will *not* let them ruin my evening...." The unspoken words, "the way they've all ruined my life," hung heavily in the air.

She rolled the Beamer into her garage, collected her leather Pineider briefcase from the car, and couldn't help but smile smugly as she stepped inside her spacious home. At the entrance of the foyer, a wrought-iron staircase wound its way up to the second floor. Custom-made window treatments framed the windows, and sunlight streamed in through them from every direction. She stopped inside and breathed in deeply, immediately noting the intoxicating combination of Clorox, Pledge, and Lysol that alerted her senses. *Ahhh,* Kate had forgotten that today was Josetta's scheduled day to clean and probably wouldn't have even recognized the woman's efforts if not for the over-the-top clean smell.

Early on—in one of the few times that Josetta had ever directly questioned Kate about anything other than cleaning supplies or her payment—the small Filipino woman had meekly asked her a question. "Ms. Harriman, why you pay for me to come to you every week? Your house too clean with jes' you and your husband here. You not need me."

After only a moment's hesitation, Kate envisioned the small, barely middle-class home she had grown up in and quietly answered, "Because if you'd seen the house that I grew up in, Josetta, you would understand why. I like things to be nice and clean."

The biting answer that she'd reluctantly held back from her house cleaner of so many years had been much more real—"Because I can."

Kate set her purse down on the polished side table and walked into the grand kitchen, her hand gliding over the marble island counter top. She never failed to appreciate the visual impact of her kitchen. The room begged for nightly entertaining and six-course meal preparations, if only their careers would allow it. But with hectic work schedules and courtroom demands, she and Ethan rarely did such entertaining. She knew that their neighbors frequently got together to share cocktails and martinis and enjoy epicurean dinners that lasted well into the night. Each one attempted to outdo the others. She spurned those women, though—the stay-at-home wives with their silly tennis matches, long martini luncheons, and pseudo-volunteerism—and preferred not to mingle with any of her neighbors.

Having a house full of driveling and judgmental dinner guests is not for me, she thought with an indifferent shrug. She grabbed a Perrier from the fridge and headed upstairs to the master bedroom to change out of her work suit.

Choosing a pair of loose-fitting black yoga pants and a simple Ann Taylor top, she undressed and caught sight of her reflection in the full-length mirror. She paused for a moment, gazing up and down the woman's body standing before her. Clad only in panties, Kate couldn't help but be pleased with the figure she saw—a flat stomach, sculpted arms, and firm breasts that were still in the right place. Turning around to glance behind her, Kate thought that even her backside still looked good enough to compete with most thirty-year olds. She smiled with satisfaction.

Kate took pride in not becoming fat and frumpy like many women her age. And she felt little pity for women who let themselves go. Running five plus miles in the dark most mornings before work and doing weights at the gym on days in between had earned her looks, and she was proud of herself. She knew she had the lungs of a twenty-something after countless hours on the trails, and each local road race she entered was easier than the last. The Fleet Feet store where she regularly replaced her worn trainers, knew her about as well as anyone did. She received appreciating looks from boys around the neighborhood who were half her age as she ran through the subdivision; and caught the long stares from the young interns who came in and out of the firm when they thought she wasn't looking.

She deftly got dressed, cast a quick glance at the rows of race medals that lined her dresser, and walked back downstairs to the library. The stately room housed a well-stocked wine bar with rows of merlots, cabs, and shirazes lining one entire wall. Eying the alphabetized bottles, she finally decided on one of the more expensive wines—a Heitz Celler cabernet from Napa Valley, priced at a hundred and twenty five dollars a bottle. It was one of her favorites, usually bought by the case, which she had enjoyed with Ethan on many occasions over the years. With no one else there to partake, she talked to herself as she expertly opened the wine bottle and set it aside to allow it time to breathe.

"A nice glass is just what I need to celebrate another case. And… some alone time before Ethan gets home," she spoke to the empty room then added dryly, "Hopefully, on time."

Kate noticed how small her voice sounded as it bounced off the fifteen-foot high ceiling and became lost in the room. The realization surprised her more than anything, for even when Ethan was home, they often did their own things in different parts of the house. After dinner together, they would each head to their own places to read, catch up on some work, or watch a show on TV. They rarely found themselves in the same room on any given night. Kate wondered how couples who spent so much time together could find anything to say to one another, night after night. *Tonight will be a nice reprieve!*

Her thoughts turned to their anniversary and the night ahead; she anticipated a delicious meal and something bright and sparkly from her husband. She then let out a loud sigh, knowing that even though it wasn't Saturday night, they would likely still end up having sex tonight, given the occasion and the fact that alcohol would be involved.

She and Ethan had agreed on their Saturday arrangement a few years back after a lagging and inconsistent sex life. Kate knew they'd hit the "post-honeymoon blues" when sex became an afterthought, at best, in their career-driven lives. One day she suggested that they mimic a couple who they occasionally went out with, Mark and Teri. For years, the couple had been having sex regularly every week on Tuesday and Saturday nights; Teri confided in Kate one day during an unusually personal conversation that she had seen the idea on a couples talk show, and it had worked well. Kate managed to omit the Tuesday part of the plan when introducing it to Ethan, but Ethan had, of course, agreed, and the arrangement remained. Since then, they had rarely deterred from their commitment to Saturday night sex. Ethan had been happy—*of course*—and Kate was relieved the rest of the week that she didn't have to think about pleasing anyone other than herself, if she chose, when the day ended.

It wasn't that she didn't enjoy sex; she did—*well, at least, usually.* No matter what anyone says, though, after a few years with the same person it just doesn't leave room for too many surprises in the bedroom. Their lovemaking was good, though they weren't into "back door surprises" as a college girlfriend used to call it or any wild tie-ups to the headboard. And, yes, their positions did tend to remain the same week after week, but she could almost always come on those nights—even if she had to help herself get there in the end. Ethan often encouraged her hand between her legs and said he liked to watch her touch herself. In the back of Kate's mind, though, she felt she did enough "self-indulgence" on the days in between and shouldn't really have to do so when she was with him.

Kate wondered how couples with kids managed to have a sex life at all. After hearing the sounds coming through the phone from Molly's house earlier, Kate felt like sex must only be an afterthought for Molly. Then thinking of Molly's accusation about their mother made her bristle all over once again, and all warm thoughts of pleasure promptly dissipated.

"Seriously! Just because I don't go back there doesn't mean that I can't talk with my own mother," she called in defiance.

She sat heavily onto the couch, pouting like a child who'd been admonished for taking one too many cookies, and forced herself to try to relax. She took a sip of the wine, savoring the oaky warmth as it slid down her throat, and smiled as the expensive liquid settled inside. Gazing around her at the life she had created for herself, Kate felt overly satisfied for everything she had accomplished—her career, her reputation, and making a name for herself as a woman where others had often tried and failed.

"My family will *not* ruin my night," she said a little too forcefully, with yet another smile that didn't quite reach her glinting eyes. "Just like they tried to ruin my life. Nothing will get in the way."

She threw her head back and took another long swill of her wine with her eyes closed and a hardened heart.

16. THE MISTAKES WE MAKE

ALL I EVER WANTED WAS a happy family that second time around. Yet it seemed as if the changes that swept into our lives were more like a hailstorm in the summer—unexpected, destructive, and too much for everyone, for Robbie, my Kate, Molly, and sometimes even me—as I tried to form a new life for all of us.

It seemed that nothing worked out, no matter where I turned.

Right from the start, Robbie had a difficult time trying to become Katie's stepfather. He always seemed oddly uncomfortable around her, and she never understood his awkward attempts to joke around with her. As time went on, he tried less and less, and Katie behaved as if we were dragging her into a life of torture. She gave Robbie a hard time, and she never gave in.

As for me, I just kept hoping that everything would be all right. And I simply pretended it was.

Looking back now, I'm sure that the weekends she spent with her dad were the only times that Kate felt any amount of joy. They are so alike, those two, in both looks and disposition. I know they shared a lot of good times together. And no matter what he may have done to me, Tom *was* a good dad. When Friday evenings rolled around and he brought her back to me, I could see it was tough for Kate to start all over again with us. Every week it got harder.

As Katie grew up, she started giving us more and more attitude, the way many kids will do. I think that's when Robbie began to really push her aside and leave her out of the activities we did together. Her defiance would emerge over the smallest of things; her temper flared up when we least expected it. The tension was high, my nerves were frayed and Robbie's patience wore thin. Maybe it's just that Kate *was* an uncommonly difficult child—God knows she was! Maybe Rob resented her being in the middle of our lives. Who knows? I could "maybe" myself into the nut house... Ha! I guess I almost did. All I know is that the discontent between them was worse than I allowed myself to believe.

Rob's indifference to Katie depended on his mood which turned out to be as predictable as our Maine weather. Sometimes he would joke around and get a small laugh out of her. With him or at him, I didn't really know. Other times, he took things too far and upset her, causing angry out bursts and biting comments to fly. Sometimes I'd catch him sneering at her or shaking his fist at her when he thought I wasn't looking. But I was so desperate to believe that he was just being playful then that I convinced myself it was so.

Robbie never physically hurt Kate. It was just a push or a rap on the arm whenever she got sassy, like any parent will do. Especially when she got snippy with me. He didn't like it when she talked back to me or gave me lip, as she often did. She would push me to the limit with her sass, and though I knew she did fine at school and had no problems with her teachers, I think she came home and let it all out on me. The worse she behaved with me, the worse Robbie was with her, and it became a vicious cycle of anger and hurt between us all. From Robbie's biting, sarcastic remarks to Katie's emotional outbursts and my pleadings for her to stop, our home ended up in constant turmoil. I couldn't make Kate happy, and I couldn't control her, either. I can still hear Rob's words to her.

"Look, Missy, your mother doesn't mind that shit you pull, but I don't like it one bit, so cut it out!"

A few times, I heard him laugh at her for something she had said to me or for some teenage outfit she had on.

"You're not going out of the house like *that,* are you? You look like a tramp!"

She would fight back, though. It wasn't right, but I have to give that girl credit for her spirit. She always fought back.

"Leave me alone, Robbie! You're not my father, and I don't need to take fashion advice from some dumb old fisherman."

The funny thing is that I never really saw Katie get upset. Their angry banter would just get louder until a raised fist from Robbie ended it. Katherine would stomp off to her room with a face full of anger. But she never cried.

Soon after Katherine turned ten, things went from bad to worse, though at the time I wouldn't have thought they even could. I asked her to come sit down beside me. I can still remember how excited I felt, like a kid in a candy store. I'm sure she must have known that something was amiss. I patted the cushion next me to; Robbie sat by me on the other side. But Kate sat down as far away from us as she could across the room. She sat there and stared, waiting for me to speak, with her eyes darting back and forth between us. Finally, unable to hold it in no longer, I blurted out the news.

I thought she'd be thrilled, and I waited for her to shriek with delight, but that was not at all the reaction she gave.

"Honey, Robbie and I are going to have a baby. You're going to be a big sister soon!"

As soon as the words left my mouth, she cried out, "Noooo!" and ran away, straight out of the house, slamming the door behind her.

It took me by surprise, and I just sat there, dumbfounded. I was shocked and confused. I felt like I'd been slapped in the face when she didn't share in my—in *our*—enthusiasm for a new baby. As my only child for so many years, I thought Katie would be thrilled about finally having a sister or brother around. What little did I know…

I turned to Robbie for help, trying to understand, "Why isn't she happy about this for us, Hun?"

Robbie shook his head and mumbled something about "stupid girls." He put his arm around my shoulder and tried to comfort me. Unconsciously, I touched my already slightly swelling belly and felt that imaginary flutter of life growing inside. Smiling the silly secret smile that expecting mothers do and foolishly thinking once again that everything would be okay once things calmed down, I gave him a small smile and let it go. He blew off

Kate's reaction, but I thought at the time that he was just trying to make me feel better.

I didn't run after my first baby girl to make sure she was okay.

Six months later, on the exact date that she was due, my little Molly was born. I have to admit that she quickly became the light of my life. She was such an undemanding baby, sweet and adorable, and easy to please. She learned to eat, crawl, walk, and talk in the blink of an eye, it seems now, and every day was exciting and new.

Compared to Katie when she was that little, Molly was happy all the time and rarely fussed or complained about anything.

I think I spent more and more time with little Molly because she turned out to be the one living thing in our home—in my life, really—that loved me unconditionally.

As soon as she arrived, it seemed like Robbie gave to his own daughter all the kindness and caring that he had kept from my Kate. He turned out to be a doting father, giving Molly expensive birthday presents and letting her do pretty much whatever she wanted. I used to tell him to stop, that he would end up spoiling her with all that, but she was such a sweet little girl. She would thank him for the gifts and obediently do her chores around the house, and she always came home at the exact time that we told her to. None of Robbie's spoiling ever seemed to change her. A few times, I even caught her giving some of those gifts away to her friends.

Eventually, Rob seemed to simply ignore Kate all together. She spent less and less time at home and pulled away from all of us. I have to admit, things seemed easier then, because the fighting had all but gone and our house was calmer for it.

There were a few times amidst the round-the-clock diaper changes, the sniffling noses, and teething that I tried to reach out to Kate.

"Katie, you know, I love you very much," I'd offer, hoping to connect with her. But she would just look back at me with that "whatever" stare that teenagers give and turn away.

"You know, even though your father and I weren't meant to be, you are still dear to me."

"Yeah, but I wasn't enough to keep you together, was I?" Kate would retort with undisguised bitterness in her voice.

"Hun, our marriage didn't have anything to do with you."

"How *couldn't* it have something to do with me, Mother? I was part of it!" she spat back before turning away.

I would try to pull her close to me and tell her how special she was, that she was my first and always would be. But she was never one for affection. She'd let me hug her for just a second before mumbling something about going out with her friends and pulling away from me. I would watch her go but only for a moment before Molly needed my attention. Eventually, my attempts with Kate tapered off, mainly through the struggles and demands of being a new mom and the frustrations of not knowing what else to do.

I see now that each new change that I brought into Kate's life pushed her farther and farther away, and I hate myself for it. But I eventually stopped going after my oldest daughter to make sure she was okay, and I let her go.

Although I knew that things weren't perfect, *I* was content with Robbie and our lives together, and I foolishly hoped that all our problems would somehow just be blown away with the wind.

Of course, I couldn't see how deep those problems ran. Nor did I have any idea that things were only going to continue to get worse. It's amazing what the mind can ignore when it doesn't want to see something.

I didn't know it then, but the reason my Katie left us was so awful that I shouldn't have blamed her at the time. I never thought that the man I married had it inside him to do something so terrible and wrong to my girl, something that would change her life forever. I thank God with all my might that she is a strong one. Who knows what would have happened if my Katie wasn't a born fighter.

Had I known about that night then, I would have left him. But I didn't know, and now I can't face the pain of my daughter's life or the burden that I've become to everyone. God, the suffering that we've all gone through because of me…

All those problems that we tend to push away or hide under the rug just fester there and eventually become a searing, gripping pain just under the surface. It's a pain that slowly eats away at you day after day, and eventually, it kills you from the inside out. Eventually, you can't think straight, you can't eat, and you can't do anything, because all you can think about is how you ruined everything for those you love and about how much hurt you received from those who scorned you.

I do believe that if this life had been better to me... that if I'd been better to those I love...that I wouldn't be ready to just let go. But I feel that it's time for me to move on now and end the pain and suffering. It's time to stop the hurt that's ripping apart me and everyone around me.

17. MOLLY

AFTER KATE ENDED THEIR CALL, Molly turned to Jack and barely stifled a small scream before it escaped her lips, "Jack, my sister actually hung up on me!"

Molly stared off in the distance in disbelief. Her mind raced around their conversation, still stunned to find out that her sister and her mother talked so often. *For heaven's sake, it sounds like they talk almost as much as she and I do!* Standing there with her hands on her hips, she shook her head in disbelief.

In the living room, the girls were engrossed in the *Dora the Explorer* cartoon their parents had let them watch. Fortunately, it was loud enough to keep her angry words from reaching their ears.

Jack watched as the emotions played across his wife's face. She had a fire in her eyes that he had never seen before. This sudden, spirited transformation was so out of character for his usually compliant wife.

"Molly, hun. You have a look of something starting there. What is it?" he prompted her gently with a hand on her shoulder.

It took her a few seconds to respond. She looked back at Jack as if she'd forgotten he still stood beside her. "What, Jack?"

He repeated his question slowly, with a trace of impatience and something else she couldn't identify, "What did your sister say?"

She turned to face him, and she spoke the words that her mind was still trying to wrap itself around.

"Jack, Kate told me that she and mom talk almost every day, but I just can't believe it. I mean, Mom has never even mentioned their conversations to me."

"Oh! Well, maybe she did at some point and you just forgot about it," Jack replied, trying to downplay what he saw brewing in his wife's mind. "You know, with everything else going on right now."

"I don't think that's something I would have forgotten, Jack," she retorted dryly. "The crazy thing is that Mom never mentions Kate's name at all. And I just always assumed that it was because they didn't talk any more than Kate and I ever do."

"So… was she mad at you for not knowing that? Is that why she hung up so fast?"

Molly looked up at him questioningly, "Yes, that was exactly it. How'd you guess that?"

"Oh, I don't know," he stammered and turned away from her, "It just seemed that way from this end."

With his back to her, Jack began arbitrarily pulling dishes out of the cupboards, grabbing at plates, cups, and salad bowls and piling them onto the counter.

"Jack, what are you doing?" Molly asked sharply.

He turned around to face her, but before he could answer, she jerked her head to the already set table, "Didn't you see that I already have everything out for dinner?"

Chagrined, he looked over to where their place settings were laid out and quickly began putting the extra dishes back in the cupboard while avoiding Molly's eyes. She seemed too wrapped up in trying to think through Kate's call to notice his behavior, for nothing more was said. After a few moments, she grabbed him by the shoulders and spun him around to face her again.

"I just don't know what to think about all of this!" She threw up her hands, looking as if she would burst into tears at any moment.

"Well, that's a change," he said with a small grin, attempting to lighten the air and his wife's mood.

Molly gave him a half-smile and a light rap on the arm. She relaxed a little and took a deep breath, "Seriously, I hope Kate calls me back soon. Or, better yet, that any minute *Mom* will call me like she always does. Then, I can stop all this worrying all together."

Even as she said the words, they both knew it wasn't true.

She peered down at her cell phone on the counter, as if doing so would cause it to ring on cue. Jack put one hand under her chin and made her look up at him. Putting on his most confident face, he tried to reassure her that everything would be fine.

"She will, Molly. She will."

"Who, Jack? Kate or Mom? Because at this point, I'm not sure I'll hear from either of them."

Jack didn't respond, not knowing what else to say. Molly shook her head as if to rid her mind of the worry and angst. She glanced at the oven timer and pulled away from him, calling out over her shoulder to Emma and Alice that dinner was ready. A disheartened "Uhhh" sang out in chorus as Alice begrudgingly turned off their favorite TV show. The two pixie-like girls dragged themselves to the kitchen table, asking as they did every night why they couldn't have macaroni and cheese, their favorite dish. Molly retorted, just as she always did, that if they ate any more of that they'd turn into pasta. The girls giggled in unison, even while sensing a slight curtness to their mother's tone that wasn't usually there.

Molly set the salad and lasagna out on the table and quickly put away the additional place setting that she had set for her father. She didn't want to be reminded of his absence. She put one hand up to her temple with a frown as she turned away from her family, giving Jack a fleeting look to see if he had noticed the gesture. She could feel the tension in her head like a rubber band about to snap, and she wondered if it finally would. Almost daily, she had crazy visions of collapsing to the floor, in the grocery store or some unfamiliar place, in a wild state of panic and scaring everyone. Or even worse, of driving with the girls in the car and swerving off the road, killing them all. She often wondered where she'd be and what she'd be doing when the moment happened. When she first started feeling this way, Jack would scoff away her worries. Later, he'd try to comfort her, promising her that nothing was wrong. He said it so often, though, that she finally stopped telling him about her spells.

It was always the "what ifs" she lived with that seemed to drive her to the brink. *What if I start feeling depressed? What if I get sick? What if I end up like my mother?* Those worries were like a shawl of shame that she wore every day.

As she sat down heavily at the table, her mind reeled from the disappointing phone call with Kate. Between Alice's observation of the family picture and the unsettling conversation with Kate, Molly thought she had every right to feel real fear. She finally understood just how mired things with her family had become.

Peering through the kitchen window, she thought fleetingly about running off and leaving all her problems behind, though knowing that she never could. Then reaching up to rub her temples again, she willed herself not to start crying and turned to face her family with the brightest smile that she could manage sitting precariously on her haggard face.

18. THE END OF THE BEGINNING

A HALF HOUR LATER, AFTER finishing a few final emails of the day, Kate glanced at the time. She realized that Ethan would soon be home, and putting her emotions and anger aside just as she had done a thousand times before, she jumped up from the couch and decided to grab a quick shower before they headed to Le Noir—determined as ever to enjoy her evening.

However, just as she stepped away from the living room, her cell phone rang again. She hesitated for a minute before turning around, a look of annoyance already forming on her face. She glared at the disruptive device then crossed the room in a few short strides to find out who else could be disturbing her tonight. Seeing Molly's name on the caller id screen for the second time instantly reignited her anger.

"Seriously?" Kate called out in exasperation as she stared at the ringing phone, yelling at it as if it was a living thing. "Haven't you done enough to me already?"

Yet in that next second, Kate's feeling of annoyance was somehow, perhaps instinctively, replaced by a sense that something might be wrong. She quickly grabbed the phone and hit "accept" and headed back toward the stairs. Before she'd even brought the phone to her ear, Kate could hear her sister's whimpering voice.

"Katie! Are you there? Katie?"

Kate stopped mid-step, "Yes, I'm here, Molly. What is it now?" Her voice was much curter than she intended.

"Something's wrong—I don't know how… I- I just needed to call you."

Molly's sobs made it difficult for Kate to understand her words. She continued heading upstairs to her bedroom in the back of the house. She tried to remind herself to be patient, but she was annoyed with her sister for being feeble.

"Molly. You need to slow down. What is wrong?" The agitation in her voice was clear.

"Kate, it's Mom," Molly hesitated just a moment longer then screamed out three small words that would change everything, "She's been shot!"

Kate stopped abruptly inside her bedroom door; her eyes flew open and one hand unconsciously grabbed for the wall.

"Oh my God, what, Molly? What did you say?" Though Kate heard the words, her mind refused to register them.

"Katie, mom was shot," she repeated more quietly, barely able to get the words out in between her sobs. "She's not good."

"Shot? But how!" Kate's disbelief echoed in the room. The words didn't—couldn't—make sense. *Shot? How?* Before Kate could work to get the words out to ask, however, Molly's frantic words spilled out.

"Dad found her at home. He just called me. He found her lying on the bathroom floor. Katie, he said she was covered in blood. She's in the ambulance now. They're headed to Portland Memorial Hospital now."

"Molly. I don't understand. Shot by who?" Yet even as she spoke the words again, Kate knew. Somewhere, deep inside, she knew the answer that she didn't want to hear—the words that Molly couldn't bring herself to say. Kate closed the door behind her and leaned against it. Tears began to tumble down her cheeks as the realization of what Molly had said began to settle in. She felt like an ice cold fist had reached in and grabbed ahold of her heart—squeezing it tighter and tighter with each frantic pump.

"You have to come up here…" Molly said, her voice wavering. "They said she will probably fall into a coma… Kate, it doesn't look good."

"No!" Kate cried out; the primal shout echoed loudly in the empty confines of the house.

Explosions of pain ripped through her insides as grief began to take hold. Her tears became a convulsive, uncontrollable outpouring of sobs. The feeling was unlike anything her body had ever experienced before. Raw emotion poured forth, and in that moment Kate felt nothing except splintered, spearing pain as the understanding of Molly's words ricocheted inside her mind.

Again, she screamed in pain, and her knees buckled, dropping her body to the floor. On her hands and knees, she managed to crawl toward the bed and propped herself against it. As she half sat, half lay beside the bed, the phone fell out of her hand and slid onto the floor beside her. She could vaguely hear Molly's sobs on the other end of the line. A guttural sound from within her involuntarily came out. Something more primal and animal-like than any human should be able to make.

Kate became oblivious to everything around her as tears that she didn't know she had inside of her poured forth.

19. BETH

I FEEL A SENSE OF peace inside now, knowing what I have to do and that it will all be over soon. I love both my daughters. I could never have known back then that they would be born into a web of pain and struggles, that I would cause them such angst, or that they would never feel the connection of siblings that parents always wish for. I truly thought they would be there for each other as sisters and friends. But that road was not meant to be taken in our little family... at least not yet.

My sweet Molly, she is such a dear girl—warm, sensitive, and open. She wears her heart on her sleeve, and I know the smallest things can hurt her. She's so different from Kate that even *I* sometimes find it hard to believe that they are both my blood. Oh, but she loved her older sister so.

Molly was only seven years old when Katherine left home, just a few years older than her Alice is now. Her memories of having an older sister around are few, yet I know she holds them close to her heart. She looked up to Katie so much; it was a total and complete love that my poor Katie never could see. Molly swears that she can remember the day that Kate left home. She insists that she can recall standing in the doorway of Kate's bedroom, watching as Kate raced around her room yanking clothes and shoes out of the closet and tossing them onto her bed. Then every so often, when Kate couldn't find something she wanted, she yelled out words that Molly knew were on the naughty list. Covering her ears, Molly simply stood there and watched as Kate furiously packed her things, oblivious to the heartbreak that her younger sister already began feeling inside. Yes, Molly is quite adamant that she can describe the very moment that Kate walked out our front door.

She remembers odd little details about that day… that Kate's hair was gathered up in a ponytail, that her shoelaces were undone, and that her face was all flushed from darting around. She remembers chasing after her sister outside in the yard, squeezing her legs tight and begging her not to leave, though I can't even recall all of that. Like my wedding, the day my Katherine moved out is just a blur.

I'm sure Molly would say something like, "It was a hot July day, Mom, and I really can still feel the dust from the driveway swirling around us as Katie sped away." My poor Molly.

In truth, she may only have created those memories with my help. I always knew Katie would leave us as soon as she could. Even if I didn't know why back then. I had been telling Molly before Katie's graduation that her sister would someday move out, preparing my youngest girl for the loss of her one and only sister.

The days after Kate left, Molly cried every day. It broke my heart. It took a few weeks before she stopped looking for Kate in the house or waiting for her to walk through the front door after school. It was months before I think she finally let go of her hopes that Kate would come back home. Over time, my youngest daughter learned to replace the absence of her sister by surrounding herself with friends—children from the neighborhood, kids from school, even summer tourists just in town for the precious summer months. Molly never rose to the top of her class. She wasn't the fastest on the soccer field, but she understood that being genuine could turn a stranger into a friend and slowly help replace her loss.

Sadly, after Katie moved out, she came home just twice during the rest of Molly's childhood years. Once, when Molly "graduated" from the eighth grade and again for her high school graduation. Molly learned to fill the void at home like a carpenter fills a hole in a piece of wood, filling in the space with putty then painting smoothly over it, so on the outside everything looked all right, as though the hole had never been there.

I understand that, because that's exactly what I've done. Filling the holes of my own pain and trying to pretend that everything was fine. But both of my husbands cheated on me, and both of my marriages were failures.

I saw women in town, old friends from high school, who had married after college and happily spent years and years with the same man. With smiles on their faces as they shopped and went about, they looked so content, so perfect. They married the good guys, apparently, but I didn't. No, I knew how to pick 'em... two different men who tore me apart inside when they said "to hell" with our vows of eternal life together and screwed around with other women. Discovering that one husband cheated on you is tough, but the second time? By then you just feel like a piece of garbage that's been torn up and thrown away, tossed into the trash like last month's spoiled food, rotten and festering. Used up, worn out, and worthless. Something that nobody wants anymore.

It hurt, and that disappointment and pain is always there in those holes life gave you, burning from the inside out.

Oh, you try to go through the motions and pretend it's not so, but as time goes on, more and more holes are made by the lies and the deceit, until you can't take any more. One day you wake up and realize that you're a piece of Swiss cheese inside and you're falling apart. You know that you can't pretend anymore. That the only way to mend the holes is to make the pain go away, once and for all.

And that's what you do.

PART II

20. ETHAN SHEPHARD

ETHAN WOUND HIS LEXUS THROUGH the subdivision, smiling broadly. Rechecking the clock on the dash, he felt confident that he would arrive home on time for his celebratory anniversary dinner with Kate. Their reservations weren't until nine *and*—he looked in the rearview mirror at the bag hanging behind him—he had remembered to pick up Kate's dry cleaning, just as she'd asked.

More importantly, though, he was anxious to give Kate her anniversary gift. Glancing down again at the signature turquoise bag lying on the seat beside him, he felt nervous all over again.

For months, he had asked the women around the office, hoping to get a gift idea that would be suitable for the occasion *and* would equal Kate's high expectations. After receiving numerous suggestions from them, he finally decided on a signature necklace from Tiffany's. It was an exquisite piece of diamonds and opals, the most expensive jewelry he'd ever purchased for Kate besides her wedding ring.

Ethan gripped the steering wheel tighter. He hoped that she would love it as much as his secretary—and the Tiffany sales clerks—had promised she would. As he pulled the Lexus to a stop in the driveway, his heart raced in anticipation of giving Kate her gift and watching her open the box.

Exiting the car with the dry cleaning bag in one hand and the gift bag in the other, Ethan entered the front door. He stopped at the doormat to remove his shoes, remembering as he did that Josetta had come to clean the house today as he breathed in the clean aromas. Appreciating the clean around him, he gazed up at the grand foyer entrance, admiring the magnitude of their home. Though proud of what they had accomplished together, he would still readily admit that their success was primarily due to Kate and her unstoppable ambition. Ethan knew he was smart—top of his class at Northwestern—yet his own drive and ambition had paled in comparison to Kate's over the years.

"God, she'll probably want to start her own law firm soon," he muttered with a small resigned smile, not knowing how close to the mark of Kate's relentless quest for success he had hit.

Ethan sighed thoughtfully. He knew that, if it weren't for Kate, he would probably still be working in the nowhere office back home, scraping by on fifty thousand a year and hanging out with his buddies drinking Pabst Blue Ribbon with the rest of the single guys, wondering where life went wrong. Definitely not the life he led now, rubbing shoulders at the country club with men who drank ten-year-old bourbon and women who gazed on languidly from their lounge chairs as nannies chased their children around.

As he hung the dry cleaning bag on the hook in the adjoining formal room, his eye caught sight of the photo of their wedding on the stand nearby, and another thoughtful sigh escaped him. In it, he and Kate were standing in front of the Bermuda hotel where they had exchanged their vows. Ethan had hoped to get married at home, and his mother had pitched a fit when he told her they were going away by themselves. But Kate wouldn't budge on the idea and deftly made the arrangements herself in her usual manner of non-compliancy and over-efficiency. The hotel brochure that Ethan had shown his parents stated that the location was "the perfect blend of beachside class and charm" for special occasions. What he recalled most, however, was that the drink prices were the cost of an entrée and the hotel staff was overzealous in their tip expectations from him every time he turned around.

As he peered closer at the image of Kate, Ethan felt a sense of wistfulness tinged with regret. He hadn't seen that easy, relaxed look of happiness on his wife's face in a long time and wondered when exactly it had disappeared. He sat down in the decorative chair by the side table and thought back to the day they had met.

He still remembered the thrill of the first moment he saw her. It was at a small coffee and bagel shop in Boston; it was one of the few places on Newbury Street back then to get some homemade muffins and bagels and real coffee that didn't taste watered down. It was a morning that had started out like any other, as he'd headed into town to grab a coffee and a dozen of their finest. He could still remember how she had casually, confidently pushed a lock of her thick, red curls behind her ear as she stepped in through the front doors of the shop and stopped to glance around. Her auburn hair shined in the sun as she strode to the counter, and her cheeks were flushed against an otherwise picturesque and porcelain face on that cool summer day.

She was dressed impeccably well in a place where formal attire was still reserved mainly for weddings and churches and jeans were a given on most days. Ethan saw instantly that this was a woman who was unique—different from the other girls he had called his girlfriends over the years—and he was instantly enamored.

Before he realized what he was doing, he approached her at the counter—his body had seemed to move of its own volition toward her. He stood awkwardly beside her and just began to talk, about what he cannot recall. Ethan knew that it would be his boldest move ever, and when she turned to him with an open face that seemed to radiate warmth and draw him in, his heart melted. Much to his surprise, the beautiful redheaded stranger returned his light and nervous banter with a candid openness that both intrigued and humbled him. She asked him to join her at a table, and as he sat stiffly in the seat across from her, he was overly aware of the strong and confident woman before him.

Normally, confidence was a trait in females that would have caused him to shy away. Yet there was something soft, almost vulnerable in her that he was inexplicably drawn to. It was something he couldn't identify, but it gave him a measure of courage like never before.

The excitement of what *could* be with this amazing woman captured him. The feeling took hold of his mind and squashed it like jelly, leaving him tongue-tied and out of breath.

They talked for a while, as customers came to the shop and left with their breakfast treats and piping hot coffees in hand. Though the conversation details were hazy, he still recalled that she ate not one but two donuts with her coffee that day. This stood out in his mind because—although she consumed coffee as if it was water—he had not seen her eat so much as a bite of a donut since that day.

Hours later—who knows how long exactly—as he scrambled to figure out a way to ask for her number, she suddenly blurted out the words that no one wants to hear.

"You know, I actually just ended a short though difficult relationship, Ethan."

It was as if she had read his mind, and Ethan's heart had lurched as he struggled to compose himself and respond. Before he could say anything, she dropped another bomb and told him of her imminent plans to leave the Northeast and relocate south just outside of Atlanta, Georgia.

For a moment, Ethan had felt that his world had crumbled beneath him. A heavy feeling of disappointment and loss already weighed him down like a sinking ship, even though the logical part of his mind recognized that it was a loss of something that he'd never actually had. Unable to articulate a single artful sentence and desperately trying to figure out how not to let this woman walk away, Ethan just sat there and watched as Kate got up to leave. He knew that his face reflected his emotions like a foolish teenage boy as he gave her his phone number before she turned and walked away, but he didn't care. With a wave and a frown, he followed her like a puppy dog out of the coffee shop to watch her go.

To his surprise, however, Kate had stopped after crossing the street and turned around. She had called out to him, above the passing traffic, "I do hope that we can stay in touch, Ethan," then lifted up her hand in a small wave.

She surprised him when she called a few weeks later, after she'd moved, just as she had promised; those weeks, however, had been the longest time of Ethan's life. She immediately began talking to him as if their conversation back at the bagel shop had never ended, and Ethan found it comforting and oddly moving at the same time.

He called her a few times a week over the next few months, trying to space out the calls to not appear too needy or desperate. Yet with each call, he felt that she needed him just as much as he knew he needed her. Their conversations were scattered with humor, heart-felt discussions about life, and intimate references to what could happen between them if and when they would be together again. He wanted her like a junkie wants a fix, and he was crazy for her. Whenever he made a joke, her throaty laugh on the other end made him want to do things to a woman that he'd never imagined.

Finally, a few months later, he found the courage to tell her that he wanted to move down to be with her. Holding his breath, he heard her quick and tense response come across the line. She said no, telling him that she needed more time and that it wasn't right just yet, then she quickly ended the call. If he tried to bring the notion up again on other days, she would deftly divert the conversation away to other more mundane things with a sharp reproach.

She left him no choice but to wait for her, and wait he did, even if he hadn't known why.

One day out of the blue about four months later, after countless conversations together over the phone Kate called and stoically stated, "Ethan, you can come down now."

Although the request—or was it a command, he was never sure—took him completely by surprise, Ethan agreed before he could even think about his decision or his action. He gave his resignation at work, gave up his apartment, and uprooted himself from family and friends to move down South.

They were married twelve months later, and since then, Ethan had watched as Kate's career and their financial status simultaneously took off. They quickly acquired and accumulated everything they had wanted. Their home was enormous. They drove luxury cars. There were few daily wants that could not be readily met and life had, seemingly, given him all that he could ask for.

He looked around again at the massive house they called home and thought, not for the first time, that despite all the money and success, Kate had not been an easy woman to be married to. Distant and aloof, she pushed him away when he tried to hold her close. She needed very little from him by means of support or concern, and she neither offered nor asked for much in return. Ethan felt in his heart that she loved him and that the thick armor she had so deftly armed herself with had been donned long ago. He'd learned to steel himself for the sour taste of rejection and the jerky pull from his affectionate touch.

For although he'd never told Kate, he felt that only someone who could be so exceptionally vulnerable and sensitive on the inside would feel that they needed such a strong shield surrounding them. Ethan understood that Kate gave of herself everything that she could.

And as he looked around their home at all the designer pieces whose names that he couldn't pronounce, he was proud of his wife and all that they had accomplished. The years together had been good. He grabbed her anniversary gift, jumped up from the chair, and excitedly called out her name.

"Kate! Kate? I'm home!" Ethan called out as he walked through the kitchen and then to the living room. Hearing no response, he walked upstairs, holding her gift bag tightly with the impatient excitement of a child.

Yet as he neared the master bedroom, he stopped short. He could hear the faint sound of sobbing coming from inside. He hesitated, for it was a sound that he had never heard before in their home. Approaching slowly, he rounded the corner to the bedroom and the sight before him was so foreign, so incomprehensible, that it didn't immediately register in his mind.

Kate lay in a heap on the floor next to the bed.

Low-throated sobs and guttural groans came from somewhere deep within her. The noises seemed as if they were being forcibly wrenched out of her. As she lay there crumpled, she looked like a rag doll that had been beaten and tossed aside rather than anything human. For a moment, Ethan was too stunned to move. Kate was usually so proud and determined, but in that moment he saw a beaten and battered woman, and he didn't know what to do.

He felt like a stranger, a voyeur, in his home as he stared down upon her.

Kate became aware of Ethan's presence. Slowly, she raised her head as if it was the last thing she could physically do. Her face was blotchy and reddened; her curls were matted to her cheeks. Wet patches littered her shirt, and she exhibited an overall list-lessness. The image was physically disturbing for Ethan. His stomach wrenched in pain at the sight; he felt for a moment that it would give up its contents inside and he covered his mouth as if to stop it from happening.

But when he looked into her eyes and saw her utter despair, all uncertainty passed. The anguish that seemed to ooze out of every fiber of Kate's body ripped through his own tender soul. He took a few quick steps toward her, with the sole intention of making her pain go away.

At that moment, he wanted to grab her into his arms and ex-tinguish whatever tormented her body and soul.

However, as he neared where she lay, he understood at once that he would never, ever be able to do so.

When his eyes caught sight of Kate's cell phone on the floor next to her, Ethan instinctively knew what had happened.

Over the last few years, he had overheard the troubling phone calls between Kate and her mother. He had picked up on the frustration in his wife's voice, witnessed the pleading silences be-tween them. And he had understood from the numerous phone conversations that there were significant problems occurring on the other end that had worsened as time went on. He understood all this, perhaps even when Kate had not.

Just as someone looking in from the outside can often see through another's life with more clarity, Ethan simply knew.

Tossing the Tiffany bag onto a nearby stand, he quickly covered the short distance between them. Bending down, he scooped Kate up into his arms. She did not resist. Normally so fiercely proud and independent, Kate wordlessly allowed him to carry her to the settee like a small child. He lowered her down gently, his mind desperately trying to comprehend what to do to make things okay. To make it better.

Ethan's heart ached with love like never before. He came down to his knees beside the couch and wrapped his arms protectively, tightly around her. As she lay there next to him, clinging to him in desperation, tears streamed down her face and sobs racked her shoulders. His own outpouring of emotion began, and they cried like that together—fiercely and without abandon.

At some point, Kate managed to utter just one word, "Mom."

Ethan simply said, "I know," and hugged her tighter. Somewhere deep inside, Ethan felt grateful that, for once, *she* was clinging to *him*. Like a life preserver thrown into tumultuous waters for a drowning passenger. He felt needed by her now, more than ever, and relished the new feeling, even amidst her pain.

21. MOLLY

AFTER HER CALL TO KATE, Molly went through the motions of living and breathing, just trying to hang on. The moments when her sorrow became too much to bear, she hid herself away and let her tears gush out in wild, convulsive sobs.

At some point, with Jack by her side, she told the girls as casually as she could that Grandma had had an accident, and that was all. She and Jack had agreed that at their age, they didn't need to know more. As soon as their neighbor could make it over to watch the girls, Molly and Jack hurried out and headed for the hospital.

With Jack behind the wheel, the forty-minute drive to Portland Memorial was made mostly in silence; only the sound of Molly's stifled tears could be heard. When they walked through the hospital doors, Jack supported her elbow and guided her across the foyer to the receptionist desk. The older woman behind it swiftly directed them to intensive care with a sympathetic eye and a pat on Molly's hand as she checked in. She watched Molly and Jack walk off with a sad and knowing smile.

As they made their way down to the ICU, Molly felt as if she could barely breathe. She gasped for air, squeezing Jack's hand tightly as they wound their way through the corridors. At the room number that they'd been told, Molly's legs stopped moving. Jack had to help her press forward as he slowly opened the heavy hospital door. Inside the darkened room, a young and apprehensive staff nurse stood stiffly by the bedside. She gave them only a sideways glance as they entered then left without a word, looking back quickly at the chart she held onto, seemingly too inexperienced or ill-equipped to handle the situation.

Molly barely noticed her. She stood motionless and just stared down at her mother's prone body as it lay in the sterile, white bed.

Still in disbelief at the site before her, her mind tried to register what her eyes could clearly see—the tubes and machines, the bandages, the lifeless body before her. For a moment, her legs buckled beneath her, and she had to grab hold of the cart table next to her for support as a gasping sob escaped her body. Jack steadied her, and the nurse quickly bustled out, mumbling something about allowing time with family, leaving Jack and Molly alone in the room with Beth. Jack reached over to hold Molly, and they stood like that for a moment as she desperately tried to keep herself together.

Finally, she found the courage to approach the bed and tentatively reached out to touch her mother's cool hand as it hung limply outside the starched sheets. She sat down heavily in the chair next to the bed and stayed like that for a while, holding her mother's hand and whispering thoughts of love, knowing that Jack was right behind her all the time.

At some point, a doctor clad in a worn white coat sauntered in, startling them both. Jack could immediately see that the man knew what he was doing as he greeted them warmly, offered his condolences, and reviewed Beth's chart. Murmuring a few words about "excellent hospital care" and "feeling no pain," the aged doctor then informed them with obvious compassion that Beth was in a coma due to the significant injury to her brain. He reiterated that they were doing their best for her, though her prognosis was still unknown.

Jack looked over at Molly. By her troubled face, he knew that she needed to hear something more. As the doctor began to walk out, Jack swiftly grabbed at his arm then just as quickly let it go when the elderly physician looked down at his grasp.

"I'm sorry. Please," he uttered, "is that really all you can tell us now?"

"Yes, I'm afraid it is." He stared back at them with the sadness of having seen it all a thousand times before, then mumbled another apology and walked out, leaving Jack and Molly alone again.

She gently picked up her mother's hand again, holding it lightly as if it would break into a thousand pieces. She stroked her mother's palm and talked to her softly. With tears streaming shamelessly down her face, she begged her to stay with them and come back. Jack looked on helplessly as the minutes ticked by. After some time like that, the same young nurse from before knocked and quickly entered the room. She awkwardly ushered them out with mumbled words about hospital policy and after hours then quickly scuttled off.

As Jack and Molly left the ICU, stoically retracing their footsteps back to the lobby, they heard a voice call out to them from down another hall.

They stopped and looked back to see an older nurse from a nearby nurses' station looking at them. She had a plump, round face and gave them a small smile as she approached them in her scuffed white shoes. She introduced herself as the head night nurse and said they hoped to have more information on Ms. Harriman's condition tomorrow. She encouraged them to get some rest, and though the bone was small, it was exactly what Molly needed—something she could hold onto that would not slip away. Molly gave the nurse a heartfelt smile then impulsively leaned over and hugged the woman fiercely. Emitting a surprised "Oh," the nurse graciously returned the gesture then stood there for a few minutes and watched the couple leave.

The walk back to Jack's truck on the other side of the parking lot felt long; the drive home felt even longer. Few words passed between them in the darkened cabin of the truck, as none were sufficient to express their pain.

When they arrived home, Alice and Emma were exhausted but still awake without the comfortable routine of their parents putting them to bed. The tired neighbor hugged Molly tightly and mouthed her apologies as she scurried out the back door and headed home.

Molly tried to wrap her head around the scene before her as she scanned the rooms littered with toys and books. Spotting a ragdoll lying limp on the floor near her feet, she looked back up at her girls, and when her eyes found Jack's, they spooled over with tears. She could no longer hide her desperation. She ran out of the room and away from the girls. Jack quickly followed. He closed the distance between them, hugged her, and nudged the door shut behind them. He murmured over and over in her ear that everything would be okay, trying to hold back his own tears.

Eventually, Molly left Jack's embrace and bustled out to gather up the girls for a quick bedtime snack and some warm milk. As they ate in tired silence, Molly went about the house picking things up here and there as best she could. However, when she stopped to look around, she realized that her attempts to organize were more of a replacement of items rather than actual cleanup. She felt foolish, useless. She stopped and stood still, staring straight ahead, lost in her own anguish.

"Hun, are you okay?" Jack called out to her gently, startling her back to the present.

Molly turned to look at him, like a deer in headlights, but said nothing.

"Babe, why don't you go lie down now and take a break. I'll take care of the rest tonight."

"I think, I think I just need to keep myself busy," she replied and turned away as she continued her attempts to pick up.

Jack said nothing more, even though they both knew her response was a lie, and Molly avoided his eyes as she scooped up an arm full of dirty clothes and rushed off to the laundry room.

Alice and Emma, knowing something was wrong but not what, obediently and quickly went through the final rituals of the night. Tempering their usual fusses and complaints, they donned pajamas and brushed their teeth then hopped into bed. At one point, while Molly hastily brushed out Alice's tangled hair, the little girl looked back around at her mother, "Mommy, why are you crying? Did I do something to make you sad?"

"No!" Molly retorted a little too forcibly, unaware that she had been weeping in front of her daughter and was instantly ashamed.

Harshly, she wiped her tears away and drew her daughter in close. As she held Alice's small frame, her mind struggled with the understanding that life may never be the same for them again. *May never or will never?* She thought with utter sadness. Releasing Alice from her clutches, she tucked both exhausted girls in their beds. When she leaned over to Emma to tuck her in and kiss her goodnight, Emma reached up and pushed a stray hair out of her mother's face.

"It's all right, Mommy," she whispered quietly.

Molly smiled at her as best she could and brushed the side of her daughter's soft cheek, "What is, honey?"

Emma took her mother's face in her little hands and said very earnestly, "Dinner was yummy. Even if it wasn't mac n' cheese."

Molly laughed at her daughter in spite of herself. She scooped Emma up in her arms, and as the little girl's arms encircled her neck, Jack swooped in behind her and sat down next to Alice. The girls giggled, glad to see their parents smiling. As Molly listened to their innocent laughter, her heart ached with love and fear for the future of her family.

She stood up and turned away, squeezing her eyes tight and trying to block out the worry from her mind. Yet all she could see was a thick blackness that made her stomach lurch and her heart sink. She put a hand on the wall to steady herself.

"Mommy, are you okay *now?*" Alice asked.

Before she opened her eyes, Molly did her best to force a smile and turned to face them. "Yes, sweetie, of course. Everything's fine."

She avoided Jack's eyes and leaned over to kiss the girls then motioned to Jack that she would leave the room. As she closed the door behind her, her legs almost collapsed beneath her. She barely made it down the hall to her bedroom before racking sobs overcame her all over again. Falling down upon the unmade bed amidst piles of clothes and pillows, she succumbed and let the waves of grief overtake her as her head pounded its usual deadly tune. She felt a firm hand on her back and jumped. She turned to see Jack kneeling beside the bed, tears freely falling down his own face. She moved over to give him room and he lay down beside her, his long body cradling hers. And though his embraces had always been able to make the bad go away, this time they both knew that things were different. Molly pushed even tighter against him, seeking a refuge in her husband that wouldn't be there.

When she finally found the strength to speak, she quietly asked Jack the question that had haunted her thoughts, "Jack, am I going to end up like her?"

Jack gently turned her over to face him while carefully formulating an answer in his head.

"Am I, Jack? Do you think I'm like that? Because some days, I just feel like *I'm* really losing it. That I'm no different than...."

He interrupted her with a careful finger on her lips, "No, Molly. You are *nothing* like your mother. You are one of the strongest people I know. Don't you ever forget that."

She managed a small smile at his fervent response. "Thank you," she said, then rapped him lightly on the arm, "You aren't biased at all, though, right?"

"Ha, maybe. But only a little."

They were quiet for a moment before Molly said quietly, "It's just that some days, I don't *feel* that strong, you know?"

"Some days, Hun, none of us do."

22. PLANNING TO GO HOME

FOR KATE, ETHAN'S TIGHT EMBRACE in those moments after he arrived home may have been the only thing that prevented her from spiraling into a place of unknown terror, a place from which she might not have returned. She held onto him in sheer desperation, for how long she didn't know, as her mind tried to block out the tormenting images that threatened to tear her apart inside.

Later that evening, she allowed him to take care of the details of the trip to Maine. Since there were no more evening flights into Portland, she had no choice but to take the first flight out in the morning. He set up the flight itinerary, secured a rental car, and presented it all to her. Yet with a stiffened back and darting eyes, she interrupted him immediately and told him that she would be going alone.

At first Ethan was speechless, but then he fumbled his way through a request to go back to Maine to be with her. It was a request that he couldn't believe he had to make.

"Kate, please, let me be there for you." he pleaded. "You are *going* to need help there. You know that, right?"

When she just shook her head, he beseeched, begging her to allow him to go. Yet her stoic response was simply "No." It was a word so devoid of emotion that it made him gasp inaudibly. She followed up her terse response with the usual string of deceptions that logical people will tell themselves during an emotional crisis when they are wretched and desperately trying to hang on.

In the end, shaken and thrown off by Kate's resolve to go alone, Ethan had no choice but to acquiesce. Sullen and worn out, he booked her flight to Maine. She told him to schedule the return trip in three days, because that's all the time that she said she'd need to be there. Then, matter-of-factly and without a word, she walked away.

Ethan looked after her in sadness, amazed that someone so accomplished and successful could sometimes be so blind.

In their bedroom, she methodically began to pack. Her arms and legs felt as if they bent and angled of their own volition as she moved about the room tossing slacks and sweaters into the suitcase for the colder weather she knew she'd soon face. Habit caused her to throw her running shoes and clothes in, as well; she never left home without them, so she grabbed for them automatically, not realizing that running may be the last thing she would be able to do. Before she knew it, the suitcase was fully packed. Her mind began to meander back through memories of the last year and what had transpired with her mother.

Kate had received calls from Beth every week, at all hours of the day, and she talked with her mother more than ever before. Occasionally, the calls occurred during her evenings at home when Beth would call and tell her something about her day in hushed tones. Some of the more desperate calls were received in the middle of the night with Beth crying on the other end and apologizing through muffled tears, for what exactly Kate could never understand. She would end the calls baffled and confused, trying to understand why her mother had even called her in the first place.

Most times, Kate's cell rang its chirp-chirping crickets sound—the ring tone reserved only for her mother—at the worst of times. During work hours, while she was meeting with a client, or when she was in the courtroom. Kate took the calls whenever she was able to and struggled to be patient with her every time. Beth usually sounded harried on the phone, nervous and almost afraid, or she would say something that had no relevance to their conversation. Other days, the ones Kate dreaded, her mother said nothing but simply wept while Kate listened uncomfortably and struggled to stay on the line. She'd try to offer her words of encouragement, though for what she didn't even know. For despite her demanding and probing questions—so typical of a lawyer—Kate could never get a straight answer from her mother as to what was wrong. That unknown, the lack of structure or reason, left Kate feeling even more frustrated and annoyed and trying not to dread the next call between them.

Thinking back, Kate could recall some good days here and there. Days that Beth sounded cheerful and seemed to be doing well when she would inquire about Kate's life, about her job and Ethan—behaving as if everything was fine. She even laughed sometimes. However, Kate now understood that those fits of laughter had undoubtedly been forced and that the person emitting them had not been well at all.

Why didn't I see this coming? She chastised herself internally and felt the urge to hit herself in as the question mired inside her head. She wrapped her arms around her body to prevent herself from doing so and sat down on the edge of her bed, the packed suitcase beside her. Kate thought back to all the times she felt that she had tried to help, to convince Beth to get away from it all and come visit.

"Mom, why don't you just come here?" she'd toss out, while reading an email or scribbling down notes for work. "You can stay with Ethan and me for as long as you'd like. It would be a nice break for you."

She had no idea how heavy and absurd those words were to someone who couldn't even drive herself to the grocery store alone anymore. Beth repeatedly refused the invitations with excuses that sounded hollow and lame, though at the time Kate accepted her excuses far too easily. Kate was focused more on the work in front of her than on the desperate person on the other end of the line.

"Kate, I can't! I... I uh... it's just too much... the airplane ride. You know I don't like to fly. And being around all those people? I couldn't do it."

"But wouldn't it be nice to just get away for a while?"

"I just can't."

"Okay... well why don't you go away by yourself then? Go somewhere fun. Take a cruise!"

"Go away by myself? But where on Earth would I go?!"

Kate's impatience would finally prevail, and she would give her Mother some reason to quickly end the conversation. After each of those calls, Kate attempted to convince herself that the next one would be better and that she had done all that she reasonably could as she went back to her job and her life.

Now, Kate shook her head and squeezed her eyes tight. The astonishment that she'd once felt at her mother's ineptness, especially for someone who had once been so vibrant and focused, now felt bitter and dirty inside her. She thought about Beth lying in a coma in a hospital bed and hung her head as the tears fell freely. Kate knew that deep down inside, she had really wanted her mother to come stay with her more for herself than for Beth. For in all the years, in all of their conversations, they had never once talked about the past. About what almost happened with Robbie. About what could have been.

What Kate wanted most, was to hear her mother say, "I'm sorry. Sorry for the divorce. Sorry for bringing Robbie into your life. Sorry for ruining everything."

Kate stood up suddenly and flung her arms out wide. "How did this happen to me?" she yelled out to the empty room before collapsing onto the bed with a renewed fit of tears.

As she lay curled up on the bed, she heard footsteps outside the door every now and then and saw Ethan's shadow underneath the door. Each time she held her breath, watching the doorknob to see if it moved, and willed Ethan to walk away. To leave her alone in her misery.

At some point, she remembered through the haze of her anguish that she hadn't called Molly with her flight information. Numbly, she called her back. Their conversation was stilted and brief. Molly said that they were on their way to the hospital, and Kate told her that she would land around nine in the morning and head straight to the hospital. She would plan to arrive at Molly's house later in the afternoon.

Neither of them knew what to say, and too quickly they were saying their goodbyes.

Then before Kate could stop herself, she blurted out the one question that plagued her, "Molly, I don't understand. Didn't you see this coming?

"Of course I didn't," Molly barked back, instantly defensive. "How could I have?"

"But you see her! You are there with her, I just talk to her on the phone..." Kate's voice trailed off.

Molly's response was bitter, "No, Kate, I—*we*—did not see this coming."

"I just don't understand..." Kate stopped herself there, knowing even in her grief that no good would come from more words. "I'll see you tomorrow, then."

Sitting alone with the phone in her hand, Kate closed her eyes tight. She knew that she could be cold, even unforgiving, at times. She had no toleration of anyone or anything that wasn't logical, didn't meet her standards, or didn't do right by her. That mentality had helped her achieve all that she had—earning more money than she'd ever imagined.

If I'd let my emotions rule, I would have never made it this far. I may be cold, but I always survive! Between the divorce, growing up with Rob, and living second best around Molly, what else was I supposed to do? She sneered at her own self-questioning.

Kate felt exasperated. She knew that her survival was primarily due to living a life in which logic ruled and life's disappointments could be tightly shelved away. Her heart had become a place where all feelings had been pushed aside, leaving only the rhythmic pumping of blood and a hollow shell. In just one phone call, however, all of that had come crumbling down. She saw now that she had been living a life of false security, far removed from everyone who could remind her of the pain of her past and foolishly believing that she could actually leave it all behind. Those wounds from the past were nothing compared to the pain that her heart now experienced with every beat.

Fighting back another deluge of tears, she realized that she hadn't yet told her father what had happened. It took three attempts before Tom finally picked up. By then, Kate had added irritation to her already overwhelming stew of emotions, and her voice reflected them all when she spoke.

"Tom, why can't you ever pick up the damn phone the first time I call you?"

"Easy, Kate, easy. It's late, and I just didn't hear it ring. Is something wrong?"

"Yes, obviously," she retorted with sarcasm coating each word then paused to gather the strength to say the words. "Tom, Mom's been taken to the hospital. I'm going to Maine first thing in the morning to see her. She's—she's in a coma."

Her voice broke as she choked back tears, not wanting to let her father hear her weakness or pain.

"What? Oh, my God, what the hell happened?"

As her mind formulated a reply and remembered the words that her sister had spoken just a few hours before, her stomach lurched. She forced herself to hold back the bile that threatened to rise up. When she finally managed to get the words out, they did not sound like her own.

"She's—she's been shot."

"What? What do you mean, shot?" The incredulousness of Tom's words reflected her own reaction to Molly's earlier call. Hearing it in her father's voice, however, made her disbelief now seem stupid and naïve.

You should have known, Kate, you should have seen it coming.

She managed to sputter out a reply. "I… I really don't know all the details. Just that she's in a coma now."

Kate could not bring herself to say the one word that already began to haunt her soul.

"But shot? How?" Tom pressed again, this time in a softer tone. Though her parents had barely spoken to each other in more than three decades, the concern that came across the phone in her father's voice was so real that it created even more tears in her heart.

"Tom, she hasn't been herself lately, after everything she's been through…" her voice trailed off, not wanting to say more.

The heavy silence hung like icicles in the miles between them. The silence lasted for seconds, yet it felt like an eternity before Kate stood up and hastily ended their call.

"I'll call you tomorrow when I'm in Maine and know more."

Her father said a sad goodbye, and Kate remained standing in the middle of the room, staring ahead without seeing anything. The room was oddly quiet. Only the constant screams of *why?* that crashed around inside her head disrupted the stillness. She turned off the bedside lamp and noticed that the street lamp outside had burned out; the bedroom was engulfed in an eerie darkness. The shadows that loomed around her felt like harbingers of death.

After speaking with her father, she couldn't help but remember how different her parents had always been in so many ways. Kate had always felt that she was the product of a conflicting combination of DNA from both her parents, as well as the unplanned byproduct of a teenage romance that couldn't sustain itself into marriage and real life. When her parents ended up behaving like archenemies, a far cry from the supposed star-crossed lovers of their youth, she knew that the genes that had created her could potentially be a horrible concoction of discontentment and angst inside.

Yes, I have every right to live a life of conflict! I'm the result of the mixed up DNA pool that couldn't help but screw things up, she thought with bitter sadness.

As all the negative thoughts swirled and cursed through her mind, Kate squeezed her eyes shut and suddenly had an abrupt sensation of falling from a high place, like falling through trees. The sensation was so strong that it seized her lungs tightly, and her limbs began to flail as if she was trying to break her fall through the dense, prickly branches. She felt herself tumbling further and further, down through bristly branches that seemed to have no end as they scratched and clawed around her. The feeling of falling was so strong that, with her eyes squeezed shut, Kate could actually feel her body thrashing through the thick canopy of treetops. The pain it caused was a welcome relief against the pain she carried inside. She screamed. *Was that out loud?* she thought with surprise and a measure of disgust. She almost lost her balance. She had to reach out and hold onto the wall to keep herself from toppling onto the floor. She gasped, opening her eyes.

Kate shook her head, trying to ward off the loss of consciousness that threatened to overtake her. With her head bowed and tears streaming down her face, Kate knew that the pain she felt was merely a prelude of the days to come.

She also knew that the control she had worked so hard to maintain had been stolen the moment her mother put a loaded gun to her muddled head.

Clutching a hand to her stomach, Kate shuffled off to the bathroom like an elderly woman in a nursing home. Methodically, she washed her face and brushed her teeth then silently padded down the hall to one of the guest rooms. She wanted nothing more than to be alone. Closing the door behind her, she made her way to the crisply made bed and turned the covers down.

As she crawled under the king-sized duvet, her last thought was of her mother when Kate was very little. Beth would rub the side of her cheek, a perfect smile stretching across her face as she gazed at Kate and murmured the words, "Don't ever forget, you were my first, and I'll *always* love you."

A soft knock on the bedroom door abruptly brought Kate out of her reverie. She saw the shadow of Ethan's presence under the door and barked out to him, "What is it, Ethan?"

Ethan slowly pushed open the door and stood awkwardly in the doorway. He stood a moment, allowing his eyes to adjust to the darkness, "I wanted to see if you needed help finishing packing…"

"No, I'm done and obviously going to bed now. You can go," she said sharply and rolled over so her stiffened back faced the door.

Involuntarily, Ethan took a step back as if he'd been hit. Then without a word, he left the room and closed the door behind him. His footsteps could barely be heard as he walked away from his wife, down the hall to their bedroom.

23. MOLLY

JACK LEFT MOLLY AND THEIR bedroom and headed downstairs to lock up the house for the night. Molly lay still as a statue and stared at the ceiling. Her numbed mind struggled to explain what had happened to her mother and all that had gone wrong with their family. The "whys" and "what ifs" battled one another like demons inside her already tormented head.

At some point her cell rang, and Molly looked down to see it was Kate. As promised, she had called to give Molly her flight schedule, though she'd ended the call with a question so obtuse, so thickheaded, that Molly still shook all over in anger just thinking about it.

"Didn't you see this coming?" Kate had demanded.

The question left Molly wanting to rip out her insides and scream at the world. She'd asked herself the same damn question over and over again, churning the words around in her grief-stricken mind until they almost lost their meaning.

When she followed Jack downstairs for a glass of water, he said he'd heard her talking and asked if it had been Kate with her travel plans. His lame attempts to look more casual than he felt went unnoticed, and when Molly answered, her voice seemed far away, even to her own ears. He put a comforting hand on her shoulder that she barely acknowledged.

Molly knew why her sister had kept her distance, at least from Jack, anyway. She looked over at him now and her breath caught. She wanted to shout out at him, to tell him that she knew what they had done. She had never talked to Jack about what she had discovered as she cleaned the house one day a few years before. In her mind, the past was the past and should be left behind. Besides, with everything going on—the kids, her spells, and her mother's declining state—it was easier to move on and let it go.

She loved her husband and felt that she knew him well enough to understand that he had done nothing wrong. Staring back at him now, she wished desperately that he could read her mind—just this once—so they could get past it all and move on.

Yet Jack, of course, could not read her mind. Nor could he understand the emotions that traced across her face. In his defense, he could have never known that his wife knew about his past with Kate, for she had never said a word.

Molly simply wanted to understand why her sister had chosen to live so estranged from her for all these years. She recognized that a chasm had been built between them—of past and personality, of future and forgiveness, of misunderstanding and pain. Kate was older, and she lived a completely different life as a high-powered attorney. They didn't have much in common, and that, coupled with Kate's standoffish and sometimes curt behavior, was too difficult for even Molly to make a connection with her.

But why the cold-shoulder from her? Molly's sadness enveloped her like a veil.

Kate had never shared any intimacy with her, and her parents never brought up the past, so the only clue she had as to why Kate had stayed away from them all these years was from a conversation that she'd overheard between them many years ago. It happened one night shortly after she'd gone to bed. She'd heard them arguing and crept down the stairs, only to hear her mother's voice get increasingly louder with each step. Hidden in the darkness, peering at them through the handrails, she saw her mother, angry and red-faced, with her hands waving in the air in front of her.

Elizabeth was yelling loudly at her father, accusing him of not treating Katie well.

"Robbie, you *knew* what you were getting into when you asked me to marry you! What happened to you? What happened to making us a family?"

But her mother's anger was met with silence.

"Robbie, are you even listening to me? Kate never comes home. What did we do wrong? She's gone, and I never see my oldest daughter anymore!"

"Beth, I think you're getting a little worked up…"

But she quickly cut him off, "Worked up? Is that all you have to say for yourself after the way you treated her?"

Her father hadn't argued; he just shrugged and walked away, leaving her mother standing there, tearful and exasperated. When her mother reached out and grabbed a book on a nearby table, raising her arm to throw it, Molly turned away and dashed back upstairs. She did not want to see if the book made its target. Molly heard the muffled sounds of her mother crying in their adjoining bedroom long into the night.

Was my father really that awful to Kate? Could he have treated her so badly that she'd want to stay away from us like this?

It had always been difficult for Molly to grasp the disparity between her own childhood experience and what Kate's may have been. Her early years at home were wrapped in a middle-class package of "just enough," with loving and doting parents. Her father had always been there for her. He took her camping and taught her how to catch a fish. He brought her on hiking treks deep in the woods, and he came to most of her tap dance recitals. He was right beside her mother on Molly's prom night, taking pictures of her first official date and warning them not to do anything foolish as they waved goodbye. He may not have been the most affectionate—hugs and warm touches were not given often—but he was there for her.

Yet by then, Kate had long been gone, and with each passing year, she had less and less to do with any of them. She almost seemed to vanish from their lives.

Kate *had* sent gifts to Alice and Emma for Christmas some years and occasionally for their birthdays, as well. Yet even those attempts were usually overly expensive items, ill-suited for the girls' ages. They often ended up on a back shelf of the closet or being given away to charity. Kate had remembered Molly's birthday only sporadically over the years, but Molly treasured each one of those cards as if it could be the last.

Through it all, Molly's never-failing optimism made her believe that things would someday, somehow, get better between them. Sometimes, she would cry about it when she found herself alone in the house. Most of the time, it was just another problem that got swept under the rubble and wreckage from the difficulties in her life, another problem that she sadly avoided. On a few occasions, exasperated and disheartened, she had turned to Jack, seeking answers. She hoped for an answer, but she also hoped that he would recognize and accept her invitation and tell her the truth about the past.

"Jack, why do you think we rarely hear from my sister? She hasn't come to see us in years, and we barely talk to each other. Gosh, I can't even remember what she looks like!"

But he was of no help, and his uncomfortable placations and lack of disclosure only upset her more. "Molly, honey, don't you think you're being a little dramatic?"

"I am *not*. I don't even know Kate anymore. And wouldn't it would be nice if the girls actually *had* an Aunt in their lives... if I had a sister..." she added as her voice trailed off.

"I don't know," Jack would mumble in a half-hearted response, busying himself with something to avoid her stare. Then, with his eyes averted, he'd quickly go off to play with the girls, and Molly would stand there and sadly watch him go.

Molly had tried to call Kate a few times over the years. They were short and often uncomfortable conversations that left many things unspoken. It was a gulf that seemed to grow farther and wider every year. What she didn't know—couldn't know—was that there was a secret buried inside Kate, a secret that festered in the silence between them all like an old wound that could not heal. And every time Molly called her, that wound would open up again, and the pain from Kate's past would rise to the surface.

Finally, exhausted from her tormented thoughts and the ordeal of the night, Molly headed upstairs to bed. With no more words between them, she and Jack slowly drifted off to a fitful night of sleep, clutched together in each other's arms. Molly's mind fretted in and out of bad dreams. Jack woke up every time she stirred and hugged her until she fell back to sleep. The night seemed to go on forever for them both. Eventually, Molly rolled away from him in the bed, clutching her stomach and careful not to wake him. Over and over in her head, she prayed that sleep would take her away from the pain.

Sometime before the morning arrived, Molly dreamt her old, childhood dream. In it, she stood alone on a deserted island blanketed by roses. The flowers were beautiful and bright— eye-catching. Their vibrant petals represented all the colors of the rainbow. Their brilliant hues swirled and swished by her legs as she danced around the island. Her arms were swept up in the air, her face turned toward the sun. However this time, the flowers slowly began to mutate. Like dominoes, one at a time they started to wilt and they turned black as coal in the midday sun. As the rainbow of colors disappeared, the sand beneath her turned to charcoal. The water's edge crept up slowly around her feet. Not knowing what to do, she just stood there, watching helplessly as the deadened island became smaller and smaller around her.

The morning light streamed in through windows and waved across her face. Molly slowly opened her eyes, tired yet grateful to be awake and out of the dream. She saw that Jack was already up and trying to tiptoe out of the room, trying not to awaken her. She closed her heavy lids again and laid still, hoping to have a few moments alone. She could hear the girls in their bedroom next door. They were, of course, awake and playing quietly together. They were innocent and oblivious to how their world had changed, and their laughter trickled through the walls.

Molly could barely hear them above the roaring pain in her head. With difficulty, as if her limbs were made of cement, she twisted around to get out of bed and start the day.

She stopped short when her eye caught another family picture with her mother that sat on the nightstand beside the bed. It had been there for the last two years; Molly had "seen" it every day. Yet now she could see it more clearly. Molly could see that the smile on Beth's face hid the many troubles that she had been carrying around inside.

Molly had never felt so helpless or inept, and the sadness inside her crept into the marrow of her bones. She lay back down on the bed and curled up, squeezing her knees tightly to her chest. One tormenting thought escaped her lips; it was the one question that Kate had demanded of her.

"How *did* I not see it before?" She spoke the words in barely a whisper, as she curled up tighter and tighter, trying to shut out the world.

24. SAYING GOODBYE

TO KATE, THE NIGHT OF Molly's fateful call felt like an eternity. She did not know what the next day would deliver—when she would have to head back to Maine and face the demons she had long since left behind. The fear of the unknown was almost overpowering and tore at her insides.

Alone in the guest room, ashen and cold, she'd lain on her back like a vampire in a coffin. She stared up at the ceiling as steady, silent tears streamed out for much of the night. A disturbed restlessness allowed for only an hour or two of real sleep. Some of the dark hours brought forth such a rage of tears that it left her with a numbing pain that seemed to swallow her whole. After, with her arms covering her head, Kate tried to rock herself back and forth and go back to sleep.

The sound of the alarm early the next morning jolted her awake. Like a looming shadow on a dark cold night, the memory of Molly's call the previous evening clawed its way to the surface of her mind. Shaking her head roughly, she struggled for clarity, but there was none to be found.

When she sat up to get out of bed and touched her feet to the cold wooden floor, the horror of it all hit her with lightning speed. She jumped from the bed. Kate stumbled to the bathroom and lurched over the toilet, just in time. Her stomach dry-heaved over and over again as if trying to rid itself of an undigested pain. The spasms lasted for minutes before her body was finally spent. Slowly, Kate pulled herself up from the floor and hung onto the sink basin, terrified of her own asthenia. With great effort, she pulled herself up and turned to face the framed mirror. The reflection before her caused an audible gasp. She peered through blurry eyes at the stranger before her, seeing pain so raw that it was as if she could look right through to her soul. Kate knew that the woman before her was not the same person. Yet there was something more that she saw in the reflection. She saw someone who had been stripped of everything, someone who was now as defenseless as a newborn baby.

Kate almost didn't recognize herself in the glass.

At first, she was scared then she turned away in disgust at her own vulnerability. She dragged herself down the hall to her bedroom and began to get ready for the flight. Though it was still dark out, Ethan was gone, and the bed was already neatly made.

As she got showered and dressed, she didn't notice the new cocktail dress that still hung in its protective sheath on her bedroom door, nor was she aware of the Tiffany bag on the small dresser by the door. The anniversary plans with Ethan for the night before had all but been forgotten in her pain and misery.

Donning a pair of grey Clasiques slacks, a grey cashmere sweater, and conservatively heeled boots, she grabbed her suitcases and walked out. As she left the room, she half-noticed the dry cleaning bag hanging up in her closet and realized that Ethan *had* actually remembered to pick it up for her. Her eyes still didn't catch sight of the tell-tale turquoise bag laying nearby. With a grimaced smile, she saw that what had been so important the night before now held such a meaningless triviality in the wake of tragedy. With her Louis Vuitton suitcase in hand and her head bowed, Kate walked quietly downstairs to the kitchen.

Ethan was there, sitting alone at the breakfast table. His face was shaved and he was dressed for work. The bowl of Cheerios before him looked soggy, and Kate wondered how long he had been sitting there.

Before she could even stop herself, she spat out a question, accusingly, "For God's sake, Ethan, how could you eat at a time like this?"

His face blanched as he looked up at her. It reflected such an obvious sadness that she regretted her words and turned away from him to hide her own self-loathing. Ethan did not answer, but simply asked in a quiet voice if he could at least drive her to the airport. Kate shook her head.

"Ethan, I'm perfectly capable of driving *myself*," She drew the last word out crisply, either from exhaustion or irritation, she wasn't sure.

Ethan dove his spoon down into his cereal bowl in silence, but with eyes downcast he didn't raise it to his lips. Kate collected her keys, purse, and a few last minute items. With each thing she grabbed—vitamins, tissues, hand sanitizer—she was vaguely surprised that her mind was coherent enough to remember anything at all in her mental state.

Ethan's child-like question interrupted the silence in the room between them. "Kate, why won't you let me go home with you?"

The pleading sound to his voice disgusted her and made her resolve harden and her back stiffen. Any previous doubts about her decision to go alone were quickly dispelled. Without even turning to face him, Kate just shook her head and walked out the door, wrongly interpreting her husband's love for her as the self-imposed pity that she hated him for.

Ethan said nothing more and quietly followed her to the garage. Before she could stop him, he lunged forward and helped load her bag into the Beamer then abruptly ran back inside and reemerged quickly with a thermos that he thrust into her hand. He tried to draw her in for a quick embrace, the coffee mug awkwardly wedged between them. She allowed the gesture for just a moment before pushing him away with mumblings of needing to get on the road. Then, almost as an afterthought, she leaned back in to try to kiss him goodbye, but the motion became lost in the air between them.

Surprising them both, Ethan took her forcibly by the shoulders and turned her to face him. The behavior was so unexpected that Kate just stared up at him with wide eyes.

"Tell me that you are okay to go back alone. I need to hear you say it, Kate."

With her shoulders stiff and her soul swinging by a thread, Kate did just that.

She left Ethan standing there with his hands in his pockets and slid into the car. As she backed out of the driveway, she caught a glimpse of him standing there, one arm half waving and the other hand hanging limply by his side. She had failed to see the suitcase by the door in the garage which Ethan brought back inside, before he closed the garage door.

Kate drove toward the airport, winding the car methodically through the subdivision then out onto the highway. She passed by her favorite running store, Fleet Feet, and in her exhausted haze couldn't remember if she'd packed her trainers. With a frown, she glanced at her suitcase in the backseat yet still couldn't recall, and she hated her mental feebleness. She took one hand off the steering wheel and banged her forehead as if the action would somehow fix it.

The airport was located on the other side of town, but she had plenty of time and minded the speed limits. She'd left much earlier than planned, to get away from Ethan and his loathsome pity as much as to not be rushed before the flight.

Her thoughts about the unknown ahead struggled inside her head, creating a surreal feeling of imminent panic. The feeling reminded her of the day she got caught in a rip-tide current at the beach as a little girl. She had been playing in the cold Atlantic waters, her mother lying on the beach nearby, and had swum out a little too far. The pull on her legs seemed to come out of nowhere, and immediately she struggled against it, even though that was exactly what she had always been told not to do. The forceful tugging on her limbs strengthened, trying to pull her down and away from the shore, before she remembered in a panic what she'd been taught. She forced her body to stop fighting and go limp in the swirling waters. And as soon as she did, the hidden grasp of the ocean released her and set her free. She quickly swam back to the sand and played in it, just near the water's edge for the rest of the day.

If only I could let go like that now, maybe I could be freed again.

But as she peered in the rearview mirror and saw her haggard face, eyes that were dark and heavy-lidded, she knew she was not yet free.

Eyes back on the road, Kate noticed that she was fast approaching the turn to her office in town. Without thinking further, she checked the dashboard clock and side mirrors then quickly swerved to veer off the highway onto the exit. Hearing angry honks as nearby drivers sped past, she looked up quickly in the rearview to be sure that her transgression had not been caught.

"That would be just my fucking luck today…" she mumbled.

She drove the few short blocks to her office and parked directly beneath the building. Peering up through the window at her office suite seven stories above, she convinced herself that she needed to stop in the office for some sense of normalcy as she reached over and grabbed her purse.

"I should just tell Sam that I won't be in the office for a few days and pick up a few things." Kate talked herself into going up and abruptly left the confines of the car.

She walked into the building and onto the elevator. The building's one hundred year old elevator creaked and squealed its way to the top as it dutifully carried its dispirited rider. Normally, Kate liked that the inside of the car emitted a faint smell of old cologne and sweat from its riders. She loved the way the old metal doors opened slowly when the car reached the top, making her feel like a present about to be unwrapped as she stepped out on to the weathered wooden floors in a sheath of semi-darkness. Today she noticed none of that as it made its way to the top floor. Struggling to remain calm, she took a few deep breaths and closed her eyes to avoid the mirrored reflection inside. She knew that her hastily applied makeup could not hide the suffering of a tormented soul.

When the elevator lurched to a stop and the doors opened, she stepped cautiously into the firm's foyer, instantly relieved to see that Sam was the only person there. Yet as soon as Sam saw her, his eyes widened and his mouth dropped open to form a large "O." Kate's relief quickly turned to threatening tears and she found herself unable to either move forward or step back into the safety of the elevator in a state of panic.

"Kate, Hun, what *happened* at dinner last night?" he asked with one hand placed saucily on a hip. "Did Ethan not give you a decent anniversary gift?"

When she stood there without replying, Sam slowly walked toward her and asked the question again, in a softer tone.

"Kate, what is it? You look like death warmed over."

Though as soon as the words left his mouth, Sam instantly regretted it, for tears that he didn't know resided within his boss immediately spilled out onto her face.

Sam gasped out loud, "Oh, my God, girl, come here!"

Sam deftly ushered her down the hall to her office and closed the door behind her. Leaning in, he gave Kate a fleeting hug then in between her controlled sobs, Kate confided in her only semblance of a friend about the details of the last twelve hours. She told him about her sister's call, glossing over the history of her mother's mental problems, and her mother's hospitalization. She managed to relay her plans to fly to Maine, saying that she would be back soon, the same errant lie she had told Ethan just hours before.

When she gave Sam her flight itinerary, he glanced around melodramatically as if pretending to look for someone. "But Kate, where the hell is your husband? Shouldn't he be going with you?"

Pulling herself up, Kate looked defiantly at Sam and informed him that she'd told Ethan not to come. She followed it up with the similar string of excuses that she'd said to Ethan, though even as she spoke she realized they sounded lame and almost cruel. Before Sam could say any more, Kate turned to her desk and mumbled something about Sheffield's case as she grabbed some files and stuffed them into her bag.

Attempting to maintain what little composure she had left, Kate stood up and behaved as if she was headed off to an impromptu vacation getaway, rather then on a trip full of pain. She told Sam goodbye and walked quickly out of her office, clutching Sheffield's folders tightly to her chest as if they held the answers to all of life's problems.

Somehow, she managed to put a constrained look of impassivity on her face as she walked through the office suite. The façade was good enough that anyone who saw her may not have noticed anything different about Kate Harriman. She was so concentrated on leaving before breaking down into tears that she didn't hear Sam calling after her to say goodbye.

The remainder of the drive to the airport and check-in and security seemed timeless as she went through the motions. As she approached the gate, a family of five hustled by her, obviously late for their flight. Their laughter danced playfully in the air behind them as they bustled down the ramp to the plane. Yet Kate saw none of their glee.

She took a seat at the gate and waited stoically for her zone to be called. With her arms crossed protectively in front of her and her chin tucked under, Kate's mind drifted in and out of the past and future. She felt like she was in a nightmare that she couldn't wake up from. She squeezed her eyes tight, praying for the nightmare to end.

A young girl walked by and tripped over Kate's luggage. Kate opened her eyes and watched as the girl ran past. The girl's pigtails bounced as she skipped down the aisle, seemingly carefree and with no understanding of sorrow or regret.

In a flash of remembrance, her mind went back to the day that Molly was born. With so many years between them, Kate had always felt more like a mother than a big sister right from the start. She'd had no choice but to help with feedings, change diapers, and babysit her at night while her mother and Robbie went out. The daily disruptions of having a baby in the house were huge, and the midnight disturbances with inconsolable crying were often unbearable.

From a teenager's point of view, the rewards of having a baby seemed few and far between.

Kate had already been avoiding Robbie and her home life as much as possible, finding reasons to stay after school, visiting her father's place more, and hanging out with friends at night—anything to be away from the place that no longer felt like home.

The arrival of a child onto the scene—one who turned her mother into a hypnotized fool—proved too much too bear.

The annoying little infant that everyone made such a fuss about took even more away from her than she felt she had already lost.

However, the ultimate tipping point of separation with her sister may have resided in their very own DNA, for it quickly became evident to everyone that the half-sisters would look nothing alike. Kate often wondered in those early years if they could have emerged from the same womb, as Molly was a female version of her father, and Kate looked too much like her own. In college, Kate would joke humorlessly with her friends that no one would be able pick out her sister in a crowd… *even* if they were the last two left women standing in the room. And since Kate had spent most of her life trying to ignore, then eventually forget, Robbie, her sister's likeness to him unconsciously wedged Kate even further apart from her.

The loud cackle of the attendant's announcement over the intercom interrupted her thoughts. Hearing the call of her boarding zone number, she checked in and walked down the ramp onto the plane. It wasn't until she dropped down into her business class seat that the reality of the situation began to take shape in her mind. She was going back. Heading home, to a place where memories were difficult and the past had been pushed aside for a reason.

Ultimately, she was on the way to face a family full of strangers with whom secrets had been hidden and left behind.

Kate sighed and closed her eyes as the plane's engine hummed loudly in preparation for takeoff. As smiling stewardesses began to roam the cabin and take drink requests in the last few minutes before takeoff, Kate heard the tick-tick of laptops keys and the buzzes and trills of cell phones

In that moment, even in her mental haze, Kate envied the simplicity and normalcy of their lives. She was keenly aware that less than twenty-four hours before, her life had been just the same.

Or was it? Damn, I'm starting to think that nothing in my life has ever been good. She turned her head to the window, trying to control the desire to scream out at everyone that she was still like them and that everything was all right. With her eyes squeezed tight, she suddenly realized how exhausted she actually was. Her body felt spent, her mind was worn out, and before the Boeing's wheels had left the ground, Kate fell into a catatonic slumber for the duration of the trip.

The two hour and fifteen minute flight north to Portland, Maine allowed her to dream. Her dreams were wild, the sort that only emerged from a state of exhaustion and emotional turmoil, scenes full of twisted, tangled memories of childhood and family, with crystal-ball visions of the unknown.

In one dream, her father was a famous baseball player. She was sitting in a school class room, and he sat at the desk next to hers. He leaned over, trying to explain to her that he had to leave her to hit the road to pursue his lifelong dream of a pitching career. Her mom wasn't there, or maybe she was the teacher pacing in the front of the room? The one from grade school who was so mean and strict. Yes, it was Beth, and she was teaching biology. Then, she yelled out to the class that everyone had to write down five hundred times, "I will not eat donuts during class." Kate kept getting up, trying to ask her why they had to write this, but the teacher or Beth or whoever it was, stifled her questions and sharply told her to shut up and sit down. Then the woman walked over with a long ruler in her hand and rapped on Kate's desk over and over until the ruler broke. Kate looked up from the pile on the floor and saw her mother's face smiling down at her, telling her that she loved her and that everything was okay.

Then, suddenly, Katie realized that she was in a boat, floating at sea. At first she thought she was in it alone. Then, peering through the fog, she saw that Rob was sitting in the boat with her at the other end. He had the oars in his hands, and he started rocking the boat back and forth, leaning from side to side with his tongue hanging out lavishly from his mouth. It made her feel scared and vulnerable, and she gripped the sides of the canoe and started screaming for him to, "Stop, stop!" But he just kept rocking back-and-forth, his head thrown back in laughter, a deep, throaty laugh that reminded her of the Joker character in *Batman*. She held on tightly. The evil laughter echoed across the water's sloppy surface and seemed to come at her from all directions.

More and more water sloshed into the boat. It looked black and murky. The boat quickly filled up, and it began to tip over to one side. Slowly, timelessly, the way dreams often do. Just as the boat's bottom was no longer visible, Kate realized that Robbie had stood up and was making his way toward her. She looked down and saw that she had no clothes on. She screamed and looked up at Rob to see if he had noticed her nudity. She wondered how she hadn't known all along that she was naked, defenseless in front of him. Gripping the sides of the boat even tighter, her knuckles white, she yelled at him to stop and leave her alone. But he was still coming toward her, as if the boat was miles and miles long yet each step still brought him closer. She was desperate to escape the confines of the boat. Fear gripped her. Her repeated screams for help only caused Rob to laugh louder.

Finally, just as Robbie reached out to grab her—just as they were about to plunge into the cold, deep waters of the sea together—she awoke with a start, still sitting in the comfortable confines of the airplane seat. Immediately, she looked down to reassure herself that she was dressed then half-laughed at herself for doing so. She could still almost feel the icy cold waters from her dream sloshing all around her. She shuddered.

As she glanced around, still not comprehending her immediate surroundings, she allowed her mind to think back on her childhood.

The days of living with her mother and Robbie... the childhood that gave her only desire to get away... and the one night that she had worked so hard to forget.

25. MOLLY

MOLLY GATHERED HER COURAGE TO face the world and headed downstairs to join her family. She avoided talking as Jack got breakfast started for everyone—oatmeal, toast, and eggs—and the girls gratefully filled the silence in the house with their usual chatter. Molly plastered a smile on her face that somehow stuck.

See, I am just like her, her mind screamed out inside.

She was a fit of nerves as she worried about seeing her mother again and what the day would bring. Seeing Kate for the first time in so many years brought equal anxiety, and her heartbeat quickened.

After breakfast was through and the dishes hastily cleaned and put away, Jack took the girls for a quick walk in the woods while Molly got the downstairs guest room ready for Kate's arrival. It took her thirty minutes to change the sheets, bring down their best pillows, and clean the room. As she walked out, she plugged in a nightlight to give the room a touch of warmth. Standing back one last time to look the room over, she cringed a little, knowing that it was probably far less than the grandeur her sister had become accustomed to in her level of upper-class living.

"Well, it will just have to do," she called out to no one as she shook her head and left.

Back upstairs, she went to the kitchen to make sure that she had everything she needed for dinner tonight. The blackboard list read steak and potatoes, but remembering even in her tired mind that Kate didn't eat red meat, she decided to make chicken potpie instead and hoped it would be okay. She couldn't remember one single dish that her sister liked to eat, but she decided that potpie—something she had made so often she could do it blindfolded and a dish that was almost universally liked—would have to do.

She darted to the fridge to make sure she had everything she needed, thinking *How would I know what she likes, for heaven's sakes? I barely know her.* Molly shook her head in exasperation.

Finally, she and Jack prepared to leave for the hospital for the second time to see Beth. Sally Johansen from next door came over again to watch the girls. She arrived right on time, knocking gently on their porch door, and Molly let her in with a heartfelt hug. After seeing how badly Beth looked during the previous night's visit, Molly was thankful that she and Jack had agreed to go to the hospital alone. They swiftly walked out the door as Sally distracted the girls with the prospect of finger-painting and a scavenger hunt, producing loud cheers.

Enduring another seemingly uneventful drive to Portland Regional, Molly gazed out the window for most of the ride. She managed a sideways smile at Jack every now and again when he squeezed her hand. They talked about small things, because that was all that Molly could manage to do. When they walked into the hospital lobby forty minutes later with heavy steps, the large room now bustled with a flurry of motion and activity that had not been present the night before.

Molly recognized the same woman working behind the information desk, yet today she looked busy as she scurried about, putting files away and making loud clucking sounds as people came and left her desk. Molly noticed that the woman was older than she'd thought last night. She was dressed in the typical baggy blue nurse's outfit, and she had a plump body that showed signs of inactivity and middle age. As they approached the desk and she turned to face them, Molly again saw her offer them a warm and welcoming smile. Friendly, calm, and attentive, the woman exuded a warm aura that Molly knew must comfort everyone who walked through the hospital doors.

"Can I help you two?" She called out to them. She had a round and kind face. Molly thought she looked like a grandmother who should be home baking cookies in her cottage.

"We're here to see my mother again, Beth Stevens, but we were…"

"Okay, dear, let me check that for you."

Though Jack and Molly remembered their way, they stood patiently at the counter and waited. The woman squinted over her glasses at her computer screen then let out a sighed exclamation. She looked back up at them with sympathy in her eyes and peered a little closer. Almost at once, recognition swept across her face.

"Oh, I'm so sorry. You were here last night, weren't you?"

Jack opened his mouth to respond, but Molly quickly and quietly answered first. "Yes, we were. Thank you, and we know the way."

She took Jack's elbow and turned away. He looked at her questioningly as they walked off. It didn't take long for her to give him an answer in exasperation.

"You'd think she would have remembered us right off, for heaven's sake," Molly hissed sharply under her breath, "We were just here!"

Jack smiled and put a protective arm around his wife's shoulder. "I'm sure she sees a lot of people every day," he assured her, knowing that any form of conceived rejection or disappointment could put his wife over the edge.

Keeping her close, they wound their way down the halls and around the white, sterile corridors of the hospital to the ICU. As they approached her mother's door, Molly's footsteps began to slow. Jack stopped his stride along with hers and turned to draw her in. For just a moment, she foolishly wished that it could all be taken away. The pain and sorrow, her mother's depression, even the hospital—and especially that voice inside her head that quietly told her every now and again that she would end up like this someday. Her tears flowed freely onto Jack's shirt as she buried her face in his chest, attempting to block out both the light and the darkness that surrounded her. Finally, she looked up at him with a desperate openness in her face and took a long, deep breath.

"Jack, would you mind if I visit with Mom alone this morning? Just for a while?"

Jack's face showed his surprise. Yet there was something else there... *Was it relief?* She wasn't sure, but in her tiredness and sorrow she couldn't identify what exactly it was—or even why—and didn't question him. Too tired to try to figure it out, she let the thought go, and Jack hastily agreed. Mumbling something about needing to take care of a few errands in town he started to leave then turned back and asked her, as if in afterthought, "Are you sure you're okay to go in by yourself, though?"

"Yes, I just need to spend time with her alone," she paused, before asking again, always needing assurance that things were okay, "Are *you* sure you don't mind?"

"No, not at all," he answered, a little too quickly, before hurriedly kissing her goodbye with a promise to return to the hospital in a few hours.

Molly turned back to face her mother's hospital room. She took a deep breath, opened up the door, and walked inside. The idea of being alone with her mother in such a physical state was more than unsettling, but she felt that she needed to do it, to face reality alone, for once in her life. The back of her mind screamed out that this couldn't be happening. In the short time that it took her to reach the bedside, Molly already regretted letting Jack go and she forced herself not run after him. She willed her racing heart to slow down and her feet to keep moving toward the bed. Slowly, she sat down next to it and carefully took her mother's hand in her own. She laid her head down and for a long while said nothing, but simply cried a steady river of silent tears.

By this time, Jack had left the hospital and was scrambling into his truck with his keys in hand; his hands were shaking with nervousness. He panted heavily from the effort of sprinting across the parking lot, and his heart raced. Quickly, before he could change his mind, he drove away from the hospital, feeling more like a criminal about to commit a crime than a husband attempting to avert more pain for his troubled wife. He hated himself for it, yet as he cut through the side streets, Jack kept telling himself over and over that this was the right thing to do.

No matter what, Jack knew he had to see Kate before Molly did.

26. SURPRISE AT THE AIRPORT

How do you disregard a child's cries for help? Kate sat low in her plane seat, staring out the small oval window at the clouds below, and shook her head in disbelief at all that had happened. Her mind reeled through disheartening memories of her childhood days, trying to make sense of what had gone wrong.

Kate felt that her mother had let her down. From the beginning, it seemed as if Beth had chosen Robbie over her. And when Beth didn't intervene to save Kate from Robbie's cruel barbs, Kate grew to understand betrayal and heartbreak. Early on, she had tried to make her mother listen, to tell her mother what went on with Rob when they were alone together. To ask for her help.

"Mommy, Robbie is so mean to me when you're not home!" she had protested.

But her complaints were shrugged off, met only with admonishment and a pat on the head.

Years later, as a teenager, Kate would demand that her mother explain why Robbie continued to treat her so badly. "Mom, I'm trying to tell you that Rob is a jerk to me most of the time. Why won't listen to me?"

But her mother ignored her pleas and smiled back at her as if everything was okay. All stormy accusations about Robbie were quickly cast aside. After Molly was born, her mother seemed to forget about Kate all together.

"Mom... you're so wrapped up in your life that you don't even see what's going on right in front of you!" she cried out.

Appealing to her mother did not work, so Kate turned to outbursts to get her attention. Those outbursts were laced with disappointment, hurt, and anger—they were cries for help that never received it. Eventually she stayed away from home. Kate turned her back on them all, and her belief in her mother's love slowly eroded like the rocks lining the Maine beaches that she often escaped to.

When she was sixteen, her life was turned upside down. It began as a night like any other, but it was one that she would never forget. She was alone in the house with Robbie; her mother had gone out to a friend's house with Molly. Robbie opened the door to her bedroom. She remembered the way he stood there with that odd look on his face. He walked over to the bed where she was doing her homework and grabbed her arm, throwing her back onto the bed. At first, Kate was surprised; she didn't know what to do or how to react. Then, as he leaned over her body and she saw the expression on his face, she knew that something was wrong, so she kicked at him with all of her might. Her foot missed its mark, and he laughed and pinned her arms down, pressing his body hard against hers. Just as his hand snaked inside her shirt and grabbed at her breast, her knee flew up and found its target. With a loud "Oomph," Robbie rolled off the bed, clutching at his crotch. Kate ran past him out of her room and out of the house.

"Hello, this is your captain speaking," The loud and scratchy pilot's announcement jerked Kate out of her reverie. "We are now approaching Portland and will soon begin our initial descent."

Shaking her mind free from the terrible memories, she hastily began to gather her things around her. The business class stewardess bustled around the cabin picking up after passengers, and the captain's voice continued its scratchy discourse overhead.

"Folks, we hope you've enjoyed your flight on Delta today. Flight attendants, please prepare the cabin for arrival. We should be landing at the Portland International Jetport in less than ten minutes."

Even in her state of despair, hearing the airport's name—far too grand for such a small airport—brought forth a sneer and a half-hearted chuckle. A tap n her elbow startled her, and she turned to look at the man sitting in the aisle seat next to her for the very first time.

"Inside joke, miss, or would you be laughing at the 'International' aspect of our little airport up here?" He asked with a warm smile.

Kate realized that despite their proximity for the last few hours, she had not once noticed the man sitting beside her. As a lawyer, she found her lack of observance disconcerting. The man was not particularly distinguishable she realized after giving him a once over. He was average looking, with receding grey hair that gathered in tufts around his ears and a kind, unobtrusive face. As Kate took him in, he continued to peer back at her questioningly. Kate finally opened her mouth to reply, a look of defensiveness on her face, but the stranger interrupted her before she could speak.

"Oh, I was just teasing you. After twenty years of traveling the country, I *still* laugh at it myself sometimes," he said with a twinkle in his eyes as he leaned in a little closer.

Kate tensed up, forcing herself not to noticeably pull away from him and tried to put a smile on her face. She felt the jerk of the plane's wheels touching down and looked away, afraid that if this stranger looked at her any longer he would see the pain inside of her. Or worse, that he would ask if something was wrong. With so many unfamiliar emotions swirling around inside, Kate knew that she could burst into tears at any moment, so she kept her eyes glued to the window.

Not picking up on her cues, the man continued talking to her as if they were old friends. "Well, with one security checkpoint here and a handful of gates, Portland sure is a nice reprieve at the end of a busy day when you're coming home… If you're heading home, that is…"

He paused as if waiting for a reply. She turned back to face him. His head was cocked slightly to one side, but when Kate didn't offer anything, he simply pressed on.

"Well, are you? Heading home, I mean?" he asked her with an encouraging nod of his head. "Or are you going away?"

Kate looked him directly and smiled wanly, wishing that she could have been sat next to someone a bit more taciturn than this man appeared to be, "A little of both, I guess."

"I'm going home and my wife will be glad to see me… Well, I hope she will be, anyway," he added with a wink. "She works to keep herself busy since I travel so often, though I think she just likes to know what's going on with everyone in town."

To Kate's relief, the captain's final announcement over the speaker interrupted them, giving passengers permission to unbuckle and disembark. Grateful to be freed from the conversation with the talkative stranger, she stood up so quickly that she bumped her head on the compartment overhead. Swearing under her breath and averting her eyes from anyone who may have seen, she impatiently waited for the man to get up so she could leave the confines of the plane.

There was a flurry from business class to the back of the plane as everyone reached for their bags and personal items. As Kate tried to reach up for hers in the overhead bin, the man placed a hand lightly on Kate's elbow. He patiently remained in his seat and looked up at her with a grin.

"Let me help you get that. It's the fancy brown one, right?" he asked her, his eyes smiling as he stood up.

"How did you guess?" she asked in an attempt at humor, though knowing that sarcasm was all that had come through.

"Ahhh, years of experience, my dear, years of experience," he said as he deftly grabbed her suitcase and brought it down into the aisle. "And, well, you look like you could use a hand today."

He turned and looked at her straight on before continuing. "Let's face it. Everyone needs a little help now and again, right?"

Kate mumbled her thanks, avoided his gaze even more, and shifted her weight from one foot to the other, anxious to leave the plane. As they waited those last few seconds, she sighed heavily and remained in silence.

When they were finally able to walk off, the stranger spoke up again, calling after her. "You take care now, miss. I hope your trip to our quiet little state is everything it should be."

She paused before answering and took a deep breath. "So do I," she responded over her shoulder, making one last attempt at politeness before briskly walking off the plane ahead of him.

As Kate walked along the ramp to the gate, her mind went numb with dread. Returning to Maine for the first time in so many years was like opening the floodgates of time. Memories that she'd worked hard to suppress clawed their way to the surface. Every step felt like walking the gangplank on a pirate ship. Bags in hand, she walked through the terminal with a forced look of impassiveness on her face. Trying to keep her worries at bay, she relied on the old standbys of logic and control and ran through the course of the day in her head.

Pick up the rental car, head to the hospital, then to Molly's. I wonder if getting in and out of here and having this all over with soon is too much to ask?

A few paces from the escalator that would take her down to the car rental, Kate heard a deep voice call out her name. Not expecting anyone to be there, Kate barely slowed her stride. It took a second, equally loud shout above the din of the busy terminal to make her stop short. She stepped out of the flow of traffic and suspiciously scanned the room for the source.

"Kate! Over here!"

It was then that she spotted him standing there, on the other side of the terminal. Her heart skipped a beat. She knew that her face registered her astonishment before she could mask over it.

He looked uncomfortable and sweaty despite the cool October air that Kate knew must be waiting for her outside. He awkwardly waved her over; his demeanor reminded Kate of someone trying to lie under oath—darting eyes, body signals misfiring in the wrong direction. Her mind furiously tried to register his image as she forced a lopsided smile and walked toward him. Inside, her emotions were askew as she worked to make sense of his presence there.

Jack Curtis, her sister's husband, was the last person Kate expected to meet when she stepped off the plane.

* * *

Kate immediately noticed that Jack looked older than she'd remembered. He had gained some weight around the middle, but he was tall, so he hid it well. She remembered his body well enough, though, to know that lean muscles once resided there. *Apparently, marriage has softened him up a little.* It was a somber thought, since they were the same age, their birthdays just weeks apart. Self-consciously, she wondered if he was thinking the same as she made her way toward him through the crowded terminal. She noted that the graying at his temples and his steel-rimmed glasses gave him a mature look and finally decided that Jack had eased into the cycles of life without too much of a fight. Kate ran a hand through her unruly hair as she faced him.

"Hi, Jack. What are you doing here? I didn't expect to be met by anyone," she stammered, looking around nervously to see if Molly was nearby. The unspoken words, "especially, by you," hung awkwardly next to the silence in the air between them.

In the recesses of her mind, a quote from Michel Foucault's *The History of Sexuality*—a book she had read in graduate school— suddenly came to mind, "There is not one but many silences, and they are an integral part of the strategies that underlie and permeate discourses." Kate laughed bitterly inside at her own ridiculous thoughts as she stared openly back at Jack.

"Yes, I know. It was a bit last minute. But I wanted to see you… before you came to the house." As he spoke, his eyes barely meeting her own, Kate wasn't sure which one of them was more uncomfortable which gave her strength.

Jack shifted uneasily from one foot to the other; he looked much more like a guilty client than her brother-in-law. She was surprised to realize that she felt somewhat sorry for him.

Clutching her Louis Vuitton bag tightly, she willed herself to keep breathing and finally managed to blurt out a response.

"Thank-you, Jack, really. But I should probably get to the hospital," Kate said, hoping to be able to walk away from the uncomfortable scene. She then realized that Jack must have already seen Beth and would be able to share the news of her condition. Quickly, she started firing questions at him while searching his face for answers.

"Hey, you've *seen* her already, right? How did she look? Do we know anything more this morning? What's her prognosis?"

"Yes, yes," he said putting his hands up in front of him defensively, "Molly and I did visit with her late last night, and she's there again with Beth now. I... uh... don't know what to say, though, Kate," he stammered, his voice low. "There's really no new news yet."

"Oh," the disappointment in that one word was unmistakable. Somewhere in the back of Kate's mind she thought, with blanched humor, *so this is what someone looks like with a 'crestfallen' face, the one you always read about in novels.* She looked away from Jack, trying to collect herself, anxious to find a way to leave him and escape.

"We *are* waiting to hear from the doctors with an update, though. It should be any time now from what they told us last night." He looked expectantly down at the cell phone in his hand, as people will do, as if doing so would prompt it to ring and deliver news right then.

For a moment, they stood there in the terminal in clumsy silence. Most of the passengers had already headed down to baggage claim or left the terminal. Except for a few stragglers, the two now-strangers found themselves alone.

"Okay... well, I should probably be going then," Kate replied as she started to turn away.

"Kate," he said sharply, then added more softly when she stopped and looked at him with surprise, "I'm sorry, it's just that I came here to tell you that Molly still doesn't know about... well, I've never actually told her about us."

Kate paused for a fraction of a second before his words finally registered. "You what?" Molly shouted loudly.

"She's just been through too much lately with..." but he stopped his own words, and in Kate's immediate anger, her attorney skills failed to pick up on what was left unsaid.

"Jack, I don't understand. I thought we agreed that you would. Years ago!" she spat out.

"Ka-"

But Kate quickly cut him off. "Why the hell not?" The question came out in a snarl; Jack unconsciously took a step back.

A few stragglers walking through the airport glanced toward them before quickly looking away as strangers will do. For a moment, Jack either didn't attempt to answer or didn't have an answer to give. He just shrugged and stood there in front of her, both hands jammed into his jeans pockets, eyes downcast.

As Kate's mind processed in full what Jack had just told her, she could feel her nerves fraying. Her stomach was on "E" and with the few hours of sleep last night, it was all of a sudden more than she could handle. Once the meaning of Jack's words sunk in and she realized that Molly hadn't known about their affair all these years, Kate felt herself hitting the wall. Her face paled. Her fingers went numb. For a moment, she didn't know if she'd be able to keep herself standing up. With shaking hands, she reached down for the handle of her suitcase to steady herself. Wordlessly, she looked around the terminal as she felt her sense of control slipping away once again.

"Kate," Jack gasped as he instinctively grabbed her elbow "Are you okay? You don't look so good."

Kate slumped precariously onto her luggage. The impact of Jack's words had left her mind out of sorts. Finally, she spoke quietly, as if to herself. Jack could barely hear her words.

"I don't know what to say, Jack. I think I just need to sit for a minute. I'll be fine."

Her words sounded far off to her own ears. The conviction that she tried to muster belied her emotions. Her clouded mind scurried around itself, trying to make sense of it all. It was a Pandora's box that, once opened, let out too many questions and confusing unknowns.

If Molly doesn't know about us… then why doesn't she call me?

In that moment, Kate remembered the day that Molly had called to share the news of her engagement to Jack five years ago. It was just one month after Kate and Ethan had gone off to St. Bart's in the British Virgin Islands to get married. She had just arrived from work, it was later in the evening, and she was enjoying a glass of wine after a long day in court. Kate remembers that she actually accepted the call by accident when she picked up the phone to see who had called.

Molly had sounded like a little girl as she almost yelled out, "Kate, are you there? Guess what! I'm getting married! Can you believe it?"

Yet when Molly told Kate the name of her future husband, Kate had choked on her wine and spit it out. The blouse she had on ended up at Goodwill as the spattered stains never washed out. Kate had been relieved that this conversation had taken place over the phone so that Molly couldn't see her reaction. And as she congratulated Molly, trying to ask the usual questions one should about an engagement, Kate's mind shouted the same questions over and over—*How could this be? Jack Curtis? What are the chances!*

Since the marriage, Kate's relationship with her sister had become even tenser. Kate had always assumed that it was because Molly knew about her brief time with Jack. Molly was not the confrontational type, so Kate knew that she would never have brought up the subject directly.

Though Kate and Jack's relationship had been brief, over and done with before Jack had even met Molly, it was a part of their tangled and troubled history nonetheless. Kate had felt that it was something left unspoken between them—just one more piece of uncomfortableness that further wedged them apart.

Now, as she stood before Jack in the airport, unable to answer any of the questions that raced through her mind, Kate could not collect herself to speak coherently. She simply sat on the top of her suitcase and stared off into the crowd that had started to form near the security gates.

"Kate, are you sure you're okay?"

Jack placed a tentative hand on her arm, jolting her back to the present. He stared intently at her as she struggled to bring her mind back into focus. When again she didn't respond, he tried to explain himself. "Your sister's just been through too much lately for me to tell her..."

His voice trailed off. Kate looked up at him and attempted a wan smile. When she finally responded, her voice was laced with bitter sarcasm. "Yes, you said that already, Jack.

It was that old self-defense mechanism that she had learned as a child and brought out when all else failed. Jack's face seemed to harden in response.

"Well, you just can't say anything to her about it right now, and that's it," he said, then enunciated the final word slowly, as if it was actually a few words strung together, "Okaaay?"

Jack stared back at Kate pleadingly, but Kate could clearly see on his face, as their gazes locked, just how much Jack loved her sister. *Enough to risk coming here to tell me this, apparently*, she thought wryly.

"Of course. Nothing will be said," she said stiffly. She then added humorlessly, "Let's face it, Jack, I wouldn't even know where to begin."

Kate thought she could actually hear the relief sighing out of him as he loudly exhaled. They stood a second or two in silence, not knowing what to say to each other. This time, it was Kate who recovered enough to attempt to alleviate the awkwardness that swirled in the air between them.

"So, are you still running, doing any races these days?" she asked, offering him a small smile.

"No, not so much with the girls," he said, laughing a little as he patted at his midsection.

He looked at her slender frame and said as casually as he could, "You look like you still are, though, huh?"

"Yeah, I get out whenever I can," Kate shrugged, feigning indifference.

"Well, Molly is looking forward to seeing you today... even with this going on. You'll be by later today, right?"

"Yes. Before dinner, I guess."

"Alright, we'll see you then."

With that, Jack said goodbye and abruptly turned to leave. It was as if his continued presence would make Kate change her mind about saying something of their past to Molly. But he took just a few steps and stopped, turning back to face Kate.

"Thank you, Kate."

"It's fine."

"Did you, uh... need any help? A ride or something?" he asked sheepishly. Both knew that his offer was an afterthought.

"No, thank you, I have a rental car reserved," she replied with a small smile.

Then, in an uncharacteristic act of humanity, she spoke again before she could stop herself. "I could use some company, though, if you can stay a little longer."

Jack smiled at the request and glanced at his watch. "Sure— for a few minutes."

He walked back to her and reached over to grab her suitcase at the same time she did. They laughed awkwardly. Kate quickly withdrew her hand before it could touch his any longer. Letting go of the bag, she mumbled apologetically.

"Sorry, I'm rather used to doing things on my own."

"What? Doesn't that husband of yours—Ethan, is it? Doesn't he help with your bags?" he tossed back lightly. "And where is he? He didn't come with you?"

"Of course he helps. Well, he would if I'd ever let him," she grudgingly admitted with a somewhat sheepish smile. "He... ah... he couldn't get away from work on such short notice, though."

Jack looked at her oddly; the lie didn't quite make its mark. They both knew that it didn't make sense under the circumstances.

But Jack didn't question her further, and as they left the terminal Kate wondered—perhaps for the first time—if Ethan ever felt upset when she didn't ask for or accept his help. It didn't even occur to her as strange that the thought should have occurred to her before.

When she and Jack stepped outside into the crisp October air, Kate couldn't help but shiver. Even though she'd known the colder temperatures were waiting for her, her body automatically braced itself in resentment. She pulled her sweater tighter around her and mumbled something about her thinned blood. Mercifully, Jack found a way to end the quiet between them as they walked to the rental terminal. He told her about his job, about the girls, about life in Maine. He was careful to avoid talking about the past. Yet in her head, each mundane comment was like a siren alerting her to the fact that there was so much more that they should be talking about. She stepped up the pace as they made their way to the rental office, trying not to regret her decision to ask him along.

The rental attendant greeted them at the counter as if they were a couple, making for a few additional awkward moments between them. But Kate quickly signed for the car, choosing the only SUV available, despite the out-of-state plates that she knew would cause her to be shunned by the locals. Grabbing the keys, she turned to Jack and quickly thanked him for staying, as anxious to end their time together as she knew he would be. She assured him that she was fine when he prompted her—just as she had with everyone back home… Sam, Ethan, and especially herself.

You shouldn't be reassuring anyone of that right now. You're be-having like a fool, Kate Harriman, a damn fool, and this is only the start.

27. REMEMBERING THE PAST

AS JACK WALKED AWAY FROM the car terminal, Kate just stood with the rental car keys in hand and watched him go. Her mind couldn't help but flash back to the summer they had met. She trembled as memories that had long been tucked away grasped and clawed their way to the surface.

It was over a year before Jack had dated or known Molly; it was the summer before Kate had met Ethan. She was living in Boston during law school and had accepted her first position as an associate lawyer in a large firm. It must have been late fall, like now, she remembered, because it was still dark that morning and cold. She had been standing in the middle of a crowd of die-hard runners at the starting line of one of the city's annual road races—one of many 10ks that she regularly did.

She hopped up and down to keep warm, waiting for the gun to go off. She heard a loud "Dammit!" behind her and realized that she'd landed on someone's foot. When she turned around to offer an apology, she saw a good-looking guy with a fit runner's body and startling blue eyes. With a kind but strong face and sandy blond hair that accentuated his eyes, he definitely stood out in the crowd.

When their gazes met, she saw that he was gawking at her, with a foolish smile plastered on his face. He assured her that his foot was okay and said that he still had another leg to run on. Without meaning to, she smiled at his silliness. They made some quick small talk in the moments before the race began. She recalled a joke he made about those doing the shorter 5k race, mocking it as wimpy and hardly worthwhile, right before they took off at the starting line.

They ran side-by-side for the first quarter mile before Jack nimbly pulled ahead and finished the race in just under forty minutes, second in his age group. Kate placed first in hers, not far behind him. As she approached the finish line, she was both surprised and pleased to see that he was waiting there. He cheered loudly for her and called out, "Hey, you!" giving her a thumbs up as she crossed the finish line. He would later joke that he hadn't known what else to yell to get her attention as he hadn't gotten her name. He said that he'd just known that he wanted to see her again, right from the start.

During the first few dates, they'd found that they had a few things in common beyond running and had a decent time together. He'd treated her well, and she could tell that he was a good guy. Almost too good, she thought, to be involved with such a warped soul as herself. He was easy-going, happy, and people-focused—all the things that she was not. After a few months, and one attempt in the bedroom, she decided that the right spark just wasn't there. It wasn't that he didn't know what to do to please her. They'd simply spent too much time laughing and joking around as opposed to having sex for her liking. Kate knew she could be demanding in the bedroom, but Jack just hadn't been able to satisfy her the way she liked.

Good guys always make better friends than lovers, she thought bitterly.

It wasn't long before they amicably agreed to end the relationship. Soon after, the awkward friendship—that never seems to last between past lovers—ended. A few months later Kate had met Ethan, but the timing wasn't remotely right for them then. At least not for Kate. The dread of what had happened to her had already begun to consume her. It was unlike anything she'd experienced before. Jack had already left Boston and moved to Maine to be near his parents. Kate was left alone, having to make the most difficult decision of her life.

The day she chose to let it go caused her heart—already hardened after a troubled childhood—to finally turn to ice.

Because of that decision, she never spoke to Jack again. She didn't return the few phone calls he made. After they split up, Kate was like a machine going through the motions—mechanically mobile yet devoid of emotion and pain. It wasn't until her sister, Molly, had called almost two years later with the news of her pending marriage that Jack's name again passed through her lips.

During such an intensely difficult time, Kate surprised even herself when she connected with Ethan at a bagel shop one day. And even though she had needed to move far away soon after they met, she genuinely liked him and decided to stay in touch as she'd promised. With his kindness, his attention, and his obvious adoration, he was like a savior for her. He was, perhaps, the only piece of her life that she could hang onto, something that was solid and worth waking up for. Ethan helped to keep her grounded. Some nights, their lengthy phone conversations deep into the night were all that kept her from falling apart in the months after she'd had to say goodbye.

She grimaced now at the thought of that time and felt that same naked vulnerability engulf her soul once again. The feeling was so strong that she looked around to see if anyone could see through her to the raw emotions inside.

Picking up her bags, Kate briskly walked out of the rental office in search of the rental car. Adeptly, stoically, just as she had been doing for the last seven years, Kate forced herself to focus on the present, pushing all thoughts of the past away. Ignoring that part of her life that she couldn't bring herself to think about— let alone to dwell on—had always been her survival mechanism. Now, she felt that it was all that she had.

Stuffing her errant thoughts down inside like dirty laundry, she loaded up the rental SUV and got inside. Feeling the chill of the darkened garage, she wrapped her arms around her body, mentally refusing to let guilt ruin her soul. Sitting there, trying to collect herself, Kate took a deep breath and willed herself to start the car and go. She dreaded the unknown ahead more than she'd ever thought possible.

The past raged against the future. For that moment, alone in the dark confines of the garage, Kate despised the world and everyone in it.

"Mom, why would you do this?" she shouted out loud.

God, what does someone who has been shot even look like? Maybe I don't need to go to the hospital. Maybe it's enough that I just came up here.

Yet knowing there was no escape, she resigned herself to the inevitable and input the address for Portland Regional into the vehicle's GPS. As the unit searched, she slowly and grudgingly navigated through the darkened terminal up to the exit ramp. As the SUV emerged above ground, Kate felt like a storm chaser heading toward the eye of a hurricane—minus the adrenaline rush and positive anticipation.

Ten minutes later, just as Jack was pulling back into the hospital parking lot, Kate pulled into a Dunkin Donuts drive-through. She ordered from the faceless voice that scratched its way to her through the little black box. When the attendant didn't understand her simple order—one large coffee with cream, no sugar—she repeated it curtly. Her tone was rude, she knew, but driving away with a large piping hot coffee in hand a few moments later, she had already forgotten. She merged onto the interstate and headed for the hospital. The autumn leaves still clung to the oak trees in brilliant shades of orange, red, and brown at the height of their autumn peak. Some of the foliage already blanketed the ground, a preview of the colder winter days ahead. Every once in a while a gusty wind from a passing eighteen-wheeler would swirl the leaves up into a spiral of crisp color. However, Kate didn't notice any of this as she guided the car along a road that she'd traveled dozens of times in her youth.

All the reasons she'd wanted to leave Maine in the first place crept back to the surface as she drove along the quiet roads. She remembered how strong the desire to leave had been growing up here. Even as a young girl, deep down, she had always felt that there was something more out there—something better. The divorce, Molly's arrival, and the trouble with Robbie had only served to harden her longing to get away and find what it was she so desperately sought. She had felt trapped here. She used to stand at the window, staring out and wishing she could be somewhere, anywhere, else and be free.

Kate laughed out loud at her own bitterness, as she thought about her hometown and what little she thought it had to offer.

Wellington was a small town "stuck in the middle of nowhere," but it was just a half day's drive to Boston and not more than an hour to the main airport. Yet *stuck* is exactly what it had felt like for Kate growing up here. The town had no chain restaurants, no theaters or cinemas, and only a few stores. It was quaint and rustic at best; uncouth and unpolished at worst. The front lawns of most of her childhood friends' homes had shown the same state of disarray as her own did. They held more cars than there were drivers, old tires, a small fishing boat or Old Town canoe, and knee-high grass that sprouted up everywhere in between. Kate was sure that town locals would still boast that Wellington was the ideal place to live and raise a family, a place where everyone knows everyone else, crime is limited to the occasional petty theft, and the post office never has a line.

Yet, right from the beginning for Kate, that life had felt small and restricted, cut off from the rest of the world. She knew deep down that there had to be something more and decided early on that there were two kinds of people who lived in Wellington. The first kind stayed because they didn't have what it took to leave. They looked the same, talked the same, and practically lived the same. The second kind were biding their time before they got out.

Remembering how mad she used to make Robbie and her mother in those days when she complained about Wellington made her laugh bitterly now. Beth could never understand why her daughter couldn't just be happy there.

"Katie, sweetheart, it's a *good* thing that we all know each other around here."

But Katie just rolled her eyes in response.

"And we have such nice neighbors—it's just not like that everywhere you go."

"I know, mother, that's why I can't wait to leave. I don't want *everybody* to know me. It's just weird!"

Kate's exasperated responses held equal passion, and their disagreements often ended with Kate charging out of the room mumbling swear words under her breath and Beth throwing up her hands in exasperation behind her.

As Kate drove through towns that resembled Wellington so much they could all be the same, she turned her thoughts back to Jack. She still felt shaken up after seeing him so unexpectedly at the airport. His repeated descriptions of Molly "having been through a lot" kept playing in her head like a skipping record. She struggled to make sense of it all. She decided that she needed to focus on her surroundings—just in time to see the blue and white hospital sign ahead. Her sharp veer off the highway caused a few honks behind her for the second time in one day as annoyed drivers slammed on their brakes then sped past.

Peering up through her windshield, she saw the hospital looming ominously on the hill ahead. It was a massive brick building that looked sinister, even in the early afternoon sun. Her heart quickened in fear as she knew that she would soon be inside its sterile walls, seeing her mother and facing the family that she had left behind.

28. EMOTIONAL OVERLOAD

AS JACK LEFT THE AIRPORT and raced back to the hospital, Molly still sat dutifully by her mother's bedside.

During her visit, doctors and nurses had periodically entered the room to check Beth's vitals. They took copious notes on their charts and consulted one another in private as they left to see other ill-fated patients. Each time Molly heard the sound of footsteps outside the door, Molly angrily brushed away her tears before someone walked in. Then, when she was alone in the room again, she cried out in pain, demanding questions of her mother who lay in a coma. They were questions that Molly knew deep down might never be answered. At times, she felt like picking up her mother and shaking the answers out, only to feel guilty immediately after for even thinking such a thing.

Despite Molly's constant requests for updates on Beth's condition, no one seemed to be able to give a definite prognosis or any solid information about what to expect. They simply didn't know what Beth would be like when she recovered, or even if she *would* recover.

Molly's thoughts turned to the past, to her childhood at home. She remembered all that her mother had done for her. She remembered the smell of freshly baked cookies after school. She remembered how her mother had volunteered to chaperone field trips when no other mom would, how she had encouraged Molly to try new activities, how she had told Molly that she was beautiful, even when Molly could look in the mirror and see that she was not. It was those loving, encouraging words her mother had offered over the years that helped create and define her, Molly knew. She felt a surge of sadness for the loss of it all. Dropping her head in her hands, she sat for a while and cried. When she was eventually able to lift her head, she gently squeezed her mother's arm and spoke with more force than she intended.

"Mom, you need to pull out of this. I know you've always been there for me. And now… I wasn't there for you when you really needed me. Please forgive me." Molly leaned over and hugged her mother's inert body. She kissed her un-bandaged cheek and softly whispered goodbye.

Just as she stood up to leave, one of the younger doctors entered the room and briefly touched Molly on the elbow. She looked up, startled at not having heard him enter, realizing that she had seen him earlier in the hall. With a disquieting sadness on her face, she stared at him and waited for him to speak.

"Uh, I know how difficult this is for families," he paused, then continued a bit stronger in his words. "We just have to take things hour-by-hour. Comas do not have predictable outcomes, but we are monitoring her closely and hoping for the best."

Molly's face softened as the doctor delivered the first piece of comforting news she'd heard all morning. She thanked the young doctor and watched him walk out. Before she left, she leaned over and whispered near her mother's ear, "I love you."

When she left the room, softly shutting the door behind her, Molly saw her father coming down the corridor. They hugged tightly and spoke quietly. She shared with him what the young doctor had said then Molly left her father to have time alone with her mother. She met up with Jack just as he was entering the front lobby. He looked flustered, as if he'd been rushing around, but when she asked him about it, he brushed it off with a comment about not wanting to be late for her. He gave her shoulder a quick squeeze, and they headed back home to relieve their neighbor from taking care of the girls.

Once again, the forty-minute ride was made mostly in silence.

29. HEADING TO THE HOSPITAL

KATE SLOWLY WOUND THE SUV up to the hospital parking lot. As she was about to turn into an open spot in the back, an elderly nun in a black and white habit came out of nowhere and walked directly in front of her. She pressed on the brakes, and as the woman whisked by, she peered over at Kate and smiled with her eyes.

"Well, I guess that's better than a black cat crossing my path," she said in a voice devoid of humor as she watched the nun pass.

It was there, with her SUV stopped in the middle of the lot, that Kate's mind turned to God. The feeling was so strong that she actually found herself looking around, as if some ethereal being would be hovering nearby. Yet as the sun shone down through the clouds, shattering rays of sparkling light, there was nothing celestial to be seen. Kate blinked a few times and inhaled sharply. She hadn't thought about God since the sporadic Sunday school attendances of her youth. These days, superior court judges were the highest powers that she had to deal with, and the very idea of a God above had been more unnerving than comforting. However, with the nun's sudden appearance and her subsequent urge to pray, Kate decided to offer up some spiritual words for her mother.

She pulled the SUV fully into the parking space and closed her eyes tight, struggling to remember a formal prayer from her childhood, yet unable to recall even one. Feeling compelled to say *something*, Kate spoke the first words that came to mind.

"Uh, God... I realize that it's been a long time. If you *can* hear me, I'm presuming you already know what I'm asking for. Please help my mother and our family and... well, that's it." Then without knowing what else to say, she dropped her face in her hands and sat for a moment in heavy silence.

Eventually, Kate willed herself to get out of the car. She took a deep breath and stole a disapproving look in the rearview mirror then hastily exited the SUV. As she made her way across the parking lot toward the hospital's entrance, it occurred to her that she had never been inside this hospital building.

How is that possible? Portland Regional was the only hospital for miles, yet as quickly as the question came, the answer hit her.

You left, dumbass, remember? Before college friends starting having their stupid babies and before family started to get old or Mom tried to…

She willed her legs to keep moving forward, and the automatic doors of the hospital opened up wide. The gust of air that enveloped her as she stepped inside smelled like antiseptic cleaner. To Kate, the smell only masked the imminence of disease and death, and she involuntarily grimaced. She approached the receptionist desk. At first, the older woman who bustled about behind the desk didn't notice her standing there. As the woman stopped and leaned over to scribble something on a pad of paper, Kate saw the skunk-like streak that ran down the crown of her head. Not used to being kept waiting, Kate cleared her throat loudly and spoke firmly, "Excuse me."

The plump woman jumped off her black swivel seat in surprise and threw a palm to her ample chest. "Oh, my! You startled me, dear," she exclaimed. "I didn't see you standing there."

"I know," Kate responded dryly. She had to lean over the desk to read the woman's nametag, "Marge Smith." *A commonplace name befitting a dowdy looking woman,* she thought. "Could you direct me to Beth Steven's room?"

Marge started fanning herself with a piece of paper and stared at the woman standing before her.

"Yes, I'm so sorry. I've been trying to get these notes finished all morning."

Kate gave a half smile and waited for Marge to answer her question.

The older nurse looked down at her computer and tapped a few keys. "Well, let's see here… What name did you say, dear?"

"Stevens. Beth Stevens," Kate murmured, barely loud enough for Marge to hear. She knew she needed to walk away soon— away from the desk, down the hall, and away from this overly cheerful Marge Smith person before any tears appeared.

"Stevens? Hmmmm… I don't see—Oh, dear. That's right," she said, looking up again at Kate. "I remember the name from her other visitors. She's not in a room, though, honey. She's down in intensive care."

Kate knew from the look on her face that this woman, this stranger, understood from a glance at her computer what her mother had done to herself. After so many years in the courtroom watching jurors' responses to plaintiffs' pleading glances, Kate knew. And Kate hated the woman for it. Hardening her resolve and the shell that had protected her for so long, Kate snapped back in defense.

"Could you *please* tell me where exactly that is," she said through gritted teeth. Kate stared back at Marge defiantly, with more fierceness than she had intended.

But Marge wasn't at all fazed and kept her smile on her plump face. After twenty years of working the front desk, she had seen it all. She gave Kate her warmest smile and directed her to the ICU. Though Marge had seen thousands of doleful faces before, her heart still went out to every one of them.

"Sweetie, you just need to go on through these doors, then head down the hall. Take a left after the lab, then left again, and you'll see signs for ICU on your left. Ms. Stevens is in room number 110."

Kate thought for a moment then blurted out, "With that many lefts, it sounds like I'll end up right back here, Marge."

Yet even as the words came out, Kate knew that her attempt at humor was lost, replaced instead by another thick spoonful of sarcasm. It was difficult for even her to swallow, as she stood there facing Marge's open and kind face, a face that looked as if it's owner had never experienced any pain or suffering. Kate struggled to maintain her composure as Marge's smiling eyes stared back then tearfully turned her face away. Marge, ever sanguine and understanding, looked down at her desk to "find" something on it—giving Kate the time she needed to collect herself.

"Miss, are you another relative or a friend of Ms. Stevens?" Marge asked as she stood up behind the desk then asked more softly, seeing Kate's fragile state, "Is there something I can do to help?"

Marge reached across the desk for Kate's hand, but Kate instinctively pulled it away as she answered curtly, "I'm fine, thank you."

Marge continued on as if she didn't notice the rebuff and said softly, "Honey, you just need to go be with Ms. Stevens right now. That's all you can do. You go now, and if you need anything at all, come back and let me know."

Kate nodded wordlessly and quickly turned to walk away. Before she'd made it to the first set of doors, however, Marge's voice echoed through the foyer.

"Miss? Wait! You forgot your purse," she called out.

Kate turned to see the woman holding Kate's Versace bag out toward her. She hastily came back to grab it, murmured a barely audible "Thank you," and then scurried away.

As she watched Kate go, Marge said under breath, "Lord, you be with that one. She's going to *need* you."

Kate ran through the first set of doors as quickly as she could, out of Marge's sight. To Kate, it felt as if a stranger had peered into her soul. The vulnerability she felt in the moment shook her to her core. Angrily, she pushed through the next set of double doors and almost knocked down an older man who ambled through them from the other side. She apologized with a forced smile and brushed past him. In the adjoining hall she stopped short, realizing that she couldn't conjure up a single word that Marge had said. Willing herself not to cry again, she desperately tried to let logic take over and looked up in the hopes of seeing a sign for intensive care. As she did, she wondered briefly if looking skyward could prevent crying the same way it was supposed to stop a sneeze. However, when a single tear escaped each eye and rolled down her cheeks, she chastised herself for the foolish thought and brushed the tears away.

Walking briskly down the sterile white corridor, she made her way to the ICU. As she neared the room, it occurred to her that her mother might not be alone. Kate's heart sank at the prospect of seeing her for the first time with someone else there, and her steps slowed. Yet as she rounded the last corner, a low voice spoke her name from the other end of the hall, and her worst fears were realized. It was a familiar voice, one that brought back memories that clamped around her heart and iced her soul.

"She's in here, Kate," the man said with a small jerk of his head toward the room behind him.

At first, Kate was too overwhelmed with emotion to respond. The man whom she had spent most of her life avoiding now stood just steps away.

Time seemed to stand still. Her mind slowly began to register what her eyes saw. After more than twenty years of carrying a basket full of heated and hateful words that she would one day say to him, all Kate could do was stand there facing Robbie in awkward, angry silence.

30. PAIN FROM THE PAST

WHEN KATE LOOKED AT THE man whom she had despised for so long, she was at first struck by how old and tired he looked. Rob stood there, obviously uncomfortable. He did not at all remind her of the heartless stepfather from her childhood days. The realization was unsettling. His hair was unkempt, his plaid work shirt was wrinkled, and the brown Dickey's pants that she remembered him always wearing were now faded and unclean. A loose boot string dangled onto the floor from under the cuff of his pants. The tips of his boots were scuffed and smeared with grease-like stains.

When she brought her eyes up to meet his gaze, she saw that his eyes were also red and swollen. For that moment, Kate almost felt a sense of compassion, knowing what he must be going through with his wife of twenty years in a coma.

"Beth isn't doing much of anything now, Kate, so don't go in there with high expectations. Molly just left a while ago, and I didn't know if she'd be able to walk herself out of here today."

"Have you been here long?" Her spoken question barely hid the one hidden behind it, *will you be leaving soon?*

Robbie averted his eyes, looking instead at the floor as he repeatedly kicked at some imaginary spot of dirt.

"No, not long," he finally answered, still avoiding her gaze.

Kate couldn't tell if he was holding back his emotions or trying to avoid her. She couldn't decide if she wanted to run in the other direction or head straight for him, and once again she hated herself for her uncertainty.

"The doctors don't know if she can hear us or not, so..." Rob looked away as his voice trailed off.

She said nothing, and the silence became awkward before Rob continued.

"Kate, your mother just doesn't look like herself in there, so you need to be prepared. The... ah... the gun went off through the top and side of her head, so it's swollen pretty bad and bandaged up. I just don't know what happened..." Rob stopped and turned away again.

With those words, Kate's heart beat fast, and the floodgates opened. Any momentary compassion she had felt quickly slithered away, and all of the anger and hurt from her childhood and the last day coursed through Kate's body like an electrical shock. Kate stared back at Rob with a smoldering hatred—the man whom she felt was responsible for ruining her childhood had failed to prevent the destruction of her mother. Not able to hold back any longer, she lashed out.

"What the hell happened up here, Rob? How could you not know that she was this bad off? Huh? You lived with her for God's sake, you saw her *every day!* I don't understand what was going on!"

Rob's mouth fell open. He looked as if he'd been punched in the stomach.

"Of *course* I didn't know, Kate," he retorted defensively, "I just thought..."

But Kate the attorney abruptly cut him off and fired back with venom in her voice.

"No, Rob! I don't *care* what you thought, and I simply cannot understand how you didn't see this coming! Mom and I talk a lot, but I could have never known that she was thinking about doing something like *this!*"

The last word came out in a snarl as her arm jerked toward the door behind them. His face betrayed his own anger, and Kate knew that her face wasn't hiding the raw emotion that surged within. With hate boiling and rumbling just below the surface, she and Rob stared at each other like fighters in a ring.

When he finally spoke, Kate learned that someone *else* was unaware of her communications with her mother and was aghast.

"I didn't know you two have been talking," he finally managed to mumble.

"Good God! That's the same fucking thing Molly said!" Kate almost screamed the words as she spun around on her heel and threw her hands up in the air. "What the hell was Mom doing? Sneaking off to call me so *no one* would know? Was talking to me so bad?"

"I just didn't know. I mean you haven't exactly been up here much…" Rob managed to stammer before Kate cut him off again.

"You fool! Why do you *think* I haven't been here?" Kate hissed at him, "Don't you know that the reason I haven't been around is because of *you?*"

His face registered an unexpected look of surprise that only served to anger Kate more.

"Rob, you *ruined* my childhood!" her voice escalated with every word, "You made my life miserable. Have you forgotten all about that?"

"Kate, this isn't the time for that."

Kate clenched her hands into fists, and Rob took a half step back, unconsciously leaning away from her.

"Don't you dare tell me this isn't the right time!" she half-shouted. Her voice seemed greater in the empty hall, resonating with anger that had been bottled up inside her for years. "I have been avoiding you for most of my life, and you know *exactly* why."

His face blanched at those words, and he said nothing. He wouldn't meet Kate's hate-filled stare.

"Well? Do you have nothing to say for yourself?" she demanded. Her words almost screamed out through clenched teeth.

"Kate, your mother is…"

But she quickly stopped him, pointing her finger accusingly as she took a step closer. "Do *not* speak to me of my mother!"

Then Kate took a deep breath and finally spoke the words that had never been spoken before.

"I remember that night that you came into my bedroom, Rob. Oh, I remember. And we both know that if I hadn't fought back, something terrible could have happened, you sick bast…"

At that moment, a young female nurse in a stiffly starched uniform rounded the corner and stopped short. She glanced back and forth between Rob and Kate then spoke quietly, with her eyes still darting.

"Is there… ah… anything I can do to help you two here?"

When neither Kate nor Robbie spoke, the nurse looked back at Rob. "Mr. Stevens, is it? Is this woman here a relative of your wife's as well?"

"Yeah," he said through clenched teeth. "This is Beth's older daughter, Kate. She just flew up from Georgia," Rob replied before adding quickly, "And I was just heading out."

He avoided Kate's cold stare and took the opportunity to get away. Robbie walked stiffly around the corner and out of sight, leaving Kate alone in the corridor with the young nurse. Kate was shaking all over, and her heart pounded fast inside her chest.

Her hands clenched and unclenched themselves as her eyes bore into the floor directly below. Tears fell as Kate began mumbling softly to herself and repeating the same mantra over and over. "It's all okay, it's okay..."

Kate felt a gentle tap on her arm. She looked up, startled, surprised to see the nurse still standing there. Kate hastily tried to wipe the tears from her wet cheeks.

"Miss," the nurse asked softly, "Is there anything I can get for you?"

Numbly, Kate answered the first thing that crossed her mind. Her voice did not sound like her own.

"Water. I could use water."

"Sure, I'll just go grab you a cup at the nurses' station," the nurse said as she bustled off, seemingly glad to be free.

Kate stood outside the room where her mother lay, feeling alone and out of control. *This must be what it's like to get caught in the center of a storm*, she thought, *eerily quiet and perfectly still, yet fearfully aware of the wild and tumultuous rage that was imminent, threatening to destroy anything in its path.* She willed her legs to take the few steps toward the door. They felt wooden as she lumbered forward. She wondered if some internal survival mode was shutting everything down inside, for she felt almost inhuman, like a robot without thought or emotion.

Slowly, she reached for the cold heavy handle of the door and turned it. As she pushed the door open, she had the sensation that she was entering a place from which she could never return rather than a mere hospital room. She walked inside hesitantly and saw her mother's motionless body lying in the bed. Panic began to rise from within, choking the air out of her as she gasped for breath.

Approaching the bed, she spoke her mother's name in a quiet hush. Then she uttered just one word, a word that seemed to be ripped out of her very soul. "Why?"

3 1. COMA

MOMENTS AFTER KATE ENTERED HER mother's room, the young nurse on duty returned to check on her. The nurse stopped a few steps behind Kate and tentatively set a small paper cup on the stand near the bed. Murmuring something about coming back later to check on them both, she softly padded back out of the room. Kate barely noticed the woman come and go as she stood there struggling to take in the horrifying scene before her.

Her mother was motionless in the bed. She lay covered with a stiff white hospital sheet. IV tubes went into both arms, and various other tubes disappeared under the sheet. The ventilation tube in her nose assisted her breathing, making her chest move up and down regularly. And as Robbie had warned, a thick bandage encircled her head, leaving only part of her face visible—a part that Kate could barely recognize as that of her mother's.

At first, Kate couldn't bring herself to believe that the body lying before her was the mother that she knew and had loved.

She forced herself to take a step closer. Peering down with the keen eye of a lawyer used to looking for details, Kate could see how darkly bruised and swollen her mother's body appeared. As her eyes strayed downward, she saw her mother's hands and cringed. They were bloated and distended, protruding out from under the hospital sheet. In the back of Kate's mind, she remembered something about a buildup of fluid that caused swelling. Kate slowly reached out and touched her mother's lifeless form, afraid to actually make contact. Yet that touch forced a breath that she didn't realize she'd been holding to come out of her body in a loud gasp. It felt as if a heavy weight had rolled off her chest. The feeling was so palpable that she clutched her other hand to her chest, directly over her heart, wondering briefly if it would give out right then and there.

In those first few seconds—moments that seemed like hours— Kate wanted to run away. Yet her legs wouldn't move; they were locked in place by a fear that made her almost as immobile as her mother's body before her. Staring down, with tears tumbling out onto her face, Kate knew that running would not make it go away. *Running is what I've done for most of my life, and look where I am now…*

She had run from the hurt, anger, and frustration of feeling unwanted and unloved and from the terrible feeling of rejection that consumed her childhood years. For the first time, she understood just how strong her flight response has been during her life. She had run away from everyone around her who had hurt her. She slumped down into the seat next to the hospital bed, wanting desperately to say all of this to her mother. She could almost taste the need for absolution. The bitterness of that need coated her tongue.

Yet, more importantly, Kate wanted—no, *needed*—to hear her mother admit her own wrongdoings in return. For her mother to admit that she had abandoned her daughter when Kate needed her most. With the understanding that such an admission may never happen came an emptiness for all she had lost—and what she may never have—that settled deep inside her heart. She felt the weight of the years of anger and hurt she'd been carrying like a heavy yoke around her neck. She sunk further down in the chair, her head hung low, as the possibility of death tried to smother her soul.

"Mom, what have we done?" she sobbed the words through her tears. The hopelessness of the moment was a cross too great to bear, and her body felt weak and frail.

She went limp and she half fell onto the side of the bed. In despair, Kate cried next to her mother's lifeless form with a suffering that tore through her. Kate rarely cried, but after the floodgates opened up, it seemed as if everything that had been stored inside for so long burst out. She cried until she felt she could cry no more, and she laid her head down next to her mother's stomach. It was just like she used to do as a small child. Though back then, her mother would stroke her hair or cheek as she lay and tell her that everything would be okay. She stayed like that with her eyes squeezed shut, hopeless that she would ever again feel that gentle touch on her head.

Finally, her anguish and tears were spent. What remained in their wake was a heavy, somber stillness that descended on her body and soul. She sat in silence and gently caressed her mother's hand over and over, unaware of the passing time. At some point, Kate knew that it was time for her to go, that she had to get out of the hospital room and away from the hospital, so that she could once again breathe.

"Mom, I don't know if you can hear me, but if you can, you have to come out of this. You *have* to get better, ok? I need you. Molly needs you... I love you, Mom. I'm going to see Molly now, but I'll be back first thing tomorrow."

Kate whispered a kiss then slowly stood up and walked out of the room.

Eying the exit sign ahead, she left the hospital's thick brick walls, already feeling like a different person than the one who had walked inside just a few hours before. She looked up to see that it had turned into a cloudy, overcast day. She slid into her rental car, pushed the uneaten bagel aside, and sat for a minute in the crowded hospital parking lot, looking around at the other people coming and going from the hospital. Even through her anguish, she knew that there were dozens of other tragedies beyond her own, tragedies that lived and breathed and died inside those walls.

As she rested there, head bowed, Kate spoke for the second time in one day to someone whom she hadn't thought of since her early childhood days.

"God, it's me again. Kate. I'm sure that people only come to you when they are at a loss for anything else, but please take care of my mom. Help her through this and help me. God, if you can hear me, please give me a sign that we'll be okay."

She turned the key in the ignition, and as if on cue, one heavy raindrop appeared on the glass. It was followed by another and another, the start of a driving rain. Kate watched in amazement as the raindrops poured down from the heavens above. The low, monotonous murmur quickly turned into a loud roar as the pelting rain hit the roof of the SUV. Soon the raining noise was almost loud enough to drown out her misery.

Typical of Maine weather, an unexpected and heavy rainstorm had rolled in on a bright, sunny day to wash everything away.

"Seriously, God? Is this my sign? A torrential rain?" she yelled out loud.

Kate began to drive carefully out of the parking lot, the wipers of the SUV barely giving her enough visibility to drive, then abruptly slammed on the brakes. As she sat, she realized that she had no idea how to get to her sister's house, and she laughed bitterly at herself. She felt foolish as her mind scurried to search through years past, trying to remember the last time she'd been back to visit family. It finally settled on the time right before Molly's older daughter was born. Kate grimaced at the memory, both at how long ago it had been and at the awkwardness of her stay here. *It's no wonder I haven't been back.*

Molly had begged Kate during her pregnancy to come up to visit them after Alice's arrival. Yet Kate had a big court case pending—*Pinson vs. the City of Atlanta, was it?*—and said that she needed to be back at work well before Molly's due date, in time for the trial. She had flown up one month before the baby was due for just a few days, and somehow she had managed to get through it. She deftly declined the invitation to stay at their house, despite Molly's many objections, opting instead to have her escape at the end of the day in a nearby hotel room, to try to find a measure of peace in the solitude there. Kate could still picture how grossly huge and swollen her sister's stomach had been; the sight had made Kate's stomach turn and her heart seize up. The two days were a blur—trying to talk with Molly, being around Jack, watching the happiness that seemed to seep out of their every pore. Kate had made it through the ordeal as best she could, counting the minutes until her visit was over, then raced back to the airport and her own home. She was so relieved to escape the guilt she felt while she was there that she promised to never put herself through that again, and she hadn't returned, despite Molly's announcement of their second child a few years later and despite her mother's problems and—now obvious—cries for help.

Has it been four years? Or five? Shit, I don't even know how old Alice is now.

Feeling guilt creep up on her again, she typed Molly's address into the GPS and saw that the drive time would be about forty-five minutes. Missing her Beamer's Bluetooth technology, she hit "Molly Curtis—Home" on her cell phone to let her know that she was on her way. Just lifting the phone to her ear, however, brought up the memory of the previous night's call. It flashed through her mind like a mushroom-induced drug trip she'd once had in college, creating swirls of discontent and sorrow. Her stomach lurched. For a moment, she was worried that her coffee would come back up as she struggled to overcome the sensation.

"Hello? Katie, is that you? Are you here?" Molly answered breathlessly as if she'd had to run to the phone.

"Hi, Molly, yes, I'm here. I just left the hospital with mom, and I'm headed your way," she replied, not bothering to correct Molly's annoying use of her childhood nickname.

"Well, how did she look to you? I mean, did she look okay?" Molly asked.

To Kate's utter amazement, her sister's optimism was shining through despite the horror of the situation. Her first thought was to shout back, "No, Molly, *of course* she's not fucking okay!" But Katie shook her head in disbelief. She held back the reality that threatened to ooze out, knowing that the bitter truth was the last thing that Molly needed to hear right now. And perhaps the last thing she could say.

"Well, I didn't see her yesterday…" she paused then rushed on, "but I did expect worse, and it looks like she's getting all the help she needs there." Kate was surprised at how easy it was to say this lie. However, she knew deep down that saying the truth would have been even more difficult, and Molly's enthusiastic response verified her lawyer's instinct.

"Oh, that's good, Kate," Molly's words gushed out. "So you're on your way here now? We are looking forward to seeing you, even through all of this..."

The relief in Molly's voice was almost palpable. Kate's mouth turned up in disgust.

"Yes. Well, the GPS says I'll arrive in just less than an hour. I guess about four o'clock, then?" Kate replied, then added as an after-thought, "I mean, if that's okay..."

"Of *course* it's okay! Yes," she said, before adding somberly, "Drive carefully. It's pouring here. I'll start getting dinner ready. Do you still not eat meat or is a chicken potpie okay? We call it comfort food around here, and I think tonight we could all use some of that."

"Anything's fine, Molly. Don't go to any trouble. I'm not sure if I could really eat anyway." Though as she voiced the words, Kate realized that she couldn't remember the last time she'd eaten. She eyed the now cold, hard bagel on the seat beside her, and her stomach heaved again in response.

They ended their call, and moments later the rain stopped, just as quickly as it had started. Kate looked up through the wind-shield in amazement as the sun reappeared behind the fast-moving clouds in a burst of yellow, making it feel like the beginning of a new day. She wound the car out of the parking lot and drove the rest of the way to Molly's in the crisp October sun, appreci-ating the quiet around her even as her mind buzzed with all the questions that swarmed in her head.

Why me? Why my mom? Why this? Why? Kate then realized that she hadn't asked Molly if Jack would be home. She experienced a surge of panic. Having to face Robbie and her mother had been just about enough to handle for one day. She didn't know if she could handle seeing Jack again as soon as she walked through their door. Or if she would even know how to react after their strange encounter at the airport. Kate knew she could put on an act in the courtroom, but outside of that venue was another story. *If I'd asked about him, though, Molly would have thought the question out of place anyway, so it's probably just as well,* she worked to convince herself as she followed the GPS guidance and sped up Route 1.

By the time she reached Molly's little town of Windsor, just one town over from Wellington, their childhood home, she had resigned herself to having to deal with Jack. Coasting to a stop at the end of their long narrow driveway, she parked the SUV and took a deep breath to prepare for the evening ahead. The first thing she noted was the front yard's overgrown state. An old Jeep was parked off to the side, weeds and shrubs practically hid the front porch, and toys littered the yard. Just as she remembered, the scene was typical of Maine homes and so very different from the polished, manicured appearance of the homes down South. She shook her head in loathing.

Some things just never change, she thought cynically.

Just then the front door flew open and two little children ran out screaming. Pigtails flew behind them, and both girls had big smiles on their faces. These were her nieces, whom she had never even met, Alice and Emma. Kate noted Alice's resemblance to Molly in an instant, with her curly brown hair and big brown eyes, and couldn't help but smile. For a moment, the resemblance was so uncanny that she experienced a sense of déjà-vu as her mind brought her back to almost twenty-five years ago, to the time when Molly was about that age. Kate shook her head and forced a smile on her face as the girls stopped and more cautiously approached the SUV.

"Aunt Kate! Auntie Kate!"

The girls cheered in unison when Kate stepped out. Little arms and legs quickly encircled her waist, bringing a short burst of laughter out of her that she didn't know she had. "Hey, guys! Look at you, look how big you are," she said as she hugged them back rather awkwardly.

"I'm not a guy, Auntie Kate. I'm a girl!" Alice pulled back with a pout on her face and placed her hands indignantly on her hips.

Kate got down on her haunches and looked back and forth between them in earnest as if she was evaluating them, "You are indeed correct. And you are pretty, at that—just like your mom."

"You talk funny, Aunt Kate," chirped Alice, with a child's uncanny ability to see through to the truth.

"Am I pretty, too?" Emma piped up.

Kate assured Emma that she was just as beautiful. The two girls beamed up at her with delight. *They are probably the only ones who could smile at a time like this*, Kate thought ruefully. She envied their oblivious innocence. Their enthusiasm was a bit overwhelming, though, for Kate's reserved, adult-centered life. She stood there a moment and awkwardly stared back at them before Molly's voice saved her.

"Emily! Alice!" Molly's voice rang out as she hurried down the front porch steps. "C'mon, girls, give your Aunt some room to come inside, please."

Alice obediently pushed away, and Emma followed her lead. Then they ran back inside the house yelling, "Aunt Kate! Come see *our* room."

Kate looked at Molly as she stood there on the porch and was instantly surprised to see how much older her sister looked, *God, what the hell's been going on up here?* The image of her sister standing there in the sun did not at all equate with the one Kate had carried around in her mind, and she was confused.

Jack was the same age as Kate, so Molly was ten years younger than both of them. Yet seeing Molly stand there, Kate saw that Molly didn't look to be younger than either of them. The lines on her face made her look much older, her middle was round and soft, and her hair splayed around her shoulders, unkempt with old highlights on the ends. Kate waved, trying to keep a smile on her face, and turned to grab her bags out of the rental so her face wouldn't give away her thoughts. She started walking toward the house, but Molly quickly came down the porch steps and met her halfway across the yard. The two women stopped short and clumsily hugged, tentatively at first, then more tightly when neither of them pulled away. When their embrace finally loosened, they stood back to look at each other. Up close, Kate saw weariness on Molly's face and a tiredness that did not at all reflect her younger age.

Kate suddenly remembered Jack's repeated comments about Molly—*she's been through so much*—and wondered if there might be more to her sister's tired appearance than she knew about.

"Let's go in," Molly finally said. "Lord knows what the girls are doing in there by themselves. I still can't leave them alone for a minute, you know."

She turned and led Kate inside, looking behind her a few times as if to make sure Kate was still following her. Or still truly there.

When Kate stepped into the house, her senses were assaulted with a variety of unfamiliar sights, sounds, and smells. Toys covered almost every possible inch of space on the floor. Baby blankets and miscellaneous clothes were strewn on the furniture. The tantalizing smell of something hot cooking in the oven permeated the air. The TV was on in the living room, and a radio was playing country music from another room. The scene was so very unlike the crisp clean quiet of her house in Brookside that it was startling, but at the same time it made her home seem almost sterile and artificial in comparison.

As Kate's eyes scanned the small rooms before her, taking everything in, Molly looked back at her and said rather defensively, "I, uh, wanted to pick up before you got here, but when you told me what time it would be, I decided to have dinner ready instead."

"It's fine, really. It looks—ah—fun here," she responded, unsure of what exactly to say.

"Ha! Fun is an understatement, I guess. Anyway, sorry it's such a mess. Jack will hate it, too—he should be home from work soon. His buddy is dropping him off. He put in a half day after driving to the hospital with me this morning. Is chicken potpie really okay? I tried to make one side with meat and the other without, just in case."

Yeah, then he left you to pay me a surprise visit, I know, Kate thought caustically, but she kept the smile on her face.

Molly prattled on and on, nervous and not quite sure of what to say or do. After she finally stopped, Kate decided it was time to fall back on her courtroom skills and smiled back at Molly as reassuringly as she could. "Chicken pot pie sounds great, Molly. And everything's fine. It really looks… homey here."

"Great!" Molly relaxed, obviously comforted by Kate's efforts.

Yet when Kate saw how quickly Molly accepted the shallow words, she felt a surge of jealousy inside that she fought to stifle, again wishing that her life could be that easy. For her, the world had always held more questions, too much angst, and fewer acceptances. She was never able to simply take someone's words at face value. She processed them over and over until she couldn't even remember what they were about in the first place. She could never accept kindness without looking for an ulterior motive lurking behind the smiling faces.

Emma and Alice suddenly ran down the stairs, yelling wildly for "Auntie Kate" to follow them back ups to their shared room.

"Okay, girls, okay. Your Aunt can come see your room later. Daddy will be home soon, and Aunt Kate probably wants to settle in for a minute before we eat. Go wash up for dinner now."

Molly had to yell over the din of their squeals, but she didn't seem to be bothered by it; Kate realized that the noise level was nothing out of the ordinary, remembering their conversation from the day before. The girls voiced their objections, but they obediently hustled to the bathroom. Kate wondered if their compliance was due to her presence or if they were always so well-behaved. She knew no children with which she could compare these two, so she could only guess from the sullied reputation most children had that it was probably the latter.

"Kate, we eat dinner early around here. And go to bed fairly early, too, I'm afraid. If you want to head down to the guest room to freshen up," Molly stopped herself and smiled before continuing. "It's the first room on the left, and it should be all ready for you. Can I get you anything? Maybe something to drink?"

Kate looked over the cluttered kitchen counters for signs of a coffee maker, determined to keep herself caffeinated for the remainder of the day. She finally spotted an old Mr. Coffee tucked between a toaster oven and an ancient Oster blender. She thought of her own kitchen at home, with counters free of clutter and high-end appliances deftly hidden behind cupboard doors.

"Would it be too much to make a pot of coffee now?"

"Oh, sure! I can do that." Molly said agreeably, bustling over to the coffee maker.

Kate murmured thanks and headed downstairs, feeling relieved to be alone once again. She could see upon entering the guest room that Molly had done her best to have it ready for her arrival. Unlike the rooms upstairs, it was neat and tidy, without a toy in sight. The twin bed was dressed with a multi-colored quilt, the window was partially open to allow in fresh air, and folded towels lay on the dresser. However, upon closer observance, she saw that the quilt had survived many a washings and the towels were a far cry from the thick Egyptian cotton she wrapped herself in back home. There was a tiny bathroom adjoining the bedroom; Kate peeked in and wondered if two people could be inside the small space at the same time.

She turned back and noticed the *Sleeping Beauty* nightlight on the side table next to the bed and couldn't help but smirk. *Once a mom, always a mom, I guess… and a ridiculous one, at that.*

Feeling out of her element and glad for the reprieve, Kate lay down on the bed and rested her eyes. As she listened to the muffled pitter-patter of footsteps above and felt the crisp October air, everything around her reminded her of her childhood. It was a reminder that growing up in Maine was simpler. So very different from her life now which was full of harried courtroom appearances and highbrow country club functions. Molly's life at home with the girls was straightforward and undemanding. It was a smaller existence that, to Kate, now seemed to carry far fewer complications than she experienced in her own life. *Maybe it's due to the lack of the competition or status here—never feeling that pressure to have more than the neighbor next door.*

Of course, there's not much to aspire to here, anyway, she thought bitterly.

As her sleepy mind trailed off, it drifted back in time. She thought longingly about the few good memories from her childhood. Weekends with her father, playing catch in the yard together. Riding bikes to the Daisy Dipper for ice cream with friends who lived nearby. Going to the beach and the taste of the salty air and the feel of the rough sand between her toes. Playing Scrabble every Friday night. She had learned to love the word game as much as her father did. They played together almost every weekend, though she rarely won even into her teenage years. Her dad had confided in her much later that he would watch her eyes during their games to see where her next move would be. Then he'd aggressively play that exact location on the board. She was so angry when he told her. "That's not a very nice way to compete against your daughter," she'd haughtily informed him.

He just laughed in response and playfully batted her arm. "Yeah, but I taught you how to be a top-notch player, didn't I?"

Kate set the alarm on her phone for a quick power nap and allowed herself to drift off to sleep. The muffled sound of children playing echoed from above, and for once, the memories of the past didn't torment her.

32. FAMILY TOGETHER

"AUNTIE KATE? ARE YOU AWAKE?" Kate was awakened, not by her phone, but by a child's whispers in her ear.

After a follow-up gentle nudge on her shoulder, Kate rolled over to face her human alarm clock. She looked directly into Alice's unblinking brown eyes as the girl stood by the side of the bed. Alice smiled tentatively at her. The uncertainty of being around someone unfamiliar in her own home was plainly visible on her pixie-like face.

Am I that much of a stranger to her? I've sent her Christmas and birthday presents every year, haven't I? Kate tried to reassure herself as she struggled to shake off the grogginess and wake up.

Kate thought that she knew her nieces—at least through the pictures Molly had sent to her over the years. Baby pictures, first smiles and first steps—she'd been in touch with them. *Haven't I?* Yet this little girl's hesitance presented a different picture that even Kate couldn't ignore.

Kate, you had no idea how to even drive here, for God's sake, she mentally berated herself as she rose to a sitting position on the side of the bed.

She realized then that she'd been foolish to think that she knew this family at all. For a moment, Kate felt a twinge of sorrow, remorse that she and her sister had not been involved with each other's lives. A sense of loss for what had been missing between them for so long. They had barely spoken over the years; each time they had to learn about each other all over again. Their conversations never had the plain familiarity of close friends, picking up where they left off—no matter how much time has gone by.

Angrily, Kate pushed the thought away, determined as always not to let regret rule her life. She shook her head free of the guilt and let it go. Her inadequate relationships were just the tip of the iceberg of a disappointing family life, and that's the way it had always been, but that's all.

Kate murmured derisively under her breath as she looked down at her niece, "Maybe I'm getting soft in my old age…"

"What'd you say, Aunt Kate?"

"Nothing," Kate ran a hand self-consciously through her unruly curls. She looked down at the expectant face before her and hesitatingly reached her arm behind Alice, encircling the girl's small frame. Kate tried to behave casually, as if she had done this with her niece a thousand times before, but she felt more awkward now than she had ever felt standing in front of a courtroom full of critics, jurors, and reporters. Kate's eyes darted around the room. After a few seconds, she realized that she had been holding her breath. She peered down at the little girl and tried to behave as if all was normal and she knew what to do.

However, the reality was that this was the first time she'd been this close to a child, let alone reached out to hug one. The feeling of her loss was so strong that she felt light-headed and weak, and tears threatened to spill over again. When Alice looked up at her aunt to speak, she saw a strained look on her face. The little girl said nothing; she simply leaned in closer to this woman who was more of a stranger to her and rested her small curly head on Kate's side. They sat together like that in silence before Kate finally spoke, holding back her tears.

"Well, Alice, should we head upstairs with everyone?"

"Oh, yeah! Mommy said dinner's ready. That's why she tol' me to come get you," Alice responded cheerfully. She then playfully pounced off the bed and beckoned Kate to follow.

Kate stole a peek in the dresser mirror before they left the room. Upon seeing the glass, however, she decided not to look anymore as each glimpse proved to be more disappointing than the last.

"A hot shower will most definitely be needed before this day is done," she said as they left the room.

Alice bounded up the stairs ahead. She looked over her shoulder every few steps to make sure Aunt Kate still followed. *Just like her mom,* Kate thought bemusedly.

Back upstairs, Kate noted that things were somewhat more organized and it was oddly quiet. Alice immediately scampered off to the playroom to be with Emma. Kate spotted Molly and Jack talking in the adjoining family room. Jack held Molly's hands tightly within his own. The two were sitting oddly close together on the couch, engaged in a serious conversation. Molly's back was facing Kate, so only Jack's face could be seen. He had watched Alice come in, so he hadn't caught sight of Kate standing there yet. He looked serious, almost stern. He reminded Kate of a defense attorney before the final delivery. Standing in the hall, she felt like an intruder observing them together. She assumed they were talking about her mother—*maybe they'd received an update?* She wondered why they wouldn't have waited to include her in the conversation. She felt uncomfortable and now somewhat miffed, but she decided to curb her anger before it took hold of her.

But when she turned to walk away, the movement caught Jack's attention. He jumped up from the couch. Immediately, his face took on a half-hearted smile, and he stood there beside Molly awkwardly, as if caught in the act. His smile was an obvious attempt to cover up the concern that had been plastered on his face just moments before.

The cover-up only served to make Kate angrier with them both. Kate knew it, and she could tell by his expression that Jack knew it, too. *All right, Kate, this is not the right time to get your feathers ruffled,* she reminded herself.

Molly jerked around to look at Kate, seeing Jack's reaction, "Oh, hey, Kate," she called out a little too cheerfully.

"Is... uh... is everything okay?"

Yet when Kate walked toward them and saw the pained look on Molly's face, Kate knew everything wasn't okay. Molly quickly tried to cover up the moment with a thin smile and jerked her hands out of Jack's grasp before turning to face Kate.

"Hey, Kate. Did you get some rest?" Molly asked as she quickly pulled herself up from the couch.

But Kate didn't respond. Intuitively, she recognized that her sister and her husband were trying to hide something from her. That, coupled with her anger, gave her an unsettling feeling of being lost and out of control, a feeling that she loathed. Away from her own surroundings and in someone else's house, Kate felt as if she didn't belong anywhere. The sensation was alarming and disturbing; her body tensed, and her empty stomach clenched tightly and heaved in response.

With mumbled words about getting dinner, Molly walked briskly past Kate to the kitchen. She called out questions behind her without a breath in between, all the while avoiding Kate's curious stare.

"Are you hungry, Kate? I think the chicken potpie is almost ready. Should we all sit down now?"

Kate silently followed her and mentally prepared the questions she would ask Molly about the scene she'd just walked in on—just as she would do in the courtroom. However, Molly didn't stop chattering or moving around long enough to give Kate the chance to voice any of them. In an overly cheerful, singsong voice she called out to the girls.

"Alice! Emma. Go get washed up for dinner, please."

When they started to argue, Jack barked at them from the kitchen, startling them all.

"Girls, go wash like your mother said!"

The girls jumped in response; they had already cleaned up for dinner, but the sound of their father's stern voice was enough to dispel any further arguments and they scooted off to the bathroom. All eyes went to Jack, and he instantly looked chagrined. Knowing Kate and Molly's eyes were on him, he asked the girls in a softer tone as he followed them down the hall, "C'mon, let's all get ready for dinner. Go on now."

Kate knew that the moment to ask Molly what she and Jack had been discussing was lost. Kate was normally assertive and brash, but in her tiredness, she decided to let it go, wondering if the real Kate Harriman was still on the plane or back in Brookside. *Because she didn't get off the plane and she's certainly not standing here now.* Kate then realized with a start that this was supposed to be the first time she and Jack had seen each other since her arrival. She looked at him questioningly to see if he had realized the same. But her question was quickly answered. For Jack quickly spun around, faced Kate, and attempted to speak as nonchalantly as possible.

"Hey, Kate... ah... sorry, it's a little crazy around here. How are you? It's good to see you... it's been a while."

Kate knew then that the façade had been created; the lie, the deceit had been set. He walked to the kitchen and began to help with dinner. The unspoken agreement between them only served to increase her concerns as she stood there staring at them. For now she knew that Molly and Jack had been talking about something else other than their airport meeting—and quite seriously. The uncomfortable scene she'd witnessed now held even more ambiguity.

Kate rolled her eyes and shook her head in frustration then met Jack's gaze head on and adroitly replied.

"Hi, Jack. It's good to see you, too."

With Molly's back to them, Kate's eyes bored into Jack with a look that said, *What the hell is going on here?*

He looked away and pretended to be intently involved in tossing the salad that Molly had already made. Molly glanced over and told him to stop before he ruined it. Jack looked back up at Kate and, seeing the unsettled and irritated look still on her face, offered up something in return.

"Ah, Molly and I were just talking about everything that's been going on. This has been a tough time, you know," he said, echoing the exact same words he'd said to Kate earlier at the airport.

"Yeah, so I keep hearing," Kate mumbled under her breath, not quite loud enough for Molly to hear.

Kate's sixth sense screamed inside her head. From Jack's tone, Kate could tell that something was wrong, but due to either sleep deprivation or emotional override, she was too exhausted to work through it. Attempting to feel out the situation, she offered a statement of conciliation, just as she would with a client who was not being completely truthful.

"Yes, well, I'm sure. I probably don't understand everything that's been going on here," she said louder, waiting for a response from either of them.

Kate's eyes still searched Jack's face for an answer, but he turned away again—either not noticing or pretending not to.

Then suddenly, Molly turned to face Kate and blurted, "What? You *probably* don't understand?"

Unusual sarcasm dripped off of every word. Her hands were on her hips, and her eyes were ablaze with an anger that seemed to come out of nowhere.

Jack and Kate both jumped in surprise, startled at the unexpected volume and tone of Molly's voice. They looked back and forth between them, then with barely a pause, Molly yelled at Kate again.

"You're damn right you don't understand, Kate. That's because you haven't been the one who's had to handle *everything* around here with mom. *I* have!"

And with those words, the room went quiet.

Jack and Kate stared back at Molly, and their jaws dropped open. Molly's outburst was so startling that Alice and Emma, who had just left the bathroom, scurried back down the hall and behind the door. They peeked out, their eyes as big as saucers. Even Molly herself looked taken aback by her outburst.

Kate was the first to speak and attempted to alleviate the pressure in the room, "Molly, of *course* I realize…"

"No, Kate, you don't. I'm sorry, but you just don't realize *anything* because you haven't been involved! In fact, you've been about as *uninvolved* as anyone could be!" Molly shouted back.

Molly started to turn away, but Kate's curt response stopped her short.

"That is *not* true. I told you on the phone that Mom and I have talked frequently. And half the time I'm at the office in the middle of a client meeting, for God's sake! I do work, you know."

With that, Molly sharply drew in her breath, turned, and took a step toward Kate as if to come at her. Though normally aggressive, Kate involuntarily stepped back in surprise. The two sisters stood there, staring at each other; one's face displayed anger and frustration, and the other displayed disbelief at seeing a side of her sister she had never seen before. When Molly spoke again, her voice was so low, so controlled, that Jack quickly ushered the girls back into the bathroom when they started to come out. Neither sister even noticed him leave as their stare down continued.

"Kate. A few calls here and there that *mess* up your day are *not* exactly the same," she said bitingly. "I have dealt with Mom's crying spells, the calls for help because she can't remember how to drive herself home, and the panic attacks that freeze her into some zombie-like state! I have handled it all!"

"I'm sure it's been difficult," Kate retorted defensively. "And I know I haven't been around, but I have a busy career, and I can't just leave whenever I want to!"

"A career, huh? What the hell do you think I do all day, Kate? Watch TV and get my hair done?"

Kate's eyes flitted over her sister's unruly brown locks and smartly stifled a laugh. She tried to respond to Molly's accusations again, this time with logic behind her words.

"Molly, my work requires me to…"

But Molly cut short her response again.

"Kate, my *girls* are my work—they *are* my career. I am a full-time mom, and trying to take care of *our* mother has been a full-time job, as well!"

"Yes, well, I can see that they keep you busy here," Kate said, trying to lighten the situation as she nodded at the disarray of the room.

But the effort came out with more sarcasm and less humor than she'd intended, and Molly fought back with an unchecked fury.

"Oh, I don't have a career *and* I can't keep a clean house? Why the hell did you come up here, Kate, if all you're going to do is put me and my life down?"

Molly's voice escalated with every word.

"No, Molly, no. That's not what I meant."

Kate took a deep breath. Putting on her best trial face—impassive, yet confident—she tried once again to regain control of the situation the only way she knew how—placation and logic stirred together, which unfortunately do not work as well in life as they do in the courtroom.

"Molly, you have a nice home here with the girls. I can see that. And I do wish I'd been up here more often to help with Mom. It's just that…"

"Don't use that condescending tone with me, Ms. Lawyer Smarty-pants. You may be older and a hotshot lawyer, but it doesn't mean you're any better than I am—law school or not."

Molly glared back at her sister defiantly as they stood opposite one another in the kitchen. The tension between them was palpable. Kate was pissed off at both the words Molly threw back at her and at herself for losing control of the situation. A cold stillness hung in the air between them like an animal carcass dangling from a hook. Kate saw naked anger on Molly's face and realized that neither one of them would win this argument, so she talked herself into ending the conversation before it spiraled down further. *Come on, Kate. You've handled stickier situations than this in court. Get it together.* She took a deep breath and spoke softly.

"Molly. What's happened is a horrible state for us all to be in. I, like you, am terrified. I wish to God I could make it right again. But I can't override what has already happened; it's done. But I am here now to help."

"But you can't, Kate," Molly pleaded. "You can't somehow make this all better and pretty it up so it fits into your perfect little life."

Kate felt all of the anger drain out of her as the truth of Molly's words hit her.

"I know. But that was my version of an apology," she said, shaking her head slightly. "And as Ethan knows, I don't exactly apologize to people very often."

"Yeah, I can believe that," Molly replied, still tight-lipped. She then added under her breath with a half grin, "Though I didn't realize that *was* actually an apology."

Kate grinned back at Molly's attempt at sarcasm and humor. *Now that's something I can work with,* she thought. "Where is Ethan, by the way?" Molly asked. "I didn't even think to ask why he wasn't here with you."

"Because I told him to stay home," Kate answered, more curtly than she'd intended. She pulled herself up straighter, as if doing so would somehow validate her words, and forced a confidence that she did not feel.

"Oh," Molly said in surprise. She peered back at Kate as if she didn't understand what she had said, "But… why?"

"I just told him that everything would be fine, that mom would be okay, and that I'd be home soon," she replied with a shrug as she turned away from Molly.

However, as the words came out of her head, Kate realized how empty they sounded. When she turned back to face Molly, she saw that her sisters eyes were brimming with tears. Kate tensed up and hesitated. She searched the rooms, looking for Jack, hoping that he would magically appear and take care of her sister so she didn't have to.

"Will it, Kate?" Molly's voice was now soft, full of desperation. Tears rolled down her face. "Will everything be okay? Because I'm not so sure anymore."

And with those words, Molly leaned over the counter next to her as if she was an elderly woman and began to cry in big, racking sobs.

Tentatively, Kate crossed the room. Ill-at-ease with another's display of emotion, she stood next to her sister for a moment and did nothing. Then slowly, with a cautious hand as if she was reaching into a fire, she gently patted Molly's arm. Molly jumped at her touch and stepped back. She tried to wipe her tears away. Struggling to compose herself, she avoided Kate's eyes and searched out the window as if there was something out there that would swoop in and save her at any moment.

Just then, a faint sound came from the foyer entryway, and two little heads appeared around the corner from the bathroom. Alice and Emma looked up at their mother and aunt expectantly, waiting for approval of their presence. Jack came up and stood behind them, shaking raindrops off his shoulders. He stopped and looked over at Molly, then Kate, trying to essay the situation and decide if the coast was clear.

"Is… ah… is everything all right in here?" he asked, directing his question at Molly.

"Yes… we're fine now, Jack." she replied softly.

Kate looked over her sister's head and silently nodded her head in agreement toward Jack.

"Well, it sure smells good in here. Shall we get some food on the table and eat?"

Jack's attempt at levity was not in vain. The mood in the room lightened with the mention of dinner, and the girls cheered. Jack motioned Alice and Emma toward the dinner table. They bounded toward it with nervous giggles and big smiles.

Molly went to the kitchen to set the dinner on the table. Jack jumped in to help. The family was in motion in every direction. Kate took a step toward them to ask how she could help but stopped when she saw Molly rubbing her head with a troubled look on her face. Kate saw Jack staring at her with the same anxious expression she'd seen before. A look passed between them before Jack walked over to Molly and squeezed her arm firmly. He nodded his head and whispered something in Molly's ear that Kate couldn't catch. Jack turned back with a big, obviously forced smile on his face.

The moment that Kate witnessed between Molly and Jack began and ended so abruptly that Kate wondered if she'd imagined it. In her sister's home, Kate felt like Alice lost in Wonderland, spiraling down a never-ending rabbit hole and desperate to know what was lurking, waiting for her on the other side.

33. AFTER THE FIGHT

KATE AND MOLLY WERE OVERLY careful around one another after their heated exchange. Smiling politely, they worked hard to say nothing that would spark a flame of discontent between them. As Molly and Jack put dinner on the table, Kate stayed with the girls in their playroom. She sat on the flowered overstuffed chair and tried to pretend that she knew what to do as the girls chatted and bounced around her.

Once dinner had been set and they all sat down around the table, Alice and Emma remained in their chairs and quietly ate. Jack broke the uncomfortable silence to make a joke about Molly's cooking that did not produce any laughs. The girls had each asked to sit beside Aunt Kate at dinner, so their sporadic comments about school and dolls and other things she couldn't relate to came at her from both sides. They were well behaved, and Jack and Molly smiled a secret smile to each other, the smile of parents who had children that were good. Once again, Kate felt overwhelmed and out of place.

The adults avoided mentioning the reason for Kate's visit in front of the girls. Molly had told them the day before that Grandma had been in an accident, and that seemed to be enough. Dinner conversation was limited mostly to small talk; it was the best the two sisters could do. Kate tried to share information about her work and some of the more interesting cases that she'd worked on, but she stopped when Molly gave her a quick shake of her head and motioned to the girls. It took a minute before Kate realized that she needed to censor her words around them. She decided to stop talking.

"Girls, we should have your Aunt here for dinner more often if you're going to behave *this* nicely," Molly said to break the awkward silence. The girls gave a rousing cheer and big toothy smiles in response.

With each heaping bite of her food, Kate became increasingly aware of just how little she'd had to eat in the previous forty-eight hours. She remembered the term Molly had used to describe the dish—"comfort food"—and understood why it was such an appropriate term... particularly in an otherwise uncomfortable situation. It went to her stomach without issue and settled in as if it had been there all along. When her plate was half cleared, she told Molly how delicious it was. Her sister beamed in response, obviously pleased and grateful for the compliment.

When dinner was almost done, Molly had to intervene during a tiff between Alice and Emma. Emma had snuck under the table to pull Alice's shoe off. Kate took the opportunity to turn to Jack and ask him small questions about his job while Molly was distracted with the girls. He provided brief and succinct answers— just enough, not too much. The girls simmered down for the remainder of dinner. After a while Alice spoke up loudly.

"Aunt Kate? How long *are* you going to stay here with us?"

Kate looked directly at Molly for assistance on how to answer, but Molly averted her eyes. Kate looked back at Alice and responded with a hint of guilt in her voice.

"Uh, not long, Alice. Just enough to see you guys and my Mom... uh... your Grandmother, then I fly back the day after tomorrow."

Alice's face fell into a frown before asking, "But why can't you stay longer? We haven't seen you in forever. Right, Mommy? Isn't that what you told Daddy the other day?"

Molly looked at Jack and blushed deeply before blurting out defensively to Kate, "Well, it's true! You *haven't* been here in a long time."

"I know," Kate replied. Then she turned back to Alice, "My work truly does keep me busy. I'm often in a courtroom working trials, and I'm busy preparing for cases the rest of the time. It's an interesting though very demanding career."

Kate sat back in her chair proudly. She felt that she had handled her niece's question quite well. She didn't see the lack of understanding on the girls' faces; they stared back at their aunt as if she had spoken to them in another language. Again silence hung over the table. Finally, once her mind had had a chance to process her Aunt's words, Alice piped up with another question.

"So, do you catch bad guys?" Alice asked innocently. There were chuckles of laughter around the table.

"No, Alice, she doesn't," Molly interjected, ever the protector of her children. Not wanting to upset the delicate balance they'd achieved over dinner she continued, "Kate, I think Alice was just trying to tell you before that she'd like to see you more often. That's all."

"Yes, thank you," Kate replied, without knowing what else to say.

"As would we," Molly continued, looking to Jack for support. When he said nothing she pushed, "Right, Jack?"

Though before he could muster an answer, little Emma shouted out loudly, "Me too, Auntie Kate!" breaking the ice and making all of them laugh.

For the remainder of dinner, the girls snuck peeks at each other every few minutes in their own secret way. Emma dropped food onto the floor a few times and laughed each time like it was the first. Jack was the first to finish his meal and got up from the table to start clearing away the dishes. Molly then tried to start another conversation with Kate.

"So, is your room okay downstairs, Kate?"

"It's great. Everything's fine."

"And how's Georgia these days? I saw you had a pretty hot summer this past year."

"Yes, summers there are difficult. I don't think I'll ever get used to them, especially running outside in the heat."

"Hey Jack, you used to run a lot, didn't you?"

Jack turned around at the sink and stared at his wife as if she'd stuck a pin in him. He turned to Kate with the look of a sailor hanging on to the side of a sinking ship. She was about to interject and save him with a comment, but Molly jumped in.

"Hun, what's that look for? You look like you just saw a ghost." There was an edge to her voice that both Jack and Kate noticed, but didn't understand.

"Ooooooo…" Emma cut in, making ghost sounds and raising her arms up over her head in a mock scare. Alice tittered behind her, Kate's face showed no expression at all, and Molly stifled a laugh as she looked back and forth between Jack and her sister.

Jack stared at his daughter and laughed too loudly in response then he abruptly brought his attention back to the dishes. With his back turned, he gave an offhand answer about his running days and rattled the dishes loudly in the sink. Kate, avoiding eye contact with anyone, mumbled something about needing another napkin. She started to get up from the table to escape.

"Kate, the napkins are right here." Molly said lightly, pointing to the middle of the table with a smile.

"Oh, right, thank you," Kate smiled weakly and slowly sat back down, wishing inside that she could just go home.

Then she remembered that she'd forgotten to call Ethan, and she wondered at the same time why she hadn't heard from *him*. Grateful for the excuse to leave the room, she turned to Molly.

"You know, I haven't even called Ethan yet…" she said, already pushing her chair back from the table. "I'll come help with the dishes right after I give him a ring."

Kate excused herself and darted to the foyer. Molly called after her and said not to worry about the dishes. A playful smile hovered on her tired face as Kate scurried outside.

Just as Kate walked out the front door, she heard Alice ask her mother with childlike innocence, "Mommy, why did Aunt Kate say 'excuse me'? I didn't hear her burp or anything." This produced chuckles from the adults.

Kate stopped then and turned around and saw Molly and Jack laughing together. Alice and Emma were looking back and forth between the adults and giggling—even though they didn't quite understand why. Then Emma knocked over her cup of milk, spilling it onto the table and into Alice's lap. Both girls screeched.

Alice jumped up screaming, and Molly yelled, "No!"

As Kate turned away again to go outside, she took with her the mental picture of a chaotic but happy family.

Outside on the porch, she sat down heavily and rubbed her arms against the brisk October air. Typical of Maine, there were no street lamps to illuminate the backcountry roads, so the darkness surrounded her. The combination of the darkness and the wind that whispered through the trees created an eerie calmness, causing Kate to shiver in response.

As she looked down at her cell, she immediately discovered why she hadn't heard from Ethan or anyone else since her arrival. In the last few hours, there were dozens of missed calls from him, from her father and Sam. She hadn't heard any of them because she'd obediently put her phone on silent at the hospital and forgotten to take it off.

Ha, that's what I get for conforming to rules.

She hit "Call Return" for Ethan; he picked up on the first ring. She could tell by the near panic in his voice that he'd been anxiously waiting for her. She immediately felt guilty for not remembering to call him sooner.

"Kate? Are you okay? I've been calling you all afternoon, for God's sake. What's going on up there?"

Exasperation was clear in his voice, but she also thought she caught a hint of irritation in his tone as well. Something she wasn't at all used to. Instantly defensive, she retorted, "Ethan, it's been a difficult day. I forgot to take my phone off silent after visiting mom at the hospital. Why didn't you just call me here? At Molly's?"

"I *would* have," he paused for effect before continuing slowly, "if I'd had your sister's phone number."

"Oh, right…" Kate's voice trailed off.

"Well? What's going on? How is your mother?" he demanded.

"I'm at Molly's now and we just finished dinner. Chicken potpie—you and I haven't had that in ages."

"Kate, I was asking you about your mother." Ethan surprised her once again by interrupting her sharply. She hesitated before responding, used to dealing with that show of aggressiveness in court but *not* with her husband.

"She's—well, she's in a coma, as Molly had told me. One of the doctors said that they don't know what to expect. He just said they're hoping for the best."

"Oh, ok." His tone made it clear that he was disappointed to not hear any new information. Kate realized that it was similar to her own response to Jack at the airport earlier in the day.

"So that's all? Nothing more?" he prompted her.

Kate paused and looked behind her to make sure no one had walked outside. Her voice got quiet as she started to relay the details about seeing Robbie.

"I saw him today, Ethan," she half whispered into the phone. "After *all* these years. Robbie was just standing outside mom's door at the hospital when I first arrived." Kate hesitated just a second then admitted before Ethan could ask her, "It wasn't good."

"Oh, Kate," he replied with a heavy sigh. "What did you do? What did you say to him?"

"Well, we did exchange a few words. There was quite a bit of yelling—until a nurse interrupted us, anyway, which was probably a good thing."

"Kate..." he only had to say her name in a sigh; she could tell what was behind it.

"I know, Ethan, I know. And I *could* see that he's as upset about Mom as we all are." Kate tried to laugh, but it came out like a snort. "Small justification, I guess."

"I'm sorry you had to see him already, though."

"I knew I would at some point, right? Anyway, I'm heading back to the hospital first thing tomorrow with Molly. Hopefully, we'll get some better news then."

Even as the words came out, Kate heard the false ring of positivity in her own voice and wondered if Ethan had also heard.

"Alright, but please call me right after you see her again tomorrow, ok? Let me know what's going on there." He then added as an afterthought, "And say hello to Molly and Jack for me, okay?"

"I will. Well, I should go back in and help with dinner clean-up. It looks like they have their hands filled here with the girls." She paused then blurted out, "It's kind of nice though, Jack. It's odd, but it looks like a real home here."

"Well those are words I certainly never expected to hear come out of Kate Harriman's mouth," he said wryly.

Just then, Kate heard a low "Psst" and turned to see Molly's head peeking around the porch door.

"I was just checking to make sure you were okay out here," she said. "And if that's still Ethan, tell him we said hi," she added quickly before ducking back inside.

Kate nodded her head and ended her call with Ethan with promises to call back.

Molly had a huge grin on her face as she slipped back into the house. She had overheard Kate's last comment to Ethan about their home and family. When she stepped inside, she gave a small shout and clapped her hands in front of her. Jack and the girls looked up at her questioningly then went back to their game of Candyland. She smiled back and continued cleaning the kitchen and humming a song, for once not thinking about the pain and craziness inside her own head.

34. ANOTHER SURPRISE

AS SOON AS SHE HUNG up with Ethan, Kate was angry with herself for not sharing with him all of the emotions that she'd been dealing with. She was angry for not telling him about the emotional time she'd spent with her mother. And she was angry for telling him to stay home.

Next, she called Tom, her father, though—of course—she only reached his voicemail. She tried to keep the irritation out of her voice as she left a message. She then texted Sam at the office to tell him that she was okay and promised to call back as soon as she returned. She was about to head back inside when her phone beeped with a new text. She glanced down, expecting it to be from Ethan again, but saw an unknown number and an odd text.

"Katie, is this u? Sorry abt ur mom. Meet me at Perch tonite? 9:00?"

Kate had no idea who could know that she was back in Wellington. She foolishly glanced around, as if the person who had sent the message would be standing nearby, then immediately texted back.

"Who is this?"

After a few long minutes of waiting in the cool darkness on the porch, the reply came.

"Curt."

For the second time that day, Kate felt like the wind had been knocked out of her.

Curt was her old college flame and an all around great guy. They had dated for a few years. They had also had some *great* sex, and some good times together, but that was a long while ago. *Why is he texting me, and how in the hell does he know I'm even here?* They had barely talked in the twenty years since they parted ways.

Trying to decide how to reply, Kate remembered the good times they had shared. Curt was happy with life and either didn't want or didn't need anything more. He was also one of the few guys she'd ever known who had talked longingly of having a family and children someday. For a driven young woman with big dreams in her head and dollar signs in her eyes, that was enough to end their relationship after just a few years. They'd shared passion, though; they'd made more memories in the bedroom than out of it. He was good in bed—he'd proven that much night after night—but he'd never shown enough interest in a career for Kate's liking, so she'd ended the relationship before graduation.

For a while after college, Curt had sporadically kept in touch with her by email. Eventually, though, life moved on and they went their separate ways. They both got married, Curt years before Kate. A few years ago, Kate saw on Facebook that he had updated his relationship status to "single." When she'd clicked on his page out of curiosity, it didn't look from the pictures as if he'd had any children. This had surprised her as much as the divorce. He was such a fun-loving, happy-go-lucky guy that she always thought he would make a great father and husband.

God, he was a good lay, she smiled and tried not to feel guilty at the thought of all those nights—and many days—in his dorm room, exploring every inch of each other's bodies. These days, she only thought of Curt when pleasuring herself and shook the steamy memories from her head, feeling a measure of guilt.

Kate remembered that she had mentioned Curt to Ethan early in their relationship—one of those nights when new partners tell each other about their sexual encounters in the past. Of course, Ethan's conservative list of partners had paled in comparison to Kate's dozen or so emotionless conquests and short-term relationships; she had opted to pare down her list so as not to scare Ethan off. Since then, there had never been cause to talk about Curt.

Before common sense could prevail, Kate let her curiosity get the best of her and responded with, "Sure—c u then." Then she hustled back into the house to a scene that was quite different than the one she had left. The kitchen was fairly clean, and counter space was visible. The dirty dishes were gone, the sink rack was full of drying pots and pans, and the dishwasher hummed quietly in the background. The plethora of toys that had covered the floor before were—mostly—picked up and put away, and clothes were folded and sorted into piles in the basket.

Hearing the muffled giggles of children coming from the living room, Kate walked around the corner to see Molly and Jack awkwardly entangled on the floor with Alice and Emma between them. It took Kate a moment to figure out that they were playing some kind of game. Walking closer to peer over the couch, Kate saw a Twister mat on the floor. The four of them were laughing and so intertwined on the mat that they didn't notice her standing there.

She looked around the room for a clock before remembering that she still had her phone in her hand. Glancing down, she saw that it was just after eight o'clock. Just then, the phone pinged indicating an incoming text, and Curt's response appeared on the screen, "Super! C u soon."

Molly's head popped up around Jack's arm at the sound of the ding, and she smiled warmly, her face reddened by the exertion of the game. "Oh, hi, Kate!"

"I'm—ah—going out to meet an old friend for a drink, if that's okay. I know you all go to bed early, so hopefully..." her voice trailed off.

Molly and Jack looked at each other in their knotted positions on the Twister mat. Then Jack blurted out with a mock angry look on his face.

"Sure, go out! I guess Twister isn't exciting enough for you."

"Jack!" Molly laughed and swatted at his arm, causing both of them to topple over on the play mat. The kids then followed suit, and all four of them rolled around the mat laughing loudly.

Unable to judge whether or not she was being taunted by them both, Kate continued with her excuse to head out.

"I just haven't seen her in a long time, you know, and well—while I'm here…" she stopped there, not wanting to say more and further incriminate herself in her little white lie.

"Kate, I was just teasing you. Yes, go out. We'll all be getting ready for bed soon, anyway." Jack looked at Molly for backup, feeling a little chagrined.

"Yes, Jack was just teasing," Molly assured her, as her face shadowed over. "We'll have time together tomorrow."

No one said anything for a moment. Then Molly interrupted the silence.

"Don't worry about locking up when you leave. I'll have breakfast ready in the morning around eight," Molly, ever the caregiver, said. She then turned to Jack and rapped his arm again.

"Thank you. I'll see you in the morning, then. Bye, girls."

Kate turned to leave amidst cries of "No!" from both Alice and Emma. But hearing Molly's next question stopped her short.

"Which friend are you meeting up with, anyway? Do I know her?" Molly asked with a total absence of guile in her voice.

"No, she's… uh… just here working for a few months, and she heard I'd come up for a few days," even as Kate rolled out the lie, she hated herself for it. "We're going to head into town for a coffee or something."

"Coffee at night? You do like the stuff. Okay, well have fun," Molly accepted Kate's answer without question and turned back to the kids who were still lying on the mat. She tickled them both.

This may be one lie I'll have to remember, Kate thought as she ran downstairs to grab a quick shower. A half hour later, freshly scrubbed and brushed, Kate snuck out while everyone was busy upstairs getting ready for bed.

As she drove toward the Pelican Perch on the other side of town, she tried to figure out how Curt had learned that she was in Maine. *I only landed this morning, for heaven's sake. I guess news still travels fast in a small town.*

Lost in her thoughts, she wound the rental car along the narrow back roads. She'd forgotten how dark it got at night in Maine. With few street lamps on the road to light the way, she sped along in almost total blackness, the only light coming from the SUV's headlights. A few other cars passed by here and there on the road, but for the most part it was eerily dark and quiet.

Just as she looked down to note the time and her speed, she saw bright blue lights in the rearview mirror. As always, her stomach did a flip and she swore loudly.

"For God's sake, can this day get any worse?" she lashed out as she slowed down and pulled to the side of the road.

As a hard-ass attorney, she had to laugh at seeing her hands shake with nervousness as she pulled her license and registration out of her wallet. Even though she knew it was coming, when she heard the sharp tap on her window, she jumped in her seat. Her nerves were frayed and as she rolled down the window and looked up, she hoped she didn't look guilty of anything other than speeding. Attempting to put a smile and an appropriate look of innocence on her face, she squinted up at the officer through the flashlight shining in her face.

When the light came down, both Kate and the policeman standing next to her exclaimed in unison, "Oh, it's you!"

They both laughed, and then the slightly overweight uniformed officer standing next to her car said in a booming voice, "Katie Harriman! I didn't know you was in town!"

She smiled up at him, trying not to laugh at his lack of proper grammar. She stared back at an older version of a face she knew well from grade school, a face that was unmistakable even with the signs of aging. Seeing her old friend's name on the badge— Billy Benton—brought back childhood memories of the two of them playing hide-and-seek in the woods across from her house and finding frogs in the pond behind his. Billy was her next-door neighbor growing up; they used to play every day after school before it got to be awkward that they were not of the same sex. By junior high, he was as popular in his own crowd as she was in hers, and he turned into a decent guy. As they found their own circles, though, their friendship became limited to waves in the hall and passing conversations on bus rides home.

She could see that he hadn't changed much at all since then—besides the telltale "donut" paunch that small town cops often seem to acquire—and she knew that she could have picked him out of anywhere. Kate saw the same boyish look on his face and crooked grin that she remembered from their childhood days and smiled up at him with a small shake of her head.

Billy was always everybody's good guy, and she wondered if being a policeman had toughened him up at all. Picturing Billy roughing up a perp was almost laughable. Kate wondered briefly if he had ever even had to pull out his firearm in the line of duty—*probably not,* she thought. "Hi, Billy. Yes, I uh, just flew up today."

Kate waited for him to say something appropriate, though awkward and uncomfortable, about her mother. But when he didn't, she was grateful that perhaps *all* news didn't travel so fast.

"Well, that's great. It's good to see you here! You livin' down in the South as some big-ass attorney, I hear?" he asked with a chuckle.

She inwardly cringed at the description, though she knew that Billy meant nothing by it. She answered him with a small smile. "Yes, I'm in Georgia, just up for a few days. I'm headed to the Perch now to meet up with an old friend."

It occurred to her, then, that he knew something about her life, though she had not known anything of his, even that he'd chosen the life of law enforcement. She'd forgotten that Wellington was a small enough town that everyone knew something about everyone else here. *That's just one of the many reasons you left, girl.*

"Well, listen, Kate, I don't want to harass an old friend, but you was going almost sixty and it's forty-five through here, so you need to slow down, ok? I'll let you go, seeing as how you're up here visiting. But you drive more careful, you hear?"

"Yes, of course. Thanks, Billy. I just forgot the roads," she replied with a heartfelt smile. "Thank you, really."

Billy handed back her license and registration card. Kate noted with some satisfaction as she rolled up the window that this was the first time she'd ever been pulled over and *not* been issued a ticket. *Maybe it does pay to know people. I guess that's one advantage of living in a small town.*

He rapped lightly on the car window again then gave her a rather formal salute and waved her on. As she slowly pulled back onto the road—using her turn signal—Kate thought to herself with out-of-character optimism that maybe, just maybe, things would turn out okay.

35. SEEING CURT AT THE PERCH

APPROACHING THE PELICAN PERCH A few moments later, Kate realized—with even more disdain for small town living—why the roads had been so empty. The parking lot outside of the bar was jammed full; there was hardly a vacant spot to be seen.

She saw that the place still looked much the same. It was an old wooden structure with a few domestic beer signs hanging near the front door and a lot full of Ford cars and Chevy trucks. The Perch was one of the few places for miles that stayed open past midnight. Kate thought that this was the only reason it had stayed in business over the years. Kate knew that her out-of-state plates may be the only ones in the entire lot and laughed out loud. The Perch had a "locals only" vibe.

Just as she remembered, she could hear loud music rumbling from inside, even with her windows rolled up. As she parked and exited the car, the sound of the music was as loud and obnoxious as it used to be. Well, *I guess some things just never change.*

Stepping inside the bar felt like walking into another world after so many years of living the sheltered, cosmopolitan, and classy life in Brookside. Loud country music blared from a band in the back corner, and clouds of smoke from the barely separated "Smoking Allowed" section filled the air. A line of pool tables sat in the center of the hall; faded jeans and t-shirts surrounded them all. The walls of the bar were decorated with rows of license plates, old deer heads, and an assortment of car paraphernalia.

Kate scanned the room for signs of Curt, not knowing quite how to find someone whom she hadn't seen in years. But apparently she didn't look any different or she stood out as a stranger, for she soon heard her name called out.

"Katie. Kate, hey, over here!"

She looked toward the direction of the voice and saw Curt sitting comfortably on the edge of his bar stool. He held a beer in one hand, and the other beckoned for her to come over. He had a huge smile plastered on his face.

Kate could see right away that he had grown up from a cute but gangly college boy into quite a handsome man. Strong looking and a little weathered, with unkempt hair that seemed almost wild on his head, he was clad in khakis, Vans sneakers, and a plaid button-down shirt. His stature and good looks definitely made him stand out in the crowd. As Kate stood there, feeling like a worn-out woman, she hesitated for a moment before approaching Curt at the bar.

He pointed to Kate with a nod of his head and smiled at another woman who attempted to approach him as he waved her off. Even from across the room, Kate could see the carefree ruggedness about him that she remembered. The sight of him brought back memories of their fun and wild days together.

Well, let's see what he thinks of me after all these years.

She started to walk toward him rather tentatively, but just as Molly had hours before, Curt jumped right up and quickly covered the distance between them. He picked her up, swung her full around—eliciting a squeal from her that she couldn't contain—and set her back down in a big bear hug. When he finally pulled back to look her over, he nodded his head up and down a few times as if he approved.

"Katie, girl, you haven't changed a bit. Damn, you look good, woman!" He drawled out the last word a little too long, making Kate blush and pull slightly away.

"Thanks, Curt. So do you," she said, feeling quite uncomfortable now that she stood before him.

She started to wonder if she'd done the right thing by meeting him and couldn't remember at that point why she had even agreed to it in the first place.

Curt must have seen her hesitance; he grabbed her by the shoulders and shook her just a little. "Uh-oh. What is it? You don't look like the fiery girl I once knew," he replied. He then stopped short and looked at Kate more seriously, as if waiting for her to respond. "Are you okay?"

When she didn't answer, he cocked his head and blurted out, "Kate, I know, I'm sorry. I heard about your mom. I'm very sorry. I know she's in the hospital now, but that's all. Is it serious?"

The concern in Curt's voice came out loud and clear. As Kate looked into his eyes, she felt her heart tighten at the passage of time and all that may be lost.

She couldn't tell from his face if he knew what had actually happened, but the disquieting look in his eyes was enough. She slumped down on the closest bar stool with a hand on the bar to steady herself. Her head started to spin. She questioned her decision to meet him, she worried about her mother, and she thought of the past; it was all suddenly too much to handle. It took every ounce of strength she had not to break down in the middle of the bar in front of all the strangers and—worse—before Curt, someone who had known her better than almost anyone else. She looked up at him with pleading eyes, and he instantly handled the situation, just as she remembered he could.

Curt nodded his head to a waitress standing nearby and in a sweeping move, scooped Kate under his arm. He ushered her to a private table at the back of the bar. The waitress brought over two draught beers and set them down on the table before quickly moving away with averted eyes. After allowing her the time he knew she needed, Curt reached across the table, took Kate's chin in his hands, and forced her to look up at him. "Kate, you don't have any control over what has happened here. You just need to take things one day at a time right now."

She understood then that he knew exactly what her mother had done. Her heart sank. When she didn't respond, he continued talking. "Life is not always easy, and sometimes we just need to let it go. I know that's difficult for you. I remember what a strong will you have—Kate Harriman, the woman who was hell-bent on going places in life and making something of herself. Oh, I remember!"

Kate smiled a little then cocked her head to one side and tried to make light of the situation. "Yeah? When did *you* get to be so old and wise?"

"The day that *I* learned to just let things go, that's when," he said, letting go of her face to take her hands in his own and setting back against the bench. "Kate, life just doesn't always work out the way we want it to. It's how we handle it that defines who we are, though."

"Yeah, what fortune cookie did you get that out of?" Kate tossed back at him, still trying to use sarcasm as a shield.

He continued as if she hadn't said a word, "Look, I know you probably have a high-powered career and have learned a lot living in the big city down there in Atlanta. But you don't always have to make a lot of money or go far away from home to learn some valuable lessons in life."

Eyes downcast, she thought about what he said for a moment as they sat together in, of all places, a loud and crowded country western bar. As his words slowly sunk in, she looked back up at her college friend, this past lover sitting before her, and was met with an odd and startling image. With the way Curt was seated, the hanging bar light behind him gave him an almost angelic, halo-like glow. The sight made her gasp; she thought of the nun who had walked in front of her just a few hours earlier. For just a moment Kate wondered if this was the sign from God that she had asked for, but then she chided herself for the foolish thought with a shake of her head.

Like God is going to talk to me in such an unholy place as the Pelican Perch, she thought as she laughed out loud at her own crazed idea.

"Hey, I'm being serious here, Kate. What's up with the chuckles, girl?" he looked wounded.

In that moment, his obvious hurt, the angelic image, and the smoky bar were too much for Kate. As Curt fidgeted in his seat, the halo that had surrounded his head seemed to shimmer and shake, and the absurdity of the moment took hold. Not being able to handle the slew of emotions that swarmed inside of her,

Kate began to laugh. And though she tried to respond to him in between her giggling fits, to reassure him that she wasn't mocking him, she couldn't seem to stop. Finally, holding her side from the effort and wiping tears from her eyes, Kate looked up at him and saw the offended look still hanging on his face. She reached across the table to squeeze his hand.

"Curt, I'm sorry," she said, between fits of giggles. "I promise, I was *not* laughing at you. This has just been a tough few days. I don't know what to think anymore! I'm sure you are right, though. Letting go is just not something I've ever been very good at."

He gave her an odd look, but she barely noticed. She picked up her beer and proffered a toast "to getting older and letting go," which he accepted with a genuine smile and joined in her toast. For the first time since she'd arrived, Kate had been able to forget for just a few moments why she had returned to Maine.

The rest of their evening passed by quickly. They moved to the back of the bar farther away from the band that still played on into the night and had two more draught beers, reminiscing about the old days like old friends. Curt brought up one night that they partied at the local fraternity houses, when a few of the frat boys ate goldfish out of a children's pool. They laughed and talked longingly about younger times.

A few times, Curt made an off-color remark about the way things used to be between them—the passion she had showed, even as a young woman. Such memories brought heavy color to her cheeks as she sat before him. She couldn't blame him, though. They'd experienced many steamy times together—exploring each other and themselves in total abandonment—and it was one of the most carefree times of her life. He even brought up their failed attempt to have sex in his dorm room closet and how upset he was that he couldn't play hockey for weeks after due to the broken arm. They both laughed at the memory.

As Kate glanced around at the other patrons in the bar, she realized how much she stood out. With her urban style of dress and an obviously fit body, she was clearly not one of the locals anymore. She thought she even saw a hint of pride in Curt—or was it cockiness—sitting across from her.

Keeping things in check the way she knew she should, she flirted with Curt a little, though not too much. As he was a single guy again, Kate was well aware that Curt did not have the same limitations as she did. She did her best to keep their conversation light and redirected him away from any additional talk about their sexual past.

Curt was not hesitant to open up to her about his life, though. He told her about his short-lived marriage, then asked Kate about hers. Kate was careful talking about Ethan to a past lover. She deftly moved the conversation to her work and talked to him instead about what life was like as an attorney and all the reasons why she loved her job. She talked freely and without censorship about her accomplishments and aspirations, while Curt sat and listened attentively. He nodded his head encouragingly, and Kate shared more about herself than she had in a very long time. She laughingly admitted that her social life was scant, as she didn't have time for much else beyond her work. At some point she let her words trail off, worried that she had said too much.

As their conversation began to wind down, Kate felt Ethan's absence more and more and she couldn't recall in that moment why she had forbidden him to come home with her. Seeing Curt again reminded her of all of the reasons why she'd known that he wasn't the right one for her back then—and why Ethan truly was.

She missed her husband more than she could have expected, and in that flash of understanding, Kate realized something about her mother, something that she had never thought of before.

Did Mom take to Robbie after being married to my father the same way. Was it because Robbie was so different from Dad that she was drawn to him? I never thought about her and her life like that.

"Hey, Kate! What's going on up there in that mind of yours?" Curt snapped his fingers in the air between them with a small smile.

Kate sighed in resignation. Curt was a great guy back then and still was, perhaps even better now with some maturity and experience under his belt. She knew it wouldn't take him long to find someone new. She still missed her husband and understood that seeing Curt like this was the best thing she could have done to realize that. Kate looked directly at him and smiled back.

"Nothing. I am just experiencing my umpteenth epiphany of the last few days, that's all," she gave him another half-smile.

"Your what? Oh, never mind… listen, I'd really like to get together again. How long are you up here for?" he asked her hopefully.

"Oh, sorry. I leave the day after tomorrow—first thing in the morning. It was a quick visit, just to be here—you know—for Mom." A shadow passed over her face.

With the mention of her mom's name, the mood shifted and Curt sighed as he stood up from the barstool. "Okay, well, let's get you home then. It's getting late, and I'm sure you're tired."

Then he stopped short and looked pointedly at her, "Oh, I almost forgot. My Mother asked if she could see you. Is it okay if she gives you a call in the morning?"

"Sure, um, do you know why? I mean, I loved your mom, but we haven't exactly spoken in a long time," Kate replied.

"I know. She just said something about wanting to talk to you about *your* mother, though."

"Oh? Well, okay, sure. I'll head back to the hospital around ten with Molly, so maybe have her call me before then?"

She knew that Lena and her mother had talked a few times while she and Curt had dated. But she had no idea what Lena could have to say to her about her mother now. Though Kate had to admit, she didn't know much about her mother's life at all these days. *If I did, I may have at least seen this coming,* she thought bitterly once again. Then she asked Curt again, "And you don't know why she wants to see me?"

"No, she said something like, 'I have to tell her something she needs to hear.' You know how dramatic my mother can be, though, so who knows."

"Okay, just give her my number," Kate replied, unable to keep the concern out of her voice.

As they left the bar, Kate allowed Curt to pick up the bar tab without making it a big deal. She was pleased with herself for relinquishing control and letting him pay.

They left the Perch and Curt spotted her SUV right away—her eyes scanned the lot, noting that it was indeed the only foreign-made vehicle there. He walked her over to it in silence. Kate knew she was overtired and groggy from the beers and hoped she wouldn't fall asleep on the drive back to Molly's house.

When they neared the SUV, Curt surprised her by moving in close. Before she knew what was happening, he pushed her gently yet firmly against the SUV then quickly lowered his head to hers. His hard lips were on her mouth, moving, exploring, and she could feel every inch of his muscular frame as his taut body pressed against her. She sensed his growing excitement as her clouded mind tried to register the reality of what she felt. In that moment, all of the emotion of the day came pouring forth, and before she realized it, Kate found herself kissing Curt back with a fierceness that wasn't her own. In a moment of abandonment, her mouth sought solace in his as her heart cried out for love.

Just as his arms encircled her body, though, her mind snapped into action and she extracted herself from his embrace, abruptly pulling away. Unconsciously wiping her mouth with the back of her hand, she tried to move back, yet still caught against the SUV she had no place to go. She looked up at Curt, pleadingly.

"Curt, I didn't—I mean—you know, I wasn't trying to lead you on," she said quickly, then placed her hands on his chest as if to hold him back from swooping in on her again.

He took a quick step back and dropped his hands by his sides, "Kate, I'm so sorry. I don't know what that was for. Old times sake, I guess?" he said in an attempt to make light of the moment.

Kate looked up at him, not knowing what to say and grateful to be away from his touch. Her eyes must have portrayed all of her uncertainty and sadness even in the darkness outside the Perch, because Curt's voice was apologetic and contrite.

"You are a beautiful woman, Kate, and we used to have something. But I honestly didn't intend for anything like that to happen tonight. I didn't. I don't know what came over me." With downcast eyes, he moved away from her and kicked at the dirt in self-reproach.

Kate stepped toward him, tentatively putting a hand on one arm.

"It's okay. You're not so bad looking yourself," she teased him, trying to alleviate the compunction that he was so obviously feeling. "And we did have something… *once.* But thank you for understanding that that was then and this is now."

"I just don't know why—and I won't be an asshole and try to use beer as an excuse," he said, trying to alleviate the awkward situation.

"Hey, it's okay. Things happen," she admitted. "Sometimes you don't have control over them, right? Isn't that what you just told me?"

She offered him another small smile when he didn't say anything. She felt bad for him, seeing him standing there with his hands thrust in his pockets and head hung down. He looked like a perp caught with his hands in the register and she held no malice toward him.

"That's not exactly what I meant, Kate," he replied with a small grin. "But thank you. I really am sorry."

They exchanged a brief, awkward hug, and Kate told him to stay in touch as she scuttled away and climbed into the SUV. She peeked at the clock and was shocked to see that it was after midnight. *No wonder I'm so beat.*

She drove back to Molly's, mindful of the speed limit, especially with a few beers in her system. It was her mind, instead, that raced through what had just happened with Curt.

Still shocked at Curt's kiss, and more importantly at her brief but passionate response, she tried to think if she had led him on in any way. But with a muddled mind and a twisted heart, she couldn't determine where things had gone wrong.

Finally, without any answers, she pushed aside any thoughts of their brief encounter in an act of self-preservation—she had experienced enough emotions for one day. Kate turned her thoughts instead to Curt's mother and her request to meet up. Desperate to find out what Lena wanted to talk to her about, she wished it wasn't too late to call tonight and wondered if she'd be able to wait until tomorrow to find out.

Fortunately, the drive back to Molly's was uneventful, and the house was still when she quietly walked in. A variety of smells still hung in the air, but all was calm. She tiptoed downstairs to the guest bedroom, kicked off her boots, and lay down on the bed. It took every ounce of self-control she had not to phone Curt's mother right then and demand to know why she wanted to meet with her. Pushing the phone out of her reach on the bed, she stared at the ceiling in uncertain desperation.

As she sat up up to take off her clothes and get ready for bed, she noticed a piece of paper at the edge of the bed. She reached over and grabbed it. The words scribbled on it made her heart lurch.

"Doctor called tonight. Mom's the same—no update." Kate's heart sank, and the guilt of the evening came up like bile in her throat.

There was a small frown face and an "M" underneath the one line on the paper. A line that could have brought hope for the future but instead added another hardened layer onto her heart.

As she sat alone, crazy images from the past and the present lurched inside her head—her mother in the hospital bed, Ethan when they first met, Emma and Alice playing in the yard, Curt as an angel hovering from above.

Eventually, still dressed and smelling of bar room smoke, Kate reached over to turn off the light and closed her eyes against the world.

36. MEETING LENA

THE NEXT MORNING, KATE WAS awakened, not by the pitter-patter of feet as she'd expected, but by the ding of a text. She fumbled for the phone on the dresser in her hazed state. The message read, "It's Lena. Could we get together this morning?"

With a quick glance at the phone's clock, Kate noted that it was only seven–thirty.

"Ahhh," she groaned and grabbed her head. She had expected to hear from Curt's mom, but not by text and not so early! With another groan, she texted her response, "Sure, Lena. Where? When?"

Kate had barely swung her legs off the side of the bed before Lena wrote back.

"Café Crème on Front Street, 8:30?"

Kate was anxious to learn why Lena wanted to meet up, and she knew the time until they met would not pass by quickly enough. She was so anxious that the name of the breakfast café did not even register in her fogged mind. Kate agreed with a quick "okay" text, and despite her hangover, she glanced longinly at the cross-trainers that lined her suitcase. As she quickly undressed and stepped into the shower, Kate knew that she wouldn't have time for a run. She also suspected that even if she did have time, she wouldn't have the energy.

It wasn't until she got dried and dressed and had hastily applied eyeliner and mascara that she noticed the list of phone messages on her cell. All had come in while she and Curt were at the Perch the night before. Her phone hadn't been on silent, but the music had been too loud to hear the ringtone.

"Damn, why can't I keep up with this?" she mumbled, hating the responsibility of getting back to everyone with updates that she didn't have.

Seeing her father's name first, she called him before she realized that he would probably still be asleep. But for once, he answered after just a few rings, much to her surprise.

"Hey, Kate. What's going on up there?" he asked in a sleepy voice.

"Hi, Tom. I saw Mom yesterday, though she doesn't at all look like herself. I don't know any more yet… it was hard."

"I'm sure, Kate. I know you're strong, though. Just be there for your mother now. That's all you can do right now." He echoed the words Marge had said to her the night before.

Before she realized what she was saying, Kate blurted out the question to him that had weighed on her soul for so many years. "Tom, why did you leave Mom like that?"

She knew she had caught Tom off guard; the silence on the phone was louder than any words either of them could have said. Though Kate already knew the answer to her question—about Tom's affair—she just wanted to hear her father admit to what had happened.

"Kate, that was a long time ago…"

"I know, but why? What the hell happened between you two?"

"We were very young, Kate, and things weren't easy. Your mother and I just grew apart."

Kate paused before asking her father the question that had scoured her mind for years, "Yeah, but why did you do that to her?"

She heard Tom catch his breath on the other end, and for a moment she felt remorse for asking the question. But remembering the reason she was in Maine and how she had seen her mother yesterday quickly dispelled her regret.

"Kate, I don't need to explain my life to you. I've made mistakes just like everyone else, including you. I may not have always been right in my choices, but it was my life to live." Tom's tone was lined with defensiveness and tinged with anger.

"That may be true, Tom, but I was in it too you know."

He paused and then sputtered something out about needing to end their call. He made her promise to call him again, though, before saying goodbye.

Kate hung up with a heavy sigh. Though as soon as the call ended, she realized that, once again, she hadn't even thought to ask him about his back or how he'd been feeling after his surgery. *Shit, who is worse—me for being a lousy daughter who holds a grudge for twenty years or him for cheating on my mother?* Without having an answer, she hurried upstairs to see who was awake... and to get a much needed cup of coffee. At first, she was surprised to see Jack standing in the kitchen, but then she remembered that it was the weekend and he would be off from work. He nodded to her with a short smile before donning his Columbia jacket and old work gloves and darting outside. She looked out the window and saw the kids already playing in the yard, both bundled up against the October cold.

Well, that explains why the girls didn't wake me up.

"Good morning, Kate."

Molly's voice startled her. Kate turned to see her sister lying on the living room couch with an Afghan blanket covering her. Molly looked so pale that Kate involuntarily took a step back; sickness was a form of weakness that she had little tolerance for. The few times Ethan had been down with the flu, she'd avoided him like the plague.

"Uh, are you not feeling well, Molly?"

"No! No, I'm just laying down for a bit," she retorted a little too forcibly. "I sent the kids out back to play so you could get some sleep this morning, but you're up awfully early. Are we going to try to head to the hospital together later this morning?"

Kate nodded, but she only half-listened to her sister's words; she was too disturbed by what she saw before her. Molly had dark circles under her eyes and a haggard look that didn't match her smile. Her face was worn, but it was her eyes that concerned Kate; they held no warmth or life. *Shit, she looks worse than I feel,* Kate thought.

Kate hesitated before deciding not to ask Molly what was wrong, again, and upset her or the morning. Instead, she opted instead to inquire about the coffee that she so desperately needed to start off the day, since it didn't look like a run would be happening before her early meeting with Lena.

"Is there—ah—is there any coffee made, Molly?" she asked with a jerk of her head to the kitchen.

"Yes, I hope so. I told Jack to be sure to save you some."

Molly tossed off the blanket and got up from the couch, slowly ambling toward the kitchen. Watching her move like an old woman, Kate knew in her gut that something was wrong. She headed to the kitchen, but before she could figure out how to formulate another question, Molly threw Kate off with a question.

"Hey, how was your friend last night? Jack and I didn't even hear you come in."

Kate's spoon stopped stirring her coffee. Without turning around, she stammered a hasty reply for Molly before changing the subject.

"Oh, good, good. It was good to catch up... By the way, do you know any of Mom's friends? A woman named Lena?"

Molly, always the Mom, had been keeping an eye in the direction of the kids in the yard. She hadn't noticed Kate's abrupt change of subject.

"Lena? Of course, she and Mom have gotten close these last few years. Lena moved in just a few houses down from them a few years back, you know. I've met her a few times. I actually called her the other day to ask if she'd talked to or heard from Mom, right before I called you." She paused "Why, how do *you* know her?"

"Oh, well, I used to know her son. Back in undergrad," Kate blew off her response with a shrug of nonchalance. "I asked because she texted me this morning. That's why I woke up. She wants to meet with me. Do you find that at all strange?"

"Huh? Yeah, I guess, but..." Molly cut her sentence short. "For heaven's sake, where is Jack?" She jumped up from the couch as she ran to the window and threw it open, "Alice, Emma! Come back here and stay close to the house, please!"

Molly tossed the words "Hold on" over her shoulder to Kate as she ran out through the back door calling out to the girls, "Hey, you two know you need to stay near the house and not go past the yard!"

Kate glanced outside as she made her coffee and saw Molly chasing Alice and Emma around front, looking more sprite than she had since Kate had arrived. The girls were giggling and laughing, turning their mother's chase into a game. Kate could hear their delighted squeals through the window and see the impish expressions on their faces. Jack joined them in the backyard and began to chase all three of them around in a circle. Molly grabbed at the girls playfully, and they all tumbled to the ground.

Kate watched impassively from inside, feeling like an outsider, like she was a spectator watching a movie. She held onto her coffee cup with both hands and tried not to down the steaming liquid as if it was an elixir of life.

Her cup nearly empty, she quickly made another thermos of coffee to go and scribbled a note to Molly, telling her the time she'd be back from meeting Lena so they could head to the hospital together. Taking one last look outside, she left the note on the corner of the counter for Molly to find. And while everyone was still out back, Kate dashed out the front door to escape, just as she had done her whole life.

Unwilling to take any chances, Kate drove mindfully to the bagel shop downtown. She laughed at how empty the roads were on a Saturday morning compared to busy streets back home in Brookside, yet for once she appreciated the quiet solitude of the country life.

She arrived at the little mom and pop bagel shop a few minutes late. Inside, the smell of coffee and baked goods permeated the air, and Kate's stomach lurched in response. She scanned the busy tables for Lena and almost immediately identified Curt's mother in the corner of the shop. She appeared not to have changed much since Kate's college days. Her perfectly styled hair was piled high on her head. Her clothing showed a preference for bright colors, and her ample bosom was barely contained under her shirt.

She looks so much like Curt, anyway. I'd have recognized her anywhere. She's like a plump, female version of her son, Kate thought wryly.

As Lena jumped up to greet her, Kate saw that her affinity for high-waisted jeans hadn't waned either and smiled inwardly. She and Curt used to laugh at wearing jeans "at her age."

Her defense on the matter was firm and unapologetic, "I may be old, but that doesn't mean I have to dress old!" she'd retort, hiking her jeans up a little further on her waist.

They just rolled their eyes back then, but looking at her now, Kate had to give the woman credit. Lena didn't dress like a grandmother. She remained true to herself, even in a small town where no one could hide. Kate liked people when she respected them, and Lena had earned her respect. Plus, she had always been good to Kate, and she knew Lena was sad when she and Curt went their separate ways. One day, the older woman had jokingly told Kate that if they'd all been living in India she'd have *made* them get married.

As Kate wound her way to Lena's table, she smiled broadly; the good days of college life flooded back in her mind, days that held so much promise and less hate for the world. Lena immediately stood up and gave Kate a big hug. Kate's thin frame was engulfed in Lena's, and a warm maternal feeling settled on Kate, but with it came sadness. Feeling that warmth again reminded Kate how nice it would have been if Lena had become her mother-in-law. Ethan's parents had passed away in a car accident a few years before, so she never got to meet them. That, coupled with the difficulties of her distant and difficult relationships with her own parents often made it feel as if they were completely alone.

Having someone like Lena in my life would have been nice, she thought with an unusual touch of sorrow and regret. Then she quickly pushed the moment of weakness away and greeted her old boyfriend's mother.

"Hello, Lena, it's good to see you again."

Lena stepped forward and drew her in for a hug that Kate did her best not to push away from. She felt her thin frame meld into Lena's plump body and for once was not bothered by it.

"Oh, Katie, dear, it's so good to see you, too! You look wonderful," she said before pulling away to give Kate a long once over. "Truly! *Just* as Curt described you."

"What? You two have already talked?" Kate asked incredulously, "But we didn't leave the bar until almost midnight last night."

"Ha, yes! Curt and I have already exchanged a few texts. Now that he showed me how to do that, I just love it. I text him all of the time… he's probably sick of me some days," she said with a knowing wink.

The comment put a bad taste in Kate's mouth as she thought about her own mother and her face immediately turned up in a grimace. She looked away from Lena, nodding in the direction of the coffee bar, so the older woman wouldn't notice.

"Shall we get some coffee then?" Kate asked as she reached for her wallet in her bag. "I'd forgotten how good it always smells in here." She breathed in deeply, noting the sweet smell of baked goods and rich coffees that permeated the air.

But Lena took over and almost pushed Kate into a chair in her haste to take care of things.

"No, dear, you sit down and I'll go order for us," Lena said. She then added in a somber tone, "I'm so thankful to have a little time with you while you're here, even under these circumstances."

Kate sank down somewhat gratefully in her chair. Without asking Kate what she wanted, Lena went to the counter and placed their order. Kate looked over the shop's clientele, half expecting to see a familiar face from her childhood days. She recognized no one, though there were people of all ages eating, talking, and laughing. Most were engaged in conversations, a few worked intently on their laptops or read from Kindles and Nooks, and some sat alone.

I'll bet no one else here is going to the ICU to check on a comatose loved one today, she thought dolefully.

"Here we are!" Lena suddenly appeared before her with two coffees, two croissants and a bagel in hand. She sat down and proceeded to slather butter and cream cheese over her croissants as Kate looked on in disgust and awe at her friend's complete lack of concern for healthy eating.

Kate avoided Lena's probing eyes, but she could feel Lena looking intensely at her before she started firing off questions. Lena demanded to know how Kate was faring given her mom's condition, and she asked about her visit to the hospital. To Kate, it felt like Lena's piercing eyes could bore into her very soul. Kate was usually no-nonsense herself, but Lena's straightforwardness took her by surprise and she caught her breath in her throat.

She knew her face was a traitor to her feelings. Lena recognized it and quickly tried to cover up her probing questions with a reassuring smile and a pat on the arm.

"I'm sorry, sweetie, that wasn't very sensitive of me. This is a difficult time. How *could* you be okay? With your mom in the hospital... I am *so* sorry. Beth is such a dear woman and she's been a good friend to me... well, before all this happened to her."

Lena lowered her head and murmured something under her breath. It took Kate a few seconds to realize that Lena was saying a prayer. Kate held her own breath and looked around at the other people in the restaurant, not knowing what to do. Fortunately, the prayer ended quickly, and when Lena looked up again, she smiled calmly and squeezed Kate's hand tightly.

"Katie, I don't know if you are aware, but your mother and I have been friends for a number of years now. That's why I asked to meet with you," she stopped as if gathering up her courage, before continuing.

"Well, this past year... well, let's just say that we've become close," she paused before continuing, her voice slightly lower. "Close enough to confide things in each other... you know, the way women will do."

Kate heard the words, but in her exhaustion, she couldn't understand what Lena was implying. For just a moment, her thoughts had gone to the gutter, as she thought Lena was going to say that she and her mother had been lovers. *Well, at least I still have my humor.*

"Kate, do you know what I mean?" Lena prompted her, squeezing Kate's hand tighter.

Yet without any girlfriends of her own, Kate really didn't. It reminded her of her early high school days when all the other girls talked about getting their periods, and Kate would laugh and joke along with them even though as a late bloomer she still hadn't started hers and had no idea what they were all talking about.

God, how much personal information do girlfriends divulge to one another? It's been so damn long since I've had one. Unless Sam would count, she mused. Though under the circumstances—he *was* her employee and a younger gay man—she was fairly certain he would not qualify as an actual girlfriend.

When Kate didn't offer a response, Lena continued.

"Well, your mother has been going through a lot lately, you know. What with her anxiety and all…"

"Lena, it seems that everyone up here has been going through a lot, because that's all that I keep hearing."

"Well, it's true. Your mother… and yes, I know, she told me about your sister—well, life's been tough for a lot of people, and that's just the way life is sometimes. But for your mother, it's different…"

Lena paused as if wanting Kate to finish her statement. Kate waited, not knowing what to say, and tried to keep an annoyed look off her face. So used to facts, logic, and detail, Kate found herself becoming increasingly annoyed by Lena's seeming determined ambiguity. She wondered if she could pull her hand out of Lena's sweaty grasp without being rude.

"Oh, Kate, honey, I can see I'm just going to have to come right out and say this…" she continued with a shake of her head. "Do you know anything about your mother's relationship with Robbie?"

"What? What do you mean? About Robbie specifically, or about their *marriage*?"

"Well…" Lena paused then with a heavy sigh pressed on, "I know from things your mother has mentioned that Rob wasn't always very good to you early on. But do you know how *they* have been together? I mean, as a couple?" Lena's voice dropped a full octave with the last line. She stressed the last word. Kate continued to stare back at Lena with a blank look.

Lena tipped her head down and peered up at Kate with her eyebrows arched expectantly. The look on Lena's face implied something big, Kate knew, yet hearing that something was wrong with her mother's marriage was the last thing that she expected.

"Lena, in all of our crazy conversations over the last few years, Beth had never once said anything to me about Rob or their relationship."

Kate had always assumed it was because her mother knew Kate didn't care to hear anything about him that she never spoke of him, *not* because there was something amiss.

"Well, how he treated you growing up was just the start of it all for that bad seed. He's not always been a very good man, I'm afraid."

Kate's face turned white, unsure of just how much of the past Lena actually knew. She held her breath, trying to remember if she could have confided in Lena while she and Curt were dating. She allowed the attorney in her to rear its ugly head and retorted with impatience, "What exactly is it that you trying to tell me, Lena?"

Yet as the words came out, Kate felt fear as she awaited Lena's response. Lena didn't make her wait long.

"You see, Beth wasn't happy with Rob for good reason," Lena said slowly. "Lately, he's been gone too much, doing *a lot* of weekends away, supposedly on fishing trips and camping with guys from work… I mean, c'mon! What kind of guy goes camping with his friends that much?"

Lena made a face at the thought of Rob and crossed her arms over her ample chest for emphasis. She stared pointedly at Kate. It was obvious that she thought Kate would grasp what she was trying to say. However, when Kate just looked back at her blankly, Lena understood that Kate did not and finally blurted out the statement she had been trying to lead Kate to for the past fifteen minutes.

"Katie, dear, that awful man was cheating on your poor mother!" Lena suddenly shrieked.

Kate was dumbfounded, at a complete loss for words. Lena hadn't intended for her words to be that loud, but as most of the patrons' heads turned their way, they both realized that it was.

"Wh- What?" Kate eventually managed to stammer out in return.

Kate was once again at a loss for words. She ducked her head down to take a quick sip of coffee, trying to collect her thoughts and process what Lena had said. Lena in turn had a huge bite of her cream cheese smothered croissant. It left a fleck of creamy white on the side of her mouth that Kate tried not to stare at when she looked back up. Both women sat for a moment in silence; Lena reached over and patted Kate's arm.

It was Kate who found her tongue and asked softly. "Okay, so when exactly did this happen? And for how long?"

"I don't know exactly, but he's been at it for quite a while, I'm afraid."

Of all the things that Kate had thought of, this scenario wasn't one of them. With the hatred of Rob that she had carried around for so many years, she couldn't fathom that there could be *other* women who would be attracted to him. *The idea of jumping into bed with a married man who reeks of fish scales and truck grease was not appealing. Let alone one who likes young girls,* she thought bitterly.

"With who, Lena? Do you know?"

"Not exactly. We think it was one of the floozies from work. It's been going on for a few years. Who knows if there were others, though I wouldn't doubt it."

Lena paused then pushed on, her words gathering speed as they came out.

"Kate, the thing is that your mother recently found out, and I think she just couldn't handle it. That tramp had the nerve to call over at the house one night looking for Rob. She *apparent-ly* thought it was Rob's cell phone. Anyway, when your mother confronted him about it, he didn't even have the decency to deny the affair! I think that was the last straw for her, with all of that anxiousness and sadness that I know she's had going on inside her... I think, I think she just couldn't take any more."

Kate was speechless as she listened to Lena talk on and on about Rob's sexual encounters. Kate could see in her delivery that although Lena hated what had happened to her friend, there was also a part of her that relished having something sordid to talk about in a town where so little excitement occurred. Kate tried not to feel loathing for the woman beside her, knowing she was good at heart.

Rarely in her adult life had Kate ever been at a loss for words. Yet for the third time in three days, it was as if she had forgotten how to speak. As Lena rambled on about Rob's indiscretions, Kate's thoughts chased each other like a cat after its own tail. *First Tom cheats, then Rob? It's no wonder she did what she did...*

"Kate?"

Kate's attention was brought back. She looked at Lena as if seeing her for the first time.

"I hate this for you, dear; I can see how terrible it is. As I always say about life, though, 'It is what it is.' Worry and anger aren't going to change anything. And it's certainly not going to change that bastard of a man she married. But I just thought that you should know what happened to your mother, in case..." But Lena stifled a tear and turned away, unable to finish the sentence.

She reached out to Kate in an attempt to find comfort. Kate willed herself not to pull away. Lena then said something else about being sorry to have to be the one to tell her, but by then Kate's mind was already far away, deliberating in multiple tangents, trying to make sense of how such a tragic thing could have happened to her mother again!

Ever the lawyer and determined to have all the facts, she somehow managed to ask Lena if she was certain about every-thing she'd told her. Lena said yes, that eventually Robby had admitted to having the affair. He'd spilled his guts to Beth and told her everything. It was at that point that Kate decided she'd heard enough. She put on a reassuring face and told Lena that she should be getting to the hospital soon and that she had plans to meet Molly there—their plan to meet back at the house beforehand was all but forgotten. She hurriedly got up to leave, her dry toasted sesame bagel left untouched on the table. Seeing that Lena was upset by their conversation—*I don't know who is worse here, the one who delivered the news or the one it affects!*— Kate attempted to reassure her that she had done the right thing. However, she knew that her body language and her haste to exit made that hard to believe.

As she rushed out, thoughts of her mother living through two marriages with two different men who cheated weighed on her mind. *Apparently, she only had it in her to divorce a husband once, so she chose to stay with Robbie. God, it must have torn her apart.*

Kate fled the café without turning back, leaving Lena calling out after her to take care.

Lena's words were lost in the noisy room. As Kate dashed out the door, the memory of her fleeting kiss with Curt the previous night came flashing back. It left a sour taste in her mouth and an eerie heaviness in her heart.

Kate turned to cross the street and looked back to see if Lena has followed her out. It was only then that she realized that this café had the same name as the place she had met Ethan in Boston years ago—Café Crème. She looked up at the large sign over the door and wondered how she had missed the connection... and what *else* she had missed in her mind-numbing state. Kate frowned and fought back threatening tears as memories of the past fought like demons inside her head. That time was just another point in her life that was fraught with anxiety and pain— and choices—and she resisted the urge to throw up her hands and cry out. Standing there in the middle of the street, staring at the coffee shop, Kate understood why people sometimes did things without thinking through the consequences of their actions. Without concern for others and without hope, they make decisions about life and death that may not be correct but are the only decisions they can clearly see at the time.

A honk from a turning car jarred her out of her thoughts and out of the street; she darted across to the sidewalk and headed toward the safe confines of the SUV.

As Kate sat behind the wheel and stared ahead, yet seeing nothing, she let out a solemn sigh. In that moment, she felt like everything in her life had been yanked away. Forcing back the tears that once again threatened to spill over, she turned the key in the ignition and gunned the engine. A few passersby jumped at the sound of the revving SUV, but Kate hardly noticed as she sped away.

37. THE PAST IS...

IT WAS SEVEN YEARS BEFORE when she first met Ethan, just three months after she had ended things with Jack; shock, dismay and fear were all that Kate could feel inside. The day she left the doctor's office felt as if it was the last day of her life, and the days that followed felt hollow and surreal.

Stunned and in despair, she had walked through the next few weeks like a zombie. She went to work as usual—she was an associate lawyer in the law firm then—and she did her best to continue to process everything as it should be. But she knew that with each passing day, each minute, things were changing more and more. It was gut wrenching to know what she had to do to survive.

She continued to run most mornings, fast and hard. She tried to block out the notion that her body would soon be changing. She tried to run away from everything.

That morning, she'd been out walking for hours, trying to make sense of what had happened and decide how to prepare for the future. By the time she walked into Café Crème, Kate had already made up her mind about what she would do. It quickly became a decision and nothing more, and her resolve to take care of her life firmly set in. She was merely biding her time until the ordeal was over, when her path would reroute itself to the way it was intended to be. With dogged determination, she chose not to ever again think or feel anything about her decision, once the events that could have reshaped her life had passed.

That morning had been terrible, and her life would never be the same, but it was also the morning she had met Ethan. The man who would show her open adoration and a secretive sort of kindness that she had never experienced with another.

When Ethan approached her at the coffee counter, she didn't notice his looks at first. Or his beautiful green eyes. She didn't see his strong features or his sandy-brown hair that looked like it would never disappear. She didn't pay attention to the quiet strength that emanated from within him. Yet for some reason, as the stranger stared at her in a comforting and unalarming way, she ordered her coffee and chose not to send him away. Her mind was still a thousand miles away as she spontaneously asked for two donuts, and when the man began to talk about the origin of coffee beans, she gave him a moment's notice, nothing more.

Any other time, she may have thought that his comments were odd, even a little nerdy. She had been hit on and asked out plenty, so she knew how to handle these situations and could do so swiftly and effectively. However, when he started to explain the process of growing coffee beans and why beans from Panama produced some of the best coffee, at one hundred dollars a pound, she turned to see him. With his eyes slightly downcast, he'd then told her that one very expensive coffee bean out of Indonesia wasn't processed until after it's been eaten and excreted by a palm civet, a small mammal also known as a toddy cat. When he had shaken his head at his own words, his hair had fallen a bit over his eyes, making him look more like a teenager than a grown man.

She had laughed then, more at his boyish looks than his joke. When their eyes met, Kate Harriman realized that there was something different about him; something unique and moving behind his hazel eyes. Eyes that felt as if they could pierce through whatever they gazed upon. She surprised herself by asking him to join her at a table. He had hesitated enough to make her question his interest in her before agreeably following her to a nearby table.

Once they sat down, their conversation had quickly turned from coffee to careers—something they both seemed interested in. He nonchalantly told her what kind of work he did then asked her where she was employed. But as soon as the words left his mouth, her face had clouded over. She had tried so hard not to think too far into the future, but she knew that she would need to move away soon, and she knew that leaving her job would be the only way that she could get through the upcoming months. She needed to be far away from everyone and anyone who knew her. She'd already given her notice at the law firm in town and initiated plans to begin a new life and a new job in Atlanta — once the year had passed. Her references were stellar, so she knew that even if she took the time off, she would find work again in no time. She was just grateful that she'd had enough money already put away to get through it on her own.

So, although it wasn't at all the right time in her life to meet someone new, Kate felt more comfortable than she ever had before with another human being. She enjoyed talking with Ethan, and they stayed at the café for more than two hours, getting to know one another and laughing together. She was relieved to learn that they shared the same political views and fiscal goals. He had attended good schools, secured a decent job, and he dressed well without being garish or over the top. She loved that his leather belt was a shade darker than his Buck shoes and that his shirt didn't look overly ironed, yet didn't have any annoying wrinkles all over it the way bachelor's clothes will do. Overall, she noted that he was a good-looking guy with the right credentials. After just a few hours with him, Kate knew enough to recognize that there was something between them.

As they'd left the shop, she had felt compelled to inform him about her upcoming plans to relocate South, but she quickly followed it up with promises to call and stay in touch. She could read people well enough to see that he was disheartened by the news and didn't believe her promises, yet with her own insecurities about the future, she didn't have it in her to try to reassure him. She had reached out fleetingly to touch his arm. The action had felt odd to her, as she rarely initiated physical contact with others, particularly with strangers, yet it also somehow felt right.

Kate said goodbye and that she hoped to see him again, though even as the words left her mouth she wondered if she was in a position to make such a promise, considering what she had to face in the year ahead.

When they parted ways, she'd walked down the street to her Volkswagen Beetle, and Ethan had headed in the opposite direction. Above all the other memories from that morning, the one she recalls most vividly is when they both turned around, ostensibly to get one last look at each other. Caught in the act, they'd both smiled self-consciously and waved. Kate had stepped into her car, hoping that she would see Ethan Shepherd again… someday, after the horrific ordeal was over and behind her.

PART III

38. SEEING THROUGH ANOTHER'S EYES

MOLLY AND JACK BEGAN THEIR drive to the hospital in silence. They'd once again left the girls under the care of their neighbor, with hurried but sincere promises of doing something nice for her in return as soon as they could.

They decided to take Jack's truck, and Molly had asked him if she could drive to help keep herself occupied on the trip. Jack had obligingly, if awkwardly, moved over to the passenger seat and handed her the keys. He did his best to avoid being a back-seat driver as she drove ten miles below the speed limit down Route One, back to Portland Regional. Molly was upset that Kate hadn't called her yet, and she kept looking down to check her phone screen for the duration of the ride, despite Jack's warnings about taking her eyes off the road.

As they had discussed after Kate woke up, Molly thought they were going to the hospital together. When she read in Kate's note that Kate was heading to meet with Lena first thing, Molly's heart had sank—she had such limited time with her sister during her visit. Now it was already after nine o'clock and Kate hadn't yet contacted her, nor had she answered Molly's repeated texts; Molly stared straight ahead and tried to contain her hurt.

At one point, she reached over to turn the radio on, switched through all the channels, then abruptly turned it off again. As the solitude once more surrounded them, Jack got out his iPhone and started playing one of his racing game apps on it. He alternated between muttering cheers and curses in between the plays. After a few minutes passed, Molly blurted out in frustration.

"Jack! How could you play games at a time like this?!"

Sheepishly, he looked over at her, shrugged his shoulders, and stopped his thumbs moving on the screen. "I'm just trying to pass the time, Hun," he said.

She took a deep breath and sighed.

"I know, I'm sorry. I just can't believe this has happened, you know? It's like, I know I'm going through it, yet at the same time, it just doesn't seem possible."

He reached out and gently squeezed her knee in response.

"I know. I feel the same way. Your mom is a good woman, and she's always treated me like one of her own."

After a few minutes, when Molly didn't add or say more, Jack asked quietly, "Is it okay if I just finish this game?"

Molly rolled her eyes, smiled slightly, and nodded. She thought once again how it often feels like she has three children instead of two. Her girlfriends all said the same, so she knew she wasn't alone. When they got together, they talked about the craziness of raising kids and the trials of living with husbands—both of which were equally difficult on many a day.

Men are just different, Molly, she told herself for the thousandth time as she peered over at Jack playing his game. *And there's no sense in trying to figure it out.*

Jack's voice interrupted her thoughts. "Well, it looks like my phone's out of battery anyway," he said as he moved to put his cell down.

"Oh! I actually picked up another car charger at Target for you the other day. Here," she said as she opened the middle console. "I put it in here. Didn't I tell you?"

"No, I don't think so," he replied, smiling at her just a little— she often forgot to tell him things.

She opened up the console and looked down. She did a double take, though, quickly taking her eyes off the road. For there, sticking out of the compartment was a bright blue ticket that Molly knew very well. She had obligingly dropped off and picked up enough friends at the Portland International Airport over the years to recognize that parking slip anywhere. With two fingers, she picked it up out of the console and brought it in front of her so she could read the time stamp.

It was dated October 6. *Yesterday!*

She looked over at Jack. He was looking straight at her; his face was pale and his lips didn't move.

"Jack, could you tell me what this is for?"

"Molly, I can explain..." his voice trailed off.

With one quick look in the rearview mirror, Molly swerved the car onto the upcoming exit ramp and pulled off the highway. As she slowed down and stopped on the side of the road, Jack spoke quietly, still looking straight ahead.

"Molly, I did that for you. I went to the airport... for you."

Molly turned and faced him squarely in the seat, "Okay, but please explain to me why you happened to be at the airport the day my sister flew in?"

For a moment, emotions played across Jack's face—fear, sadness, and remorse. He drew in a sharp breath before gathering the courage to answer her.

"I just wanted to let her know that this has been a tough time for us... for *you*, before she got to our house," he said again, this time more forcefully.

He stopped and took another deep breath. Molly said nothing, and when he turned and looked at her directly in the eyes, Jack could see that she was waiting for him to go on. But there was something else in her eyes, an expectation of sorts, which compelled him to finally say to her what he had wanted to for so many years.

"Molly, I'm so sorry I never told you before now. There was just never a good time—but before we were married, before I even knew you, I knew Kate..." he spoke hesitantly before his voice trailed off, unable to continue.

He looked over at her, waiting for Molly to say something—anything. But she remained silent, looking down at her hands, which she held tightly in her lap. When she looked back at his face, Jack saw that it still held an eager expression.

"Dammit, Molly, you're not making this easy on me! Your sister and I knew each other a long time ago…" he cut his sentence short then almost shouted out the next. "And we dated briefly! I just never knew how to tell you when I found out that she was your damn sister!"

He looked at her, his face pleading and pained. He waited for the screaming and lashing to begin, but he was unable to read the odd look on his wife's face.

"Well… Dammit! Aren't you going to say something?" he finally demanded. "Don't just sit there without saying *anything* to me."

The desperation in his voice finally brought a small smile to her face. She reached over to him in the confines of the truck and squeezed his hand as she said two simple words.

"I know."

It took a minute for him to comprehend what she had said, before his mouth dropped open in astonishment. After a few seconds, he blurted out, "You what?"

"Jack, I've known about you and Kate for a while now."

Her voice was matter of fact, as if she was telling him about the weather forecast.

"You knew? What the… And… and you never said anything to me?" his voice was incredulous.

"Hey…" she chided him. Then with a tilt of her head she said, "Shouldn't that be my line, Jack?"

"But, how? How did you know? And for how long?"

Jack was in total disbelief. He could tell by his wife's reaction that what she had just told him was undeniably true, yet he couldn't grasp what it meant. He stared back at her dumbfounded, with a mixture of awe and uncertainty. He didn't realize that his mouth was hanging open until she told him to close it. He shook his head and waited for the deluge of anger that he anticipated would follow. However, after she paused for just a moment, Molly spoke in a hushed tone with her head slightly bowed. It was so low that he could barely hear her.

"In your defense, Jack, I think you did try to tell me a few times. When we were still dating… I seem to remember some awkward moments when Kate's name was brought up, but you never seemed to be able to get it out."

Looking back at her, he finally asked softly, "But how did you find out, Molly?"

Then Jack's disbelief slowly turned to relief as his wife told him how she knew. He looked through the side windshield a few times and shook his head in amazement as he listened.

"I found an old race medal of hers in a box one day when I was looking for something in the upstairs closet. There's a picture of the two of you in it. It looked like you guys had just finished the race. You were smiling at each other. There was a note she'd written with it, something about getting pizza and beer after."

Jack sat in silence, taking it in, before finally asking her the big question on his mind.

"And you weren't mad or upset?"

"Jack, I could see from the date of the race that it was well before you and I had met. And... I looked it up online to confirm it," she said with a smile. "I knew that she was already living down in Brookside when you and I had started dating, so there wasn't much to worry about... Was there?"

Jack smiled at his wife; she *really* was an amazing woman. He stared at her a minute then blurted out one last question.

"But I still don't understand—why haven't you said anything all these years?" he asked incredulously.

She just cocked her head, and he knew that it was he who should have said something.

He said nothing at first; he just reached out and grabbed her hand. "Molly, I wanted to tell you the moment I realized you were sisters. There was just never the right time to say it. At first, I thought I would risk losing you. You and she haven't exactly been best friends, as you know. Then, as time went on, the girls came, then your mom started getting worse... then *you* started feeling bad..." his words trailed off, but she allowed him to continue.

Molly squeezed his hand and offered a smile. "It's okay."

"Shit, how do you think *I* felt about it? I didn't even *know* that Kate was your sister until even after you and I were engaged!"

"I guess that means she never talked about me, huh?" Molly said ruefully once the full meaning of his words settled in.

He ran a hand through his hair and exhaled loudly, knowing how much his wife wanted to have a connection with her sister—a woman who just happened to be his ex-girlfriend! The day that Molly brought up her sister's name and he realized that it was the same woman he'd dated before, he had silently asked for the earth to open and swallow him whole.

Molly interrupted his thoughts of the past with one question, "So, I still don't understand. Why *did* you meet her at the airport yesterday?"

"Ironically, it was just to let Kate know that I'd never told you that we had dated," he quickly replied with a contrite look. He then added, "And she was equally pissed off at me, if you can imagine."

"Oh, I have no doubt," Molly smiled.

"It's just not like you two were—are—close."

"Yes, I know," she replied sarcastically. She let out a big sigh.

Then with eyes downcast she responded gently, choosing each word carefully as she spoke. "Thank you, Jack, for telling me the truth. You could have lied, you know, and you didn't." She looked over at him and continued with a small grin, "Although your right eye always twitches a little when you're not being honest with me, so I would have known."

"What? It does not!" he said, playfully swatting at her. His relief at finally having the conversation with her was immense; he felt a thousand times lighter. He shook his head, wondering not for the first time how he got so damn lucky to have found a woman like Molly to marry him.

"Actually, it does twitch. You didn't know that? Huh, I guess I shouldn't have told you," she laughed then swiftly grabbed the handle of the car door, opened it up, and jumped out.

Jack apprehensively watched her dart around the truck to the passenger side and rap lightly on the window. He looked out at her and cocked his head, not understanding why. She motioned for him to get out of the car and stepped aside so he could open the door. As he got out of the truck, she immediately reached up and drew him in for a tight embrace. They stood like that on the side of the road for a few minutes before Molly pulled away and glanced up at him shyly.

"Thank you for falling in love with me, Mr. Jack Curtis, and not with my sister."

He threw his head back and laughed then squeezed her so tight in his embrace that she gasped. At her prompting, he darted around the truck and hopped into the driver's seat. He maneuvered the truck back onto the highway toward the hospital then sped along as eighties music played quietly in the background. The air in the truck was noticeably lighter, and Molly found herself humming to the music.

As they neared the hospital exit, Jack looked in his rearview mirror and was surprised to see bright blue lights fast approaching behind them. He glanced at Molly apologetically then obligingly pulled off to the side of the road. Jack glanced at the side mirror to see a hefty police officer approaching the side of the truck. He glanced at Molly as he rolled down the truck window. The officer rapped on the driver's side door then barked out his command.

"Folks, could I see your license, registration, and proof of insurance, please?"

"Yes, yes, of course," Jack said as he shifted in his seat, scrambling to get the license out of his wallet.

He looked up at the policeman and said, "Was I going that fast, Officer? I didn't realize."

"No, no, I jest pulled you over for a busted tail light. You weren't speeding at all!" the policeman responded, more cheerfully than either Molly or Jack expected.

"Oh! Well, that's good," Jack said, looking back at Molly with a big *see-I-told-you-so* smile. Jack put his license and registration into the officer's outstretched hand.

"I still gotta run you through the system, though. You know, pro-to-cahl," the officer said almost apologetically. "You sit tight, and I'll be right back."

The officer walked back to his car, so Jack rolled up the window to keep the truck warm. "You got lucky on that one, Jack," Molly said.

"Lucky? What do you mean? I wasn't even speeding!"

"Well, Lord knows you certainly could have been," replied Molly with an air of worldly knowledge. She then added, "Hey, do we know him? I think we used to live on the same road growing up, but I'm not sure. He was much older. He may be around Kate's age."

"Hey, thanks," Jack mock protested—he was also in the "much older" category.

"You know what I mean, Jack." She looked back at the flashing blue lights on the police car parked behind them, as if she could affirm her suspicion by doing so. Then abruptly, she turned around in her seat and faced the front like a student who had been called out in class.

"Jack, he's coming back," she whispered.

A tap on the window prompted Jack to roll the window down once again.

"Well, all's good, folks. You will need to take care of that tail light, though, okay?"

He started to walk away then turned back to the window before Jack even had time to put it up again. He leaned over so he could look across at Molly in the passenger seat.

"Hey, you wouldn't happen to be little Molly Stevens, would you?"

Molly looked back at the officer in surprise then smiled slyly at Jack—she had been right.

"Yes, I am. I was just trying to figure out if I knew you, too," she responded.

"Well, you wouldn't remember me. It was actually your sister, Katie, that I grew up with. We graduated from Belleview High together."

"But how did you know it was me?" she asked him after a second's hesitation.

"Well, naturally, cuz you look so much like each other!" he replied back earnestly.

Jack and Molly looked at each other in surprise before Molly blurted out, "What? But we look nothing…"

But Billy the police officer quickly cut her off with a wide grin, "Uh, I was just messing with you. You two look about as alike as an elephant and an orange!" he replied, laughing at his own lame joke.

He looked back in through the window at Molly again. "No, I just knew it was you. I remember you chasing us around when we was trying to play. You haven't changed much at all," he said with a male's lack of tact.

"Uh, thanks, I guess," Molly retorted with a small grin.

"Gosh, that reminds me of the days Kate and I was friends… jumping in the creek, we used to play hide-and-seek in the woods behind my house," he looked off in the distance, reminiscing. He then peered back at Molly and grinned, "You know you were always trying to chase after us, and your momma always told you to come back to the house and leave us alone."

At the mention of her mother, Molly's face suddenly fell. She quickly turned her head away before he would notice. His next words were even more upsetting, though in a very different way.

"Your sister—Katie—though, she was so good to you, you know. Even when your Momma would tell you to leave us be, she'd always bring you along if you pestered us enough. And it was odd, but it seemed like the farther away from the house we got, the better she was to you. Including you in our fun, taking care of you… She was real good to you like that even though you were so much younger than we was."

Jack grinned at hearing Billy's words; he knew the affect they would have on his wife. He reached out and grabbed her hand to give it a firm squeeze. Molly just looked over at Billy as if the officer had told her she was going to grow wings and fly right then and there.

"Thank you. That's very sweet to say. I'm sorry I don't really remember all that, and we don't get to see Kate very much these days…"

But again, Billy cut her off, "What? But you must have seen her!" he said in surprise, "I just saw her here in town last night, myself."

"You what?" Jack and Molly suddenly exclaimed in unison, looking back and forth at each other and then back at Billy.

"Yes ma'm, I pulled her over, too," he smiled at Molly, somewhat shamefaced.

"But," he continued with more confidence, "she was going *way* past the speed limit over on Old Franklin Road to the Perch. She said she was on her way to meet up with a friend there. You must be real happy to have her up here visiting with you."

Molly and Jack stole another quick glance at each other. Molly's eyes narrowed to mere slits as she listened to Billy talk.

"I just gave her a warning since she was an old friend an' all," he smiled smugly then half stood up and half saluted them. "Okay, well I gotta' run, go take care of some real po-lice business. You all take care now and enjoy your sister being here!"

As he sauntered back to his police car and drove away, questions began to fire off Molly's tongue at Jack.

"How come I don't remember her being nice to me when we were kids? She actually brought me along to play? And what the hell was she doing on that side of town last night? Headed to The Perch?" She spat out the name of the old bar as if it left a bad taste in her mouth.

"Whoa, whoa… easy there. She *said* she was going to meet a friend, and it sounds like that's just what she did," Jack said in Kate's defense.

"Yeah, but not at the Perch! Who would she meet there? No respectful girl in town would go…" Molly cut herself off short and looked at Jack with saucer-eyes before asking, "Do you think she was meeting a guy last night?"

The incredulous tone in her voice rang loud and clear.

"Hey, she used to have guy friends here, too. So what if it was a guy?"

"Yeah, but..."

Jack interrupted her. "No. There's no 'yeah, buts.' Kate's a grown woman and can have whatever friends she wants to."

Molly peered at him suspiciously, "Why are you defending her like this, Jack?"

"I'm not. It just seems absurd that you're jumping all over her for it. Let's give her a break, okay? Especially after what Billy just told you, Molly."

And with that, he turned to face the front and started up the truck, revving it a little more than he'd intended to. He pulled the truck sharply onto the highway ramp, and as he did, Molly reached out and hit his arm a little too hard.

"Hey! What was that for?"

"For getting pulled over. Now, my sister and I need to talk," she said. "Let's get going!"

They rode the rest of the way to the hospital in silence, lost in their own thoughts about what was right and wrong, about the differences between men and women. But mostly they thought about Kate—the woman who was a mystery to them both.

39. KATE

AROUND THE SAME TIME, FORTY miles away, Kate had driven away from the coffee shop feeling stunned and in disbelief. Numerous texts beeped on her phone during the 45-minute drive to the hospital; she read them all but did not have the strength to respond to any of them. Curt apologized for last night. Lena apologized for breaking the news. Ethan asked if she'd call him as soon as she could.

Her mind was in turmoil after learning of Robbie's infidelity, and at the same time she hated herself for her own indiscretion with Curt the night before. She drove to the hospital in heavy silence, feeling angry, hypocritical, and many other emotions that she couldn't name. The biggest question that repeatedly popped up was whether or not Molly knew of her father's cheating.

"Is *that* why Jack keeps saying that Molly's been through so much?" She asked the question out loud, trying to work through the logic in her head. "Because Molly's known all along about her father's affairs?"

However, her unanswered questions hung heavily in the empty space inside the SUV. She berated herself for never once asking her mother about her relationship with Rob. At the same time, she tried to let herself off the hook for not being privy to these details; she lived so far away.

As she neared the hospital, she felt a confusing mix of anger and sadness. For her mother—for anyone—to have to experience the pain and heartache of having a marriage end due to cheating was just wrong. At the same time, Kate was apoplectic with both Robbie and her father for causing her mother so much pain. Through that scorn and pity, much of the resentment that Kate had felt toward her mother over the years was replaced by sorrow.

She walked into the hospital and saw an empty reception desk. As she headed to the ICU, Kate looked around the lobby and felt herself actually missing the opportunity to interact with Marge.

She wound her way down the sterile halls, her mind a thousand miles away. When she turned the last corner, she stopped short. Robbie was just leaving her mother's room, and before she knew what was happening, Kate hissed out his name in the echoing corridor.

"Rob!"

Startled, he turned to her, but before he could say a word, Kate went in for the kill.

"You know I always *thought* you were an asshole, but now I *know* you are. How could you do this to her?"

"Kate, you have no right to speak to..."

"No right? Let's talk about what's *right*, shall we? What the hell have you been doing to my mother?"

Her retort was so quick, so biting, that Robbie was taken aback and said nothing. He simply looked back with his wide eyes.

"Rob, how could you cheat on her like that, especially with her depression and knowing what she'd been through already?"

Stupefied by her questioning, he blurted out defensively, "Well, how the hell do *you* know?"

"What difference does it make, Rob? All that matters is that *you* drove my mother to this. And after the way you treated me growing up? What the hell? Haven't you done enough to our family?"

Kate spat out the final question and willed herself not to cry. Every fiber of her body was taut and ready for a fight. The last thing she wanted was to lose control and show this man any more weakness than she had allowed him to see while growing up. Kate pulled herself straight up, determined not to break down, and stared back with unwavering eyes.

"Kate, I know that I may not have always treated you the best, but it wasn't easy back then, and you weren't exactly an easy child."

Yet his half-hearted, half-assed attempt at an apology only infuriated her more.

"Is that the best you can do, tell me that things weren't *easy* for you?"

Standing there with her fists clenched at her side, she could feel anger beginning to boil inside her. She felt like a volcano about to erupt. She breathed deeply, trying to regain control. Then Rob said a few simple words that she couldn't bear to hear, words that were so condescending that they made her body shake with a rage from her very core.

"Kate, aren't you being a little dramatic about all this?"

"*What* did you say?"

Her fury must have shown on her face, for Robbie unconsciously took a step back. Kate took a step toward him and used the full force of her commanding courtroom persona.

"Robbie, you knew back then that you were treating me like shit and you did it anyway. You gave me nothing—except what you had to—and you almost took something away from me that night in my room." She lowered her voice for the last words so that only he would hear them. "You are a disgusting human being."

She stood, shoulders down, and stared at Robbie with a look of total wretchedness. The next line came out in barely a whisper, "Just go, Rob. You are no longer welcome here."

"What do you mean? That's my wife in there," he responded incredulously.

"Yeah, well that fucking changed the day you made the decision to cheat on her. Now I'd like to have some time alone with my mother, so leave us. Now!"

Robbie opened his mouth to talk, but when he saw the look of controlled hatred on her face, he quickly closed it. Wordlessly, he turned around and walked away down the hall.

Once he turned the corner and was out of sight, Kate let out a long slow sigh of relief. Looking down at fists still clenched tight, she exhaled loudly and slowly unclenched her hands. As she willed her body to relax, she felt more emotionally depleted than ever before.

Surprisingly, the visit with her mother at the hospital was initially uneventful and calm. Kate sat by the bedside and talked about her life, about Ethan and her job. While she waited for Molly to show up—not remembering that they'd discussed coming to the hospital together—she talked to her mother with barely a pause. At some point in the quiet of the room, Kate began to tell her mother about the night with Robbie, the night that changed everything. There were no tears, no accusations, simply an outpouring of things that needed to be said. While she spoke, the question of whether or not her mother could hear her buzzed in her mind like a mosquito. It was the longest personal conversation she'd had with her mother—it was probably the longest personal conversation she'd had with *anyone*.

After some more time had passed, Kate said softly, "Mom, you know I have to go back home tomorrow. You just need to get better, okay? Put this all behind us. I'll be here today, then I'll be back to check on you in the morning right before I go."

She walked out the door and down the hall. She didn't see Molly, so she decided to go outside for some fresh air. As she left the hospital and walked into the brisk October air, she inhaled deeply and brought her arms closely around her body. The wind swirled past as Kate walked away from the hospital. She did not stop to think about where she would go. Not knowing which direction to head, she simply strode purposefully away from the hospital as fast she could walk without bringing her body into a run. A few tears rolled down her chapped cheeks, but the cool Maine winds quickly blew them dry. She wasn't dressed appropriately for the weather, and she soon found herself colder than she'd felt in a long time. She kept her pace, though, struggling to stay warm, but the chill crept inside of her.

Finally, she stopped and looked around. Trying to get her bearings, she scanned the horizon of a city she hadn't visited since her early college days. The skyline had changed only slightly; there were now a few taller buildings scattered throughout the downtown area. When she turned to the right, she saw something ahead that she vaguely remembered, a park called Battery Field where she used to go for her morning runs. She walked the short distance to the park and saw a statue near the front entrance. It was a dark iron piece, weathered and worn, nestled in between shrubs that hid most of it from the view of passersby. She approached the statue as if drawn to it. As Kate neared the iron sculpture and saw it up close, she almost cried out in anguish.

It was a statue of a mother and two small girls. The metal image was playful—they all had broad smiles on their faces, and one of the girls held a ball in her hand, poised to throw it up in the air. The smaller girl had a handful of flowers—they looked like daisies—and she gazed up toward her sister and mother, happy and carefree.

Kate tore her eyes away from the statue and quickly looked around. In some deranged and disturbed way, it felt as if someone had put it there just for her. She wondered if it was real or a figment of her imagination and reached out to touch the cold metal to be sure. Despite the late morning sun, the statue felt bitingly cold on her skin. She forced her hands to stay on the cold surface as she traced her fingers along first the mother's beaming face then over the young girls' faces. Their etched smiles seemed to travel like an electrical current along her arm and through to her soul.

Kate stood there for just a moment longer then turned and walked straight back to the hospital. The return pace seemed much quicker, and after just a few blocks and turns, Kate found herself once again facing the building's brick walls. She walked in through the side entrance, her feet taking her right to the ICU.

When she arrived outside her mother's room, however, the scene before her eliminated the sense of ease and comfort that she had felt only moments before.

There was a flurry of activity in the hall, and white coats moved quickly in and out of her mother's room. Kate hesitated, glancing up at the number above the door to make sure that she was at the right room. When she confirmed that she was in the right place, her heart dropped. She pushed open the door and found her sister and Jack standing facing the window. A handful of doctors and nurses stood around the bed. They spoke to one another in hushed tones. Not able to catch a word from any of them, Kate finally called out in exasperation when no one acknowledged her presence in the room.

"What the hell is going on here?"

Molly turned sharply at her sister's voice and ran to her side. Her drained face had taken on a new animation and color. "Kate, oh my God, I thought I saw Mom move! Just a few minutes ago, she moved her fingers—just a little—so I called a nurse in. The doctors are trying to figure out if it's just a meaningless flutter or something more."

One of the doctors finally spoke up. Kate saw that it was the same man who had offered her words of comfort yesterday.

"Folks, without making any hasty decisions, upon reviewing Ms. Steven's recent brain activity, we are unable to determine whether or not her finger movement was self-initiated," he announced.

Kate and Molly looked blankly at each other then back at him, waiting for more. Kate was the first to speak.

"You mean, she may have moved on her own… or she didn't. Which is it?"

"Possibly. We simply do not know for sure. But certainly, if she *did* move of her own volition, that would be a good thing."

Kate and Molly looked again at each other before firing questions at the doctor in unison.

"What does that mean?"

"Will she come out of the coma?"

"Is she going to be okay?"

The doctor held up his hands in front of him, as if to shield off their questions. Jack interjected, trying to help him out.

"Molly. Kate. Let the man speak, okay?"

The doctor gave him a nod of thanks.

"We don't know. Just let someone know immediately if you see any additional movements," he replied curtly.

Then with a quick nod of his head, he left the room. The nurses and other hospital staff trailed behind him.

"Wow, that was intense," gasped Molly as she sunk down in the bedside chair. For the moment, all of her questions about the Pelican Perch and where Kate went last night were forgotten.

"Well, this *is* the first bit of good news we've received, I guess," replied Kate.

Molly nodded her head enthusiastically.

"Yes, it is. It really is! Hey, where were you, by the way?" Molly asked tentatively, "I—we—thought we were all going to come here over an hour ago," she said with a jerk of her head to Jack, who stood on the other side of the bed.

Kate gave him a cursory nod and he delivered the same in return. With the knowledge that Molly knew of their past together came awkwardness.

"Oh, I was here earlier; I just went for a walk to clear my head. Guess I lost track of the time," Kate stopped then continued abruptly before Molly could start talking again. "By the way, do you know that park down near the waterfront? Battery, I think it's called, where there's that large bronze statue of a mother and two girls?"

"Battery Park? Yes, I know it. But there aren't any statues there anymore. There were a few until one of them was vandalized a few years back by some teenagers. Then the city decided to move them all to the smaller park right next to the police station on the other side of town. Are you sure you were at that one?"

Kate looked at Molly, dumbfounded. She said nothing and glanced down at her hand to avoid questions about the stunned look she knew was on her face. It was the same hand that had touched the statues and outlined their cool faces less than an hour before. It was almost as if by remembering the feel of the cold metal she could reassure herself that they were truly there, that she hadn't lost her mind. She looked from Molly to Jack and opened her mouth to say something, but nothing came out.

"What is it, Kate?" Molly asked.

"Nothing," Kate replied slowly and shrugged it off. "Yeah, I was probably just in a different park."

Though even as she said the words, the image of the wooden park sign engraved with the word "Battery" burned like fire in her brain. She had never questioned her own sanity before, but now she thought she should.

Molly shook her head and sat down at their mother's bedside. Jake and Kate stood on either side, gazing out the window or uncomfortably back at one another, each lost in their own thoughts. Kate's eyes saw nothing as she struggled to understand a world that seemed to be turning off-center and out-of-sync.

Eventually, Kate took a seat on the other side of the bed and gently touched her mother's arm. Staring with sadness at her mother's bandaged face, Kate tried to understand how awful life must be for someone to get to a place where they no longer wish to live. For as difficult as things had been—growing up with Robbie, what happened with Jack, the despair she felt now—doing something like this had never crossed her mind. Instead, she had allowed her heart to turn to stone. A tear rolled down her face, and she brushed it away before Molly or Jack could see. Kate decided that she needed to know why this had happened. She needed to hear something—*anything*—that made sense.

Molly had also been away in her own thoughts, trying to conjure up the memories that Billy had shared with her, trying to remember a period in their lives when her sister was there for her and actually wanted her around.

At the same time, the two sisters broke the silence in the room, each with their own burning questions about the past.

"Molly, is your father going to be here later today?"

"Kate, tell me about before you left home."

They both laughed somewhat nervously for speaking at the same time. As usual, Molly acquiesced to Kate.

"Sorry, what did you say, Kate?"

Kate paused just a second before imapatiently repeating her question. "Do you know if your father will be here again today?"

"Of course! I think he said he'll be back later," Molly answered. Then she looked sharply across at Kate, "Why are you asking?"

"Well…" Kate hesitated, turning away from Molly as she busied herself pulling the chair closer to the bed. She could tell by Molly's tone that pursuing her line of questioning might not be for the best. Ever the lawyer, however, she simply paused to collect her thoughts before proceeding.

"I was wondering how close you are with him. Any conjectures about your relationship together, after not being up here and around you both, would be just that… Do you and he talk, you know, about personal matters?"

The humming and buzzing of the machines that Beth was hooked up to were the only sounds in the room. Jack stayed staring out the window with his back to them, as if he was searching for something of great meaning beyond the glass.

Eventually, Molly interrupted the quiet in the room. She dropped each word carefully, one at a time, as if they were precious seeds. Even in the quiet of the room, Molly's words were so soft that Kate had to listen hard to hear what she said.

"Kate, if you were asking about my father because you know about the affairs, just say so."

Kate's reaction was swift and furious.

"What? Seriously?" Kate retorted before she could stop herself. "You *knew* about this? Molly, what the hell's been going on here? Why didn't you tell me?"

"You haven't been around much, Kate! Things change. I'm not saying that my father was right, but you just can't come back home and get your moral feathers all ruffled without knowing everything that's been going on here. You must know *that* from that job of yours in Atlanta." The last line was issued with a sneer, which caused Jack's heard to turn back just for a moment before he returned to his visual quest at the window.

"Dammit, I certainly can, Molly! Are you saying that you *knew* your dad was fooling around on my mother—on *our* mother— yet you did nothing about it?" Kate barked back in frustration.

At that point, Jack finally made an attempt to intercede with the two sisters. He turned back to them with a forced smile and put his hands out as if to ward off any advances. Molly cut him off. She extended her arm and put her palm straight up to him—much to his surprise.

"Jack, I can handle this." Her tone did not leave room for discussion, and Jack resignedly took a step back.

Molly turned, looked at Kate, and took a deep breath.

"This was between *them*. It is *their* marriage, Kate," Molly stated defensively. "And it wasn't *my* business to interfere."

"Yeah? Well, look how 'It's not my business' ended up for all of us!"

Kate spat out the words and stormed out of the room. She almost ran down the hall, not looking where she was going, her eyes blinded by tears. She ended up back at the first place she thought of—the receptionist desk—and felt surprisingly grateful to see Marge sitting there this time. When the older woman glanced up and saw what a disheveled state that Kate was in, she immediately called for her to come over.

"Dear, come over here. You look like you could use a drink about now."

She beckoned Kate over and patted the chair next to her. With nowhere else to go, Kate obligingly walked toward the desk while roughly attempting to brush away her tears.

"Well, to be honest, I'm afraid I can't give you a drink, but I do have some popcorn that I'd be happy to share," Marge said with a small smile.

Kate gave a lopsided smile. As an attorney, even now she couldn't help but think that only in a small town could confidentiality be flaunted in a hospital setting, with an invitation to a non-employee to sit behind the receptionist desk. As the smell of Marge's popcorn drifted from the bag, Kate slowly walked behind the U-shaped desk and plopped down heavily in the available seat. Marge extended the bag of popcorn to her and Kate put a hungry hand into the bag of buttery corn to withdraw a big scoop. She looked down at the popped white kernels overflowing in her hand and said nothing.

"Alright, Miss..." Marge stopped, looking at Kate's sizable ring on her other hand. "Well, you are definitely a 'Mrs,' I see, so tell me, what's your name again?"

"Kate. Kate Harriman."

"Well, Mrs. Kate Harriman, it looks like you are having one helluva day."

"Marge, my mother is in a coma in ICU. Of *course* I'm having a shitty day," Kate immediately snapped back, though she felt chagrined instantly.

"Sorry," Kate offered with a wan smile, but the older woman was not at all daunted by Kate's show of anger.

"Thank you. That's fine, and that may be so. But I have learned something after my twenty-six years here, and that is that life must go on. Which means that you *still* need to be good to the people who are standing beside you, no matter what the circumstances."

Marge cocked her head to one side and lifted her eyebrows, waiting for her words to sink in.

"Yes, well that's sometimes easier said than done," Kate retorted. She heard the bitterness and tiredness in her voice and hated herself for it.

"Look here.... Life is only as difficult as you choose to make it, and my guess is that you are fighting every battle you think should be fought right now. But you just don't have to. I have no doubt by your fancy clothes and your big-ass ring, that you are a smart girl..."

Kate smiled a little, both at Marge swearing and at the word "girl" used to describe her; it was a word that she hadn't heard in a long time.

"So now, why don't you start using those college-earned smarts of yours and make things right for yourself and everyone around you?"

Marge issued Kate the challenge before turning to welcome an older couple that had just approached the desk asking for assistance. In a raspy smoker's voice the elderly woman asked Marge for directions to her sister's room. Marge answered, and the pair engaged in small talk for a few moments.

It gave Kate time to allow Marge's comments to sink in. *Of course I'm smart. I wouldn't be where I am today if I wasn't, right? So why does everything feel like it's going wrong right now and I'm fucking it all up?* After having the rug pulled out from under her legs *more* than a few times in the past two days, Kate felt like all her reasoning and sensibility had been ripped away from her. She couldn't answer her own questions, and she was amazed at how quickly her life had turned upside-down, spiraling out of orbit in just a few days.

As the elderly couple shuffled off and Marge helped some other visitors who approached the desk seeking her help, Kate rolled back and forth in her chair. Her arms were crossed and her eyes stared at the floor. At one point, she looked up briefly and noticed a young couple walk by; the man reminded her of Ethan and her heart ached. With all that had happened, it felt as if she'd been apart from him for weeks instead of just a few days. For the first time ever, Kate wondered how he had put up with her coldness and aloofness all these years. She'd always known in the back of her mind that she may not have been the easiest person to be with. Yet, it wasn't until now that she understood just what that could have meant for her husband... let alone the other family in her life that she'd strayed from. *Strayed? More like ran from at a full runner's sprint, Kate. Let's be honest here.*

And before she could change her mind, Kate gave a quick nod of her head to Marge who was busy helping someone else at the counter and walked briskly away from the desk. Rounding the corner, she called Ethan on his cell, noting that he, of course, had called her three times already this morning. Once again, she felt negligent for not responding earlier.

He picked up the call on the very first ring. Before he could say anything, she quickly told her husband something that she hadn't said from her heart in a very long time.

"Hi, Hun. I love you. I do, and I wish you were here."

40. INTERVENTION OF A STRANGER

MOMENTS LATER, AS KATE TALKED to Ethan, Molly walked by on the other side of the hall. When the two sisters saw each other, Molly stopped short. Kate abruptly ended her call with Ethan, cutting him off mid-sentence with promises that she'd call again soon. She had someone else she needed to make amends with, and she wasn't going to delay. As she turned to face her sister and the two women stood there and looked at each other, Marge's voice called out at her from behind the desk.

"Mrs. Harriman, I take it this is who you were having the tiff with?"

When neither of the women spoke, Marge spoke to them encouragingly, as if they were children, "Well, go on, you two. Go talk through this and make up. You two must be real good friends to both be here so much with Mrs. Stevens like this."

And with that, the two sisters—who looked nothing alike—looked back at each other and laughed out loud.

Marge didn't understand why, nor did she care. She just felt happy to see them laughing together. She let out a long contented sigh, feeling that she had done her good deed for the day. She crossed her arms over her chest in contentment as Molly strolled over to Kate.

"C'mon, friend," Molly said with a small chuckle. The two sisters started to walk back toward Beth's room before Molly stopped Kate with a light hand on her arm.

"I was actually just going to go grab a bite in the cafeteria. Are you hungry at all?"

"Sure," she said as she nodded toward Marge with a smile. "Marge here was kind enough to share some popcorn with me, but I was too upset to eat it."

"You? Upset? You always seem like everything's fine. Calm, cool, and collected Kate, right?" Molly said. "I'm the one who feels out of control all of the time."

Kate had heard almost the same words from Sam—*God, was it just a few days before?*—and she realized just how strong others perceived her to be. *They are so wrong. If we are all in the same boat without a fucking paddle, then why does it feel like I'm the only one whose crumbling away here?*

"Molly, I might not always show it, but things bother me just like everyone else. I'm just not one to let everyone see that side of me, that's all."

The two women followed the signs to the hospital cafeteria. The aroma of food was insufficient to compensate for the antiseptic smell of the hospital, and little behind the glassed counter looked appealing. Kate chose carefully from the few items in the buffet line that looked palatable. Molly added a number of items to her tray with much less discrimination. Despite Molly's objections, Kate went ahead in line to pay for them both. The elderly cashier gave Kate her change with a big toothy grin. As the girls were about to sit down at the cleanest table they could find, Molly thanked Kate for her food again and piped up.

"Hey, I almost forgot. After you left the room, I think Mom may have moved again," she said with an impish look in her eyes.

"What?! Did you tell anyone?"

"No, I mean, I wasn't *really* sure, and I didn't see it happen again. But, I think she did."

Kate gave her a skeptical look, not knowing if it was Molly's inane optimism that witnessed a move or just a figment of her hopeful imagination. She said nothing and gave Molly what she hoped to be an encouraging smile.

The two talked sporadically while they ate, mostly making fun of the cardboard nature of the cafeteria food they had ordered. Both women were in agreement that the salad tasted downright awful, and that the Jell-O was too old and tasteless to be referred to as food. Molly joked that the hundred-year-old cashier probably made everything years ago, anyway. Kate laughed out loud, not remembering her sister to ever be so bitingly humorous before.

In the shared moments, Molly's questions about Kate's whereabouts the previous night and this morning were all but forgotten. As Kate drank the tepid house coffee—it wasn't good, but it had caffeine—Molly revealed what she knew about her father's affairs. She admitted to Kate that there were at least three other women in the last five years. And although she couldn't recall exactly when, it seemed as if the first woman had come into the picture about the same time that their mother's behavior had gone downhill.

Every few minutes, Molly shook her head in frustration, though Kate couldn't tell if it was with her father for what he'd done or at herself for not doing anything about it.

The situation reminded Kate of the chicken and egg fable. She repeatedly asked herself which came first, her mother's mental decline or Rob's dalliances with other women. She hoped for an answer, but none came. And as her mother's daughter, she wanted to believe that it was Rob who had started to fool around on their mother *well before* Beth's mental state began to change.

But we'll never know the truth if Mom... She stopped her thoughts, unable to think them through. Kate shuddered and hoped Molly didn't see. She was grateful that her sister seemed to be too engrossed in picking at the lumpy remains of her chicken casserole to notice.

Molly's phone trilled loudly with the alert of an incoming text, and she sheepishly looked up at Kate, as her phone had been left on. When she glanced down to read it, though, and after sending a response, she peered up at Kate with an odd steely glint in her eyes.

Kate said nothing, and when they finally left the hospital cafeteria, with bellies slightly fuller and hearts a little lighter, she wondered what kind of state they would all find themselves in before this ordeal was over.

Molly walked down the hall beside Kate with renewed purpose, feeling a strength that she had not experienced in a long time. She knew what she needed to do—something her mother should have done years ago. She told Kate that she needed a few moments alone with Beth and that she'd meet back up with her in a while. The two sisters bumped into Jack just outside of Beth's room. They all talked for a few minutes, making arrangements for the remainder of the day. At one point Jack said something that made Kate grin, and she swatted playfully at his arm like an old friend. Molly noted the affectionate gesture but pushed it aside, too intent on the task she needed to do at hand. She asked Kate if they could meet back near the reception desk; Kate said she should make a few more calls back home anyway, knowing her cell phone messages were undoubtedly piling up. Jack said he'd head down to the cafeteria to try to grab a bite to eat, despite the women's warnings, and the two sisters hugged briefly before parting ways.

Molly entered Beth's room and sat down to wait for her father's arrival. The text that she had received from him moments before said that he would be back shortly. She was surprised at how calm she felt inside; the minutes slowly ticked by as she prepared herself for what had to be done.

41. TAKING A STAND

MOLLY SAT IN MEASURED SILENCE with Beth in the hospital room as Kate headed outside for some fresh air with her phone in hand.

Kate scanned through the list of people she needed to call back—Sam, her dad, Ethan again. She realized, sadly, that it was the same few people as yesterday, as no one else knew where she was. *And there's no one else who cares*, she thought with bitter sadness. Still holding her now cold cup of coffee, she stepped outside into the crisp October air.

At the same time, Robbie pulled into the hospital parking lot from the opposite direction. Just as Kate turned around to throw her coffee cup into a nearby trash can, he drove past her and parked his GMC truck in a vacant spot a few rows away. With her head down against the wind, Kate scrolled through her emails to catch up on office activities and prepared to call Sam. They spoke briefly, just long enough for her to get a pulse on what she had missed; Kate put forth her best effort to assure Sam that all was well as she ended the call. She scrolled through her contact list searching for her father's number next, just as Robbie walked directly past her a few feet away and through the hospital doors. Neither of them knew that their paths had almost crossed.

Moments later, Robbie entered Beth's room to find Molly talking softly to her mother's prone body. Molly sat with her back to the door, so she was not aware of his presence as he walked in. He paused for a moment, awkwardly standing by the door, unsure of what to do. Molly murmured her final goodbyes and stood up to go. But when she turned and saw her father, she gasped—as much out of surprise as in anger as her conversation with Kate about her father's infidelity still rattled her brain. Her face contorted with emotions; her look was enough to keep him in silence as he waited for her to speak.

Abruptly and with an unfamiliarly aggressive tone, she spoke. "Dad, we need to talk."

Robbie looked back at her with a surprised look on his face; she had never shown such authority with him before. He glanced past Molly at Beth as if she would somehow sit up and interject her help at any moment. However, when she remained immobile, he faced his daughter again. Knowing that something was wrong, a look of apprehension covered his tired face, a look that Molly found unnerving yet empowering at the same time.

"Okay, Molly…" he said slowly, "I got your text. About what, exactly?"

Molly looked pointedly at her mother then turned back to Robbie and shook her head. "Not here, Dad. Let's go outside."

She walked out of the room before him, her thoughts tangled and snarled inside like climbing vines. Molly led her father down the hall opposite the direction Kate had taken. Coming face-to-face with her sister now was the last thing she wanted. She didn't turn around to look at her father to make sure he was still following her until they were outside the hospital. Finally, she stopped and swung around to face him. Then before she lost her nerve, Molly spat out three simple words. Even she was surprised at the fierceness behind each word. "Why, Dad, why?"

He looked at her blankly, which only served to anger her. Her cheeks reddened and her breath quickened. She repeated her question, though this time in a calmer tone in a subtle attempt to encourage him to tell her the truth about what had happened with her mother.

"Why did you do it to her, Dad?"

For a moment he just stared blankly at her. In his continued silence, the opportunity she felt that she had presented him, to admit to his wrongdoings, was lost. His silence infuriated her, and she finally lashed out.

"Dad, I'm asking you why! I need to know… why did you cheat on mom!"

"What, not you, too, for God's sake!"

His reaction to Molly's words momentarily confused her, but then she realized that Kate must have already confronted him. Yet there was something else, something that looked more like relief than anger or even denial. She looked at him warily.

Relief about what? What did he think I was going to say?

Then the questions jumbling inside her head were almost answered before Rob stopped himself.

"Molly, shit, I thought you were talking about Kate," he paused and shook his head, as if he'd been let off the hook.

"What? What did you *think* I meant, Dad?" Molly looked at him warily.

When he didn't speak, she demanded in a firmer tone, "Dad, what *else* have you done?"

When he spoke again, secure in the knowledge that his daughter was not going to ask him about his past with Kate, he pulled himself up a little taller.

"Molly, I don't have to explain myself to you," he began, but she cut him off.

"Yes, Dad. You do. You know why?" she stopped, as if she was actually giving him a chance to reply. But she quickly answered the question for him, "Because my mother—your wife 'til death do you part—is lying there in a coma and may not come out of it. And it may be because of you!" By the end, she found herself shouting and her hands were clenched by her side.

Molly had never spoken to her father like this. She was enraged, and she was taking a stand. Planting her hands on her hips and trying to control the accusing look on her face, her anger and frustration seeped out from every pore. After all the years of keeping silent and holding back, the embittered disapproval she felt toward her father poured out like a geyser. Molly felt a new power, a sense of control that she'd never experienced.

She asked her father the same question once again, this time more softly, "Dad, how could you have done that to her?" The quiet of her voice was more unsettling, and his face blanched.

"What's gone on between your mother and me is *our* business."

Again, she cut him off.

"Yes, Dad. I know. And that's the way I've been dealing with everything for the last few years. But now I'm realizing that isn't enough. Your actions affect others, just as mine do—for good *or for* bad—and pretending that everything's okay or that things aren't 'our business' isn't the right thing to do. I know that now."

Molly stopped talking as an orderly hurriedly walked past them and turned into the hospital. When the scrub-clad young boy avoided their eyes, Molly knew that he had heard her shouting and felt somewhat chagrined. For a moment, she wondered sadly who she was and what had become of things—standing outside a hospital yelling at her father, with her mother lying in a coma just inside.

"Molly, you have no idea what *I've* been going through with your mom."

"Actually, Dad, I do. You know why? Because while you've been avoiding her and off having your own little fun, *I've* been the one taking care of her most of the time. So I know *exactly* what it means."

"For God's sake, none of this has been easy on any of us. But being married to someone who can't even *be* with you… who can't be a *wife.*"

"What? Are you actually saying that because Mom stopped having sex with you, you found someone else? That's disgusting!"

"No! Well, yes… God, it's just not that simple!" he threw up his hands in frustration, "You're twisting my words, dammit!"

"You know what? I have always stuck up for you, Dad. Always—even when I knew you hadn't always done right by everyone. And yes, I'm talking about how you treated Kate. But this? This was just wrong," Molly paused.

Before he could respond and before she could stop herself, Molly spat out the words that her sister had never spoken to her but that she knew to be true, "Maybe Kate was right, Dad. Maybe you are just a selfish ass."

And with that she abruptly turned to leave.

But just as quickly, Rob grabbed her arm to stop her. Molly stared back at her father with a look of total shock on her face. His hand was wrapped so tightly around her arm that it dug into her skin through her sweater. She was speechless and had the fleeting thought that this man, this person who had been a good father to her, had a side that she'd never seen before.

It was that moment that she realized she knew someone who *had* seen this side of her father, and Molly's heart went out to her sister like never before.

Before her mind could formulate any words Rob released his grip and answered her sharply before looking away, "Let's *not* bring your sister into this."

"Why, Dad? Is that something else that I just don't understand?" Molly retorted, feeling a sudden and extreme sadness inside for all that had been lost for her family over the years. She could still feel the pressure of her father's hold on her arm and wondered if he had left a mark. The pain paled in comparison to the tightness of the sorrow around her heart.

"Kate was an obstinate child. She's not like you. She made *our* lives very difficult together."

"Dad, she was a *child*. That's what they do!" She threw her hands up in exasperation then demanded to know more, "What exactly do you mean by *difficult*, though?"

"Oh, you're too young to remember..." His voice trailed off, and he looked away from her.

"Try me," she said smartly.

Robbie looked up at his daughter sharply.

"Look, I heard you and Mom yelling at each other one night. Something about how badly you'd treated Katie when she was home, so I know."

"Molly, your sister had problems. Emotional problems. Maybe even psychological problems! She lied to us all of the time; sometimes she'd hide our car keys when we were trying to go out the door. She even used to pack a suitcase of my clothes for me and tell me to leave. She wasn't an easy child!" He yelled back at her with a look of indignation in his eyes.

Again, Molly looked at her Dad as if it was for the very first time. Her voice was particularly quiet when she finally spoke.

"She was just a kid. I'm sure her whole life was turned upside-down when Mom and her father got divorced."

"No," he shook his head vehemently, "it was more than that. We had problems with her! She even told the school one time that I'd died in a tragic car accident in which I'd killed a car full of Amish people!"

Molly's laughter came out before she could hold it back.

"Seriously, Dad? That's the worst you can give me? As a mother, it sounds to me like she was reaching out for help and no one was there to listen to her."

Robbie stood there defensively, not meeting his daughter's accusing gaze.

"You know that I've always been on your side, Dad. Always..." Molly stopped talking and carefully chose her words before continuing. "You were a good father to me. But for the first time, I'm wondering if that's really enough... Because it seems that you *haven't* been good to the people I love."

Molly said nothing more. Shaking her head at her father, she turned away and headed back inside the hospital. She left her father standing alone outside—which is exactly where she hoped he would stay. After delivering heated words that she did not know she had inside, she felt depleted and worn out. She leaned up against a corridor wall and closed her eyes. Her heartbeat felt fast but heavy. For the first time ever, she was proud of herself for finally standing up and fighting back.

It was then that Molly realized she hadn't had one of her spells since the moment her father had called to tell her what Beth had done.

Her eyes flew open, and she looked at her immediate surroundings in surprise. Slowly, a smile crept on to her face. She turned around and from her vantage point around the corner from the lobby she could see Marge, the receptionist, talking to a man behind the desk.

He was casually dressed though unshaven, and he looked to be about the same age as Marge. Even from afar, Molly could plainly see that her face was lit up as she stood next to him. Her cheeks were rosy, and her actions were animated; as she spoke, she gesticulated wildly, and her infectious laughter caused the man beside her to laugh with her. When he reached over and gently put his arm around her shoulder in an obviously familiar way, Molly decided that he must be Marge's husband.

Like a spy, Molly stood and watched the couple for a moment. She was unable to hear their words, but she was able to see the love that passed between them. The scene made her think of her mother and how it must be feel to be cheated on by someone you love. She made herself look away, and the genuine smile that had rested on her face just seconds before was replaced by the frown that had become so familiar lately.

A movement from the other side of the lobby caught Molly's eye, and she looked over as Kate walked through the hospital entrance from the other direction. Kate stopped short when she saw Marge and the man standing at the reception desk.

The man, in turn, glanced over Marge's shoulder and saw Kate standing across the foyer; he called out "Hey!" to her in genuine surprise.

Kate noted that the man was dressed differently than he had been the other day—the business suit now replaced by casual khakis and a bright plaid button-down shirt—but she knew from the beaming smile he gave her that he was most definitely the same person. Marge saw his look and cocked her head in a questioning glance.

"Well, hello there, Ms. Traveler," he bellowed. "What are you doing here?"

Yet with a nudge and a telling look from his wife, his open smile instantly turned to a look of chagrin. He shuffled his feet uncomfortably and looked down at the floor. Kate slowly walked toward him, looking back and forth between them.

Finally, she asked slowly, looking at Marge with a small smile, "So this man is your husband, I take it?"

Marge laughed loudly. She gazed up at him with a huge smile on her plump face.

"That he is, Ms. Harriman. Proud to say I've been with Frank now for twenty-five years and still counting!" Marge joked as she put her arm around his rounded waist.

Frank stood in silence, not knowing what to say after his slip-up. The three looked back and forth at each other before Marge finally asked them both.

"So... how do *you* two know one another?"

Frank was the first to answer with a nod toward Kate.

"Oh, we don't. This nice young lady was just nice enough to sit next to me on the ride up from Atlanta the other day."

"Ohhhh," the look of comprehension on Marge's face held nothing more. Kate saw no concerns. No "what-ifs." No jealousy. She trusted her husband implicitly, and it showed.

Molly had witnessed the exchange and saw the same love and trust. As the scene the between these strangers unfolded, it became more and more apparent to both sisters that Marge and her husband were still very much in love.

Not wanting to get caught standing watching them, Molly stepped into the reception room and walked toward Kate to stand by her side.

Kate turned to her and smiled.

"Well, it looks like you two have made up!" Marge exclaimed loudly when she saw them.

Frank, with a puzzled look on his face, glanced quickly at his wife for answers.

"Frank, these two friends are here..." Marge began to explain, as if reading his mind.

But Kate interrupted her with a sideways glance at Molly, "Actually, Marge, Molly and I are sisters."

"Oh, my!" she said, a hand resting on her chest. She looked back and forth between them then continued talking with obvious surprise, "Well, I'll be! I'm usually pretty good at these things, but I certainly wouldn't have guessed this one."

"I know. Nobody ever does," Kate said with a knowing smirk and a sideways glance at Molly.

"And yes, we have worked things out," Molly interjected.

Then looking back and forth between Frank and Kate, Molly asked them, "So you two know each other?"

"Yes, he and I sat next to each other on my flight up," Kate said with a nod toward Frank, "Though I wasn't exactly a good companion, I know."

Frank patted her arm in assurance.

"Well, as they say… it sure is a small world," Marge clucked. Then she absentmindedly reached out and laid her hand gently on her husband's arm.

From some women, the gesture may have been one of ownership or possessiveness. For Marge, however, it was a simple act of love. Though the words that Molly said next were kind, there was an edge to them that caused Kate to look at her questioningly. Marge and Frank missed the underlying tone in her voice.

"You two look very happy together."

"Happy?" Marge chuckled, "Yes, most of the time, I guess. Life *can* be difficult, and marriage isn't always easy. But I'd say we've made the best of it and stuck by each other through all of the tough times. Right, Frank?"

Before he could reply, though, Molly let out another comment under her breath, though loud enough for them all to hear, "Well, that's more than I can say for our family."

There was a moment of awkward silence, broken only when Frank decided to drawl out a near perfect imitation of Forrest Gump, "Well… life *is* like a box of chocolates. You never know what you're going to get!"

With that, they all laughed and the uncomfortable moment passed. Frank was obviously pleased with himself. Marge affectionately squeezed her husband's arm again. Huge smiles encompassed both their faces as they looked adoringly at each other.

Kate snuck a few glances at Molly, trying to understand what was going on in her sister's mind and why she was acting so strange.

"Molly, where is Jack?"

"Oh, still down at that lovely cafeteria to try to get something to eat, I believe," Kate replied sarcastically, offering an apologetic grin to Marge. Marge chuckled knowingly.

"Sorry, but I don't think we'll be going back there again, Marge," Molly said with a rueful grin.

"No worries here. Frank and I didn't get these," she patted her waist with one hand and his stomach with the other, "eating here, that much I can tell you."

Amidst more laughter, the two sisters said goodbye to Marge and her husband and left them in the lobby as they walked back to their mother's room together for one last visit of the day.

Since the earlier update, the doctors had not been able to offer any additional news on Beth's status. And without more hand movements or disruptions in her EKG waves, the prognosis did not appear to be better. While the sisters were beside their mother's bed, the younger doctor stopped by again and attempted to give them a realistic expectation of the days to come. Jack rejoined them in the room, catching the tail end of the doctor's words, and saw his wife reach out and tentatively take Kate's hand. His heart went out to her, especially when Kate did not pull away.

Kate, Molly, and Jack left the hospital soon after. Few words passed between them.

Molly and Jack drove straight home, anxious to see the girls again after a long day away. Molly interrupted the quiet only once to tell Jack the story about what had happened with her father that afternoon. He said nothing, glancing over at her with admiration every now and then as she spoke. When she was done, Jack tuned in to 104.5, the local radio station that they used to listen to before having the girls—before the need for quiet overcame their love of music. The drive home was otherwise quiet and uneventful—no flashing lights appeared behind them.

42. ONE MORE THING

WHEN THEY ARRIVED AND PULLED into the driveway, Sally, the neighbor who'd been helping with the girls, walked outside to greet them. She looked as tired and worn as Molly felt most days. Alice and Emma ran out of the house behind her, calling out to their parents with smiles on their faces.

"Mommy! Daddy!"

Alice opened the truck door for her, and the girls almost fell over themselves rushing in to give her a hug.

"Easy, girls! We've only been gone for a day."

The girls grudgingly moved aside to let her out of the car, and they all walked into the house together. As soon as she entered the main living space, Molly stopped short, her eyes wide in surprise.

The house looked spotless. There was not a toy was to be seen on the floor, not a piece of clothing on the furniture. The house was amazingly, and pleasantly, completely picked up from the living room to the kitchen. It looked more put together than any day Molly could remember. She looked over to see the girls standing prim and proper, with their hands behind their backs and smiles on their angelic faces.

"Do you like it, mommy?" Alice asked, as she swept a hand in front of her. "I cleaned up *all* morning for you."

"I helped, too!" Emma piped in.

"Yes, of course! I love it. You girls did a great job!"

Molly laughed and sent a grateful look to the babysitter who said her goodbyes and left, mentioning the need for a long rest. As Molly looked around the rooms, she could tell how much work Sally must have done; she had no doubt that she needed rest. Molly said a heartfelt "Thank-you" to Sally as she left, then scooped the girls up in another big hug before she pulled back, smiling.

"Mrs. Johansen promised us ice cream sundaes if we helped pick up. Can we make them now?" Alice asked expectantly. Then she let her face drop into an exaggerated frown, "Or do we have to wait until *after* dinner?"

Molly laughed again. Then before she could even get the words out to agree to a sundae now, both girls cheered. They ran to the kitchen, and Jack sat them down at the table to help make the sundaes. Molly followed them to help, but Jack encouraged her to take a few minutes upstairs and sent her off with a small rap on her behind and a grin.

Molly, grateful for the break after the day, headed up to the bedroom to change into some comfortable clothes. She hastily pulled off her slacks and top and stopped to take a quick peek in the mirror. With a small grimace she turned back and forth, noting the white stretch marks that lined her tummy, the sagging rear that used to be her favorite feature, and the placement of her breasts. She lifted them up to where they used to rest and frowned. She avoided looking at the little pooch that protruded above her panties and turned around once again to look at her behind. Seeing far more dimples than she'd remembered, she grimaced and turned away,

With a heavy sigh, she grabbed a t-shirt and pants from the dresser then walked over to the nightstand next to the bed to grab her deodorant for a quick reapplication. Her hands fumbled with the small cylinder, and she dropped the bottle, watching it roll under the bed. Cursing silently, she bent down to reach for it. Their old futon bed was low to the ground, so she had to fumble blindly for the deodorant. Her searching fingers encountered an old pacifier, a few socks, and finally the deodorant bottle. Next to it, she felt a crumpled piece of paper.

"Lord knows what else is under here," she muttered under her breath as she dragged everything out with a sweep of her hand.

When she looked down at the floor, her heart skipped a beat. Lying between the pink pacifier and two dusty socks was a handwritten note on light pink stationary. Molly immediately recognized her sister's messy scrawl without even having to read the signature at the bottom. She got up from the floor with some effort and sat down on the bed to read what could almost be described as a love note to her husband. The words were not flowery or overly romantic—typical of Kate—yet it was definitely written from a lover's perspective. Molly read through to the end just as Jack bounded upstairs to the bedroom. He had whip cream smeared on his cheek and a splash of bright red on the front of his shirt, presumably maraschino cherry juice.

Molly would have smiled at the sight had it been another time, but she just stared up at him blankly with the paper in her hand.

Jack didn't know what she was holding, but the look on his wife's face told him that something was very wrong. Her head was cocked to one side, and she peered at him as if for the first time. He stood in the doorway, uncertain of what to do. When she finally spoke, her voice was quiet and controlled.

"Jack, is there anything else about my sister that you need to tell me? Because frankly, I'm not sure if I could handle much more right now."

Jack found her tone even more disconcerting than if she'd yelled at him.

Molly then held the paper out to him, her arm extended and eyes downcast. Jack strode across the room and cautiously took the paper out of her hands with his thumb and forefinger as if it was on fire. He looked at the note and began to read. Realization dawned on his face. He jerked his head to Molly and started to explain.

"Molly, there's really nothing…"

Yet before he could finish, Molly cut him off and put one hand up between them as if it could ward off his words. Her voice got louder with each word.

"Nothing, huh? Then can you please explain why there's a fucking love note from my sister under our damn bed? You told me today that what happened between you guys was nothing!

This does not sound like nothing, Jack!" she shouted, flinging the paper in front of his face.

Jack flinched as if she had slapped him. Instinctively, he reached back and closed the bedroom door behind him.

"Molly," he took a deep breath then plunged forward, "I told you the truth earlier. My relationship with Kate *meant* nothing. It was over and done with before it even started."

"Yes, but I saw the way she touched you today. And the way that receptionist was with her husband. So loving. I don't know, Jack! Am I losing my mind, here? Was there something more between you and Kate, Jack? Was there?"

He paused for a second before blurting, "There was nothing between us!" He shook his head dejectedly. "It was just a fun time for a few months, that's all…"

"I don't know, Jack, this note definitely says something very different to me!" Molly spat back more harshly than she'd intended. "How the hell did it even get under our bed?"

Jack stood in the doorway, trying not to let the hurt show on his face. Although he knew Molly was right to be upset, the look of anger on her face was difficult to accept.

"I have no idea, truly. I hardly remember it, Molly. Maybe the girls found it somewhere. You know how they are always getting into things around here." Molly stared up at him as he talked. The mention of their daughters took some of the wind out of her sails. As her shoulders slowly relaxed, she looked down and read the note again. Finally, she broke the silence.

"Jack, you know I have to ask you…"

He gave her a nod as he waited for the questions that he knew were coming, questions that would have come out earlier today if his wife were a less trusting woman, questions that he knew she wouldn't have to ask if he had told her everything right from the start.

Softly yet sternly, Molly asked, "Did you love her, Jack? Did you? And did you sleep together?"

He sat down next to her on their bed. The only sounds that could be heard from downstairs were those coming from the television. Fortunately, the girls were too heavily engrossed in their favorite cartoon show to notice that neither parent was with them.

Though their legs were almost touching, Molly felt that the distance between was vast. They both stared down at the floor then Jack tentatively reached for her hand. Molly instinctively pulled away then relaxed and let him hold her tightly.

She prompted him again, "Did you, Jack?"

Jack turned to Molly, looked directly into her eyes, and spoke the words that he'd been holding inside for six years.

"Of course I didn't love her," he said quietly but emphatically. "Molly, if it weren't for you being her sister, Kate would have long been forgotten. Your sister and I may have been together for a short while, but you were the one that I was meant to be with, Molly. You. And, yes, we—ah—slept together, but just once, nothing more."

Jack scooted off the bed and knelt down on the floor in front of her on one knee.

"Molly, believe me when I say that the minute I met you, I knew that you were the one."

"Ha! Now I know you're lying!" she scoffed and looked away, brushing off a stray tear.

"What? I did—it's true!" he exclaimed.

"For heavens sake, it took you months to propose to me, Jack. You *told* me that first day at the football game that you had just gotten out of a bad relationship. That you needed to take things slow. Don't you remember?"

Then the realization of the timing hit Molly like a brick. "Oh my God! That was her, wasn't it? That was Kate?"

Jack let out a half laugh, and Molly looked at him with wide eyes, obviously confused. She yelled again, "What was *that* for? This is not at all funny, Jack."

"You don't know much about guys, do you?" he said teasingly.

"Well, since I've only been with one, I guess not."

"Molly, yes, that *was* Kate. But I liked you the instant we met. The guys just told me to play the broken heart card—'girls *love* that'– so I did. I was trying to win you over, you goof."

"You didn't need to… you had me at hello," Molly offered a soft smile.

Jack sat back down next to her. Molly leaned in close to him as he reached his arm around her to hold her tightly. She exhaled and slowly melted into his embrace. Her head felt like a thousand tiny pins were stuck inside of it. She began to rock back and forth, tears rolling freely down her cheeks.

Jack was the first to stand up. He reached out an arm to help Molly off the bed. Once standing, he took her by the shoulders and made her look directly at him.

"Everything's fine, Hun," he said with a smile. "You are my only girl."

"So that's it? One time? There's *nothing* else I should know about?"

"No, babe. Nothing."

And with that, they hugged tightly again and walked back downstairs together hand-in-hand.

What they saw when they reached the bottom of the stairs caused them both to gasp. Alice and Emma looked up at them sheepishly with ice cream on their faces. There was also ice cream on the counter and hot fudge drippings everywhere around them. Colored sprinkled were splattered all over the floor. The girls had tried to make their own ice cream sundaes.

"What happened here?" Molly and Jack called out almost in unison, laughing a little as they did.

At the same time, both girls shrugged their shoulders, glanced around the kitchen, and replied, "I dunno!"

Jack threw his head back, laughing at the absurdity of the moment, and put his arm around Molly's shoulder. Molly looked up at him and smiled lovingly.

43. SISTERS

KATE HAD ONLY BEEN IN Maine for two days, and it had only been three days since Molly called to deliver the terrible news about their mother, yet so much had happened since her arrival. To Kate, the past two days had felt more like weeks had gone by.

On the drive alone back to Molly and Jack's house, she kept busy returning her voicemails since the morning. First, she called Sam again and was thankful that little activity had occurred during her absence. He teased her, saying that in the few hours since they'd talked, things were still fine. But he did relay that there may be some good news about the Sheffield case. He said he should know more by tomorrow and would certainly keep her posted. Then she called Tom to give him an update—a conversation that went much better than earlier today because Kate smartly avoided any difficult questions. At one point, she pulled over on the side of the highway and just sat in the SUV with her hazards on, watching as cars went by with. She sat there alone, unaware of the passage of time, wondering what had happened to her life and where it would go.

When she finally arrived at Molly's house, she was struck by the tantalizing aroma of comfort food that she couldn't identify. It instantly made her salivate—especially after the lunch they'd had at the cafeteria. Any shyness that Alice and Emma had shown toward her was now gone. They both ran up to their aunt as soon as Kate walked through the door, bombarding her with questions and taking her hand to lead her to their toys.

"How was your day, Aunt Kate? Where'd you go? Which is your favorite Wiggle? Do you think Boots wears boots all of the time?"

Without a clue as to what the girls were asking, Kate looked over at Molly for help. Molly just laughed and shooed the girls off to the living room to play. As Kate watched in fascination, Molly moved quickly and deftly about the kitchen in multiple directions as she got everything ready for dinner. Although she was weary and overwhelmed, within minutes she had laid out a full table with rolls, a side salad, and some vegetables still steaming in the bowl.

Kate simply watched Molly from her barstool, feeling rather helpless amidst the flurry of her sister's activity. When Kate noticed Molly unconsciously touching her head for the third or fourth time, she decided that she had to know and finally asked.

"Molly, why do you do that?" Kate asked softly.

"Do what?" Molly replied. She tried to sound nonchalant, but she could not look Kate in the eye.

"Is everything alright? I'm mean, do you *feel* okay? Why do you keep touching your head like that?"

Molly turned to face Kate. She hesitated a moment and didn't answer. Instead she called to Jack in the next room. When he strolled into the kitchen, she put up her hand to stop him with a small jerk of her head.

"Jack, could you take the kids outside for a few minutes before dinner to blow off some energy?"

He looked back and forth between the two sisters—one had a firm, serious expression on her face, and the other looked as perplexed as he was at the request to leave. But without asking why, he swiftly got the girls into their coats and shoes and hustled them outside to play.

Once they were alone together in the kitchen, Molly looked her sister square in the face.

"No, Kate. Things are not okay. I mean, I don't know if they are okay." She took a deep breath before continuing, "You know what? I'm just scared to death that I'm going to end up like mom. Don't you ever worry about that?"

Kate shook her head. "I don't let myself, Molly. We are *not* our mother."

"I know, that's what Jack always says, but the pounding in my head usually says something different."

"I know it's been difficult here, and I'm just now beginning to realize what that has meant for you. I had no idea that Mom was this bad off, but I honestly don't think that either of us have any reason to worry about anything."

From outside, they could hear the girls' muffled squeals as Jack chased them around the front lawn.

"But why didn't you ever tell me that you two were talking?" Molly blurted out, with tears pooling in her eyes, "It would have helped, you know. It would have made things a little easier if I'd known there was someone else who Mom was turning to besides me every day."

Molly slumped down in one of the kitchen chairs. Feeling dejected and worn out, she put her face in her hands and let her shoulders relax—they had carried so much weight for so long.

Kate walked over and put her hand on Molly's shoulder. "I'm sorry, Molly. I truly am… I don't know what else to say."

"Well, I know that you've had your share of family problems, too, Kate. And I am so sorry about that."

Kate stiffened with Molly's words, then realized from the genuine sympathy on her sister's face that they held nothing more to them; her secret with Molly's father was still safe.

Before she even realized she was doing it, Kate knelt down in front of Molly and gently took her hands away from her face. The two sisters looked at each other and felt a bond that seemed strong enough to overcome everything—the resentment, the confusion, and all of the hurt from the past. They hugged tightly, almost fiercely, before Kate gently pulled away. She still saw uncertainty in Molly's eyes and asked softly, "What is it?"

When Molly didn't respond, Kate continued.

"Molly, you have a look about you. What is it?"

Then Molly drew a deep breath and plunged forward to ask Kate the question that she so desperately needed to hear.

"Kate, can you tell me about the time you were with Jack."

In an instant a heavy veil came over Kate's eyes. She stiffened up again and pulled away. She avoided Molly's eyes and suddenly became deeply interested in the *Care Bears* cartoon on the television.

Molly instantly regretted her question, knowing that the closeness they had just shared had vanished into the air. She reached out to touch Kate's arm, trying to save the moment.

"Kate, it's okay. Really! I know all about it. Jack told me."

Yet again, a dark shadow dropped over Kate's face. She replied without meeting Molly's stare.

"It was just for a short time, Molly." Then she threw back her head with a bitter laugh. "What are the chances, right? That he would be the same guy."

She looked out the window and watched him playing with the girls outside. Then she turned back to Molly with a vague and disturbing look.

"It's all over now, though." Her voice had a measured hollowness that echoed in the room.

Molly could feel the unease in the air and saw something in Kate that told her that something was very wrong. She tried to reach out once again to touch her arm, to make a connection and break the tension, but Kate pulled away from the contact as if she'd been burned by it.

"Kate, what is it? What's wrong?"

"Nothing," Kate answered a little too quickly. "Nothing's wrong. I'm glad you know now. That's certainly a relief."

At that, Molly laughed so loudly that Kate looked at her in surprise.

"What? Why are you laughing?"

"Kate, for heaven's sake. I knew about you guys *years* ago," Molly said, peering out the window with a smile on her face. "Jack thinks that he can hide things from me, but he's so bad at it. I mean I didn't know *everything;* just that your paths had crossed."

"What? How did you find out? When? And more importantly, why didn't you tell us—or me, for that matter—then?" The
questions poured out of her.

"Well… I guess I didn't tell *you* because we barely talk to each
other," Molly said matter-of-factly with a tip of her head. "As for
Jack, I was really just waiting for him to tell me himself. Apparently, he just needed some prompting… six years later!"

Molly offered Kate a smile, and they sat for a moment without
speaking before Molly asked Kate one final, tentative question.

"Kate, why did you look so upset, or rather sad, when I mentioned you dating him?" She paused then continued in a feeble
attempt at humor, "Was my husband *that* bad to date?"

"No, no, that wasn't it at all, Molly," Kate hastily replied and
attempted to put a smile on her face.

Then, to Molly's dismay, the smile fell and Kate threw her
hands to her face and began to cry.

Molly involuntarily uttered an "Oh!" at seeing Kate's tears,
but she said nothing more. She jumped up and hugged Kate
closely. Kate cried what seemed to be a river of tears. Molly didn't
know what to say. She just stroked Kate's hair and murmured,
"It's okay, it's okay," over and over. After a few minutes, Kate
pulled away slightly and wiped away her tears with the back of
her hand.

She looked at Molly and spoke quietly, "I'm fine… Could
we just get dinner started? And I think I need to get some more
coffee."

"Sure, sure," Molly replied obligingly as she hurriedly stood
up. "Why don't you go freshen up and come up when you're
ready? I'll get the coffee started."

And with that, Molly gratefully bustled off. She felt uncomfortable enough with what *wasn't* said to know that there had to
be something big behind Kate's words to bring her to tears. Her
hands busied themselves with the coffee as her mind desperately
searched for answers.

Kate hurried downstairs as she heard Molly call Jack and the
girls back inside. She slumped down in a heap onto the bed,

feeling resigned to all the bad things in her life—her nonexistent relationship with her only sister, her mother's state of life or death, and the life that she'd created for herself away from them all. Coupled with the piece of her past that she couldn't bring herself to think about, it was too much to bear. Kate had never felt more uncertain of herself. She curled up on the bed, alone with her thoughts, and hugged her knees in tight.

The remainder of the evening was uneventful. The girls, exhausted from being up so late the night before, ate dinner and went straight to bed. Dinner and cleanup were smooth and everyone was lost in their own thoughts about life, and perhaps death, as they retired for the night. For the first time in three days, everyone slept long through the night.

The next morning, as always, Molly and Jack were awakened by the girls, though later than usual due their late night. Alice and Emma hopped up onto their bed, their nightgowns swirling playfully around them. Emma pounced on her father's midsection, causing a loud "harrumph"; he instinctively turned sideways to protect himself. Alice snuggled up next to her mother and started talking about what she wanted for breakfast. Both girls were energetic and chatty after a good night's sleep, and as Molly struggled to open her reddened, sleep-deprived eyes, she hugged Alice tightly and looked over her small head toward Jack.

"How are you feeling, Hun?" he asked her gently.

She said nothing but gave him a small squeeze on his arm in response. They all clambered out of bed and Molly tried to get the day underway.

Molly and Kate quickly got ready to head back to the hospital once again. This time Jack would stay behind with the girls, giving Ms. Johansen some much needed rest and Kate and Molly some time together. This would be Kate's last visit before she flew back home. Molly looked questioningly at her throughout the morning for signs of their previous night's discussion, but she didn't see any. Kate was attentive with the girls, knowing that she might not see them for a while.

But inside, Kate couldn't wait to leave. Knowing that today would be her final visit with her mom left her with a feeling of dread, yet she couldn't bear to stay any longer. The weight of her emotions felt like a cloak of iron draped around her, suffocating her. Her muscles were as worn as if she had run a hundred miles. Before leaving, she packed her suitcase and took one last look at the tiny guest room then joined everyone upstairs. They ate a simple breakfast of Cheerios and toast. When Alice and Emma left the table, Molly surprised everyone by saying, "So, guys, I guess it's a good thing you two didn't work out, or I guess we wouldn't all be together like this now."

Jack spit out his orange juice and Kate almost choked on her toast as Molly sat back, folded her arms on her chest and smiled at them both. After her eyes had cleared, Kate looked over at Jack to see his reaction. He shrugged his shoulders in feigned innocence.

Kate looked back at Molly and answered slyly, "Well, I guess that means we are all copacetic then?"

"Yes, we are… if that means that we're okay, Ms. Lawyer" Jack tossed back with a grin.

Right then, Molly realized that the secret she had held on to for so long now seemed small and insignificant. She smiled inwardly and looked back and forth between two of the people whom she cared about most.

"Yes, everything's fine and it was a long time ago," Molly said with absolution as she got up from the table to clear up their dishes.

"Yes," Kate said under her breath, "It was."

"What was that?" Molly turned back to her, bright-faced and obviously content in her newfound knowledge.

"Nothing," Kate replied with another forced smile.

Kate quickly left the table before her face showed them what her words did not. Scurrying around the kitchen to finish gathering her things—and to keep busy—Kate said a quick goodbye to Jack then approached the girls on bended knee. They came right to her and she hugged them close. They pleaded with her not to leave and made her promise to visit again very soon. Kate was prepared for their request, agreeing to return sooner rather than later, and had already told herself that this was one promise that she had better keep.

The older sisters left the house in a flurry of activity and took their own cars to the hospital as Kate would be heading straight to the airport after. She arrived at the hospital first and waited in the parking lot for Molly. When Molly arrived ten minutes later, Kate playfully tapped at her watch and teased Molly for driving like an old lady.

As they crossed the hospital's foyer, Kate's cell phone buzzed. They waved to Marge who was once again working at the receptionist desk, then Kate looked down to see Ethan's name. She answered warmly, telling him that she'd just arrived back at the hospital. Despite his protests, she quickly ended their call with assurances that she would call him back after her visit. She hung up, not thinking twice about his objections and anxious to see her mother one last time.

The sisters walked straight to the ICU. As they were about to enter Room #110, Kate heard a low, "Hey, Kate," come from behind them. She turned to see Lena and Curt coming down the hall and gasped.

The beseeching look in Curt's eyes told her that nothing good would come of this, and she shook her head at him as if to ward off the moment, trying to send him away. As Curt ignored her and approached, she experienced first anger then regret, blushing at the sight of him. The feel of their short but heated kiss still burned on her lips, and her desire to run was stronger than ever. She felt like a naughty schoolgirl and hated herself for it. She hoped that her desperation wasn't obvious, and she did her best to react normally, giving Curt a small wave.

Molly was the first to speak up, oblivious to the turmoil inside Kate.

"Hey, Mrs. Connors. Thank you for coming to see Mom. Are you leaving now, or did you just get here?

She leaned over to give Lena a quick hug then looked up at the attractive man standing next to her. Lena hesitated just a moment upon seeing the questioning look on Molly's face.

"Oh, we just arrived. Molly, I guess you've never met my son, Curt. Curt, this is Molly, Beth's other daughter, from her second marriage," she explained to him.

"Other?" asked Molly, looking at Kate then back at Lena with a confused look.

At the same time, Curt looked to Kate and spoke for the first time; his deep voice was tinged with disappointment.

"Really, Kate? I don't even remember that you *had* a sister," he chastised lightly.

Kate was instantly chagrined at hearing his words as she knew the effect they would have on Molly. Feeling Molly's stare bore into her, Kate quickly turned away and said nothing.

"Well, I'm a little confused here," Molly said dryly, looking back and forth between Curt and Kate. "You two actually *know* each other?"

"Oh, Katie and my Curt used to be lovers, dear…" Lena said before being cut off.

"Mother!"

"Lena!" Kate admonished.

"What?" Molly gasped.

Kate opened her mouth then closed it, knowing that whatever came out would not be helpful right now. Curt was the first to speak up.

"Mom, that was a long time ago," he said sharply, adding gently, "And you didn't need to phrase it like that."

"Sorry, dear," she tossed over her shoulder to him as she turned to face Molly and Kate with pursed lips.

Kate couldn't tell if she was aware of the havoc that she had just created.

"Were you girls going in to see Beth now?" she asked them as if nothing had just happened. "Do you mind if I join?"

She was once again interrupted by her son.

"Actually, Mom, I was hoping to talk with Kate first," he said. He looked directly at Kate with a dip of his head. "Alone."

And with that, all eyes went to Kate.

She froze. Unsure of what to say or do and hating herself for her indecision, she chose to do nothing but pray that the ground would open up and swallow her whole. Kate had spent countless hours arguing cases in courtrooms with dozens of people staring at her, but she was now immobilized.

"Kate," Curt asked quietly, "I'm sorry, could I just talk to you for a minute?"

When she didn't immediately respond—she was not yet able to find the strength to speak—he continued in a low voice as he took a small step toward her.

"About what happened the other night?"

That brought Kate out of her stupor; she immediately cursed him under her breath and looked at Molly. Kate knew then that Molly understood that Curt was the "old girlfriend" whom Kate had left to see that first night, and she bit her lip so hard that she tasted the copper taste of blood inside her mouth.

Molly's moral compass went on high alert. Her back bristled. Then before Molly even knew what she was doing, she started yelling at her sister like a mad woman.

"Kate! Seriously? You gave me shit for my father's affairs, but *this* is what you do when you come up to visit us?" She jerked her head at Curt. "And with our mother in the hospital?"

Molly glared at Kate. Kate, in turn, stared defiantly at Curt.

"Molly, it was not like that." Kate tried to defend herself. "Curt and I used to date in college, and we've hardly stayed in touch since then. He just asked me to meet up with him when he found out I was here in town."

Then before she knew it, Kate's guilt and anger got the best of her. She suddenly blurted out defensively, "And it was just one kiss, dammit!"

Amidst the gasps that seemed to echo in the corridor, Lena was the quickest to respond. She promptly turned to rap her son's arm in reproach and chided him softly.

"Curt! Kate is a married woman. You know that! What were you thinking, son?"

Curt just looked at Kate apologetically, trying to tell her without words that he was sorry.

Molly looked directly at Kate and asked with anger flashing in her eyes, "*Just* a kiss, huh?"

Kate nodded numbly but said nothing. Curt came to her defense.

"Yes. And it wasn't Kate's fault. I'm the one to blame. I don't really know what happened… I just came here this morning to make sure that she was okay and tell her I was sorry. But maybe it's best if I go."

Then suddenly another masculine voice came from behind Kate and Molly. It was the voice that Kate knew better than any other.

"*What*, exactly, wasn't your fault, Kate?"

Kate and Molly spun around, and Kate let out another gasp. Lena and Curt looked around to see who had spoken. No one moved until Kate broke the silence, shrieking at the man standing there and causing everyone to jump. The man held a bouquet of cellophane-wrapped flowers tightly in one hand. Bewilderment and anger played across his face.

Kate stared at her husband in shock.

"Ethan, what… what the hell are you doing here?" she finally managed to stammer.

"What do you mean, 'what am I doing here?' I'm your husband," he replied sternly, looking directly at Curt like a lion marking his territory and preparing to fight.

Kate knew that he had heard their conversation. Her heart sank.

"And since your mother is here lying in the ICU," he continued sarcastically, "I thought I should fly up here to be with you."

"But—but I *just* talked to you a little while ago… You were home!"

"No, Kate. I'd actually already left the airport. You didn't bother to ask me where I was." He then added with a small smile,

"You cut me off, as usual, so I didn't get the chance to tell you that I'd landed."

Kate hesitated just a moment more. Then she closed the distance between them in a run and reached up to hug her husband tightly. As she burrowed her face in his shoulder and felt his arms encircle her body, she wanted desperately for everything—and everyone—else to fade away. When she pulled back enough to look at Ethan's face, she saw something unfamiliar in her husband's demeanor. It was a conviction of sorts and a confidence that she wasn't accustomed to. She searched his face for answers and wondered if he could see in her face the undeniable changes that she had experienced since leaving home just days before. Kate knew that she had changed from the cold, shut off person she had been into someone who could feel and suffer… and endure.

"Thank you for coming," she told him quietly. And she meant it.

With that, she drew herself away and turned around to face everyone and make things right, but the hall was empty.

She looked back at Ethan and said, rather cautiously, "I should probably explain…"

Ethan put his finger to her lips to silence her. She looked up at him in surprise but heeded the gesture. He motioned for them to go into her mother's room.

"C'mon. Let's go be with your mother. That's where you need to be."

Inside the room, Molly stood stiffly in front of the window with her back to everyone. Lena sat on the other side of the bed, holding her friend's hand. She looked over at Kate and Ethan as they walked in and said that Curt had thought it best to leave, her tone apologetic. As Kate introduced Lena to Ethan, a text beeped loudly on her phone. Even Molly turned around, though Kate avoided her burning stare. All eyes turned to Kate and again the text notification echoed off the hospital walls.

As she glanced down at the cell in her hand, Kate couldn't help but smile slightly. The text was straightforward and sincere.

"Hope I didn't cause u any problems. Take care. Remember to smile."

Kate looked up at Ethan and silently handed him her phone. He took one look at the message and gave the cell back to her with a nod of his head. From that small gesture, Kate understood that no additional explanation would be needed between them. Gently, tentatively, she took hold of his hand; he gave hers a firm squeeze.

Lena sat quietly on the other side of the bed and held Beth's hand in silence. Ethan and Kate stood side-by-side, and for the first time in days, Kate felt a sense of security. However, when she finally glanced over at Molly and saw the anger in her eyes, her stomach dropped again. Avoiding her sister's glare, Kate talked quietly to Ethan, trying to bring him up to speed about the last few days.

She didn't mention the time spent with Curt. She didn't mention her concern about Molly. As she spoke, she realized that what she *did not* say to him probably meant more than what she *did* say.

44. NEWS OF BETH

LENA STAYED IN THE HOSPITAL room a short while longer before bustling out to leave her good friend with her family. As she somberly left the room, she gave everyone a big tear-filled hug, even Ethan who kindly if hesitantly returned the gesture.

A short while later, Ethan, Kate, and Molly left the room single-file with their heads bowed. Kate could feel Molly's eyes boring into her back as she reluctantly followed Ethan out. There was only silence between them as a few other families walked quietly by. A baby's cries could be heard faintly from somewhere down the hall.

As they were about to leave, a voice called out, "Excuse me? Are you the family of Beth Stevens?"

They turned around, and Kate saw the same doctor who had offered comforting words to her yesterday in her mother's room.

"Yes, we are," she replied tentatively.

They all stood there, mired in an uncertainty that inhibited movement and speech. The young doctor, sensing their hesitancy and discomfort, smiled warmly as he said, "Folks, if you have a minute, I'd like to give an update on her condition before you go." His bedside manner was refreshing. Many of the doctors they had encountered seemed to see patients as numbers in charts.

The trio walked briskly to where the doctor stood. Molly's anger toward Kate was all but forgotten. Ethan grabbed Kate's hand in support and held onto it tightly. Kate wanted nothing more than to reach over and shake the information out of him, but she kept her arms by her sides, grateful for Ethan's hold on her.

As the doctor rifled through the pages of notes on his chart, the moments seemed like hours. Kate glanced at his nametag,

"Dr. David Smith," and barely stifled a laugh. As she looked at his face, she saw the similarities that she had missed before, and she realized why he'd seemed familiar yesterday.

"Doctor, are you by chance related to Marge at the front desk?" she asked with a small smile.

His head snapped up, but before he could answer, she went on, "And Frank, the talkative though helpful traveling businessman, is your father, then."

"Yes," he exclaimed with obvious surprise on his face. "I can see how you've met my mother. Everyone remembers Marge. But how do you know my father?"

"Oh, I don't actually know him, though I did see him when he was here earlier today. We actually had seats next to each other on the flight up here the other day from Atlanta." Kate paused before adding hesitantly, "He was quite nice, though, and your mother has certainly had some words of wisdom to share with me in the last few days."

Dr. Smith tossed back his head and laughed loudly, "Yes, well, you do already know my mother then. Words of wisdom and everything else she can throw in, that's for sure. She's never short on what to say."

Though when the last word left his lips, he stopped himself and looked at each of them apologetically. In unison, the sisters looked back down the hall toward their mother's room, working hard to hold back their tears.

"So, Doctor Smith, what were you going to tell us?" Ethan tried to encourage him.

"I'm sorry. That wasn't very considerate of me."

Ethan spoke up again, "It's fine. We'd just like to know how she is. I understand from talking with my wife here that Beth may have moved her finger yesterday, which seems like a good sign, correct..." his voice trailed off expectantly.

"Yes, that is correct," Dr. Smith said quickly, relieved that his tactless moment was excused. He then continued somberly, "However, I'm sorry to say that we don't feel she did so of her own volition. And I'm afraid there's been no increase in brain activity since then to indicate that her condition is improving."

"What? But yesterday you seemed so hopeful!" Kate blurted out. Anger tinted every word.

"Yes, I know. And we are *always* hopeful with everyone who is in a coma. We are," he said. Then he shook his head, "But sometimes hope isn't enough to change the tide and make things better. And your mother's situation is simply not improving. I'm sorry to say this, but I thought you should know before you left the hospital today."

Dr. Smith allowed time for his words to sink in.

Molly was the first to speak. Her voice was barely audible. "So are you telling us that you don't think she'll come out of this?"

Dr. Smith shook his head, "I'm sorry, but we just don't know. We do see miraculous recoveries inside these hospital walls all the time. All we can do is hope for the best. Now, if you'll excuse me, I should continue my rounds."

As graciously as possible, Dr. Smith nodded and continued past them down the corridor.

Kate had to steel herself to keep from grabbing Dr. Smith by the arm as he passed by her. All she wanted to do was slap him. As if Ethan sensed her impulse, he placed one hand gently, yet firmly, on her arm.

Startled, Kate wondered for the first time if her husband had actually read her thoughts.

"It's okay," she said, "I'm fine, really." She lightly shrugged out of his grasp.

"Are you sure?" His question was soft, yet the retort that came back at him was not.

"Yes, Ethan, why wouldn't I be?" she snapped back, more harshly than she'd intended. She followed it up with a humble apology and squeezed his hand when he said nothing in return.

He gave Kate such a look of understanding and compassion that her heart sank. This man whom she had shut out for so long, whom she had given as little of herself to as possible during their time together, and whom she had forbidden from coming home with her during a traumatic time was still looking back at her with love. Kate was dumbstruck. She felt her husband's love for her like never before. Needing some space to process her emotions, she mumbled another thank you to him before she briskly headed down the hall and walked away.

"I'm just going to go grab some coffee, Ethan," she tossed back over her shoulder. "I'll meet you guys back in the lobby in a few minutes."

Kate left Ethan and Molly standing alone in awkward silence. She didn't care. The rollercoaster of emotions she was experiencing was too unsettling. Her heart felt fragmented and splintered, even raw, but at the same time she was so grateful to feel *something* that she almost wanted to jump with joy. Kate knew she needed to be alone for a few minutes to sort out her newfound emotions.

After everything that had happened in the last few days, she knew without a shadow of doubt that she had become an entirely different woman. Like a snake that sheds its skin, she felt both a vulnerability and a vitality that she had never felt before. She aimlessly walked up and down the halls to give herself time to think, unaware of how much time passed. Then, forgetting the coffee and without knowing where else to go, she headed back toward the lobby.

She walked into the room to find Molly, Ethan, Madge, and Madge's son, Dr. Smith, all engaged in conversation. She immediately glared at Dr. Smith as if he was to blame for her mother's condition.

They were all grinning about something, behaving more like old friends than strangers who had just met. Looking in from the outside Kate felt excluded and shut out, though from what, she didn't know.

"You are all awfully cheery considering that Mom is on her death bed," she said upon approach. Then she looked directly at the doctor. "And I thought he had other patients to *not* help improve."

Once again, however, her attempt at humor failed; she instantly regretted her words. Seeing everyone's faces, she vowed right then to stop using sarcasm as a shield. Dr. Smith quickly excused himself and hurried off down the hall.

"Kate, Hun, we were just making conversation while we waited for you," Ethan said quietly.

Then Molly added in her own failed attempt at humor, "At least I wasn't making out with an old boyfriend."

Kate's face blanched as if she'd been slapped. With steely eyes, she quickly turned on her heels and walked out through the automatic hospital doors without saying another word.

Once outside, she breathed in the cold air, wondering how things had come to this point. Emotions seemed to rule everything, and the logic that she'd lived by for so long seemed to be lost. She walked around the side of the hospital building away from anyone's view and leaned against the wall and looked out at the city skyline beyond.

Glancing at her phone, she saw another missed call from her father and silently cursed the hospital's policy of no cell phone usage. Without hesitation, she called him back. Tom picked up on the first ring.

"Oh! I didn't expect that!" she said in surprise.

"Kate, I've been waiting for you to call all day. For God's sake, what's going on?"

"Drama, Dad. Lots of drama," she said. Then she added, "You'd love it."

He ignored the sarcasm. "Kate, please tell me about your mother. How is she doing?"

"Nothing has changed, which the doctors are now saying is not a good sign."

"Oh." The disappointment in his voice was unmistakable.

Ever the attorney, Kate stood up straighter and went in for the "kill" that she was known for.

"Did you love her, Tom? Did you ever love her?"

"Kate, this is a fine time to be asking me a question like that."

"Please, could you just answer me? Did you?" Her voice was low.

Tom paused for a moment then replied so softly that Kate had to strain to hear him on the other end, "Yes, Kate, I truly did. But the best thing between us was having you. Your mother and I didn't last, and God knows I wasn't perfect, but the one good thing that we got right was you!"

With that, a tear rolled down Kate's cheek, and she exhaled slowly. Then for the first time in a long time, Kate let the fight go.

"Thank you... Dad. That means more than you will ever know."

45. TOGETHER AGAIN

AFTER KATE STORMED OUT OF the hospital, Molly and Ethan walked to the other side of the lobby toward the rows of chairs. They sat down and waited for her to return. This was the first time Molly had ever been alone with Ethan, and at first she did not know what to say, but in an effort to make things right she spoke pleadingly to her sister's husband.

"I was just teasing her, you know," she said apologetically, looking up to Ethan expectantly. "She's always tossing it out, and I was trying to give a little back. I guess I thought she could take it."

"I know, Molly. It's fine, really. Let me go try to find her. Stay put and I'll be right back," Ethan assured her. Then he walked out through the lobby doors in search of Kate.

Molly stood there for a few minutes, looking around self-consciously, though the lobby was deserted except for an elderly man in the corner who appeared to be sleeping in his chair. Needing to do anything but stay there alone, she sharply turned and headed outside.

"Hey, there! We'll see you tomorrow!" Marge called out to Molly as she walked through the electronic doors.

Molly nodded to Marge over her shoulder with an attempted smile. As soon as she stepped outside, the cool air wrapped around her. Looking around, she saw no movement in the parking lot. She leaned back against the cold brick walls, just as Kate had done moments before.

Out of habit, she rubbed the side of her head and closed her eyes against the pain that threatened to creep up behind them. A few people left the hospital, and the warmth that escaped through the automatic doors made its way to her, teasing her back inside.

The chill of the air proved to be too much without a jacket, so she scurried back into the warm hospital lobby. Still feeling sad and remorseful about her comment to Kate, she slumped down in a chair by the window and waited.

Within moments, Ethan strode around the corner and called out her name. He said he'd looked in their mother's room then walked around outside, but didn't see Kate. He vigorously rubbed at his arms against the cold and muttered under his breath; Molly could see that his blood had also thinned from living in the South, and she smiled with a Northerner's haughty scorn of his weakness.

"How do people live like this?" he asked with mild exasperation as he approached her chair. Molly smiled and stood up to greet him, immediately seeing the anxiety that riddled his face.

"Where do you think she went?"

"I don't know," he shook his head, "and her phone didn't pick up. I couldn't tell if she was on it or if it's just on silent."

They looked at each other, unsure of what else to say. Molly tried to remember the last time she'd been around her brother-in-law. She realized that she had only been with him one other time, well before Alice was born. He stood beside her, his eyes scanning the halls then out to the parking lot through the hospital windows.

Looking closer at him, she sadly realized that if Ethan had been standing in a group of men on the street, she might not have been able to pick him out at all. Peering out of the corner of her eye, she decided that he was a handsome man in a classic sort of way. He wasn't ruggedly handsome like Jack, but despite the leanness of his frame and the smoothness of his hands, he was good-looking and came across as a very capable man.

What stood out most, however, were his green eyes. They were piercing and strong, and their hue seemed to change whenever he looked at her. *How did I not remember those eyes*, she thought with surprise as their gazes met. She had a fleeting thought, wondering if those keen eyes of his could see through to the fear that had gripped her insides for so long.

She smiled and decided that she liked her brother-in-law—and just for his attractiveness and his telling eyes. She liked him because he had flown up to be with her sister despite Kate's insistence that he stay back. His eye caught hers again, and they smiled warmly at each other. Ethan nodded his head in the direction of the front doors.

"Kate should come back soon, I presume. Should we just sit and wait there, then?" he asked, motioning over to the lobby chairs where Molly had been sitting before.

She agreeably walked over and sat down; he took the seat next to her. After a few moments, she was unable to contain her questions any longer. She began to ask him the questions that were burning inside of her, searching for answers about the sister she barely knew. She realized that she had the attention of the person who knew her sister best.

"Ethan, why do you think Kate has had so little to do with me since she left Maine?"

He paused thoughtfully before answering her slowly, his eyes still straying outside in search of Kate. "If I knew that, Molly, I'd probably know who my wife really was."

And although the words might seem callous from someone else, his tone was pure. The years of rejections and rebuffs that he had also received from her sister rang loud and clear. She softened to him even more, as she understood that Ethan was as lost as she was on how to get behind the wall that Kate had built up around herself.

Molly reached out to put a small hand on his arm.

"It's okay... It's just been tough to have a sister all these years that I don't even know." She paused, adding sheepishly, "You know, I wish you'd both be staying with us tonight."

"Thank you, but I'm sure you hadn't planned on having an extra guest... Hey, where *is* Jack by the way? And your father? Were they here already this morning? I'm sorry, I didn't even think to ask about them with everything going on here."

"No worries! You'd be just as welcome as my own sister, though, Ethan. I hope you know that" she said agreeably. "And yes, they were here earlier this morning. Jack's back with the girls now so Kate and I could have some time alone together with mom... look where *that* got us."

"Molly, your sister *is* a good woman. She is. I know she had a tough beginning in this world, but she means well. She just doesn't know how to show it sometimes." He grinned ruefully. "Well, perhaps *most* of the time."

"Hey, I'm not looking for much, Jack. Just something—anything, really," Molly shook her head, then continued, "to show me that she cares about me—about us!"

At that moment, they both looked up to see Kate striding resolutely down the hall toward them. She held a to-go coffee cup in one hand and a large plastic bag in the other hand. Popping out of the top was something pink and furry.

Kate walked over to where they sat and carefully set her coffee down on the floor beside them. She pulled the pink objects out of the bag, revealing two identical overstuffed teddy bears. They wore t-shirts that read "I Hug You" with a red heart below. She looked back and forth between Ethan and Molly then blurted out awkwardly, "I want us to be friends, Molly. Friends *and* sisters... I—ah I picked these out for Alice and Emma, if you think they'll like them okay."

Molly and Ethan looked at each other with undisguised shock on their faces then burst out into peals of laughter.

"What's so funny?" Kate finally demanded, though she was not able to contain the smile on her own face.

Ethan looked at his sister-in-law and nudged her arm. "Maybe there's hope for us yet."

"Maybe..." Molly nodded and smiled broadly at Kate.

"I don't know what's humorous here, but I believe that I'm the brunt of it," she said dryly. "Ethan, would you mind if I had a few minutes alone with my sister?

"Yes, of course," he nodded encouragingly and then hopped up and strode out of the lobby.

Kate hesitated before awkwardly handing over the stuffed animals to Molly. She still wasn't entirely sure if they'd be thrown back at her or tossed aside. But Molly took them from her out-stretched hand, murmured her thanks, and hugged them close.

"Molly, I'd like to explain… about the other night. Really, Curt just wanted to say hi while I was here in town. That was all. There was nothing more than old friends getting together." Kate looked down at her feet. "That kiss—shit, I don't know what happened and I feel terrible."

"It's okay. Really. I think it was just the timing, you know? I thought you were being a little hypocritical, especially after getting on me about my father." She paused, then rushed on, "And I did come down hard on him, you know. For how he treated mom! I surprised him. Gosh, I even surprised *myself!*"

"Good for you. I mean, for taking a stand. I'm proud of you."

After a pause, Molly asked, "Kate, was he that bad to you? My father?"

Kate took a minute to respond, wanting to share what she felt without hurting her sister anymore than she had already done these last few days. She knew that she would never tell her what almost happened that night with Molly's father. Letting her know how he made her feel so unwanted at home would be enough. One line continued to play inside her head like a skipping record: *No matter what he did to me, he's still my sister's father.*

"Well, he wasn't abusive, Molly, if that's what you're thinking. It was just that he didn't care, and that hurt," she explained. "I have no doubt that I wasn't an easy child, though—God knows I'm not easy now, right?" She laughed bitterly.

"That's all? Nothing more?" Molly prodded.

"No, they were just difficult times for everyone, I think, but that's all," she replied without making eye contact.

Molly sensed that Kate was shielding her from something, though she didn't know what, and it didn't matter. All she knew was that her sister cared enough about her to protect her, and that meant more to her than she'd ever anticipated. She experienced a fierce love for her that was unlike anything she'd felt before.

Molly quickly came to Kate's defense to try to let her know that she understood that she was on her side. "Well, as a mother now, I can't imagine treating any child badly, no matter whose they were... I'm sorry, Kate. Really, I am."

A cloud passed over Kate's face as she replied. "You know, I think we are all sorry for what's happened. But I would really love to see us move on now. To get past it all and start again. What do you think, could we make that happen?"

Molly smiled broadly, "I think that's the best thing I've heard all day."

She hugged Kate tightly. They stood like that for a while. Just then, an alarm went off at the nurses' station and two nurses rushed down the hall. As they passed the two sisters, one of the nurses said the name "Stevens." Kate and Molly pulled back and looked at each other—and froze.

46. SAYING GOODBYE

KATE AND MOLLY WATCHED IN horror as more nurses and doctors darted around the corridor. Kate was the first to break away from the embrace.

She grabbed for Molly's hand and ran down the hall, half dragging her sister behind her. As Kate rounded the last corner, she let go of Molly's hand and ran toward their mother's room. She heard the same high-pitched beeping sound they'd heard from the nurses' station, but it was much louder. At that moment, Dr. Smith stepped out of the room and the look on his face told them everything.

"I'm afraid you can't go in there right now," he said as he looked back and forth between Kate and Molly. "I'm sorry, but it appears that your mother's heart has stopped beating. We are trying to revive her."

He turned to go back inside and closed the door, leaving them standing speechless in the hall. They could hear muffled frantic voices for a few minutes then finally the beeping stopped; Kate could stand it no longer. She leaped forward and thrust the door open, only to find all the hospital staff standing still and staring down at her mother.

"What's going on here? Do something, will you?" she shouted out. But no one moved.

The doctor touched her arm gently. "I'm sorry, but we've done all we can."

"But you told us earlier to have hope! You said there was a chance!" Kate screamed out the words and shook her head almost uncontrollably, trying to negate what he'd said.

In that moment, the door opened and an even louder guttural sound came from behind them.

"NO!"

Everyone turned to see Molly standing in the doorway. She ran to the bed and leaned over their mother. Kate reached out to her, but Molly wildly lashed out her arms in defense and beat back at Kate senselessly. Kate yelled for her to stop, even though Molly's fists had no weight behind them.

Her cries of "No, no!" slowly turned to whimpers as Molly stopped and pushed away from Kate to stand next to the bed.

One by one, the staff walked out of the room to leave the women in their grief; neither Kate nor Molly noticed. Tears rolled freely down both of their faces. Molly reached one hand out and touched their mother's already pallid cheek. Her hand jerked back in response, and she looked down at her fingers as if they had been wounded. She turned to Kate and laid her head on one shoulder, allowing sobs to rack her body.

When the sisters finally let go, Kate leaned over to give Beth a final gentle hug, avoiding the tubes and machines that still clung to her now lifeless body. Tears continued to slide down her face as she hugged her mother close.

For the first time ever, Kate told her mother how much she loved her. Expecting nothing in return, she let her go.

Upon hearing Kate's words, Molly reached out and squeezed her sister's hand tightly. Kate squeezed back, and the two women hung on to that grasp as if it was saving them from being swept away by grief.

47. LEAVING THE HOSPITAL

MOLLY AND KATE HAD BEEN allowed to stay by Beth's bed to say their final goodbyes. Ethan, who had been passing by the lobby on his way back from the cafeteria when Marge told him the news, immediately joined them. Jack arrived at the hospital as soon as he could after he got the news of Beth's passing. He rushed in to the room and drew Molly close, murmuring words of sympathy and support that only she could hear. Ethan took his place behind Kate, allowing her the time to say the last words to her mother that he knew she needed to say.

Finally, the four paid their last respects before the hospital staff quietly ushered them out of the room.

Ethan and Jack took care of the required hospital paperwork while Kate and Molly sat beside each other in the lobby and waited for them, still stunned and in disbelief. The two sisters held each other's hands in silence. Their eyes were red from tears and their hearts ached with the indescribable suffering that comes from losing a loved one, let alone a mother.

Suddenly, Marge rounded the corner and appeared before them with her arms outstretched, clucking her condolences. She expressed her heartfelt sympathy while drawing the two women in close for a long hug as if they were dear friends. Her son, the young doctor, approached the family next and offered his own sincere, if somewhat reserved, condolences. Even in such a terrible time, Kate came out of the darkness long enough to tell Marge how grateful she was for her kindness and encouragement over the last few days, and she hugged the woman back more tightly than she realized.

"Thank you, Marge," she murmured. "Thank you for everything."

"Thank *you*, Mrs. Harriman. Your words are why I still work here. If I can help anyone in their struggles, it makes *all* of our struggles easier to bear."

A short while later, Jack, Molly, Kate, and Ethan all left the hospital together. They were solemn, and they maintained their composure enough to discuss what needed to be done in the days ahead. Jack promised Kate that all of the funeral arrangements would be taken care of quickly, as Kate and Ethan would need to fly back home. Ethan called the airline and cancelled his and Kate's return flights. He rebooked them with open tickets and called a nearby hotel that Jack recommended. Then he darted back into the hospital to grab his suitcase from behind the service desk.

The two couples hugged teary goodbyes in the parking lot. Before going their separate ways, Molly asked in a half-hearted attempt at graciousness if Kate and Ethan would change their minds and stay with them instead. Kate just hugged Molly in response and said the hotel was the easiest solution under the circumstances and that they would see them tomorrow. Kate knew that despite Molly's kind offer, the last thing her sister needed was to be hostess on this night.

She also wasn't sure if she could be around anyone else herself, anyway, and she and Ethan left with promises to call first thing in the morning.

Though Molly had driven to the hospital separately earlier in the morning, Jack took her back home in his truck so she wouldn't be alone.

Standing in the parking lot, Kate and Ethan leaned against her rental SUV in silence, each staring off in the distance. He held her close yet withheld his words, understanding that his wife would need time to grieve and time to heal, as she slowly began to process her mother's loss. When he finally spoke, he chose his words carefully and spoke from his heart.

"Kate, I'm so sorry that you have to go through something like this. I hate it—for you, for Molly, for everyone. Your mother didn't deserve this... this terrible way to go, but neither do you."

She said nothing in response, but she reached over and clutched his hand in her own. Tears fell silently down her reddened cheeks. Though the air around them was cold, she felt nothing except heartache inside.

"Should we head to the hotel now?" he asked tentatively.

"Sure. From what Jack said, I believe it's not very far from here."

Ethan turned to get into the SUV, but Kate grabbed his arm and stopped him. She looked at him with pleading eyes and a tormented look on her face.

"Ethan, part of me did want to go back and stay with Molly, you know. To be with family… But honestly, I think I just needed some time alone. Was that okay?"

"I think it's perfectly fine, Hun. Molly and Jack undoubtedly need some time alone to mourn, as well. We can just stay at the Hilton until after the funeral…" he stopped, knowing that no more needed to be said.

Her eyes glassed up, and she turned away from him. She sensed that his eyes were tearing up again, too.

"It's okay, you don't have to be strong for me, Ethan," she said, looking back at him with an attempted smile.

"Shouldn't that be my line?"

They laughed a little then slid into the SUV. They drove the short distance to the hotel. The only words spoken were Kate's mumbled directions. Jack pulled the SUV to a stop outside the Hilton and turned to Kate.

"Hun, I know this may not be the right time, but I know that your sister loves you very much. She would love to be a part of your life, of our lives. Now, I think she needs you more than ever before."

"I know," she replied softly, feeling penitent. "It's been so hard for me all these years to let go and move on. I did tell her as much, though, Ethan. I tried to, anyway. And you know I'm not good with conversations like that," she said ruefully.

"Ha, yes, I do, I'm afraid." His words bore no strife. Kate was silent for a moment, staring through the side window, and then she turned to him with resolution in her eyes.

"I do know that's what we need to do, though."

"That's great to hear. I'm proud of you for that." He gave her a gentle squeeze.

"You know, I've spent my whole life trying to be independent and not needing anyone," she said with a sideways glance, knowing that the unspoken words in that sentence were "including you."

"All I've done is run away from what and who I didn't want to face, and I fought against all the rest. But I finally think it's time to change that."

"Good! Let's work on it together, okay?" he said with a small smile. "I'm here for you, always. I hope you know that."

"I do, Ethan, I finally do." Kate shook her head at herself and looked again out the window. She felt such love and tenderness that she could not remember why she had shut out this man—and everyone else—who cared for her for so long.

"Come here," he said as he awkwardly pulled her closer to him across the center console of the SUV.

They stayed like that for a few moments before she broke away and rubbed her side. "I think you just ruptured a kidney."

He chuckled and let her go.

"It's a good thing I have three of them." She smiled and looked over at him playfully. "I do. Did I ever tell you that?"

"What?" he gasped. He could plainly see that she was serious. He couldn't believe that she had never shared that him. "Seriously, Kate, you have got to learn how to open up to people more! For heaven's sake, let us in a little. I promise you that I will never intentionally hurt you."

"That's my fear, Ethan. It's never the intentional ones that hurt the worst; it's the ones that you don't see coming."

"That may be true, Kate, but it's part of life. If you shut out the bad, you will inevitably shut out all the good along with it."

Kate sniggered and rolled her eyes. "Why does it seem that everyone around me has become wiser than I have?" she retorted, remembering the sagacious words that Marge and Curt had imparted upon her in the last few days.

"You just never gave us a chance to show you," he said with a small grin and raised eyebrows.

"Ethan, I shouldn't have told you to stay home. Thank you for coming up... for not listening to my stupidity and coming to be here with me."

"Of course. It's exactly where I should be."

Kate gazed out the window again and noticed all the pine trees surrounding the parking lot. Their branches lilted back and forth in the October breeze, and they were especially noticeable because the other trees had already lost their leaves, becoming skeletons of trunks and branches. The pine trees became the kings of nature, the sole survivors. Kate heard the wind that swayed the trees whistle around the SUV, and she shivered involuntarily. Again, she wondered how her life had come to this point. The rollercoaster ride of emotions she'd been on had made the last few days seem infinitely long, and some of things that had happened now seemed unthinkable.

With a nod of his head toward the hotel, Ethan opened his door, and Kate followed suit. She stepped out onto the lot and turned her face skyward, closing her eyes to try to feel some warmth. As if on cue, the clouds separated and the sun shone down from above. Its rays were instantly warming, despite the cool air that surrounded them. Kate breathed in deeply as if by doing so, she could capture the warmth and keep it inside of her. Her skin felt touched, somehow. She looked up again and thought—just for a second—that she saw an angel-like figure in the cloud shapes above. It seemed to hover in the sky directly above, smiling down on her.

Kate drew in her breath sharply and looked over at Ethan to see if he had seen it too, but she saw that he was busy getting his bags out of the SUV. Inside, she said a short but meaningful prayer to God for life, for family, and for showing her the way back to them. As she looked back up, the cloud shape slowly disappeared in the sky, but she smiled broadly, believing in her heart that it was a sign for her.

"Ethan, did you see..." but she stopped herself. "Nothing, sorry. Do you need some help?"

"What, babe?" he asked as he walked around the SUV to her side.

"Nothing," she said in a low voice. "Hey, I know this is going to sound odd right now, Ethan, but do you believe in God? I mean we've never discussed it—rather *Him*—before."

"No, we haven't," he conceded, "But since you're asking me, I do, Kate, and it's not at all odd. What else would explain the wonder of this thing we call life?"

He shrugged as if it all made perfect sense and smiled at her gently.

"And," he continued, "I do believe that even when it's impossible to see the wonder, it *is* still there. It's simply whether or not *you* are able to see it that makes the difference."

Kate stared at her husband intently with wonderment in her eyes. "Why have we never talked like this before?" Even in her extreme grief, his words made sense and gave her peace inside.

"It doesn't matter now, Kate. Let's just make sure that we do it from now on." he prompted her, grinning.

Kate reached over to hug her husband, and looking over his shoulder, she felt positive that she saw the cloud angel hovering in the sky over them again.

***

The rest of the evening, the next morning, and the days leading up to her mother's funeral passed by in a daze of grief and responsibility. Kate alternated between fits of sobbing and stoic silence. She did her best to be strong whenever she and Molly were together and let her emotions run free when not. Ethan stayed close to her throughout the days. He did not smother her; he acted as a rock to which she could tether herself before sadness carried her out to sea. At night he held her so close that their bodies seemed to become one in the darkness, and she slept curled up in his arms.

Ethan did not ask for anything more of Kate than she could give during her time of sorrow. Somehow, they both made it through the week, going back and forth between Molly and Jack's house, the funeral home, and back to the hotel each night.

Not once did a sarcastic comment pass through Kate's lips. Not one cold shoulder was thrust against her family. She slowly allowed the wall that she'd built around herself to crumble, and though the exposure was unsettling and sometimes even terrifying, she did not rebuild it.

Kate could see that Molly, as the youngest and more vulnerable of them, fared the worst in her sorrow. Kate reached out and held her close whenever Molly needed her to. She did her best to ignore the fears that still settled in the deep recesses of her grieving mind.

In the end, Molly made it through somehow, though her sobs rarely ceased and she often found herself clinging to Jack like a helpless child. She was only able to hold herself together and be strong around Alice and Emma.

It wasn't until after the funeral that Molly realized that she hadn't once thought of her own ailments. She had not reached a timid hand to her head in angst or consternation. She had not even thought of her own eventual demise. She had been too engrossed in what had to be done for her mother and her family.

Molly understood then that her worries and anxieties had just been in her head. And even more importantly, she understood that with her mother's passing she had somehow managed to let them go.

48. IT'S TIME TO GO

LYING HERE IN THIS HOSPITAL bed these last few days, hearing my daughters cry themselves sick, watching Robbie and the others look on helplessly, and not being able to console any of them…

Some moments, I think I was actually screaming inside at the horror of it all.

No one really knows if a comatose person can hear what's going on around them. Unless, of course, the person comes out of the coma and speaks for themself, I guess. I know doctors always encourage people to talk as if that person can. I'd always seen that on TV shows, you know, ones like *Chicago Hope* and… what's that other one? *Grey's Anatomy*.

I heard the doctors here say as much to Kate and Molly and I'm telling you now that it's true. I heard everything going on around me, and it's truly awful. I am so sorry for the hurt that I've caused everyone I love.

Molly, bless her heart, she sat by my bedside and told me over and over again how much she loved me, which she didn't need to do—I already knew. My sweet Molly has always been there for me and carried around the weight of the world on her shoulders. She's a wonderful mom, better than I was, that's for sure. At least that husband of hers will treat *her* right. And as a parent, you always want better for your children, so I pray it is so.

As for Robbie, well he was a good dad to Molly, but some people are just like that. They don't have it in them to love another's child as much as they love their own. But the worst part is that I—*my daughter's mother*—never put a stop to what was happening around me. No, I let that man push my baby out, let him make her feel unloved and unwanted. What kind of a mother does that?

I was just so wrapped up in the ridiculous hope that things were okay. I pushed the problem away like I did with everything else in my life. My Katie suffered because of it, I know.

Poor Kate, I think she may have taken this the worst. Lord knows that her bedside tears shook both of us to our very cores. I hated it for her. I know it's in part because she feels guilty that she hasn't been around much since she left home. I don't blame her for not coming back, though, I don't. She had a difficult childhood. Her world was turned upside-down when her father and I divorced, and things never righted themselves.

I cried inside for her, I'll tell you. And when she finally told me what Robbie did—or almost did to her —I felt my heart break, just crumble apart inside. That was the last straw for me. God, how I've hated myself every day for not doing more for her, but now hearing this?! It's truly too much to bear.

I keep telling myself how sorry I am about the way things turned out, but I never got to tell her. She was always so busy with her lawyer life that it was so hard to find the right time. If I could come back—just for one minute—it would be to tell my dear, determined Katherine just how sorry I am and how much I love her.

I truly would.

You know some say that the love between a husband and wife can last forever. Yet both of my husbands ending up cheating on me and it tore my heart asunder. But I know now that my marriages weren't meant to be the *real* highlights of my life in this world; no, it was my two girls. They were the highlights, and I love both of them so very much. They are good women in their own special ways, both the innocent products of the painful and disappointing relationships that had created them.

I hope that once I'm gone, my beautiful daughters will realize that they couldn't have saved their mother. That wasn't for them to take on, not their cross to bear. I believe that there is a "grand plan" to this life—to all of our lives—that's mapped out long before we are born. My family's "plan" simply includes losing me. Even though they are going to have to experience that loss,

I know in my heart that my daughters will get each other back. When all is said and done, they'll be all right.

My daughters are grown women who look nothing alike, yet inside, I know they have a bond of love that's been forgotten for too long. Now, the two miracles that I brought *into* this world will finally have each other.

I love them both, and I pray that they will love and cherish one another as much as I always have.

Goodbye, my dear daughters. Take care of each other and remember the love. I leave this earth knowing in my heart that I've at least done that for you.

Yes, I know that after I'm gone, everything truly *will* be okay.

49. CONFESSION

THE FUNERAL HAD TAKEN PLACE just a few days before, but it already felt to Kate like years of her life had passed by.

Sitting on the hotel bed with her laptop open, its eerie light the only one in the darkened room, Kate looked down for the hundredth time. She desperately wanted to see the response that she so desired, even though logic told her that it was still too early for anything to have been done yet. She scanned her emails, ever hopeful, and let out a sigh. She snuck a glance at Ethan to make sure he was still asleep next to her. Their suitcases were packed; it was the last morning they would spend in Maine before flying back home.

Kate sat, deep in thought, and stared straight ahead without seeing a thing. She became lost in memories of the last few weeks and all that happened. It seemed like eons ago since she'd received Molly's call telling her "Mom's been shot!" But that tragedy had helped reveal to her in an amazing burst of clarity exactly what she had to do moving forward.

While Ethan had been in the lounge downstairs the night before, booking their flights back home, Kate had made excuses to stay back in the hotel room. In a whirlwind of activity, through a flurry of late night phone calls and emails, she had initiated a new course for her life that would begin after they returned. It was a life that she was still attempting to believe would—hopefully—soon become true.

A tide of emotions swept in and out every few minutes, yet the uncertainty was not at all scary. She welcomed it with open arms.

Kate sighed. It still felt so hard to believe that her mother was actually gone. Kate hoped and prayed that Beth had gone to a better place, away from all of her worldly pain. She had offered many words and prayers to God over the last few days; after each one she felt a peace encompass her that somehow superseded the grief. She was grateful that both the funeral and the wake were brief. Almost all the attendees had cried.

Kate imagined that they were crying for the sorrow of all the women in the universe who had suffered and in the end had chosen to end their lives.

As the elder sister, Kate had done her best to hold herself together throughout the service. She walked through the day in a daze—smiling at offered condolences, shaking hands, and hugging distant relatives whom she couldn't quite remember. She gave a small speech in front of everyone, with Molly by her side; they held hands so tightly that ring marks were still indented in her skin two days later. Somehow, she managed to get all the words off of the page and into the air for all to hear. The mothers in the crowd had smiled sadly as Kate shared a few stories. Those in attendance who were already in the second half of their lives listened with bowed heads, mourning Beth's sudden and bitter end.

At some point during the funeral, Robbie had shown everyone his true colors. For although he'd been quietly by his daughter's side for her support, it was plain to see that he had put his marriage to rest long before his wife actually was. Not a tear left his eyes and he managed to escape the wake as soon as he could, silently slipping out through the back door like a thief in the night.

Kate saw that Molly, full of heartbreak, just stood and watched him go. Then she turned her back on him and returned to stand beside Kate.

Molly knew that she would have to forgive her father at some point, if only for her children and the grandmother that they had just lost. And she knew that people are not perfect, that mistakes are made, and that life must—and will—always go on. For the time being, though, she let all that go as her father walked away. She focused instead on the tragedy of the present and on her sister who was finally right there by her side.

Later that night, after everyone had gone home and the last of the casseroles had been taken away, Kate made the greatest decision of her life, preparing herself to face her fears.

The next day, while the husbands were off with Alice and Emma, she asked Molly to sit down with her, and she told her almost everything. She shared the many struggles she experienced growing up. She told her about her own father's infidelity with their mother and about her own internal conflicts with family all these years. She still did not tell Molly about the incident with Robbie that night in her bedroom, because she knew that wouldn't have been right.

Some lines are just not meant to be crossed.

Finally, she took a deep breath and told her before she lost her courage why she had actually moved away, down to Atlanta six years ago. Why she had needed to leave everyone behind.

Molly sat and listened without interruption or judgment. She offered nothing until the very end. Then, as both sisters held their breath, keenly aware of the pivotal point they were at in their lives, Molly said the three words that Kate needed to hear.

Taking Kate's hand in hers, Molly looked at her earnestly and said with a brilliant smile, "Go get him."

50. HEADING HOME

"SO, BEFORE WE LEAVE THIS fine state," Ethan said dryly to Kate, "Is there anything else that I should know about?"

They had just left the hotel and were headed down Main Street to the airport. Kate gazed out the SUV's window at the other cars passing by, lost in her thoughts about the wheels that she had set in motion and all that it would mean. The early morning sun streamed in through the window, blanketing them in glistening lines of light. She had barely heard him speak, but she slowly turned her head to face him.

A small but expectant smile hovered on his face. She reached for Ethan's hand and squeezed it gently. "No, I think I've told you everything now."

She knew that after their heartfelt talk last night, he knew the answer to his question, but he needed to hear her say it.

Somehow, somewhere, Kate had dug deep and found the strength and courage to say to her husband the words that had been buried inside for so long. In the confines of the hotel room late into the night, she told him about the fateful moments alone with Robbie that one night and about dating Jack. Once she started, the words gushed out, and the story of her life seemed to fully unravel and unfold as Kate told Ethan everything that she had kept inside. At one point, he reached up and gently touched her cheek with the back of his hand. When his hand dropped down, so did her eyes, and it was that moment that Kate delivered the final blow.

"Ethan... there's one other thing that you need to know. Something that will change our lives forever, either way..."

Then she told him what she had finally told Molly earlier that day, why she left Maine and moved away. She told him about the terrible thing that she had done.

Ethan's heart went out to his wife more than he ever thought possible. For it was only now that he finally, truly understood her and all that she had been through. He allowed her to finish her story without interruption, just as Molly had done.

By the time Kate was through sending her emails, it had been past midnight. She had slept for only a few hours.

Now, driving to the airport, Ethan sat up straighter in his seat, secure in the knowledge of the truth and understanding about his wife, and drove onward. For the first time ever, Kate saw how grounded and safe she felt. She no longer believed that she was in control of everything, but she didn't feel like she was out of control either, falling through the trees or into the rabbit hole. Kate knew that, despite her mother's death, everything would be alright.

As the SUV stopped at the next red light, they both looked out to see a small boy run around and around a tree off to the side of the road. A woman who looked like his mother chased playfully after him. They could tell that she was only pretending that she couldn't reach him. They could hear the boy's squeals of laughter even through the rolled up windows.

Ethan stole a glance at Kate then quickly looked away.

Kate saw the boy then and felt the nervous anticipation of her future flutter in her gut.

She turned to Ethan with a pleading, open face, "Do you think I'm a bad person?"

After barely a pause, he replied, "No, Kate, I don't. I do know that some bad stuff has happened to you. But once you get to a certain point in life, you just need to learn from it and let it go."

With that, he leaned over and kissed her on the forehead. "Everything will be okay."

"I don't deserve you, you know," she whispered under her breath as a tear fell down onto her cheek.

"I know," he replied with a smile. "You do deserve happiness, though. Hopefully life will bring that to you now."

Looking again at the boy and his mother playing by the roadside, Kate couldn't help but ask Ethan one last time.

"Are you ready for this, Ethan? I mean, really ready?"

"I guess I'm as ready as I'll ever be," he exclaimed with a broad grin. He stepped on the gas as the light turned green. "It will certainly be a new adventure for all of us."

When Kate saw the "Portland International Jetport" signs a few minutes later, she couldn't help but smile. She thought of the man who sat next to her on the plane on the way up, and she thought of his wife, Marge. Both of them had given her more words of wisdom and kindness than she ever deserved.

With just a handful of other travelers, the airport was calm, even for midday travel. She and Ethan moved quickly through check-in and security and stood by the window at gate number three waiting for the plane that would take them home. They watched in silence as planes taxied by on the tarmac below until it was their time to board. When the attendant called out their zone number, Ethan held his arm around Kate, and they walked down the ramp together.

Kate knew without a doubt that she had received blessings from the two people in her life that meant the most to her—her sister and her husband.

She walked onto the plane a new woman, ready to finally let go of the past and face her future.

FINAL CHAPTER

A FEW DAYS LATER, KATE walked back into the foyer of her law firm. She hadn't been there in more than two weeks. Despite the countless hours and days she had spent there, the office suite now felt foreign.

A hush fell over the room as she strode across the wooden floor. When she scanned the room, she saw everyone divert their eyes and busy themselves with seemingly meaningful tasks. She held her head high as she walked by them. Sam was standing outside her office door waiting for her with his arms outstretched. He rushed to her side and deftly hustled her into her office and away from curious stares, one arm held protectively behind her. For Kate, it was faintly reminiscent of when she'd first learned of her mother's tragic demise. She wondered if Sam, or even her coworkers, could see the changes in her. To her, the changes seemed to radiate from inside. She felt remarkably warm and bright.

Once inside her office, Sam started firing questions at Kate as if she was on the stand at the end of a trial.

"What happened up there, Kate? Did you know about your mom being like this? What the hell did you do?" He paused for a breath before continuing in a quieter voice, "And seriously, how did you hide this from me all these years? How?"

"Whoa, Sam. One question at a time." She smiled at how much he cared.

Kate knew that she would miss Sam when she was gone.

She sat down, not behind her desk as usual, but in the small Clodale chair near the window. She gazed out, her head tipped to one side and her legs crossed. She lazily tapped one foot on the hardwood floor so that for a few seconds, all that could be heard was the click-clicking of her heel. Finally, she looked over at Sam and gave him a slow, deliberate smile.

"Alright, Sam, want to go ahead and ask me?"

He paused for just a moment then practically yelled out the question, his arms open wide in frustration.

"How in the hell did I not know about this?" The look on his face registered his shock and amazement.

"Because, Sam, it happened *before* I began working here, that's why."

"Well, even so... don't you think that's something that I should have known?" he snapped back in defense.

Kate tossed her head back and laughed. "What are you, my father?"

Sam sat back, chagrined.

"Oh, don't look so puritanical, Sam. It all happened well before Molly and Jack had even started dating. Surely, you can imagine *my* surprise when Molly first told me who she was marrying a year later. I was shocked!"

"Huh, no less than I am now," he murmured under his breath, shaking his head in disbelief.

"Well, I've thought all of these years that Jack had told Molly about us—well, not about the *that*, because I actually never told Jack about that—and that's when I moved down here."

"Wait a minute!" Sam interrupted, putting up a manicured hand to stop her. "Kate, I may be gay but it's my understanding that in the hetero world that kind of thing is a no-no."

His tone was admonishing, and in that moment Kate loved him for it. She looked appropriately chagrined and replied, "Yes, you are correct. That was very wrong of me. I was scared, and I didn't know what to do."

"You? Scared? I've never heard *that* before," he exclaimed.

Kate thought about that for a moment and then continued, "All I ever wanted was my career, Sam. That's all that mattered to me, all I knew. And in my defense, Jack and I were by no means in a relationship that would have lasted. We were—well, are—very different people."

Then Kate added with a rueful grin, "Which is exactly why he and my sister are perfect together."

"So… all this time, your sister *didn't* know about you and Jack dating, or she did?"

"Well, that's the irony. I *thought* she did, and Jack thought she didn't, so when he met me at the airport last week and told me that he'd never told her, I, of course, immediately wondered why she and I hadn't been closer all these years."

"Okay…" Kate could see Sam's wheels were turning as he worked to figure out the dynamics. "This is like one my mother's soaps… Okay, so why haven't you and she been close then?"

"That's the catch, Sam. Because of me! Because *I* was the one who left home! I was never happy and I couldn't wait to get out of there, away from everyone. Then after I left for the…" she stopped herself. "Well, I just never had much to do with any family after that. And Molly, it seems, just missed me. That was all, nothing more! Anything else was just in my head."

Sam said nothing, trying to take everything in. Kate continued her explanation.

"That's the thing, Sam. Molly *knew* about Jack and me, but she still missed me. She still loved me." There was awe in Kate's voice.

Sam paused for a moment to take it all in, and then his face fell in response.

"Ohhh," he drew out the word slowly. "That's all very, very sad."

"I know."

Kate glanced outside again and seemed to be lost in thought. Sam waited patiently, as he always did, for her to focus and return to their conversation. Various emotions played across her face until she finally turned back to him and took a deep breath.

"Sam, this is still a lot for me to take in, too," she said, offering a small, sad smile. "And losing our mother when I finally feel like I found my family again is the worst irony of all."

"Kate, I am so sorry about your mom. I can't imagine what that must feel like. Did the flowers arrive okay?" Sam had sent a huge bouquet from the office. It was the most beautiful one at the funeral.

"Yes, thank you, that was sweet. Honestly, Sam, it's like something has gone dead inside of me, in losing her. Yet after closing myself off from everyone for so long, there's another piece inside that recognizes what's been given to me, a new life! Between my sister and now my…" she stopped again and turned to look out the window, unable to say any more.

Sam watched as Kate closed her eyes and took a deep breath. It looked as if she was cleansing herself of all the wrongs inside. She eventually turned back to him and gently spoke.

The smile in her eyes did not quite reach her face, but Sam saw it there nonetheless and knew that his friend would be okay.

"So Sam, were you able to get in touch with Sheffield regarding my emails?"

Clapping his hands enthusiastically, he practically jumped out of his chair. "Yes, and *this* is good news! Our Mr. Bocephus Sheffield is tickled pink to help you. Honestly, I don't know who has been more excited at all this, him or me! We both started working on it as soon as I read your email."

"Well, Henry is a good guy—I could tell that right from the start. So where do things stand now?"

"I sent him all the paperwork that they'd requested, and to my understanding, the wheels are in motion. We're just waiting until we get word from his office."

"Okay, will they be contacting me directly?"

"Uh…" Sam paused. "I've never done so before, but in this circumstance I gave Sheffield your direct cell to call… I hope that was the right thing to do."

She could see that he was tentatively trying to gauge her reaction, so before another second passed by, Kate reached over and gave him a reassuring pat on his arm.

He squealed in response, obviously delighted. "What was *that* for, Ms. Harriman? My, you *have* changed."

Kate grinned and replied, "Sam, you have been there for me almost daily for the last six years. I'm sure I haven't told you just how much I appreciate all your hard work and everything that you've done for me."

Embarrassed and confused by her display of emotion, Sam blushed a little and turned away. Kate reached out again and touched his hand. Sam noticed that the mosaic silver bracelet that he had given her for her anniversary dangled on her wrist. He looked at her questioningly; she was sending all kinds of warm and fuzzy signals that he had never received before.

"You've always been so good. Thank you."

He looked at Kate oddly. Her words seemed to have a tone of finality to them that he didn't understand. Yet when Kate didn't add more, he began to explain to her everything that had happened with Sheffield in the last few days—leaving out no details along the way.

Kate listened intently as if his words were describing another incoming case. Yet every once in a while her eyes got an indiscernible glint to them that Sam had never seen before, despite the numerous court wins and welcomed publicity that Kate had earned over the years. It was a look of compassion and hope, and it rested sweetly on her face. It looked as if it should have been residing there all along.

After he was through, Sam promised to take care of a few unfinished tasks and left her office. As he closed the door behind him, he took one last look at this woman who had been his boss and his friend for a number of years. She had exuded such confidence and brash assertiveness since the day he had met her that the picture of another calmer, more content person before him was oddly unsettling.

As Kate gazed out the window with a knowing smile on her face, Sam gently closed the door and walked to his cubicle with a frown—though he did not know exactly why.

With the click of her door, Kate was alone inside her office again. She looked around thoughtfully. She knew that it might be for the last time.

The large suite, which has seemed so important to her before, now seemed cold and austere; there was a feeling of loneliness that she had never noticed before. There were only a few vases of flowers scattered around the room—tokens of sympathy from the office and a few clients—that provided any life or warmth to the space. The suite was very masculine in its design; it didn't reflect a thing about her.

She opened her desk drawers and began rifling through the contents, making piles to one side of the desk and tossing other items into the trash underneath. She reached for a pen and almost knocked over the small glass paperweight of the coiled snake that she'd been given at the office last year. Her hand wrapped around its coolness, and a shudder went down her spine at the thought of her reputation in the office and in the local legal community. It was a reputation that she had taken pride in, but it now seemed wrong and out of place.

She carefully placed the snake back on the far edge of the desk and sat back in her chair. Remembering all the newspaper articles over the years about her tenaciousness in the courtroom, she couldn't help but sigh. All of those lives that she had affected clouded her head; she hoped that she had done right by most of them.

Her laptop beeped and startled her out of her reverie. She looked down, read the email message, and her heart skipped a beat:

Sheffield here. Call us as soon as you can.

Kate's breath caught in her throat and her stomach felt like it had turned upside down and inside out. For a moment, she was too paralyzed to move as the inertia seemed to take hold of her very soul. She breathed slowly and gazed outside trying to calm her nerves. Just seconds after, a second email came through, and Kate looked down to see three words in all capital letters on her screen.

WE'VE GOT HIM!

With her hands shaking, she quickly called Sheffield's office. The receptionist picked up on the first ring.

"Matters of a Lifetime," she answered in a sweet voice.

"Hello, this is Kate Harriman. I'm calling for Bo. He, uh, just sent me an email. Is he in?"

"Oh! Ms. Harriman, of course! He's expecting your call," the receptionist replied cheerily. "Wait one moment, please."

After a few seconds, Sheffield picked up the phone and bellowed loud enough that Kate had to move the phone away from her ear.

"Ms. Harriman! Kate... it's good to have you back," he said, as if they were long lost friends.

"Thank you, Bo."

"Are *you* doing okay?" he asked. Then with a lowered voice, he continued, "We heard from Sam about your mother, and we all extend our condolences to you and your family."

He asked her the last question with a genuine caring in his voice that made Kate smile.

"Yes, and thank you for the flowers. That was very kind of you. And I actually am okay." As the words came out, Kate knew that she truly was. "I understand that congratulations are in order for you, Bo."

"Congratulations? For me?" he asked. "What for?"

"Well, it seems in my absence that Ms. Greta Pearson has decided to drop the lawsuit against you after our initial response. Her legal team and I have already begun working out the details, and they should have the paperwork done soon."

"Well, I'll be a horse's ass, that's won'erful!" he yelled through the phone. "What happened to change her mind?"

"Apparently, our mayor just has a bit more influence than we thought."

"Ms. Harriman, that is great news!" His voice was laced with awe. "Thank you, Ms. Harriman. I knew you could do it."

Kate laughed. "Well, I'm not sure if I did much being away for two weeks. Sam took care of everything while I was gone. But I am happy for you."

She smiled again then looked down at the manila folder on her desk; the tab at the top read #18680 and the edges of the folder were worn and tattered. A photograph peeked out from the side, showing just the right side of a child's face in a green and blue striped shirt. Kate had already stared at it enough to memorize every detail.

"Well, Kate, I am also pleased to be able to share some good news. You read my email and you have the file, I believe, so you know that we've found what you're looking for. There's an excellent home, a bit south of the city that does an excellent job providing for children. I've worked with them before, and I know they do their best."

Even though his email had said as much, hearing the words spoken aloud brought forth a gasp from her lips. Kate closed her eyes and listened in darkness as Sheffield continued to talk.

"It did take some heavy cutting through red tape, I'll tell you, given your original notice of intent to sign him away. Fortunately, though, I know some good people at the state agencies who owed me a favor or two and helped us out. It seems as if he was with a family a one point, but that didn't work out. Since then, he's been living at the home and doing well."

He paused, but Kate didn't—couldn't—say a word in return. Her throat was tight.

"Ms. Harriman? Are you there?"

"Yes, I'm here, Bo," she responded quietly. She exhaled, unaware that she'd been holding her breath in until she slowly let it out.

"Well, it took three days of constant searching, but we finally found him there and sorted everything out... and he's actually here now! In fact, he's sitting in the room just down the hall from me." He stopped then added with a loud guffaw, "And, by golly, if he doesn't look just like you! Ms. Harriman, I would have picked him out in a crowded room anywhere, I swear!"

Kate smiled. Her eyes pooled, and a tear rolled down her cheek. She turned her head to see her own reflection in the window, vaguely aware of the distant skyline through the overcast clouds that consumed the sky. She could barely contain the excitement she felt inside and wanted to run outside as fast as she could.

For once, she did not want to run away; she wanted to run toward the thing that she knew she should have never left behind.

She thanked Bo for his help. The emails that he and Sam had exchanged over the last week were many, and Bo Sheffield had acted much quicker than she'd ever anticipated. He delivered what he had promised her, and her heart skipped a beat in anticipation. She told him that she'd be at his office within the hour then quickly called Ethan to share the news. He didn't pick up, so she just left a message on his cell.

"Hun, he's here, and he's coming home with me tonight. I'll see you soon. Call me back. Love you!"

As she laid her cell down on the desk, a thousand details raced through her mind. *How could she make up for years past, how would they get through the first night together, and how could she make the most of the time to come?* She knew that she would need to take one day at a time—maybe even one hour at a time—and her heart ached longingly at the prospect of finally having him close to her again.

Before she could think twice, she called Molly and waited impatiently for her sister to answer the phone so she could tell her.

"Kate? What's going on down there?" Molly's breathless voice was full of the same excitement that Kate knew had been in her own. "Is there any news?"

"Hi, Molly. Yes, everything's good. The agency just called to tell me that they've found him. I can't believe it, but I'm going to get him now and bring him home with us tonight."

Kate waited to hear Molly's response, not realizing that she'd been holding her breath and sitting on the edge of her chair. However, Molly's immediate and heartfelt reaction dispelled all of her fears.

"Oh, Kate, I am so happy for you! That's just what you need— what we all need—to hear after the last few weeks."

Kate asked how she was doing, and Molly enthusiastically shared with her that no spells or fears had been troubling her since the day of the funeral. Molly said that it took something so tragic to realize that everything that was going on with her was truly only in her head.

"I feel like a new woman, Kate. Besides getting you, it's another gift that mom gave me."

"I'm so happy for you." Kate paused before continuing, speaking barely loud enough for Molly to hear, "Are you sure, though, Molly? I need to know that you are *really* okay with this before I go through with it."

Without any hesitation, Molly answered, "Absolutely! Don't make it sound like a business deal, though." She laughed at her sister. "Really, this is wonderful news and I can't wait to meet him."

"Thank you, Molly."

"You promise to bring him up soon so he can meet me and the girls… and his Uncle Jack, right?"

With those words, Kate knew that Molly had given her full approval and that everything between them would be okay.

Kate's relief was palpable, and her love for her sister was even greater than anything she could have imagined. Kate surprised herself by wanting to give Molly a hug and squeeze her tight. She hoped that her next words adequately expressed the love she felt for her sister.

"Thank you, Molly. Losing mom is unbearable for us both. But having you in my life—and now him—it all just seems like too much to hope for."

"I know, Katie, I know." As Molly answered, Kate could almost see the smile on her sister's face across the miles. "But I know it's exactly what mom would have wanted."

"Maybe that's the gift that she gave us, for us *all* to be together again as a family."

The two sisters said heartfelt goodbyes and made promises to talk soon, promises that they would keep.

Kate closed her laptop and scooped up the manila folder and some papers from her desk. As she started to get up, the skies opened up and sun streamed in through her office windows. It bathed everything in warm light, and Kate unconsciously cast her eyes skyward and slowly sank back down. With the sun's bright rays streaming in, she remembered the prayers she had spoken to God while staying in Maine and paused to reflect on what she had asked for and all that it meant.

She smiled, for although she had lost her mother, she understood just how much she had gained in return. And although she might not understand the course of the events or the reasons for them all, she knew deep down that life was not always meant to be understood, or controlled. And it was certainly not intended to be run away from.

Without hesitation, and without asking for anything, she shouted out "Thank you, God" to the empty room. Clasping her hands over her heart, she looked up and said it again, quietly, sincerely, and with true grace. She knew with her sister and a husband who loved her, that she would never again be alone.

Kate scrambled up out of her chair and walked quickly around her desk. She stopped and turned back to grab the glass snake and the nameplate that read "*Katherine Harriman*" in brassy bold letters. Quickly, she stuffed them into her briefcase, and with a smile plastered on her face, she ran out of her office and left it all behind. For the first time ever, Kate Harriman felt hope and happiness and eagerness. It was clear for all the world to see.

As she closed the large mahogany doors of the old building on Mayfield Boulevard behind her, she ran as fast as her feet would take her. She was a new mother, anxious to finally meet her son.

EPILOGUE

KATE RELAXED IN THE ADIRONACK chair, watching as Sam chased Alice and Emma around the yard. The girls shrieked with delight each time Sam tagged them. The warm August sun streamed down upon them all, and Kate relished its warmth, glad to be back near the coast and away from the humid summer of the South. Maine summers were perfect in so many ways. Since she had moved back, each day had felt like a blessing.

She looked over as Ethan slid open the patio door. He was holding a tray of hamburgers and hotdogs and had a spatula tucked under one arm. He threw Kate a smile as he headed to the nearby grill. From her seat on the other side of the lawn, she could hear him whistling a tune; his head bopped back and forth to the beat, and she smiled at his adorable boyishness.

The kids suddenly tumbled down on the grass, laughing. Sam, just a few years older than Alice and already towering over little Emma, leaned over to tickle them both. They screamed his name, with threats of peeing their pants, and laughed louder

Kate giggled and looked over at them with a love that she still couldn't believe she could feel. It had been a little over a year since she'd found Sam and brought him home—and one year since Beth's death. Though the two events occurred so close in time, the joy of reuniting with the baby that she had given up years ago, now a handsome and amazing nine-year boy, outshone the pain of losing her mother.

Sam, she mused, still laughing at the name her son had been given. She loved the name, but since Ethan's last name was Shepherd, she couldn't help but think of the actor Sam Shepherd whenever she looked at her son. *Well, at least by the time he's in high school, that old actor will have been replaced by younger ones and long forgotten.*

"Kate?"

Ethan's shout interrupted her reverie. "What, Hun?" she called back.

"What time will Molly and Jack be here? I want to make sure the burgers don't get cold."

"Oh, any minute, I'm sure. She said right around four or four thirty." With that, Kate remembered to get the mail, as their mailman arrived at almost the same time every day, never any later than four thirty. Now that she stayed at home with Sam, only accepting small legal jobs on the side, getting the mail each day had become part of her daily routine.

"Watch the kids, babe, I'll go get the mail and give her a call to check," she said as she crossed the yard to the gate.

As she walked out to the street, she breathed in the sweet salty air. Falmouth, Maine was just minutes from the coast and less than thirty minutes from Molly and Jack's house, so Kate felt that she now had the best of both worlds. She knew she needed both her family and the sea to feel whole.

She smiled and reached into the mailbox. Just one envelope was inside, and as she pulled it out and saw her name handwritten on it, it donned on her that it was Sunday—the mail did not come today. With a furrowed brow, she looked down at the paper and decided that she did not recognize the handwriting. She carefully opened one end of the envelope and pulled out a folded white piece of paper. She unfolded it, and something that had been tucked inside fluttered to the ground. She reached down to pick it up. It was a wallet-size photo of a man.

Though the picture was small and worn, she could see that the man had auburn hair like hers—curly at the ends—blue eyes, and a pale face. *A male version of myself,* Kate thought. Her heart skipped a beat and her throat seized up.

With shaking hands, she read the words on the piece of paper and cried out:

I am your brother. Help me.

ABOUT THE AUTHOR

Photo by Shannon M Gillen Photography
www.shannonmgillen.com

CRYSTAL KLIMAVICZ IS A PROUD Maine native who grew up in Bath, a small coastal town with big city spirit and beautifully rustic beaches. She spent her early adulthood in Boston, Massachusetts before moving back to Maine—Portland this time—where she met her husband, Tim, through Dale Carnegie (or was it the old dive bar, T'birds? The story sometimes changes). Crystal and Tim moved to Atlanta 16 years ago, but they get back to Maine as often as possible to visit friends and family, dine at some of the country's best seafood restaurants, and shop at Maine's wonderfully eclectic shops. They now have two beautiful children, Calum and Claire, who keep them busy, as well as two dogs and one fish (though talks of adding a feline to the home can often be heard). Crystal rarely sits still, so when she is not crafting a story or being a mom, she loves to head out for a run, go for a bike ride, or play tennis with friends.

For three years, Crystal lived as an ex-pat in Kyiv, Ukraine, a country that now faces significant crisis. While in Ukraine, she taught cardio kickboxing and Pilates to a wonderful group of other ex-pats and served as president of IWCK, the International Women's Club of Kyiv, a charitable organization with over 300 women from around the world that does great good for the local community.

She began her professional life in sales in the health care sector, but she found that offices and their politics were not for her. She has achieved a master's in healthcare management from Mercer University, and she has written and taught professional development courses in Atlanta and overseas. She still has hopes of someday finding the time to pursue a PhD. Her love of the written word and her own family tragedy pushed her to create *Falling Through Trees,* her debut novel, over the course of a few years.

Crystal's passion is finding balance between joy and divine grace and the many troubles that are inevitable in our world. She and her family currently reside in a suburb north of Atlanta, but she hopes to return someday to the coast and to the sea that beckons her.

CPSIA information can be obtained at www.ICGtesting.com
Printed in the USA
LVOW06s1149110514

385165LV00001B/1/P